TOOTH AND CLAW

DS VICKY DODDS 1

ED JAMES

OTHER BOOKS BY ED JAMES

SCOTT CULLEN MYSTERIES SERIES

Eight novels featuring a detective eager to climb the career ladder, covering Edinburgh and its surrounding counties, and further across Scotland.

1. GHOST IN THE MACHINE
2. DEVIL IN THE DETAIL
3. FIRE IN THE BLOOD
4. STAB IN THE DARK
5. COPS & ROBBERS
6. LIARS & THIEVES
7. COWBOYS & INDIANS
8. HEROES & VILLAINS

CULLEN & BAIN SERIES

Four novellas spinning off from the main Cullen series covering the events of the global pandemic in 2020.

1. CITY OF THE DEAD
2. WORLD'S END
3. HELL'S KITCHEN
4. GORE GLEN

CRAIG HUNTER SERIES

A spin-off series from the Cullen series, with Hunter first featuring in the fifth book, starring an ex-squaddie cop struggling with PTSD, investigating crimes in Scotland and further afield.

1. MISSING

2. HUNTED
3. THE BLACK ISLE

DS VICKY DODDS SERIES

Gritty crime novels set in Dundee and Tayside, featuring a DS juggling being a cop and a single mother.

1. BLOOD & GUTS (a short novel)
2. TOOTH & CLAW
3. FLESH & BLOOD
4. SKIN & BONE

DI SIMON FENCHURCH SERIES

Set in East London, will Fenchurch ever find what happened to his daughter, missing for the last ten years?

1. THE HOPE THAT KILLS
2. WORTH KILLING FOR
3. WHAT DOESN'T KILL YOU
4. IN FOR THE KILL
5. KILL WITH KINDNESS
6. KILL THE MESSENGER
7. DEAD MAN'S SHOES

Other Books

Other crime novels, with Senseless set in southern England, and the other three set in Seattle, Washington.

- SENSELESS
- TELL ME LIES
- GONE IN SECONDS
- BEFORE SHE WAKES

For Al Guthrie.

Tho' Nature, red in tooth and claw
With ravine, shriek'd against his creed—

– Tennyson, "In Memoriam A.H.H".

PROLOGUE

'I see.' Rachel gripped her mobile as tight as she could without cracking the screen. 'I'm sorry you see it that way.'

Benji was tugging at his lead, desperate to sniff at the lamp post over the road. Little sod might be small for a pug, but he was strong.

Up here, she got a great view down to the Tay, shimmering in the spring sunshine. A boat was cutting up surf on its way out to sea, heading for the two bridges across the river. The honeysuckle was starting to send out its sickly sweet perfume, as sure a sign as any that summer was coming.

'Listen, you just give us the money back and we'll say no more.' His voice was harsh, distorted by her phone's speakers. 'I'm not an angry or vindictive man. That's all.'

Rachel let Benji have his way and crossed the road. 'Well, I'm afraid I can't just—'

'Listen, you sold us a pup!'

'Literally. We agreed the terms. Now goodbye!' Rachel ended the phone call and scanned through her contacts list for the man's number. Before she could block him, he was calling her back. How rude! She killed the call, then tapped the button to block him. Excellent. A wave of calm surged through her. 'Come on, Benji.'

She tugged at his lead and set off down the grass verge on this side of the lane, uneven but preferable to walking on the road.

That woman was staring hard at her over the fence. It hadn't been here a week ago, but now its varnished wood barred any view of the garden. Used to be one of the highlights of Rachel's day, but now it was... Well. 'Don't you even *think* of letting those dogs get in here again.'

Rachel shook her head. Some people just didn't get it, did they?

'I'm talking to you!' She was keeping pace with Rachel and shooting angry looks over the fence. 'Your bloody dogs should be—'

'I'm not listening to you.' Rachel tightened her grip, quickened her pace, but held her keys in her pockets in case she needed a weapon.

'Snooty cow. You and your horrible little—'

'Snooty?' Rachel chanced a look at the spiteful woman. 'If you knew half of—'

'Yeah, yeah, yeah. Just keep walking. And don't come back.'

'Gladly.' Rachel spotted that point where the pavement picked up across the road. One last look over the fence, though. 'Good day to you.'

'Good day? *Good day?* Christ! I've lost a year thanks to you!'

Rachel jogged over the road away from the harpy.

A car horn jolted her out of her rage.

Some black thing was stopped in the middle of the road. The driver was shouting something at Rachel, but the glass muted whatever it was.

'Come on, you too.' Rachel clutched the leads in both hands and dragged Benji and Jemima across the road.

'Could say thanks for not running you over!' A woman's voice, soon drowned out by the roar of the car's engine and the bitter tang of burnt petrol.

What was wrong with people?

Rachel hurried on down the pavement, eager to get away and get home in time for *Pointless*. Not too far now – she could see the back of their house off in the distance, behind the runs that filled their garden. If only there was a shortcut.

'Excuse me?' A car was coming up from behind, some dance music thumping out into the country air.

Rachel stopped, sighed, then made to turn.

Before she could, something hard pressed into her back and it felt like her whole body shook and turned to jelly. She fell forward, unable to break her fall, and landed flat on the tarmac. Her cheek scraped off some loose stones.

The dogs looked back at her, then up at someone, then turned tail and ran away, their leads trailing behind them.

That was the last thing Rachel saw before something was shoved over her head.

DAY 1

Thursday
31st March 2016

1

Detective Sergeant Vicky Dodds pulled off the roundabout onto the North Marketgait, the dual carriageway ahead giving her a clear run for once. A line of dishevelled trees obscured a new block of flats, browns and blues caught by the morning sun. She shot through a light as it turned amber, passing the pink brick of the Wellgate Shopping Centre, the famous Dundee multi-storeys looming over.

Her phone started ringing but fell silent as she slipped into the semi-darkness of the tunnel.

A row of red brake lights up ahead.

'Shit, shit, shit.' Vicky hit the brakes. What passed for rush-hour traffic in Dundee. Fumes leaked into the car. She flipped the air to recycle and snatched the phone from its cradle.

David Forrester. No voicemail. The clock on the dashboard showed 8.22.

Not late, yet. What did he want?

The cars ahead trundled forward a few feet and she dialled Forrester on speakerphone, ringing and ringing.

Stop and go.

Stop and go.

Stop and go.

She pulled out of the tunnel. More traffic queuing outside the long row of ancient jute mills, all redundant and mostly repurposed. Opposite, the brown-and-mustard ridges of the three-storey police station, a washed-out prison uniform.

Held up in city traffic, struck by visions of penal service and now a missed call from the boss. Superb...

'—please leave a message after the tone.' The phone beeped.

Eyes on the road, Vicky fumbled for the red button and killed the call.

Another shunt in the queue of near-stationary cars ahead, then finally a gap. She put her foot down, tyres screeching, and turned on to West Bell Street. The grand Sheriff Court, with its smooth Doric columns, outmuscled on either side by brutal concrete buildings. Another left and she was into the car park.

A blue BMW 1-Series sat in her parking bay, gleaming in the sunshine.

Superb...

With gritted teeth, Vicky parked in the nearest free space. She grabbed her bag and phone, zapping the lock on her black Fiesta as she stomped across the small car park. The old Tayside Police sign still outlined by the weathering, the Police Scotland replacement not quite filling the space.

Vicky smiled at the desk sergeant as she passed. 'Morning, Tommy.'

'I prefer Sergeant Davies, but you know that, don't you?' He ran a hand over his bald head, shaved to the pockmarked skin. 'And what a beautiful morning it is.'

'Don't even try to sweeten me up.' Vicky stopped and held his gaze as she rummaged in her handbag for her ID. 'Someone's taken my space again.'

'Sorry about that.' Tommy looked away, fingers combing his patchy beard. 'New lad started in your area. DI Forrester said it was okay today.'

Forrester at it again... Superb.

Vicky flashed him a grin. 'Check with me first, Tommy, all right?'

'Said he'd okayed it with you. Didn't think you'd mind, what with you being so even-tempered and everything.'

'I'll let it pass. Today.' Vicky tugged her ID over her head. 'But try my gracious temperament again tomorrow and I'll park my Fiesta in the empty space between your ears.'

'I said sorry, didn't I?'

'No bother.' Vicky flashed her security card at the reader and pushed through, hurrying down the corridor already bustling with uniformed officers.

And Forrester, heading straight for her, his long arms and legs ploughing through the crowd. He stopped in front of her and ran a hand through his hair. Hard to tell what colour it once was, but no mistaking the dandruff catching in the air conditioning. 'Morning, Vicky.'

'Sir.' Vicky moved aside to let the foot traffic past. 'Tommy let someone park in my space again.'

'Sorry about that. Tried calling.' Forrester leaned against the wall. 'That new DS starts this morning. A Thursday, of all days. But there you go. I'll be with him all morning.'

'And what's that got to do with me?'

'Means no briefing. Got a couple of disappearances passed over from Local Policing. One in Forfar, one in Invergowrie. Can you take charge?'

'Some Major Investigation Team we are.'

'Can't have murders every day.' Forrester laughed as he handed her the incident reports. 'I'd start with the Gowrie one.'

Vicky took the sheet, folded it and tucked it into her notebook. 'I'll take Karen Woods with me.'

'Actually, I was thinking...' Forrester tilted his head. 'Young Considine needs a bit of coaching, doesn't he?'

Vicky bit the inside of her cheek. *Considine... Great.*

'Cocky wee bugger needs brought down a peg or two.' Forrester grinned, a row of perfect white teeth accentuated by a glint of gold at the edge of a molar. 'And officer development is what being a sergeant is all about.' He pointed out of the door at a gleaming Subaru, dark grey in dark-grey Dundee. 'Our new pool car. You're welcome to have it, if it'll cheer you up.'

'YOU'VE STILL NOT MENTIONED HOW late you were this morning, Stephen.' Vicky took another pass at the incident report but didn't get anything new. 'You're lucky the briefing was cancelled.'

'Whatever.' DC Stephen Considine turned left off Riverside Avenue, passing through the leafy barrier transition from town to motorway. He took a hand off the steering wheel to smooth the side parting in his red hair. Sitting in the driving seat he looked solid and authoritative, quite the presence about him. As long as he was sitting. When he got up, he would have needed another few inches to sustain the impression. *What is he? Maybe five ten? Shorter than me, anyway.* He drove on through Invergowrie, low stone walls and beech hedges lining the dark-brown stone cottages and modern council houses. A couple of church spires pierced the sky at the horizon.

'Don't whatever me.'

Considine sighed as he took a left in front of a sprawling school. 'Sorry.'

'I waited half an hour. I was close to taking Kirk with me instead.'

'Be my guest.'

'Stephen, Forrester told me to take *you*. I'd like to see you explain it to him.'

Considine continued down the long road — low cottages hidden by tall trees opposite two-storey semis. Halfway along, he bumped up onto the pavement behind a squad car and killed the engine. 'I was in late last night.'

'Still need to be on time in the morning.' Vicky looked over at the houses, trying to spot a number. A uniform stepped from the nearest gate and scowled at the car. Vicky got out and met the uniformed officer at the panda car. 'DS Vicky Dodds. This is DC Stephen Considine. What's happened?'

'PC Stuart Melville.' Tall and lanky with a thick goatee that wasn't quite distracting from the male pattern baldness. The stick-thin arms of a competitive runner. 'Boy's wife didn't come home from walking the dogs last night. He's going spare.'

Vicky looked at the incident report. 'Derek Hay, right?'

'That's the boy. Wife's called Rachel.'

'Have you got a trace on her mobile phone?'

Melville looked away. 'Not yet.'

'That's standard process.' Vicky nodded at Considine. 'Stephen, can you call Jenny Morgan? Tell her it's for me.'

'Fine.' Considine sloped off back to the Subaru.

Melville stopped him and passed him a yellow sticky note. 'Here's the woman's number.'

Vicky waved at the grey-harled villa. 'After you.'

MELVILLE LED DOWN THE HALLWAY, busy with multiple doors and little in the way of wall space. The bitter tang of burnt filter coffee wafted out of the open kitchen door. Melville showed Vicky into the living room.

A gas fire burned away in a tiled fireplace, a dark wood mirror mounted above. A man sat on a settee clutching a mug, scratching at the stubble on his face. He seemed uncomfortable in his beige cargo pants, or perhaps the faded green T-shirt was a bit too tight. It certainly wasn't covering his pot belly.

Melville sat on a chair opposite and rested his hat in his lap. 'Derek?'

Hay didn't look up.

Melville nodded at Vicky to take over.

'I'm DS Vicky Dodds.' She leaned back against the window and clocked Considine out front, practically shouting into his phone. She got out her notebook and biro, fixing an appraising look on Hay. *Treat him as a suspect for now.* 'I believe your wife has gone missing?'

'Last night.' Hay leaned forward on his seat, the springs

squealing as he placed the mug on the coffee table. 'Rachel was out walking the dogs yesterday afternoon, as usual. She didn't come back.'

'Are the dogs missing too?'

'Nah, little buggers ran home, scratched at the back door.' Hay's hand twitched as he reached for his mug again, wrapping his thick fingers around it. 'This was at the back of six. Maybe twenty past. She set out at half four, something like that.'

'Does she usually go on such long walks?'

'Every day. Little buggers need a lot of exercise.'

'When did you call the police?'

'Just after half six. I waited to see if they'd slipped their leads and Rach was just behind them. She wasn't.'

Vicky made a note in her timeline. 'And you were here?'

'Day off. I'm the head greenkeeper at Downfield golf course.' Hay shook his head. 'Been on the phone since I woke up this morning, not that I slept much. Friends and family. Nobody's heard from her. They're all worried. I mean, her parents are dead, but she's close to her cousins in Forfar and...'

Considine entered the room, but didn't seem to have anything to report, just reflected Hay's vacant look.

'Here's the thing, though.' Hay set his mug down. 'They're pugs. Rachel breeds them.'

Vicky had to avoid scowling. She hated pugs as much as she had sympathy for them. Deformed beasts carried around by vain idiots, the contorted faces they thought were cute actually stopped the poor things breathing properly.

'She was walking the main breeding pair. They're worth a lot of money.'

'Pugs are great.' Considine smirked. 'My bir—girlfriend's got one.'

Hay got to his feet. 'I can show you, if you'd like?'

Considine stepped towards the door. 'That'd be smashing.'

'This way.' Hay led them into a room lined with dark oak bookshelves on two sides, a dresser at the back covered in garish rosettes and polished trophies. He twisted a key in the French doors and opened the left one wide, then propped it with a stone statuette of a pug. The long Victorian garden was filled with ten dog kennels, the real-life pugs staring at them with heavily creased brows and dark wet muzzles.

'This is the pair Rach was out with last night.' Hay knelt in front of the first two cages. 'Benji and Jemima. Took them to Crufts last year. Proudest day of our lives.'

The dogs seemed to be sharing a collective pout at their visitors. Their wheezing sent shivers down Vicky's spine. She couldn't look at the dogs for long. 'And they ran back on their own?'

'Very territorial dogs, pugs.' Hay pinched his nose tight, grimacing. 'I keep thinking that... What if it wasn't the dogs that ran off? What if it was Rachel? Could she have left me?'

Vicky took a long look at him. *The most likely explanation. Take the dogs out and run off. That would mean Rachel had no attachment to the dogs.* 'We'll do our best to find her, sir.'

BACK OUT THE FRONT, Vicky stopped by the gate and squinted at the house. 'Did that tally with what you heard earlier?'

Melville shrugged. 'Well, you asked a few more things, but there were no inconsistencies if that's what you're getting at.' He passed her a gilt-edged portrait. 'I'll get this scanned and a press release out.'

Vicky took the photo and stared at it, searching for detail.

Rachel Hay standing on a beach somewhere, her smile hiding a coy frown. Like she was annoyed with whoever was taking the photo but habit had kicked in. Lantern-jawed with blotchy skin, her green eyes catching the sunlight. Stick thin, you could see her ribs through her blouse.

Vicky snapped a photo of it on her phone and passed it back to Melville. She looked down the long street, almost completely silent save for the distant murmur of motorway traffic and the rustle of trees in the wind. 'I'm thinking this stays with uniform.'

'Your decision.'

Vicky let out a deep breath. 'That phone trace is our best option. We'll let you know if we get anything.'

'Sarge.'

'Bagsy driving.' Considine set off towards the pool Subaru. 'That's a *wizard* motor. Kind of car that needs a name.'

Vicky shook her head at him as she followed. 'I'll give you a name...'

Melville frowned at something off the path. 'Oh, it's *The Courier*.' He crouched to collect the newspaper, still folded up. 'Didn't see the Garfield this morn—' He stopped dead, a deep scowl on his face, as a sheet of paper dropped to the welcome mat just inside the door.

Classic poison pen style, cut-out letters from a newspaper glued to a blank page:

WE HAVE YOUR WIFE. SHE IS SAFE.
DO NOT WORRY. MUCH.
JUST A LITTLE THING BETWEEN CLOSE FAMILY MEMBERS.

What the hell does this mean?

Vicky stared at the note again, her gloved fingers shaking as she read it slowly. The letters were from tabloids, all red and black, hard outlines. 'It's not signed. Nobody's taking credit for it. And there's no demands.' She pointed at the note and nodded at Considine, trying to hide her shaking hand. 'Get that to the lab.'

'Will do.' Considine grabbed it, his hand stuffed inside an evidence bag like he was picking up dog mess.

Vicky nibbled at her top lip and took another look at the house.

So, this case is more complex than I assumed.

Or Derek Hay's trying to cover something.

She frowned at Melville. 'Can you get hold of the paper boy? Probably innocent, but they might've seen something.'

'Coolio.' Melville paced off, some purpose in his gait.

Vicky snatched the note from Considine as she barged past and re-entered the house.

Derek Hay was on the phone, crouched over his footstool. 'The police think they might find her, Mary.' He locked eyes with Vicky, then looked away. 'I've got to go. Bye.' He put the phone down and smiled at Vicky. 'That was her pal in the town. Mary. Hasn't heard from her in weeks.'

Vicky held up the page. 'There was a note under your paper.'

Hay took a few seconds to scan it. 'This means she's been abducted, doesn't it?' His lips were trembling. 'Is she dead?'

'We don't know anything, sir.' Vicky stayed standing. 'Can you think of anyone who'd want to harm your wife? Any enemies?'

'Not really.' Hay scratched his neck. 'She's involved with the kirk. Does work for cancer charities.'

'What about, I don't know, rivals for the pug prize or something?'

Hay snorted. 'You think this is funny?'

'Very far from it.' Vicky snatched the note back. 'This line here, "Just a little thing between close family members". What does that mean?'

Hay's nostrils were twitching. He snorted again. 'Well, Benji and Jemima are—' he swallowed hard, '—brother and sister.'

It stabbed Vicky in the gut. 'And you make them breed?'

'Pugs need to be—' Hay frowned. 'Wait. This couple bought a dog last year. Poor thing died. PDE.'

'Which is?'

'Pug Dog Encephalitis. It's like meningitis. Only pugs get it, hence the name.' Hay tugged at the collar of his T-shirt. 'We've had a few over the years.'

'How many recover?'

Hay's head slumped forward. 'It's a progressive condition. They all get... put to sleep.'

'I take it the owners weren't happy?'

'They got really angry, started threatening us. Said they'd sue. Only paid a grand for the dog, but they were asking for distress and vet bills and shite like that. Daft bastards hadn't insured it. We settled out of court. Gave them a refund and a couple hundred quid. They seemed happy with that.'

'Do you still have their contact details?'

Hay picked up his mobile again. 'Here you go.' He held it for Vicky to note the number. 'Guy called Gary Black.' He took his phone back, clasping it tight. 'She's just trying to make an honest living, you know?'

Getting a brother and sister to... Vicky swallowed down bile. *Hardly an honest living.*

'We're tracing her mobile number now. It might help.' Vicky smiled at him. 'Was there a set route your wife would walk?'

'Rachel's a creature of habit.' Hay waved out of the side window. 'Same route every day. Go to the end of the village then keep along the edge of the fields, then through the wood by the motorway.'

The regularity could have allowed for easy capture.

Melville bumbled into the room. 'Paper girl's getting taken to the Longforgan nick.'

~

VICKY NOTICED IT BEFORE CONSIDINE. 'THERE.'

Longforgan police station was a small building hidden by trees at the start of the village. Considine slowed to a halt. 'Still motorway driving there. Tell you, I want to take this car home with me.'

Vicky got out and walked across the tarmac to the squat building. She held the door for Considine. 'Let's be quick. I want to go follow Rachel's route next.'

Considine let the door slam behind them. 'Surprised this place is still open.'

'Only station for miles.' Vicky looked around, not so much as a jaded desk sergeant in sight. She tried a door and found a walk-in cupboard. Next door was a coffee room, a pair of beat cops tucking into tabloids and bacon rolls. Vicky chapped the door frame. 'Looking for a paper girl?'

'Try a paper shop.' The older of the two got to his feet, sticking his thumbs in the stab-proof vest dangling free. 'You DS Dodds?'

'For my sins.'

'Two doors down.' He picked a sliver of bacon from between his teeth. 'Follow me.' He led them down the corridor grumbling to himself. 'Young Dannii Patterson. Dannii with two I's, though she'd suit Britney more.'

Through the windowed door, Dannii was leaning back and chewing gum, stretching her school uniform to the limits of decency. Cleavage bursting through the white blouse, bare legs crossed underneath a micro skirt. *Not that I was any better at that age.*

'Had to fetch her from her house. Poor thing was getting stuck into a bowl of Coco Pops before a hard day giving blow jobs behind the bike sheds.'

Vicky prodded the cop in his sternum. 'Constable, I'm going to take that up with your sergeant, okay? You want to use that kind of language, then you're not going to be a cop for much longer.'

He looked away, eyes shut.

'Now. Have you spoken to her yet?'

He shook his head.

'We'll take it from here.' Vicky glared at the sexist prick until he waddled off. She entered the room and sat across from the girl. Considine stayed on his feet and the uniform was gone, no doubt already had his roll between his lips again.

'You going to keep me here much longer?' Dannii popped gum, straight back to chewing without missing a beat. 'I need to get off to school. Got my Standard Grades coming up.'

Vicky nodded for Considine to lead. He was clearly trying to avoid staring at Dannii's legs. And her boobs. Everything but her face. 'Right.' He cleared his throat. 'You been doing that paper round long, Ms Patterson?'

'Few months. Why?'

'We found a note underneath the paper at one of the houses.' Considine held it up. 'Outside number seventeen. You wouldn't know anything about it, would you?'

'Just deliver their paper.' Dannii switched her gaze to the door. 'That's the worst. The dogs are always nipping at me.' She ran a hand down her thigh, eyes trained on Considine. 'Lucky they've never got out. It's a busy road.'

'Mrs Hay went missing last night. The only clue to her whereabouts is the note you appear to have delivered.'

Dannii raised her hands. 'I delivered the paper, that's it.'

'Really?'

'Honest.'

Considine folded his arms. 'Not sure I believe you.'

'I swear.' Dannii leaned forward on the seat. 'I just chuck the paper and get out before those freaky dogs get me.'

Melville found the note under the paper. What was much more likely was someone had slipped the note into the paper after it was delivered. Time for good cop.

'Did you see anyone unusual on the street?' Vicky flashed a warm smile. 'Anyone you don't normally see?'

Dannii tugged her sleeves down over her hands and poked her thumbs through well-worn holes. 'There was, like, this car I'd never seen before?'

Vicky glanced at Considine. 'A car?'

'Big black one, no idea what make it was.'

Vicky noted it down — Considine could look into it, keep him from drooling over the pool Subaru any longer. 'Nothing else?'

'No.' Dannii sat back and crossed her legs, fluttered her eyelashes at Considine. 'Mind if I go now?'

Vicky got to her feet and knocked on the door. The uniform appeared in a puff of burped bacon roll. 'The constable will drop you at school.'

She couldn't tell who sighed louder.

Dannii got up and smoothed down the tiny patch of fabric covering her bum. 'I've not got my bag.'

'Then he'll take you home to get it.' Vicky handed her a card. 'If you remember anything please give me a call. Okay?'

Dannii palmed it like a magician and let Constable Bacon Roll take her outside.

'She's full of attitude, I'll give her that.' Considine stared at Dannii as the door trundled shut. 'Give her a few things, I tell you.'

'Both inches?' Vicky took Dannii's seat. 'We need door-to-door in Rachel's street.' She got out her phone. 'I'll call Forrester and—'

Her phone rang — unknown number. 'DS Dodds.'

'Hey, Vicks, it's Jenny Morgan. You with a DC Considine? Sounds like he fancies himself?'

'And he fancies an underage schoolgirl, too.' Vicky glanced at Considine, watching Dannii through the window as she winched herself in the back of the squad car. Not for the last time. 'You got anything on Rachel Hay's mobile?'

'Switched off at six oh seven last night. You want the last-known location?'

'Shoot.'

'WHAT?' Considine slowed to a crawl as they rumbled over the gravel. They passed a large field segregated into an array of smaller sections, different crops in each. Nearby, two burly men were locked in conversation, arms folded and brows creased. 'This can't be the place.'

'Jenny said it's called the Living Garden. Looks like one to me.'

'Not sure about the living part, Sarge.' Considine pulled into the car park and crunched on the handbrake. 'Heard we've got a new DS.' He tugged at the collar of his dark-grey suit. 'Should be me getting an Acting gig, not some prick from Strathclyde.'

Vicky arched an eyebrow at him. 'You really think you're ready for a DS role?'

'You saying I'm not?'

'You need to have a serious think about whether you are. An honest one.' Vicky undid her buckle and let out a sigh before she said something she'd regret. 'I'm happy to give you some coaching.'

There. Something I'll definitely regret.

Considine let his seatbelt ride up, a smirk on his face. 'What makes you think *you* can coach *me*?'

'You think you don't need any?'

'I know I don't. I'm ready.'

'Stephen, you actually need to *be* ready, not just think it.'

'What about when I caught that taxi driver last month?'

'What about it? You were doing your job. Well done.'

'I did that all on my own, though.'

'That might be the problem.' Vicky got out of the car and walked through the crowded car park, a few steps ahead of Considine. The James Hutton Institute was a low-slung set of dark-brown brick buildings. The doors swooshed open as they approached and stamped their feet on the door mat.

The receptionist looked up from a magazine. 'Can I help?'

Vicky went over to the desk and flashed her warrant card in one hand. In the other, her mobile phone screen showed the portrait of Rachel Hay. 'We're investigating the disappearance of a Rachel Hay. Do you recognise her?'

'Sorry, no.'

'Sure about that?'

'Hang on.' The receptionist scowled. 'Is that the woman whose dogs ran all over the garden?'

Vicky frowned. 'Go on?'

'Aye, that's her. These wee pugs, cutest little angels you'll ever see. But they got off the lead and started running all over the place, digging up the Living Field outside.' She waved back out the door they'd just walked through. 'You'll need to speak to the curator about it.'

A WOMAN KNELT at the flower bed nearest them, back bent in focused labour. She looked mid-forties, a greying ponytail snaking down her back. She wore shorts and a vest top, despite it being late March in Dundee.

'Excuse me.' Vicky cleared her throat. 'We're looking for a Marianne Smith?'

The woman thrust the trowel into the ground and got to her feet, rubbing her wrist against her temple, eyebrows raised. 'That'll be me.' She tore off her garden gloves and held out a hand, her skin rough and pale. 'And you are?'

'DS Vicky Dodds. DC Stephen Considine.'

Marianne nodded at them both. 'How can I help?'

Vicky noticed a few other workers looking over. 'What are you working on here?'

Marianne dusted off her hands and chewed on a dirty fingernail, slightly torn down the middle. 'I doubt the police are interested in our work. What do you really want to know?'

'We're investigating a woman's disappearance. We believe she was walking her dogs near here yesterday.'

'There are quite a few people walk up this way.'

'Name of Rachel Hay.' Vicky held up the photo. 'This is her.'

Marianne frowned. 'Nope, sorry.'

'Strange.' Vicky pointed back to the main building. 'The receptionist just told us her pugs ran all over this garden.'

'I remember her now.' Marianne stared at her for a few seconds, jaw clenched. 'Well, I didn't see her yesterday.'

Vicky held her gaze before looking away with a curt nod. 'What did her dogs do?'

'They ruined half of the garden.' Marianne sighed, then gestured around the space. 'Trampled a crop of Malaysian seeds we'd just sown, *crucial* to a PhD project. Ingrid had to start again from scratch.' She shook her head slowly. 'Pugs are the most despicable breed.'

'In what way?'

'Oh, nothing to do with them per se, just the breeders. I love dogs, but I hate dog breeders.' She seemed to shudder. 'All that incest.'

Vicky underlined Marianne's name twice in her notebook. 'Where were you between four and seven p.m. yesterday?'

'At home. In Fife.' Marianne folded her arms. 'I did a talk at the local high school in the morning.'

'And after that?'

'Reading.'

'Can anyone verify that?'

'I live alone.'

Vicky made a note then handed her a card. 'If anything jogs

your memory, please don't hesitate to get in touch.' She led Considine towards the car, glancing back at Marianne as they stopped by the Subaru. 'We need—'

Considine's phone rang. 'Do you mind?'

'Go for it.'

He answered it, walking round to the driver's side.

Vicky looked back at the Living Garden.

Is Marianne Smith involved? Is losing a few weeks' work enough to kidnap someone? Then again, she said she despised dog breeders.

Definitely need more people, though.

Vicky got out her phone and dialled Forrester. Two rings and he bounced it.

Wanker.

She tapped out a snotty text and sent it. *If nothing else, I've got an audit trail.*

'Oh ho ho!' Considine walked over with that grating smirk plastered all over his smug face. 'That was someone who *definitely* wanted to kill Rachel Hay.'

3

'What sort of name is Perspect?' Finger on the intercom buzzer, Considine shook his head at the brass plate, the purple-and-lime logo curved and twisted beyond legibility.

'A bad one.' Vicky looked down Whitehall Street, old town-houses now turned into city centre shops. A bakery and a camping store either side of Perspect Financial. Across the road, bookies, pizza restaurant, Chinese buffet. 'I remember when that was Debenhams.'

'Showing your age there.'

Cheeky bastard. Vicky nodded towards the office. 'You're leading here, okay?'

'Perfect.'

The door clicked open. A tall man in a suit beamed out at them, pale skin shaved close, clutching a tall beaker of coffee like it was his life support. His pink shirt looked box fresh, the navy suit less so. 'How can I help?'

'Police.' Considine showed his warrant card. 'We've got an appointment with a Gary Black.'

He slurped coffee. 'That's me.'

'Mind if we do this somewhere other than the street?'

'Sure thing.' Black pointed inside. 'Come in.' He pushed through the glass door with his free hand. Inside, the small unit was filled with offices, gleaming chrome, modern art filling the white walls — splashes of oranges and reds in a series of three large canvases. Black sauntered through a glass door and shrugged off his suit jacket before the door had even closed behind them. He draped the jacket over his chair and collapsed on it. Then took a long pull at the coffee. He pointed at Considine. 'You said on the phone this is about wee Boab. My daughter loved that dog. Poor wee bastard.'

Considine smoothed out his notebook on the desktop. 'Can you take us through what happened, sir?'

Black's glare showed that he saw right through Considine acting like a real cop. 'Had him about half a year. One day, the wee guy just wasn't himself, ken? The wife took him to the vet. He reckoned he'd seen it before. Called it NME, like the music paper. Said it stands for something like necrotizing meningitis, something like that. Gave us some pills but they didn't help wee Boab. Had to put the little fella to sleep a week later. The vet could only confirm it was this NME after the autopsy.'

'And what did you do?'

'What do you expect?' Black sucked up more coffee through the lid. 'I went ballistic. Pitched up at that Hay woman's house and had it out with her. Course, she denied all responsibility, said the dog must have caught it.' He clenched his fists, pressing down hard on the wooden desktop. '*Caught it.* Can you credit it? The vet told us NME's *hereditary.* Boab wasn't the only defective dog over the years. Should see her setup, man. She's breeding brothers with sisters. Cousins with uncles. Breeds from three bitches and this boy's the father of two of them. That's not right. Just not right.'

Vicky tried to ignore the sickening tear at her gut. 'Did you do anything else?'

'I'm not a violent man, but I swear I came close to swinging for her prick of a husband. We'd paid them a *grand* for that dog. The medication and vet bills came to another grand. Didn't even have insurance, which—' he held up his hands, '—is my fault, I'll admit.'

Considine scribbled in his notebook. 'What happened next?'

Black finished his coffee and tossed the cup in a chrome bin. 'We just wanted a refund and our vet fees. But the way they acted... We took them to court.' He let out a deep breath. 'But it didn't bring Boab back. We settled and got another dog. The scruffiest mongrel they had. And I donated the money we got off the Hays.' He leaned even harder on his fists. 'My wife and daughter loved wee Boab. Him dying hit them hard. I had to tell my wee girl that Boab wasn't coming home. Do you know what that's like?'

'You're saying there was some animosity on your part?'

'Course there bloody was.' Black picked his fists up and dunted the wood. 'They shouldn't breed those animals so closely. It's unnatural.'

Considine folded his arms. 'Can you give us your whereabouts yesterday afternoon?'

'Sure thing... Wait a minute. What are you suggesting?'

'Mrs Hay was abducted last night.'

Black blinked a few times. 'What?'

'You know anything about it?'

'What? No. Of course I don't. Come off it, eh?'

'I'm serious, Mr Black. We need to eliminate you from our inquiries.'

'Jesus wept.' Black tapped at his computer. 'I was working till eight, okay? Client meetings all over town. Happy to share my itinerary with you.'

'That'd be useful.' Considine smiled. 'When was the last time you saw Rachel Hay?'

'Not since she signed that cheque back in November. Couldn't get out of there fast enough in case the bloody thing bounced.'

≈

WELL, Forrester definitely got my text.

Vicky got out of the Subaru, back at the Living Garden. All around, cops were interviewing people. Plainclothes she recognised and uniforms she didn't. Showing photos. Getting statements. Progress. And not just her and Considine.

'Look into Black's background, will you?' Vicky glanced at Considine as he got out of the driver's side. 'Get someone to check out his wife and kid. See if that story was in the papers.'

Considine let out a deep breath, his lips vibrating. 'That all I'm good for?'

She thought she saw Forrester in the car park and marched off, Considine hot on her flat heels.

Give me strength. Vicky stopped. It wasn't Forrester. She locked on to Considine's grey eyes, dark shadows underneath them. 'Stephen, I've been over this with you—'

'Look, I'm a wee bit resentful of you bossing me around here.'

'Constable, you need to deal with it.'

Considine looked up and down the street. 'I should be getting that DS gig, not some punter from Glasgow.' He stabbed a finger in his chest. 'Me. I know the team, I know the area.'

Vicky tried to disarm him with a smile. 'DI Forrester asked me to coach you. That means you need to tone it down a bit. Nobody wants to hear you go on about how you need a promotion, or how you arrested a taxi driver all on your own, or how your daddy never loved you.'

Considine breathed hard through his nostrils, jaw twitching.

'If you want to become a DS, you need to *demonstrate* you're a DS, not *declare* it. Show, don't tell.' Vicky stared down at the car park's grass, cut through with mesh reinforcement, a nerve at the back of her neck thudding. 'And start with being a competent DC. Lose the attitude. Show me you can do your job and I'll put in a word with Forrester, okay?'

'What the hell...?' Considine gave a sniff, like he'd been at the Airfix glue. 'Fine, Vicky.'

'Call me Sarge. You need to show some respect.'

'Fine, *Sarge*.' Considine wandered off to speak to some uniform.

Vicky took out her mobile and tried to ignore the huff. Still nothing from Forrester.

Superb...

'Sarge?' Melville was lumbering over towards her. 'Sarge?'

'Heard you the first time.' She smiled at Melville. 'How's Derek Hay?'

'As you'd expect.' Melville scratching at his head like he had nits. He held up the portrait of Rachel, still in its frame. 'I've scanned it, press release should be out by lunchtime.' He stared at the photo. 'Wouldn't kick her out of bed for farting.'

'Excuse me?'

'Sorry, Sarge. Figure of speech.' More scratching. 'You getting anywhere?'

'The paper girl didn't know anything. Gary Black has an alibi.'

'The boy who bought the dog off her, aye? He's a suspect?'

'Maybe.'

'Well, after his name came up, I did some digging. Turns out he called us after the dog was put down. We investigated it but couldn't find a crime, so Trading Standards took over. Brought in the SSPCA. Neither progressed it past cautioning Rachel about her breeding practice.'

'You're saying she's allowed to breed and sell dodgy dogs?'

'About the size of it, aye.' Melville rubbed his forehead. 'Though if there were any further instances the SSPCA were going to prosecute. As far as they're aware, the recent sales have been clean. I don't know if she's been using a wider breeding stock or what.'

Vicky focused on the garden, a pair of workers laughing through a smoke break, upwind of Considine and his cronies.

Someone's dogs tearing the place apart doesn't seem serious enough to warrant kidnapping. Not that anything else does, so far. We know precious little about Rachel Hay.

'It's sickening, Sarge. Getting brothers and sisters to shag. Sickening.' Melville's fists curled tight. 'I had a wee chat with the Hay laddie about it. Way he tells it, that dog's death is an isolated incident. Told me it was taken to a specialist for treatment. Place called Tayside Animals or something?'

Vicky nodded slowly. 'Where the Blacks got their new dog from.'

'Worth speaking to them, do you think?'

Vicky clocked Considine, tempted to call him with a whistle. Instead, she just waved. 'I'm praying for leads, so we might as well.'

THE TAYSIDE ANIMALS kennel was just over the Marketgait from Bell Street nick, Vicky's police station. Deep in old mill territory, one of the few buildings to be repurposed, the purple *TA!* logo graffitied all over the brown stone. Trees grew out of the building opposite, next to a mosque.

Something set the dogs off, and a barrage of barking burst out.

'Making an absolute racket.' Considine stopped and pointed at the sign next door, a halal meat packer. 'Suppose they can just chuck them in there when they don't get rehomed.'

Vicky grabbed his shoulder. 'Would you like to have your throat slit and be hung up to bleed out?'

'Sorry!' Considine held up his hands. 'Didn't know you were so precious. Have I touched a nerve?'

'I had a dog from Brown Street kennels when I was growing up. Sonic.' Vicky stood glaring at him, something stinging in her stomach. '*Never* joke about that sort of thing, especially on this case.'

Considine bowed his head. 'Look, I'm sorry, okay?'

Vicky brushed past and entered the corrugated iron building through the main door, flashing her warrant card at the receptionist. 'We're looking for Alison McFarlane.'

THE OFFICE DOOR opened and six women left, all frowning at Vicky and Considine as they waited.

Vicky glanced through a window to the yard. Rows and rows of dog cages with only one family looking around, a mum and dad dragging a surly teenager.

In the office, two women sat across a desk, both wearing green scrubs with darker epaulettes on their shoulders. The computer on one side was surrounded by small pot plants, their leaves touching the beige monitor.

Vicky smiled at them in turn. 'Alison McFarlane?'

The older of the two pushed her keyboard away and raised herself to her full height. She was short with an erect posture, spiky blonde hair streaked with grey, her skin aged from a working life spent outdoors. She offered a wrinkled hand. 'That'll be me.'

Vicky shook it. 'Thanks for seeing us.'

'Not a problem.' Alison gestured at her colleague. 'This is Yvonne Welsh. The brains behind the operation.'

Yvonne blushed. Despite remaining seated, she looked even taller than Vicky. Dark hair cut short, piercing blue eyes. 'This is Alison's place.' She waved her left arm, her short sleeve lifting just enough to reveal a tattoo on her toned bicep, a cartoon cat raising its paw. 'I just help out, that's all.'

Vicky sat in one of the chairs, still warm from the meeting. 'I understand that one Gary Black brought a dog here for treatment?'

'Ah, wee Boab. Hawthorn Robin is his—' Alison snarled like a cornered bloodhound, '—*pedigree* name.' She pulled a leaflet out of her drawer and slid it across the desk. 'We provide a service for dogs suffering from congenital defects, even though we're just covering up for bad practice. NME is caused by inbreeding in pedigree dogs, especially pugs with their very limited breeding stock.' She looked away with a shudder. 'I hate that term.'

'What happened to Boab?'

'He was put to sleep.' Alison grimaced, her eyes cold. 'We had no choice.'

Yvonne's eyes were locked on the window.

Vicky waved a hand in front of them. 'Am I boring you?'

Yvonne swallowed as she made eye contact. 'Sorry, I'm not

good at speaking with people. Animals, I'm fine with. People, I just don't get.' She glanced at Alison. 'I'm almost domesticated.' She took the leaflet and passed it to Vicky. 'I've developed a way of helping them manage the symptoms, extending their lives by a few months, sometimes up to a year. Poor Boab wasn't so lucky.'

Alison waited for her to finish before jumping in. 'What's this about?'

'We're investigating the abduction of Boab's breeder, Mrs Rachel Hay.'

Alison put a hand to her mouth. 'Is she okay?'

'She's still missing.' Vicky sat back and stared out of the window —a couple were walking a black Alsatian. 'In your view would Gary Black want to harm Mrs Hay?'

Alison thought about it then nodded slowly. 'A few months ago, I would've said yes.'

'And now?'

'Now... Well, the Blacks have been seeing a bereavement counsellor, which helped Mr Black. He wrote a letter to Mrs Hay, saying he'd forgiven her.' Alison brushed some fluff off her shoulder. 'The Blacks took one of our needier dogs, a lab-collie cross. Cyclops, because he only has one eye. They gave us a good donation. It funded a pilot programme.' She passed another leaflet.

Vicky took it but didn't look at it. *Feels like dealing with Jehovah's Witnesses.*

'Mrs Hay was the first breeder we educated on their errors.' Alison got another piece of paper out of a drawer. 'She imported some pugs from China and their breeding quality has markedly improved. She received a commendation from the Kennel Club to that effect.'

'And you think this was enough for Mr Black?'

'He wrote a letter to them in support of the award.'

Vicky scowled. 'Why didn't he mention it to us?'

Yvonne flashed up an eyebrow. 'Mr Black's a strange chap, it has to be said.'

෴

'WHAT DO YOU THINK, SARGE?' Considine held the front door for Vicky. The couple from earlier were filling out a form, their surly teenager fussing over a squat mongrel. 'That put the Blacks in the clear?'

'I'm annoyed he didn't mention it.' Vicky walked past him and headed back to the car. 'Can you get someone to speak to him about it?'

'Sarge.' Considine dawdled behind her.

Vicky stopped by the Subaru and got out her phone. The dogs sent out another salvo of barking. She called Melville. 'You getting anywhere?'

'Got a wee bitty more out of the husband when I returned the photo.' Melville huffed out a grunt. 'Some cock-and-bull story about Gary Black signing a letter saying that he was happy with their breeding practises. That sound right to you?'

Vicky glanced round at the approaching Considine and got a nod. *Down a suspect already. Not that anyone else is popping up.* 'Heard it from another source.'

'Ah, Christ. Had a fiver on him.' Melville paused for a few seconds. 'Funny thing, though.' He clicked his tongue a few times. 'Only member of Rachel's family Derek couldn't get hold of is her brother in Forfar.'

Forfar? She froze. Forrester's words that morning jabbed Vicky in the face:

'Got a couple of disappearances passed over from Local Policing. One in Forfar, one in Invergowrie.'

CONSIDINE WEAVED in and out of traffic as they drove into Forfar, spending more time on the wrong side of the road.

Vicky clutched her mobile, the display still blank. 'Slow down.'

Considine eased it to below the speed limit. 'That slow enough for you, Miss Daisy?' He pulled up and winked at her. 'You not enjoying the Python?'

'The *Python*?' Vicky rolled her eyes, then got out first. She walked up the path to the grey-harled box marked with a 19. 'I don't know Forfar too well, but this doesn't look like one of the better parts.'

'I live here and it isn't.' Considine was still blushing, looking like he was about to say something as he knocked on the door.

It opened, and a uniformed officer stood there. Medium height, slightly overweight, thick sideburns drooping below his jawline. 'You Dodds and Considine?'

Vicky pulled out her warrant card, nodding. 'And you are?'

'PC Murray Watson.'

'We're dealing with his sister's disappearance.' Vicky put the card back. 'We understand Mr Joyce is missing.'

'Kirsty found this. His wife.' Watson got out an evidence bag containing a letter:

WE HAVE YOUR HUSBAND. HE IS SAFE.
DO NOT WORRY. MUCH.
JUST A LITTLE THING BETWEEN CLOSE FAMILY MEMBERS.

4

'It's a match.' Vicky took a deep breath. 'Another disappearance.' She handed the note to Considine. 'Where was it?'

'Underneath her *Sun*.' Murray rasped a hand down his bushy sideburns. 'Just back from speaking to the paper boy. Denies dropping it off. Lad swears he didn't see anything weird. Said he was half asleep and listening to Slayer.'

'Slayer?' Considine grinned to himself. 'Half asleep's the only way to listen to that shite.'

Murray handed Vicky a photo of a man, his emerald eyes shining out of the crumpled page. 'Best photo she could find.'

'And we live in the age of smartphones and selfies...'

Paul had his sister's lantern jaw, covered in dark beard hair. On top, the close shave trailed off into a widow's peak stopping a good portion of the way down his forehead.

Looked like Paul and Rachel's parents had been related, too.

Vicky caught herself. *These people are victims. Stop joking about it.*

'In all the other photos the boy was gurning or making slanty eyes.'

Vicky nodded at the house. 'We need a word with his wife.'

'She's not in a good way.'

Not that anyone would be.

Murray led them straight into the living room, a small space crammed like an IKEA catalogue, all lacquered wood. A wall-mounted TV played a news channel on mute. Next to it was one of those white-background photos, parents and kids in an action pose. A family trying hard to project easy bliss.

Kirsty Joyce was slumped on the dark green sofa, a wad of paper tissues in her hand, her red face slicked with tears. She wore a grey tracksuit, her cream T-shirt stained brown in the middle. A vacant look in her eyes. 'I'm not trying to cause any trouble. Just wanted to check he wasn't in the cells or hospital.'

'You're not causing any trouble.' Vicky sat on the adjacent sofa. 'Mrs Joyce, we understand your husband didn't come home last night?'

'Paul's a good man. A great dad.' Kirsty bit her lip. 'Only thing is... Every few months, he'll go and watch the football in town and lose track of time.'

'Who does he drink with? Mates?'

'Sometimes. Occasionally some Polish boys from his work.' Kirsty zipped her top right up to her chin, biting into the flesh. 'I called him all night but nothing. His phone was switched off.'

Like Rachel's. Shit, shit, shit.

'Usually... Usually Paul will pitch up first thing before the kids are up, reeking but, you know, *alive*. Not this morning, though. So I called you lot. Just thought I'd be on the safe side. But when I got that letter...' Kirsty broke off in tears.

The same story that played out every night in Tayside. Husband with one too many stays out with some mates or complete strangers. Meanwhile, their poor wife sitting at home, the worry about their husband's location adding to those about the kids and bills.

Sometimes, it was just a few too many with the boys. Sometimes, another woman. Sometimes, it was something else entirely.

Vicky waited for her to make eye contact again and flashed a smile. She tried to think quickly. *Too many options here. Only problem is they all match up with his missing sister.* 'When was the last time Paul spoke to his sister?'

'What the hell has Rachel got to do with it?'

Vicky focused on the painting behind Kirsty, a still life of pale flowers. 'She's gone missing, too.'

Kirsty shut her eyes.

'Were they close?'

'Hardly. Rachel shacked up with that ponce when she was eighteen. Paul says she's getting above herself.'

With a green keeper?

'Any family?'

'Their parents died about ten years ago.' Kirsty gnawed at a knuckle, the skin about to split as her teeth sunk into it. 'Their dad worked at Murison's like Paul does. Their mum was a cleaner.'

'Derek mentioned cousins in Forfar?'

'Paul doesn't have anything to do with them. Bunch of pricks. Into their horses and that.'

So it looks like an attack on Rachel, rather than her brother. 'And there's nobody who'd want to harm Paul?'

'Nobody. And I mean that. He's not got many mates. Keeps himself to himself. He likes a drink but nothing too bad. He's funny when he gets pissed. Never heard of any fights. The nights he goes missing he just loses track of time. Ends up in a mate's flat scoffing a pizza and drinking whisky. I track his location on his phone so he's not seeing some floozy.'

Vicky stared out at the street. 'Have you noticed anything odd recently? Strange cars, maybe?'

Kirsty frowned. 'Well ... Just after I got the kids off to school, I saw a car outside. Black. Big, too. Shot off when I got to the end of the road.'

'Do you remember the make and model?'

'No, just the colour.' Kirsty shook her head. 'Why are you asking?'

'We're investigating it as a lead.' Vicky perched forward. 'It's possible this is all a big misunderstanding, okay? Who was the last person to see Paul?'

Kirsty frowned hard, really concentrating. 'I spoke to his boss this morning. He said he saw Paul yesterday afternoon. After that...' She just shrugged.

VICKY STOPPED at the canteen entrance and looked around. The factory floor was littered with static conveyor belts and abandoned forklifts. A couple of men leaned against a van, chatting. 'I worked in something similar in Carnoustie one summer. A lot more basic than this.'

'Surprised they've got factories in Car-snooty.'

'They don't anymore.' Vicky pushed open the door to the busy canteen, the place stinking of frying meat and onions. She headed for the nearest occupied table and stood over a man reading a book. 'Looking for Michael Murison.'

Without looking up, the man waved behind him. 'Two tables back. Boy fiddling with his phone.'

'Thanks.' Vicky clocked him immediately. Mid-fifties, red-faced, glaring at his mobile and shaking his head. 'Mr Murison?'

'Who's asking?' Murison clocked her warrant card and jolted upright. 'Christ, who let you in?'

'The security guard downstairs.'

'Need words with him.' Murison picked up a roll and took a bite before dropping it back to his plate. *Fatty mince on a white roll. Scottish cuisine at its finest.* 'What can I do you for, hen?'

'Looking for Paul Joyce.'

Murison swallowed his mouthful, then ran his tongue over his teeth. 'Not been in today.'

Vicky sat opposite, the chair cold through her trousers, and got out her notebook and pen. 'Not coming into work this morning isn't odd?'

'Seen it all in this game, hen. Thought he'd pissed off to the boozer last night. Liverpool match on the telly. Paul's a big fan. And I'm not a dick like some boys in this game.'

Vicky checked her watch. 'It's okay for him to lie in till half twelve?'

'With me, course it is. Turnbull and Deeley down the road? Doubt it. I trust my lads until they start taking the piss.' Murison thudded the table with his fist, making sure the nearby workers heard him. 'Then I come down on them like a ton of tatties.'

'And does Paul take the piss?'

'Hardly. Paul's a grafter, if he wants a lie in, fine by me.' Murison cackled. 'Everybody likes him. Always got a cheeky comment.' He stared at the table. 'Even gets on with the foreign boys. Big drinker, but nothing bad. Few pints of lager a couple of nights a week. Occasionally he'll go off on one, like today. That's it. Boy isn't a fighter, if that's what you're getting at.'

'Does he gamble?'

'I wouldn't know.'

'Of course you wouldn't.' Vicky nodded slowly, drawing out the time. All she got was the sickly sweet smell of his roll. 'When was the last time you saw Mr Joyce?'

'Yesterday afternoon. Sent him out on a delivery last thing.'

'What sort of delivery?'

'Tatties. It's our bread and butter, hen.' Murison cackled at his joke.

'Did he take a van?'

'Course he did. My name on the side, hen.'

'We'll need the registration plates.'

'It's in the office.' Murison looked at her like that was enough to get them to leave. 'Anyway, some boy phoned up needing three hundred kilos for some fancy dinner or something. Told him it'd have to be pretty special to need that many tatties.'

'When was this?'

'Call came in about half four. Paul went out not long after.'

Vicky added it to her timeline —becoming crowded. 'Where was this delivery to?'

Murison lifted his roll and bit into it, fat dribbling down his chin. 'Delivery was to somewhere in Dundee. Can't remember.'

'Knowing where might help us. Does the van have GPS?'

'Sorry, hen.' Murison lifted his roll's top and squirted ketchup. 'Listen, we're a bit disorganised just now. My PA's just gone on maternity leave and the temp's not exactly hit the ground running.'

'That's not good enough.'

Murison picked up his roll again. 'Look, I'll check once I'm done eating, okay?'

'It's possible that Paul's been abducted.'

'Seriously?' Murison nudged the plate away, the porcelain screeching off the laminate. 'Ah, Christ.'

'Now, unless you give us a name, address and inside leg measurement of where this delivery was, I'll bring in half of Police Scotland to find out what the hell you're hiding here.'

'Look, hen. I'm an honest businessman, okay?' Murison's dark glare softened. Then he clicked his fingers. 'Just remembered. Paul took the call himself.'

Vicky furrowed her brow. 'Did he answer it?'

'No idea.'

'Do you have a switchboard? Does your temp PA answer it?'

'Kind of. When the phone in the office rings, anyone who's about picks it up. Paul told me he got a call for a shitload of tatties. Asked if he should deliver them. I'm not going to turn that down.'

Vicky inspected Murison's face. *Probably just covering his arse and the bottom line.* 'Get through to your office now and give me the delivery address and phone number of this order.'

Murison picked up his roll. 'Just let me—'

'Now.'

'You'd make a cracking Terminator.' Another chuckle from Considine, staring at his phone. 'Unbelievable.'

Vicky slowed as she approached the row of buildings. 'See what you mean about this car.'

'Wizard motor.' Considine pointed down the street. 'Unit seventeen. That blue one. I think.'

A warehouse surrounded by a heavy-duty fence, currently padlocked shut. The building was narrow but taller than the rest of the estate, save the Jewson around the corner.

'You think?' Vicky shot him a glare. 'I need better than that.'

'You saw Murison's stock system, Sarge.' Considine inspected his notebook again. 'New company, not properly set up, just a mobile number and that address.'

No sign of the Murison's van. No sign of anything, except a queue at the burger van. 'I assume he must've left.'

'But where did he go?' Considine got out first and crossed the road. He rattled the giant gates, huge padlocks keeping them in place. 'Police!' Nothing, just the echo of his voice.

A smashed window upstairs looked like a snarling dog's teeth. Even sharper.

'This is no use.' Vicky followed the fence round to the side and clocked a For Sale sign, probably visible from the Kingsway.

Considine was on tiptoes. 'Building's empty, Sarge.'

'Very well deduced, Sherlock.' Vicky gave the gate a final shake.

What was the play here?

Two missing siblings. Two weird notes and two dead ends.

'Come on, Stephen.' Vicky unlocked the Subaru and got behind the wheel. 'Let's get back to base.' She pointed at the sign. 'Can you call the estate agents?'

'A Detective Constable's work is never done...'

'Because you never start it.'

VICKY PULLED up outside Bell Street nick, filling the last pool car space. The blue 1-Series was still squatting in hers. She got out into the gale, the evidence bags holding the ransom notes flapped in the wind. 'Got anywhere with the letting agent?'

'Still on hold, Sarge.' Considine caught up with her in reception. Sergeant Davies was dealing with an elderly couple in visible distress. 'Just a minute.' Considine held his ID card over the reader but didn't swipe. He turned back to Vicky, hand muting the call. 'Letting agent says that unit's owned by some boy in Edinburgh, been looking for new tenants for over a year. Nobody's ordered half a ton of tatties.' He pulled his hand off the mic. 'If I can have a word with the owners, that'd be smashing.' Looked like he was going to hang up.

Vicky waved a hand in front of his face. 'Any security we could speak to?'

Considine turned away again to speak. Then back. 'Guard goes around once a week to check on it. I've asked for his number.'

'Get it.' Vicky nudged him out of the way and swiped through.

'Took forever, that.' Considine followed her down the corridor. 'Not even had a chance to eat my burger.' He opened the polystyrene box lid, giving a whiff of grilled meat. Didn't smell too bad. 'See that mince roll in Murison's canteen? I'd kill for one right about now.'

Vicky entered the stairwell, her stomach rumbling. 'My granny used to make them. Fry some mince, shove it on a roll with butter. Rank.'

'Surprised you've made it to forty, Sarge.'

Vicky stopped on the first step, hands on hips. 'I'm thirty-five.'

VICKY DODGED her way along the corridor, busy with uniform coming back from lunch breaks, and followed a fat man in jeans and T-shirt into the Forensics office, stinking of Pot Noodle and sour BO.

Jenny Morgan had a teacher's desk near the front of the room, looking out across her team. Shoulder-length red hair and pale skin, looking like she needed a jumpstart from Dr Frankenstein every morning. She looked up at Vicky and gave the smallest smile. *Probably so she didn't get any lines on her perfect skin.* 'DS Dodds, are those the—? Yes, they are!' She picked up the crinkling evidence bags containing the notes like they were slates carved with the word of God. 'Interesting.' She clicked her fingers and summoned the guy Vicky had followed through. 'Jay, do the doings on these, please. Fingerprints, paper stock analysis. And find out which editions and papers they're from.'

'Okey doke.' Jay took the notes, his belly wobbling out of the sides of his T-shirt.

Jenny watched him waddle off. 'Thinks the world of himself, that one.' She gave him a withering look as he sat. 'Like young Considine. Getting on well with him?'

'Like a house on fire, Jen. Preferably with him tied up inside.' Vicky slumped into the chair opposite her friend. 'You getting anywhere with the phone traces?'

'Rachel's phone hasn't been on since last night.' Jenny leaned forward and pouted. 'Bit of a weird one, isn't it? Brother and sister. Imagine if it was you and Andrew being kidnapped?'

'Not that I've seen my brother for a while.'

'You do know he's back, don't you?'

'What?'

Jenny waved over at the far side of the room. 'Doddsy!' Vicky's brother didn't look up. Huge DJ headphones like a Cyberman in *Doctor Who*.

'Back in a sec, Jen.' Vicky went over to him and pulled at his headphones.

'Piss off!' Andrew batted at her hands and grabbed the head-phones back. 'Vicky?' He frowned. Beard, purple bags under his eyes, his hair a mess, looking heavier than she'd ever seen him. 'What are you doing here?'

'Might ask you the same thing.'

'Working on finding that Airwave scanner.'

'That what?'

'You need to pay attention to briefings, sis.' Andrew rolled his eyes. 'We received intelligence that someone used a scanner to hack into the Tetra network.'

'Thought you needed access codes?'

'Who says they don't have them as well?' Andrew looked around the room. 'The Tetra system was supposed to be totally secure, but that's not necessarily the case. Ways and means, usually backhanders to pissed-off coppers. Problem is we can't trace it to a cop, so it's flummoxed us. Which is why they've got me in.'

'Right. You look tired.'

'I am tired. I've forgotten half of what I knew about the bloody Airwave system. I'm the only idiot left from the original team, so the Bride of Frankenstein put pressure on me.' He shook his head at Jenny, tapping at her computer, completely oblivious. 'Luckily, her maker hasn't installed eavesdropping software yet.'

Vicky laughed, but her frown settled back on her forehead. 'You taking care of yourself?'

'Fell asleep in the toilet. Twice.'

'Andrew!'

Jenny frowned at them, then got up and marched over, arms folded. 'You got an ID yet?'

'Jen, you only asked ten minutes ago.'

'It's a five-minute job. At most.'

'Jenny?' Vicky thumbed at the corridor. 'A word.'

'Andrew, chop chop.' Jenny followed Vicky out. 'What?'

'You need to back off. Andrew's ill.'

'What are you talking about?'

'You are his line manager, aren't you?'

'He's IT. His boss seconded him to me to get this Airwave scanner stuff nailed down.'

'He's on long-term sick. He's got ME.'

'Shite.' Jenny's face crumpled, her mask dropping. 'He's not mentioned it.'

'My brother doesn't know how to say no.' Vicky grabbed Jenny's arm. 'This is going to kill him, okay? He needs rest.'

'Fine. Fine, fine, fine.'

'Thanks, Jen.' Vicky re-entered the office and charged over to her brother. 'Come on, Andrew, I'll drive you home.'

'Great.' Andrew's shoulders sagged. 'My sister acting like the big girl while I go back to Mum's.'

'You're not well, Andrew, you shouldn't be here.'

He huffed out a sigh. 'Right. You win. Again.' He folded his laptop shut and tugged at his hoodie.

Vicky walked him over to the door. Each footstep was like a thousand miles.

'Vicks?' Jenny was frowning at her. 'Got something on that trace.'

Vicky smiled at her brother. 'I'll see you outside, okay?'

Andrew stepped off, looking like he was in severe pain.

'That call Paul Joyce received at Murison's?' Jenny held out a sheet of paper. 'Came from a burner. Pay-as-you-go.'

'Bloody typical.'

'But very suspicious.' Jenny tapped her perfect little nose. 'And his phone's been switched off since it pinged the cell site at the industrial estate last night.'

'That's his last-known location?'

'Correctamundo.'

'Thanks, Mum. He's waiting in the car park.' Vicky climbed the stairs, the metal resonating with each step, then swiped through to their office space. Ten desks with a view of the car park and the closed door of Forrester's private office. The place was almost empty, the usual smell of burnt coffee mixing with print toner and damp. 'You need to keep a better eye on him.'

'And I will, Victoria. I will.' Click and Mum was gone.

Vicky stopped by her desk. A blue overcoat was folded on her chair. A navy leather document pouch, embossed with *EMac*, lay on her computer keyboard. She picked it up and dumped it on the floor. Forrester's office looked out onto the communal space, but the lights were off inside.

'Sarge?' Considine walked over holding some paperwork. 'You got a minute?' He dropped some prints on the desk. 'Been digging into this Gary Black boy.' He showed her the first page of newsprint, looked like the *Courier*. 'The story was all over the papers in October, November time. I checked the journalist, some lassie called Anita Skinner, but she's not at the paper anymore.'

'Try and track her down, Stephen, there's a good boy.'

Considine scowled at her. 'See what I can do, Sarge.'

'Good work.'

'Don't mention it.' Considine shrugged. 'Want me to brief DI Forrester about it?'

Why would he...?

Vicky sighed. 'I'll get back to you on the next steps.' She handed him back the pages. 'Have you got hold of the guard at that building yet?'

'Waiting on a call back.'

'Never wait, Stephen. Chase him up. And find his boss and chase them up.'

'Sarge.' Considine slouched off, like he'd been expecting to be made Chief Constable for downloading some old newspapers.

Vicky leaned across the desk and waved her hand in front of DC Karen Woods' face. 'Seen Forrester?'

'Not for ages.' Karen took out her earbuds and stretched out, her green blouse riding up her slight belly. Her round face twisted into a grin, getting even rounder. Wispy blonde hair hauled back in a tight ponytail. 'He had that new DS in his office all morning. Gone for a meeting with DCI Raven.'

'Typical.' Vicky hauled the overcoat off her chair and draped it over Considine's.

Karen rested her headphones on the desk. 'You had lunch yet, Vicks?'

VICKY ENTERED THE CANTEEN, sniffing at something spicy in the air. 'Hope they've got mince rolls on today.'

'Mince rolls?'

'A Fifer like you wouldn't get it.'

'Don't you dare diss the Kingdom, Vicks.' Karen squinted over Vicky's shoulder. 'Oh, that's the new DS with Forrester.'

At the far end of the room, Forrester winched himself to his feet then clapped the shoulder of the officer next to him, obscured by the crowded canteen. 'They're coming this way.' She pulled her blouse tight. 'Been trying to call you, sir.'

'Right, sorry. We've been busy.' Forrester patted her on the arm then gestured at the new guy. Tall and athletic with a broad grin. Black suit, blue tie, white shirt. Dots of stubble, like he'd have a full beard by five o'clock. 'This is DS Euan MacDonald.'

And the EMac made sense.

'Vicky Dodds, right?' MacDonald turned the grin up another few volts. 'David's told me a lot about you.'

Vicky raised an eyebrow. 'All good, I hope.'

'No comment.' MacDonald laughed as he held out his hand. 'Please, call me Mac.'

What sort of person gives themselves a nickname?

'Pleasure to meet you, *Mac*.' Vicky shook his hand then scowled at Forrester. 'Need to catch up with you about the case, sir.'

Forrester's smile was polite at best, eyes gesturing to the door. 'Can't it wait?'

'We've got two missing persons and we need to search the last known location of one of them. I want you to approve—'

'Hang on, hang on.' Forrester waved his hands in the air. 'Vicky. I'm not approving *anything* based on a wee chat in the sodding canteen, okay?'

Very far from okay.

'Two people are—'

'Vicky. I'll phone you.' Forrester paced off.

'Nice to meet you.' Vicky smiled at MacDonald then watched them walk off, joking like old pals already. 'Bit of an improvement on old Ennis.'

Karen rolled her eyes. 'Oh, Vicky, tell me you've not fallen for him already?'

'Hardly.' Vicky tried to hide her blush by inspecting the menu. Baked tatties left, for once. 'Wouldn't trust him an inch.'

Karen smirked. 'How about nine?'

～

'VICKY! CALM DOWN!' Forrester stood by his office window, the early afternoon sun silhouetting him from behind. 'I need you to take us through it, okay?' He walked over and poured himself a coffee from the hissing machine in the corner. 'Here you are.' He stared at Vicky over the edge of his Dundee FC mug. 'And you want to raid this building?'

'Correct. DC Considine is just tracking down the security guard.'

MacDonald helped himself to a mug. 'Anyone taken credit for this?'

'No.'

MacDonald blew on his coffee. 'Any ransom demands?'

'None. Just these notes, which are fairly abstract.' Vicky held up a photocopy of the Forfar note. 'Their spouses both received them. Jenny Morgan's doing some analysis downstairs.'

Forrester slurped coffee. 'She's a good one.'

'She's the one who traced Paul's mobile to this location and I think—'

'—we should enter the building and search?' MacDonald tilted his head at Vicky.

She shot him a glare which said 'Don't you dare finish my sentences'. She added a frosty smile. 'Correct. We just need to—'

'And these notes?' MacDonald took a sip of coffee. 'Got anything on who delivered them?'

Vicky tapped at her scribbles. 'Got sightings of a black car at both addresses around the time the letters were delivered this morning.'

MacDonald yanked the picture off the whiteboard and caressed it like a lover. 'Ooh, a Mercedes. Nice one. E-class, right?'

What was it with boys and cars?

'The papergirl only said it was *like* this.' Vicky snatched it off him and pinned it back up. 'We need to show her a wider range to get a positive ID.'

'With you.' MacDonald stroked the photo again as he put the mug down. He tapped the whiteboard over Dryburgh Industrial Estate. 'I think we need to get in there and see what's what.'

'Still don't buy it.' Forrester spun his coffee mug round slowly. 'Feels very much like a hunch. Why do we think the brother's going to be in there?'

'Because...' Vicky felt her rage boiling her blood. *Come on, you know how to deal with him.* 'Because if he's in there and we *don't* look, Raven's going to come down on you like a ton of bricks.'

Forrester dumped his coffee mug and grabbed his jacket. 'Let me sort a warrant, then.'

~

'CAN YOU BELIEVE IT?' Vicky pulled in at the end of a line of four cars at the Dryburgh Industrial Estate. 'I'd been begging and begging, then bloody Super Mac repeats what I said and here we bloody are.'

MacDonald and Forrester stood by a burger van, Mac handing over a few coins. *Sneaky twat.*

'Maybe it's how he said it, Vicks?' Karen let her seatbelt flop on her lap. 'You're not the most eloquent, are you?'

'Cheeky cow.' Vicky got out and headed over. The van had a decent view of the unit across the road. Still looked dead inside, the huge gates still padlocked.

Forrester was squinting at the building. 'Which one is it?'

'Over there.' MacDonald thumbed behind them. 'Big blue one.' He handed Forrester a coffee cup from the burger van. 'Considine's got hold of the security guard.'

'Excellent.' Forrester unfolded a warrant and took a slurp of coffee, the breeze rippling the surface. 'We've no idea what's in there. I want grid searches on each floor.'

MacDonald nodded at Vicky. 'Good work getting us to this point, Sergeant.' *Sanctimonious, too.* He squinted into the distance. 'Here we go.'

Considine was charging along the pavement, leading a man with a bad limp dressed in full security guard outfit, the sort that made a uniformed cop look underprepared. *Not that he'd ever have anything to be prepared for.*

MacDonald's Airwave crackled. 'Serial Alpha, this is Serial Bravo. That's the back door secured, Mac.'

'Nice one.' MacDonald nodded at Forrester. 'We're good to go.'

'Come on, then.' Forrester parked his coffee on the lid of a bin and set off across the road. 'Vicky, you take DC Woods and four of the uniforms. Mac, you're with me, we'll secure downstairs. I want two officers on full guard of the exits, engine running.' He surveyed the group, splitting them in three with chops of his hand — four, four, two. 'Let's go.'

The security guard hobbled up to the gate, where Considine was holding the padlock like it would help. He rummaged around with his set of keys and tried one. The lock put up a fight but after a second squeeze it opened and thunked to the ground. Considine rushed inside, holding the gate open for the rest of them.

Vicky got her team close behind and entered. The floor was open, rows of ceiling-height shelves sitting empty, a couple of forklifts left sitting in the middle of the aisles.

Forrester stopped them with a clenched fist, then pointed at MacDonald and mouthed, 'Ground.' Then at Vicky, 'Upstairs.'

She nodded then headed to a set of stairs to the left. As she climbed, her team's footsteps echoing behind, she mentally divided the floor into six areas based on the layout of the ground floor. One each.

She stopped at the top of the stairs and signalled for her team to wait.

Silence. Almost. The only sound was a tap dripping somewhere to the right. Must be hammering down from some height. The place looked empty, but it was hard to tell — there was a different layout up here. Corridors twisting around, the windows of a partition wall showing an office or storage room, another revealing an empty hallway.

Superb... My plan is up the spout.

Vicky gestured to the team. 'Split up.' She formed one group with Karen, while the other four officers paired off. 'Take a third of the floor per group. Meet back here.' She glanced at Karen then led down the corridor, the windowless grey wall looking like it went right to the back of the building. As they crept forward, a clanking sound joined the dripping tap. *A broken radiator, maybe?*

Vicky tiptoed towards the sound and was soon blocked by another wall, six big windows roughly cut into the plasterwork. The noise came from a large room on the other side, filled with crates and shelves.

Karen tugged at her sleeve. 'Can you smell that?'

Vicky sniffed — nothing. Wait, something sweet and tangy. 'Is that shit?' She motioned for them to split.

Karen headed left and Vicky took the right, opening a door and inching into the room. The rattling got louder and more insistent the further she went. Seemed to be coming from a cage at the back of the room. The stench made her gag. Excrement mixed with ammonia. *Urine?*

Vicky kept going, hand clasped over her mouth and nostrils, and stopped dead.

In the cage, two people lay naked, legs and torsos smeared brown, the base of the cage wet and filthy, shaking and rocking. A man and a woman. Impossible to tell if it was Paul and Rachel.

The man was doing most of the rocking, pushing against the bars with the filthy soles of his feet, face contorted with the effort, mouth taped up. 'Mmmf!'

Karen started tugging at the bars.

Vicky searched the front of the cage for a catch, a keyhole, anything. *Nothing.* She circled around the sides, the metal almost lifting off the ground, as the man rocked it even harder.

At the back, she froze. 'Shit, shit, shit.' A note pinned to the cage at the far side:

NOT SO NICE IS IT?

6

The firefighters nudged Vicky back. 'Give us a bit of space, eh?' The chainsaw bit into the cage, sparks biting at Vicky's eyes, screeching tearing at her eardrums. A woman's scream, still muffled.

A paramedic barged through the wall of firefighters and reached into the cage. Vicky inched forward and compared the photos with the faces of the two poor souls emerging. A paramedic tore the tape from the woman's mouth — skinny, lantern jawed. *Definitely Rachel.* 'You need to find those animals!' Her scream echoed round the room. 'They need to pay for this!'

Paul was prostrate, a dead weight to the two paramedics hauling him out. Stayed silent when the tape came away from his lips.

Forrester looked shell-shocked. Couldn't stop shaking his head. Then he snapped to attention. 'Right. Mac. Vicky.' He walked away from the centre of the storm. 'We need to get on top of this. Mac, can you set up street teams here, Forfar and Gowrie?' He waited for a nod. 'Vicky, I need you with me at the hospital. That cool?'

Vicky leaned against the wall. 'Cool with me.'

'Right-o.' Forrester did up his suit jacket. 'I'll rustle up some uniform, then.' He sauntered off, tapping at his phone.

MacDonald stood next to her, hands in pockets, eyebrows raised, leaning against the window. Like he'd practised that pose. 'Penny for them?'

Vicky felt the nerve in her neck twanging again. 'Just trying to process everything.'

'Some first day.' MacDonald's grin shone.

'Nothing compared to what you're used to in Glasgow, I suspect.'

'You'd be surprised.' MacDonald flashed up his eyebrows. 'Still, rescuing two kidnap victims is a pretty good result.'

'We didn't really rescue them.' Vicky narrowed her eyes. 'Paul's mobile led us here. If I'd been on the ball, we could've got in here quicker, maybe even caught them.'

'Sorry madam, I couldn't help but notice your glass is half empty.' MacDonald laughed. 'Take the credit for finding them, eh?'

'Right.' Vicky rubbed her hands. 'I just wish we'd caught whoever kidnapped them, trapped them in a cage and welded it shut.'

'Weird how nobody's taking credit for it.' MacDonald held out a hand. 'We should grab a coffee soon. Get to know each other.'

'Definitely.' Vicky pushed away from the wall, smoothing down her trousers. 'Not today, though.'

'Naturally. Forrester's shoved me right into the thick of things. Good place to start.'

'I'll do you a deal. Give me Karen Woods and Stephen Considine and you can have the other four.'

'I'd say thank you, but I feel like you're trying it on.'

'Hardly. Forrester told me to keep an eye on Considine. Besides, you've got much more ground to cover.'

'Fair enough.'

'Catch you later.' Vicky left MacDonald with a smile and made her way through the throng of firefighters, skipping aside as the paramedics wheeled Paul away. She found Karen and Considine chatting with a pair of uniforms. A glare got them to break off from the pack and join her by the stairs. 'Right. Karen, you're in charge of the street team round here.' That got a nod. 'Stephen, can you help out?'

'Are you serious?' Considine glowered at Karen. 'I mean, I'll go along with it, but...'

'Tell you what, Stephen.' MacDonald grabbed Considine's shoulder. Vicky didn't know he'd followed her. 'How about you come out to Forfar with me, and if you're a good boy you can have that Subaru?'

Considine beamed like a child on Christmas morning. 'I'll take that.'

～

VICKY STOOD in the corridor of Ninewells hospital, drinking from a can of Diet Coke. She sucked in the drink's smell along with the sharp odours of cleaning fluids rising from the damp laminate floor.

But all she could smell was that cage — sweat, urine, shit.

'This is barbaric.' A short doctor stepped out in the corridor and took a deep breath. Maybe late thirties, but she was barely five-foot tall. Most of that seemed to be hair, a wild, dark-brown frizz. Eventually her eyes settled on Vicky. 'DS Dodds?' She waited for a nod. 'Dr Alison Rankine.' She offered a hand.

Vicky shook it.

Rankine smiled. 'I'll start with Rachel. The good news is there aren't any physical injuries, at least nothing serious.' She grimaced. 'Paul, on the other hand . . . He's clearly been throwing himself against that cage as hard as possible. It's likely that he's cracked his skull. He's definitely sprained his ankle and bruised his shoulder.'

Vicky finished her can. *No sign of a recycling bin.* 'Can I speak to them yet?'

'Rachel, yes.' Rankine looked away. 'Paul's still not speaking, I'm afraid. I'm not sure if he's suffered a brain injury or sustained some kind of psychological trauma.' She brushed her thick hair out of her eyes. 'He's just not talking.'

'Thanks.' Vicky entered the room and sat on the seat by the bed. Tried to make eye contact with Rachel but got nowhere. 'My name's DS Vicky Dodds of Police Scotland. I'm investigating what's happened to you.'

Rachel didn't speak, her eyes moist with tears. She looked about ten years older than her photo and there was no sign of a smile, coy or otherwise. Dark rings around her eyes, lined with worry. Kept blinking every second, an off-beat rhythm, hard to pin down. Then a shudder. And another. Her breathing slowed.

'Mrs Hay, can you understand me?'

Rachel nodded, her fingers screwing a tissue. 'Are my dogs okay?'

'They're fine. Your husband's looking after them.'

'Derek...' Rachel adjusted her position on the bed, the frame creaking as she moved. 'Where?'

'Your husband's on his way in. You'll get to see him soon.'

'Paul?'

'He's not doing so well, I'm afraid. He's either unable or unwilling to speak.'

Rachel closed her eyes.

'Mrs Hay, do you know who abducted you?'

Rachel shook her head.

'Did you see them?'

'Masks.' Rachel clicked her fingers, trying to find the words. 'Balaclavas. They'd... done something to their voices. Deep, mangled, like... Like the IRA on the TV, years ago.'

Vicky noted it. 'Tell me everything you remember, please.'

Rachel took a few seconds to compose herself. 'I was walking. Just past the Hutton Institute. The dogs startled. A car approached but... it's a fairly busy route. Didn't think anything of it. Then someone grabbed me. From behind. I dropped the leads and the dogs... The dogs ran off.' A tear slid down her cheek. 'I thought that was the last time I'd see my babies.' She turned her head to the side and looked out of the window, her jigging leg rattling the bed. 'Then they drove me somewhere and... put me in that... cage. They stripped me, then locked us in the cage. Welded it shut. I thought we'd die in there.'

'Was Paul there first?'

Rachel nodded.

'When did you last see your abductors?'

'Lost track of time. Maybe a couple of hours ago. I kept thinking we were going to die...'

'It's okay. You're safe now.' Vicky gave her a fake smile. 'Do you have any idea why anyone would want to do this to you?'

Rachel rubbed a tear from her cheek. 'None whatsoever.'

'What about the dogs you sold with PDE?'

Rachel's eyes widened. 'The Blacks wouldn't do this to us.'

'You sure about that?'

'We settled everything. It was amicable. Gary wrote us a very nice note for the Kennel Club.'

Vicky let her silent gaze do the asking for her.

Rachel sat staring at her hands, silent. 'I kept thinking it was Paul they were after.'

The door opened. Derek Hay ran in and held his wife close.

Vicky sighed then backed out of the room.

VICKY STOOD by the drinks machine. Another can of Diet Coke, another attempt to wash away the bitter taste. She took a long swig and spotted Dr Rankine's approach.

'You need to see this.' Dr Rankine passed a sheet of paper to Vicky, tiny text full of numbers. 'I fast-tracked the blood tests. They were both sedated. And Paul's had sildenafil citrate...' She tapped at a second sheet. 'Viagra.'

'Christ.' Vicky's skin tingled, her mouth now dry as dust. 'They were trying to get them to have sex?'

'Not for me to say.' Rankine pointed at Rachel's door. 'Mrs Hay didn't consent to a rape kit. Said she wasn't raped.'

And it just gets better...

Vicky folded her arms. 'Is Paul speaking yet?'

'He's displaying symptoms similar to catatonia, interspersed with moments of rage. I'm concerned it's a brain injury, though. But... Well. The nurses have cleaned him up... And...'

Vicky glanced at Rankine. 'Am I okay to speak to him?'

'Look, I've no objections to you trying, it's just...' Rankine shrugged. 'We'll need to monitor his condition. If he becomes agitated again, I'll have to sedate him.'

VICKY TOOK the seat next to the bed. 'I'm investigating what happened to you and your sister. I want to help, but I'll need your co-operation.'

No reaction. Paul Joyce lay absolutely still, eyes fixed on a single point at the ceiling.

'Paul you were abducted, weren't you?'

Nothing.

'Someone kidnapped you.'

No response.

'Whoever did that took your sister, as well.'

A brief flicker of his eyelids.

Vicky leaned forward, the chair tipping up at the back. 'Paul, what did they do to you?'

No reaction.

'Paul, did they try to make you do something?'

Moisture formed in his eyes. 'My *sister*.' His eyes shot up to Vicky's. 'My *sister*.' Blinking, he flared his nostrils and clenched his teeth. Swallowed hard. 'My *sister*.'

'What happened?'

Paul opened his cracked lips again and spoke in a whisper. 'They tried to force us to... do it.' A tear slid down the side of his face, eventually dropping into his ear. 'They had a thing. Like a cattle prod. Kept zapping me.' He bucked with sobs. 'They...' His breathing quickened. 'They tried to make us have sex.'

'Did they succeed?'

The bed made a grinding noise as Paul sat up, clasping his fists around his knees. 'She's my *sister*.' He slammed a fist on the bed.

'Do you have any idea why they'd do this to you?'

Paul shook his head, eyes locked shut. Then he laughed, the sound utterly devoid of humour. 'They were after Rachel.' He let out a deep groan. 'I don't have enemies. I don't follow Scottish football, I'm not religious, I'm not gay, I'm not trans, I'm not black, I'm not Polish, I'm not racist. I've got no debts. This isn't about me.'

'What about when you were attacked?'

'Got a call asking for three hundred kilos of Maris Piper to a building on the Dryburgh Industrial Estate. Mr Murison okayed it, so off I went in a van.'

'To where we found you?' Vicky got a nod, but it looked like she might lose him. 'Have you been there before?'

'Got some wood from the Jewson when I was doing our attic a few years back but never to drop off any tatties.'

'This caller, what did they sound like?'

'Male. Twenties. Angus accent. Maybe Forfar or Brechin. That's about it. They got me from behind. Zapped me but didn't knock me out.' His eyes glistened as he glared at Vicky. 'They took me into an empty room and put me in that cage. Not long after, they brought Rachel in and zapped me again. It was dark. I knew Rachel was there, but I was tied up. They'd taped up my mouth.'

Vicky swallowed, the metallic taste of Diet Coke still in her mouth. 'What did you see of your attackers?'

'Nothing. They wore balaclavas, and they did that thing with their voices like in that *Arrow* show on Sky, made them all deep and that.'

'You say *they*?'

'There were two of them.'

'Male or female?'

'Definitely one male.' Paul rubbed his nose. 'I've no idea about the other one. Didn't really see them. They kept the light shining at us.'

'What light?'

'I think it was from a camera.' Paul shut his eyes. 'I think they were filming us.'

7

'Filming them?' Forrester leaned against the wall, pinching his nose. He looked like he was trapped in the cage himself, his own sister straddling him. 'Sick, sick bastards. Jesus suffering—'

'Sir, that file could be on YouTube right now.' Vicky put her hands on her hips. 'We should get IT to monitor video traffic. A couple of analysts, at least.'

'I'll see what I can do.' Forrester almost collapsed against the wall, the energy falling out of him. 'I want to know who did this.'

Ignoring the sick taste in her mouth, Vicky walked over to the giant map on the wall, covering Tayside as far north as the Angus glens and down into deepest, darkest Fife. She circled the industrial estate on the city's sprawling north side. 'Paul was called out on a delivery to Dryburgh Industrial Estate in Dundee.' Pointing at the city's north side. 'He was attacked here and taken inside.'

Then she moved west to the Hutton Institute. 'Rachel was abducted near her home in Invergowrie and taken over.' Back to the industrial unit. 'They knew precisely when and where to abduct both victims. This is meticulously planned. You'd need to monitor Rachel over a couple of weeks to assess whether she'd take the dogs on the same route every day.'

She traced her finger through the long loop round Invergowrie, south of the M90, and tapped the Hutton Institute, then
on the industrial estate. 'They were quick, too — they jumped her
an hour after they got her brother.'

'And here was me looking for some inspiration, not more
puzzles.' Forrester scratched the back of his head. 'It's risky. And it
all hinges on this tatty order. It's a lure. Paul drops it off and they
nab him. Once he's secure, they've got an hour to grab his sister.
Agreed?'

'Very doable.' Vicky pinched the gap between Dryburgh and
the Hutton Institute. 'Just head down the Kingsway. Ten minutes,
even with bad traffic. Even gives some time in case her route's
slightly delayed.'

'Right-o.' Forrester got out his phone. 'Feels like the heat's on
the warehouse, then. Can you get back there and start kicking
arse?'

BACK AT DRYBURGH, uniforms milled around cracking open doors
and taking statements from bored-looking supervisors and
delivery drivers. In the eye of the storm, Karen Woods sat in a pool
Focus tapping away on her phone.

Vicky hauled open the door. 'What are you doing?'

Karen glanced up. 'It's called "running things".'

'Looks like you're trying for another three stars on *Angry Birds*.'

'Finished that *years ago*, Vicks.' Karen got out onto the street,
her blouse riding up to let her belly droop out before she hauled it
back. 'Got hold of the security camera up there.' She pointed at a
building then held up a standard-issue laptop, not attached to the
hamster powering it. 'Got a sighting of your black car.'

Vicky snatched it from her and squinted at a black blur. Could
just as easily have been the Batmobile. She hit play and the car
disappeared. She wound it back and played it again, just the blob
passing through.

Superb...

Vicky scanned around the nearby buildings. Satellite dishes and advertising billboards, yes. CCTV, no.

'I'm trying to get a make or model, Vicks. There's an expert in Aberdeen, got a load of photos of blurry cars, means he can work out what this is.'

Vicky didn't hold out much hope. 'When was this?'

'Last night, just before Paul got here.'

'So it could be unconnected?'

'A black car, Vicks?' Karen took the laptop back. 'We've been through the rest of the footage. The driver was smart and avoided detection, assuming it's been here more than once.'

'Have you got Paul's abduction?'

'Just got him going up to the gate.' Karen hit play again and Paul walked past the camera, his gait slightly lopsided. That was it. 'No coverage of the entrance. And he didn't come back out.' She pointed back at the road. 'The van was unlocked when we searched it. Still got all the tatties.' She waved over. Some SOCOs were milling around the van, dusting and cataloguing and photographing, but it looked like they knew they'd find nothing useful.

'Where do you want me?' PC Colin Woods sidled up to them, the sun catching the crescent-shaped birthmark on his left cheek. He was eye-to-eye with Vicky, sixteen stones of monster bulging out of his uniform. Nobody would dare mention his birthmark. 'Alright?'

Vicky smiled back at him, then took the laptop as Karen led her husband away. She played the video a few times.

So little to go on, but the car was here. Karen's expert... That case a few years back, someone matched a model and year based on similar footage. Something to do with having photographs of every car in every possible position and condition and—

'Bloody hell.' Karen stomped over, hands in pockets. 'He's pissed off he's working for his missus. I tell you, when I get him home...'

'You'll be wearing the uniform?'

'Piss off, Vicks.' Karen snatched the laptop from her and tossed it in the car. 'Colin's out tonight so I've only got two kids to feed.' A sly smile tugged at the corners of Karen's mouth, eyebrows flicking up and down a couple of times. 'Listen, he's playing squash tonight with his new best mate. Our new neighbour. Do you want to come over and watch a film?'

'I've got something on.'

'Right. Well, we could meet them after they play squash?'

Vicky didn't like the insinuation. 'What are you up to?'

'Nothing!' Karen reached in to wind up her window. 'Well, we're going out with Robert for a curry tomorrow night and . . .'

'I'm not tossing my car keys in the middle, Kaz.'

'Come on, Vicks...'

'You're not suggesting a double date, are you?'

'No! Well, yeah.' Karen reached into the car for her Airwave and checked the display. Whatever it was wasn't worth responding to. 'Robert and Colin are getting on like a house on fire. Guy's a teacher and a nice one.' She raised an eyebrow. 'Bet he could teach you a thing or two in a private class.'

'Don't be lewd.'

'You started it! Look, Vicks, we're going up to the Ferry for a curry, maybe a couple of drinks afterwards.'

'We'll see.'

Karen's forehead wrinkled. 'I worry about you.'

'I'm fine.' Vicky sighed, glancing around the area for prying ears. The closest was a man in a dress shirt and tracksuit bottoms clutching a tin of strong cider as he gave a statement to Colin Woods, the can at arm's length, glasses atop his white hair. *That won't stand up in court...*

'You can always talk to me, you know?'

'About what? Still being single at my age?' Vicky scowled at her. *Two counts of ageism in one day?* 'I'm hardly decrepit, am I?'

'Far from it. Look. The offer's there. Robert's a nice guy.'

'I'm still trying to do that "don't take your work home with you" thing. Just so many things to juggle on my own. Going out drinking with two cops isn't that.'

'It'll be fun. Let you get your hair down.'

Vicky took a deep breath. 'I'll think about it.'

'You do that.'

'Here, darling?' The security guard limped over, his leg sliding behind him. 'Just checked on that delivery, eh?' He waved a clipboard around. 'The cage turned up on Monday.' He passed the clipboard to Karen. 'Found some delivery paperwork in the office.'

'Thanks.' Karen grabbed it and start dialling a number on her phone. She quoted the reference number.

'Put it on speaker.' Vicky inched forward, trying to listen in.

'—on Monday afternoon at two fifteen.' The voice coming out of the phone crackled with static, the accent a mixture of Birmingham and Glasgow. 'Oh. Yeah. The credit card used was reported stolen, so it's with our fraud department. I can put you through?'

'More interested in who delivered it.'

'Hang on, yeah?' Some loud tapping. 'Yeah, looks like DDX Couriers based in Dundee. Dryburgh Estate.'

Vicky looked around. *The DDX depot was just down the sodding road.*

~

'SCOTT KEILLOR?'

The man in the brown and orange uniform stopped loading his van and looked Karen up and down. 'Who's asking?'

'DC Karen Woods.' She showed her warrant card. 'Your manager said we'd find you here.'

Vicky kept her distance, one eye on the delivery driver, one on the laptop screen. The CCTV had him stepping up to the door, cut as he got close, just like Paul.

Keillor's lip curled up as he returned Karen's warrant card. 'So, *this* is why I got called back in?'

'I did offer to meet you elsewhere.'

'Did you now?' Keillor flashed a smile. 'How can I help, ladies?'

'The word you're looking for is "Officers".' Karen put her card away, her face tightening as she waved at the next building over.

'Your boss said you delivered an animal cage to unit seventeen at the Dryburgh Industrial Estate on Monday.'

'Give me a sec.' Keillor reached into his van and retrieved his PDA, stabbing the screen with a stylus. 'Bloody thing.' He stabbed harder. 'Right, here we go. Delivered them in the afternoon. Just after two.'

'Was it signed for?'

'Sure was.' Keillor stabbed the PDA again. 'A bloke, I think.' He handed it to Karen.

She inspected the device. 'This is just a cross.'

'That's one of the better ones, believe me.'

Karen groaned then nodded at Keillor. 'Can you remember anything about the man who signed for it?'

He took a deep breath, arms folded, staring at the ground. 'See so many people in this game. Sorry.'

'Mr Keillor. Anything you can remember could be crucial.'

'I *think* he wore a hoodie.' Keillor stared into empty space for a few seconds. 'Had a scarf on, too. One of those Take That ones, you know, all tied back? Couldn't see his face.'

'You didn't think that was odd?'

'I didn't think much about it, hen. Dundee in March. Be weirder if he was wearing shorts.'

'What about height and weight?'

'Sorry.'

'Was it definitely a man?'

Keillor shrugged. 'Could have been a big lassie, I suppose.'

'So, a tall person then?'

'Five eleven, maybe six foot. Big coat on so I couldn't tell you about build.'

'Thanks for your help, Mr Keillor.' Karen handed him a card. 'If you remember anything, please give me a call on either of those numbers.'

Vicky led away. 'As your friend, I feel duty-bound to tell you that you ought to make it harder to get your number. Especially as you're a married woman.'

Karen glared over at her husband, still with cider man. 'See how long that lasts, I tell you.'

'Excuse me?' Keillor was back, frowning. 'Just remembered something. I had a wee smoke with the cleaner here last night. She said something about seeing some boy getting bundled into a car just over there.' He pointed back towards the empty unit. 'Amount she smokes, she sees *everything*.'

~

'COME ON, COME ON, COME ON.' Vicky pressed the buzzer. White-harled hell box off the main road. Not much better than Vicky's house, all told, but in Craigie and not Carnoustie. She nodded at Karen. 'You lead.'

Karen straightened her shoulders. 'Sure thing.'

A small, middle-aged woman answered the door, wisps of smoke coiling up from her cigarette. 'Can I help?'

Karen smiled. 'Looking for Irene Henderson.'

Irene stared at them, slowly puffing on her cigarette. 'What's this about?'

'We're investigating an abduction up at the Dryburgh Industrial Estate.'

Irene leaned against her front door and exhaled through her nostrils, red lines of scar tissue tracing up her nose. The anger in her face lit them up like votive candles. 'Did that Keillor boy put you up to this?'

'Ms Henderson, a man was abducted there last night. We wonder if you saw anything?'

Irene folded her arms. Shaking her head, she pulled the door fully open. 'In you come.'

Vicky followed her down a narrow hall to a small room thick with cigarette smoke. A carriage clock ticked away on the marble mantelpiece beneath a landscape painting — men in straw hats tending to a boat on a river, the canvas dark and brooding. She perched on the front edge of a sofa, while Karen remained standing. 'Wondering if you saw anything unusual last night? About five o'clock, say.'

Irene collapsed into a green armchair by the window and stubbed out her cigarette on a bronze ash tray, resting it so she could relight it. 'Well there's something, maybe. Had a row with my boss about my hours so I went outside for a smoke. Saw this boy standing outside the next building. Place has been empty for ages, ken? Anyway, someone pulled up in a swish motor, grabbed the boy and shoved him inside.'

'You didn't think to report this?'

Irene shrugged. 'Not my business.'

'Can you describe his attackers?'

'Wearing balaclavas, I know that much. Three of them.'

Vicky frowned. 'Definitely three?'

'Three. Definitely one woman, though, I remember that.' She gurned at Karen. 'Child-bearing hips like yours, doll.'

'What about the others?'

'I'd say there was a man for certain. The third one, I don't know.'

'Androgynous?'

'Andrew who?'

Vicky stifled a laugh. 'Could the third attacker have passed for either a man or a woman?'

Irene scowled. 'Like a trannie?'

'No. In terms of build, you know, smaller, no obvious curves or bumps.'

Irene shook her head. 'I didn't get a good look at them.'

'Did anybody else see this happen?'

'This is Dundee, sweetheart.' Irene laughed. 'Nobody sees anything.'

'And the car you mentioned?'

Irene sniffed. 'Never mentioned a car.'

'You called it a "swish motor".'

'Right.'

Vicky showed her the blurry shot on Karen's laptop. 'Was it like this?'

Irene took a long look before shaking her head. 'That could be anything. It was getting dark. Didn't get that good a look at it, like I said.'

'But it was black?'

'Must've been.'

'And it was a saloon?'

'Could've been, aye.'

'Right.' Vicky made a note. 'Well, thank you anyway.'

Irene picked up her cigarette and sparked her lighter. She blew a cloud of smoke at Vicky. 'Shut the door on your way out, hen.'

8

'I want to expand the street teams working Invergowrie and Forfar, but...' Vicky scribbled on the whiteboard in Forrester's office, the pen squeaking as she wrote. '...we need to find the driver of this car. If we broaden out the CCTV search, we might get plates or a better description than "it was like one on an advert", or it was "a swish motor".'

'Agreed.' MacDonald rubbed his hands together. 'Wondering if we should go public with it?'

'Not sure.' Forrester walked up to the board and took off the photocopied poison pen letters left at the homes. 'I'm struggling with the why. Usually, when there's a kidnapping, there's a ransom note. We've just got someone playing games here. They don't seem to *want* anything.' He pinned them back down. 'But they've got to be doing this for a reason.'

'Publicity?'

'Exactly.' Forrester clicked his fingers. 'If we go public, we scare people. Anyone breeding dogs or delivering tatties starts dirtying their undies. Is that what we want? No. These letters are unsigned.' He took a long, hard look at the board. 'We may be dealing with a new group. Some weird MO that involves filming your victims.

Have they shared it? Vicky, can you speak to the National Crime Agency?'

'I've had experience with the NCA.' MacDonald shrugged at Vicky. 'Happy to help.'

'Done.' Forrester added *Mac — NCA* to the *Actions* list. 'Now. Suspects?'

'We should speak to Rachel's husband again.' Vicky shrugged. 'Also, the Living Garden curator, Marianne Smith. Rachel walked her dogs there every day, and apparently they trashed part of the garden a while back causing a load of work and aggravation.'

'Right place, right time, but...' Forrester slurped more coffee. 'That enough to abduct her?'

'I worked in Motherwell CID for a year.' MacDonald flashed a grin. 'I saw someone stabbed over a losing lottery ticket.'

'And they say Dundee's a backwater.' Forrester gazed at Vicky as he tapped the board. 'What about Gary Black, the poor sap who bought a dog from her?'

Vicky rubbed his name out. 'He didn't do it.'

'He's got a clear motive.' Forrester wrote his name in again. 'Rachel sold him a dog with a congenital disease. And you told me he's been researching canine health. He could've got angrier the more he learned about the adverse effects of line breeding incest. We're cooking on gas with him.'

'The flame's gone out, David.' MacDonald sat back down and drank some coffee, grimacing at the taste. 'He got his money back and he donated the cash to an animal charity, right?'

'And he supported Rachel.' Vicky shook her head. 'Said she's improved her breeding practices.'

MacDonald stared at the board again. 'What if Paul's the target?'

Vicky shrugged. 'I doubt it. We've no suspects there.'

'Still, let's keep an open mind.' Forrester tapped at *Notes* on the whiteboard. 'But I agree. Someone's trying to send Rachel a message about these bloody dogs. Just... who?'

'We've got a slight problem.' Vicky folded her arms. 'Paul

described two people, but Irene Henderson saw three people abduct him.'

'The man, the woman, the ladyboy.' Forrester shook his head. 'Sounds like the start of a joke.'

'And not a very funny one.' Vicky wanted to pick him up on his transphobia, but... She sighed. 'She's maybe not reliable, but our working hypothesis should be three abductors.'

'Fine.' Forrester put the pen back and grimaced. 'Mac, you okay to keep an eye on the detectives and uniformed officers still going around Dryburgh?'

'Sure thing. Might narrow it down to two or confirm three.'

'I need to update DCI Raven.' Forrester marched towards the corridor. 'Full team briefing at nine tomorrow, but I expect you pair in earlier, okay?'

'Night, sir.' Vicky left the office and headed for her desk.

MacDonald joined her, hands in pockets. 'We didn't get that coffee, did we?'

'No, we didn't.' Vicky grabbed her bag and put it over her shoulder. 'Tomorrow?'

MacDonald grinned. 'Look forward to it.'

Vicky knocked on her parents' front door, casting a nostalgic look back along Bruce Drive as she waited. The old street looked the same, only now the neighbouring kids she grew up with had kids of their own. *Like I need another reminder of my single status. And how many of those old friends are as reliant on their parents as I am?*

Her mum opened the door, a stern frown on her face accentuated by the severe black trousers and the long hair hanging loose. 'Good evening, Victoria. Nice of you to finally show up.'

'I'm not late, Mum. Besides, I'm working a big case.' Vicky tried peering past, but she just got the smell of Dad's stale cigars. Not that he'd be stupid enough to smoke in there. 'How's—'

'Mummy!' Bella came bouncing out of the door, easily side-stepping her grandmother. She grabbed Vicky by the waist, wide eyes and flushed cheeks looking up. 'Mummy!'

Vicky picked her up, resting the wriggly little legs against her hip. 'Oh, you're almost too heavy to be carried.' She kissed her on the head. 'How's my baby?'

'Granny made tablet!'

Vicky put Bella down, rolling her eyes at her mother. 'Mum, I've told you...'

'I don't remember you complaining when you were her age.'

'The number of fillings I've got? I've got a mouth like a scrapyard.'

Bella tugged at Vicky's coat. 'What's for tea, Mummy?'

'Cheesy pasta, your favourite.' Vicky smiled at her mum. 'I'll need to drop her off tomorrow at half seven. Got to get in early.'

Mum climbed back up to the top step. 'Fine.'

'Bella, go get your things.'

'Okay.' She toddled inside, her legs almost going too fast for her.

Vicky felt a longing deep in her gut. *So much missed time while I'm at work, so much...* She wiped a tear away. 'How's she been?'

'Fine, I suppose. If it wasn't for us you'd be in real trouble young lady. You need to get yourself a man my girl.'

Vicky took a step back onto the paving slabs lining the front lawn. 'Is this my day for unsolicited advice on how to stave off early-onset spinsterhood?'

'I'm just saying.' Mum folded her arms, loose skin trembling on her triceps. 'You know best, don't you?'

Vicky pressed her teeth together.

'Oh, here.' Mum reached to the ledge in the porch. 'Here's a DVD from your brother. Said you'd like it.'

'I told him to stop doing that for me.' Vicky took the disc. *Breaking Bad series 4* written in black marker. 'How's he doing?'

'He's gone to his bed.' Mum put her hands in her pockets. 'Thank you for phoning. I didn't know he was back at work.'

'If that's how you keep an eye on your own son—'

'It's different with children, Vicky. Believe me.' Mum nodded at the disc. 'You'll thank your brother for that. Giving people CDs and DVDs really helps him.'

'Shame he's pirating them off the internet.'

Mum ignored the comment. 'Your father's said he's going to put up those shelves for you on Saturday.'

'Is he in?'

'Snooker.' Mum descended to the bottom step, resting a hand on Vicky's shoulder. 'What are we going to do with you, Victoria?'

'I'm fine, Mum, really.'

Bella skipped down the steps and Vicky caught her before she went face-first into the concrete.

'Thanks, Mum.' Vicky gave her as warm a smile as she could muster. 'Bella, say goodnight to Granny.'

'Night-night Granny!'

Vicky led Bella out to the car, her daughter's little hand tugging at her pinkie, the skin soft and unblemished. She opened the back door and put Bella in the car seat. 'Come here, you.' She kissed her forehead, drinking in the sweet smell for a few seconds, before she broke off and got behind the wheel. She took a deep breath, trying to steady herself. Then she started the engine and drove off, following the loop round to the start of the street. 'How was your day, Bella?'

'Good, Mummy. Playgroup was fun. Grandad took me to the cliffs in Arbroath. Can I get a doggie?'

'We'll see when you're a bit older, Bells.' Vicky ploughed down North Burnside Street with its rows of tall post-war houses and mothballed police station, where she'd started. She indicated right at the end, chip shop smells making her mouth water. 'You've got Tinkle.'

'I want a doggie.'

'Let Mummy think about it.' Vicky drove on in silence, adjusting the mirror to keep an eye on her daughter and hoping the dog would be another thing Bella would eventually forget.

She passed the Spar then turned left and pulled up in front of their house. She got out and helped Bella from her car seat.

Bella hopped out and walked down the path. 'Hello, Tinkle!' A small tabby swarmed around her feet, the purring audible even from the gate.

Vicky joined her at the door, fishing around in her bag for keys. 'Come on, Bells, let's get your tea on.'

DAY 2

Friday
1st April 2016

9

'Right-o.' Forrester exhaled slowly. 'To summarise, we're looking at two cases linked by these notes and similar MOs. We need to broaden our search for that black car sighted at both crime scenes. Mac, you're lead on that, okay?'

'Sir.'

'Got some... interesting news for you this morning.' Forrester cast his gaze around the room. 'Sadly, DCI Raven has taken a position in South Yorkshire Police, which means I'll be stepping up to DCI.' He locked eyes with Vicky. 'DS Dodds will be Acting DI until a permanent appointment is made.'

Vicky couldn't look away. 'What?'

She felt...

What? Sick? Pleased? Shit-scared?

'Sir, I...' MacDonald swallowed hard. Couldn't look at Vicky or Forrester, just stared at the floor. 'I thought...'

'You thought what, Euan?' Forrester glared at him, fire burning in his eyes. 'That you should get it?' His cheek flickered. Then he burst out laughing. 'April fool!'

Vicky's gut plunged to the floor. *Relief? Disappointment? The way everyone's laughing, it's like they're the ones who're relieved.* 'Good one.' She shook her head at him.

Forrester ran a hand across his mouth, mischief twinkling in his eyes. 'Right you lot. We've got people to catch, okay? Let's do it.'

Vicky slouched off towards her desk and sat down. She reached for her headphones in her bag. *Blot out the world and get on with some work.*

'Excuse me? I'm looking for DS Dodds.' Glasgow accent, lilting and slightly nasal. 'Is he around?'

Vicky dropped her bag and looked up.

A young girl, sixteen at most, giving a quizzical look from under her mop of red hair.

'You've found her.' Vicky held out a hand. 'DS Vicky Dodds.'

'Oh, sorry.' The girl blushed then shook it. 'Good morning, ma'am. I'm Zoey Jones. That's with a Y, thanks to my parents.'

'Don't start me on names.' Vicky gave her a warm smile. 'Bit early in the year for work experience, isn't it?'

'I'm your IT analyst. Jenny Morgan said to ask for you?'

'Oh.' Vicky re-examined her for a few seconds. Definitely older than sixteen. And a shining rock on her finger. She patted the empty chair next to her. 'Take a seat.'

'Cheers.' Zoey perched on the edge of the seat, barely denting the fabric, and took out her laptop. She sat back, legs crossed as she opened the machine, glancing around. The four male DCs at the next desk instantly focused their attention on their laptops, all furrowed brows and pursed lips. She turned her smile back on Vicky with a wryness that suggested she'd seen it all before. 'So, ma'am, what are you looking for?'

Vicky got out a sheet of paper. 'Based on this overview of the case—'

'Jenny briefed me.'

'She did, did she?' Vicky passed her two sheets of paper, PNC prints of Paul and Rachel. 'Well, I want you to trawl social media for these people. And do an idiot search, too.'

'A what?'

'You know, look for the sort of idiot who posts on Facebook saying they're going to go out and kidnap someone just before they go out and kidnap someone.'

'I'll see what I can do.' Zoey noted it in an app lurking in the corner of her screen. 'What about the dark net?'

Vicky thought it through. *There's a clear terror motive. Terrorists liked to hide down among the drug dealers, paedophiles and pirates.* 'Please.'

'Our search algorithms aren't perfect and TOR's designed to hide stuff, but you never know. Might unearth something, ma'am.'

'You don't need to call me "ma'am" okay? I'm just a sergeant.'

Zoey winked at her. 'Might unearth something, Mrs Dodds.'

'Vicky's fine.' She grimaced. 'And what brings you to sunny Dundee?'

'My fiancé got a job here, and my manager in Glasgow said you've not got many experts left after the restructure. So it's a much better chance of getting the experience I need to progress.'

'Miss Jones, you're *definitely* stalking me.' MacDonald appeared at Zoey's shoulder.

Her eyebrows shot up. 'What are *you* doing here?'

'Transferred up. First day yesterday.'

'What a handsome coincidence.' Zoey curled her hair round a finger. 'Good to see you again, Mac.'

A blush crept up over MacDonald's white shirt collar, though he quickly covered it by fixing his tie and turning to Vicky. 'Can I have a word?'

Vicky got to her feet, smoothing down her trousers as she stood, then followed him out to the corridor. 'You know her, then?'

'Zoey's...' MacDonald cleared his throat. 'Mmm, a real expert. Trained in Strathclyde the proper way.'

'I heard there was only a wrong way down there.' Vicky arched an eyebrow. 'Our last guy was an idiot. Only ever stared down my top.'

MacDonald laughed, tugged at his collar again and quickly raised his eyes to meet hers. 'Jesus, I'm knackered. First day ended being a sixteen-hour shift supervising the street teams in Dryburgh and Invergowrie.'

Vicky nodded as she leaned against the wall. 'How was it?'

'In short? We've got nothing more than when you left last

night.' MacDonald put his notebook in his pocket. 'Phones are the usual nonsense. I say that, but it's even weirder than I'm used to. Lots of people taking credit for the abduction, looking for attention. Put them in a room with a twenty-stone constable and they change their minds faster than Considine's Subaru changes gears.'

She smirked. 'Why do I ever hope?'

'It's the hope that kills.' MacDonald cracked his knuckles. Hard, like he'd torn a tendon. 'Got a few minutes before we have to head back to Dryburgh. How about we grab that coffee?'

'AFTER YOU.' MacDonald held open the door to the Auld Cludgie Café, nestling in the bowels of one of Dundee's long-dead jute mills just across from the station. The icy wind blew his tie over his shoulder as he smiled at her.

'Thanks.' Vicky stepped into the shelter of the café and made for the counter. The mirrors filling the walls were covered in steam from the espresso machine, smudging out yesterday's specials.

MacDonald joined her, raising a finger to attract a barista, a chunky man in skinny jeans and a tight black turtleneck. 'Americano with cold milk on the side. And what can I get you—' He smiled. 'Is it Vicky?'

'Vicky's fine. Vicks I'll tolerate. *Never* Victoria.'

'So, *Vicky*, what can I get you?'

'Diet Coke.'

'Don't drink coffee?'

'Value my sleep too much. If I have a coffee I'm up all night, twisting and turning in my bed...' Her time to blush. 'Oh, er, no innuendo intended.'

'Noted.' MacDonald winked at her and took his change from the barista. 'I'll bring the drinks over.'

'Thanks.' Vicky took a seat at a table, staring out to avoid looking at MacDonald at the counter, fiddling with his phone.

What am I playing at? Acting like I'm fifteen again, blouse pulled tight, flirting with Craig Norrie in the year above.

Play it cool, girl.

'Don't get me wrong.' MacDonald passed her drink and glass before sitting. 'I don't make a habit of skiving off work for drinks with beautiful women.' He checked his watch, the sort of chunky bling that you'd see advertised in men's magazines. *Probably got it out of Argos.* 'We'll probably be working closely together, so I want to get to know you.'

'No worries.' Vicky couldn't help but smile. 'What do you want to know?'

MacDonald returned the smile. 'Inside gen?'

'Well, you did pay.'

'That's perceptive, DS Dodds.' MacDonald made a show of giving her the once over. 'Pretty, pretty perceptive.'

'I like to think I am.' She coughed. 'Perceptive, that is.'

'Has your boss noticed? What's Forrester like anyway?'

Hands wrapped around her can, Vicky took a few seconds to consider her answer. *Brutal honesty — why not?* 'I like David, but he can be a tad bureaucratic. Likes to play it by the book.'

'Not necessarily a bad thing, is it?'

'Didn't say it was.' Vicky took another sip. 'He's good at politics, unlike me. I'm shi— really bad at that side of things, whereas he's cultivated useful connections in the force.'

'What's the rest of his team like?'

Vicky took a drink as she thought it over. 'DC Woods is the best.'

'Karen, right?'

'Right. She's been a DC for ten years. No ambition to move up the ladder, but she knows what she's doing and she's reliable.'

'And Considine?'

Vicky licked her lips. 'He'll be good once I've kicked him into shape.'

'Up himself, right?'

'He solved a taxi murder recently, but the way he tells it he caught Jack the Ripper and solved the JFK murder.'

MacDonald laughed. 'I'll bear that in mind.' He lowered his gaze to his coffee, taking a long sip. 'And the others?'

'The Three Amigos.' Vicky ran a hand through her hair. 'I try to keep away from them. They're thick as thieves or thick as pig shit. Take your pick. Decent officers, but they don't exactly respect a female boss.'

MacDonald rubbed his smooth chin. 'Let me get my feet under the table, then we'll see about divvying up the team.'

'I'd take Karen any day.'

'We'll need to sort something out if she's the only good one.'

'I'll arm-wrestle you for her.'

MacDonald smirked. 'I wasn't hoping to be pinned quite so fast.'

'Sure you need to worry about that?' Vicky's turn to give him the deliberate once over. 'You look like you work out.'

'I like to keep in shape.' He tugged at his collar again. 'Helps with the job if nothing else.'

Instead of an answer, Vicky crushed an ice cube with her teeth. A filling jolted out pain. Then she looked him in the eyes.

After a few long seconds, MacDonald broke eye contact. 'Well, eh, where were we? The team!' He laughed off his blushing. 'This Ennis guy? Feels like I'm stepping into dead man's shoes here. Want to know if I'll measure up.'

Vicky found it hard to shift Karen's "nine-inch" joke from her mind. As much as her own about Considine's two. She took a sip of Coke. 'I don't know what it's like in the old Strathclyde, but since they formed Police Scotland it's got worse up here. It's all stats, stats, stats. They want progress reports on everything. *Now.* That's why bureaucrats like Forrester do so well. Ennis was old school — liked his snouts and scrotes.'

MacDonald laughed. 'Was he in *The Bill*?'

'Exactly. Poor guy couldn't cope with being out in Stonehaven one minute, then in deepest, darkest Perthshire the next, only to be flung down to Fife or up to Inverness at a moment's notice. He was Dundee through and through.'

'How do you cope?'

'Not sure I do.'

'Oh, come come.' MacDonald took another sip. 'Good coffee in here. You been in Tayside long?'

'Had a fairly boring career to be honest.' She finished her drink with a sharp sigh. 'Two years in uniform, secondment to CID, then I got a job. Three years as a DC, then I got this DS position. Eight years later I'm still here. Guess I'm not ambitious.'

'Hardly. DS within five years is impressive, especially in a small force like Tayside. Know a few guys who managed it in Strathclyde and Lothian and Borders.'

'You've done well.'

'Thanks.' Vicky took the compliment with a dismissive wave. 'So, if you're not after Forrester's job, why are you in Dundee?'

'I'm originally from Coupar Angus. Actually started in Tayside Police. Four years on the beat in Dundee before moving south.' MacDonald beamed at Vicky. 'Eight years in Strathclyde CID then the Glasgow North MIT feels way too long. Just want to settle down. Sold the flat in Glasgow. Renting a place just now, but a house would be ideal.'

'What does your wife do?'

'Not married.' MacDonald held up his left hand, no ring on it. 'I'm hoping to make DI in the next twelve months. Get a bigger mortgage with that salary.'

Vicky ignored the bashful pause. 'Talk about ambitious.'

'Working in Glasgow was tough.' MacDonald leaned towards her and lowered his voice. 'Murders, assaults, brutal rapes. That kind of crime scars you. Don't want to become one of those embittered old cops, you know?'

'Sounds tough, alright.'

'Glad it's in the past.' MacDonald picked up a sugar sachet and pulled at the opposing edges. 'So, anything I can help with?'

Vicky fixed him with her tough-girl police stare. 'Not undermining me with the DCs.'

'What did I do?'

'Last night you let Considine wheedle out of work, using the Python as a lure.'

'The Python?'

'It's what he calls that pool Subaru.'

MacDonald smirked. 'I thought he was referring to another part of his—'

'So!' Vicky cut him off. 'You mind not undermining me?'

He held up his hands. 'I'll deal with it.'

'Fine.' Vicky finished her drink. 'This has been good.'

'Yup. But that's enough chat.' MacDonald drained his coffee. 'Need to see what the children are up to in Dryburgh. You need a lift out?'

'I'm babysitting back at the station.'

VICKY SLUMPED in her office chair. The adjacent desks were empty. No sign of Zoey or Considine.

'You owe me one.' Karen settled in the seat next to Vicky and took a drink of Dr Pepper. 'CC bloody TV. Been through all of it and the Auto Number Plate thingy. Nothing.'

'It's a big case, Kaz. That's what a DC does. Sorry.'

'I know what a DS does.' Karen smirked. 'Flirting. You and MacDonald over the road.'

Vicky coughed. 'It was just coffee.'

'You don't drink coffee.'

'Okay, it was just Diet Coke.'

'I'll remind you when you shag him.'

'We were establishing a rapport.' Vicky sat back and folded her arms. 'We're going to be working quite closely together.'

'If it's just that why are you blushing?'

'Stop it.' Vicky picked up a pile of papers and dumped it in her drawer. 'And here's you trying to set me up with some guy who's just moved in next door.'

Karen shook her bottle and let it fizz up. 'Touchy...'

'What are you doing here?'

'Checking out those cages delivered to—'

'You were supposed to be out in Dryburgh?'

Karen opened the bottle and took a sip. 'Mac called me back.'

'Have you got anywhere?'

'Oh, right.' Karen stared at her notebook. 'The supplier reckons there were five cages delivered in that box Keillor delivered. Self-assembly job.'

'But there was only one inside?'

'Right.' Karen did that thing with her tongue, turning it into a pipe. Then she frowned at her Airwave. 'Oh, crapping hell. That's Mac.' She got up and answered it, walking away.

Vicky tried to process it. *Five cages, one used. Two or three kidnappers at large. Meant they were likely to strike again.*

Crapping hell, indeed.

'Sarge.' Considine slumped in his chair chewing gum, his face flushed red. 'You look lovely today.'

'Have you been to the pub or something?'

He smirked. 'Was out for a ramble last night.'

'A what?'

'Me, Kirk and Summers are in a rambling club. Every Thursday night.'

'Destination: pub?'

'Got it in one.' Considine gurned like he was still pissed. Stank like he was, too. 'Just the one.'

'It's never one.' Vicky pointed at the desk next to her. 'Seen Zoey?'

Considine looked up. 'Who?'

'The IT analyst.'

'Eh? I thought that was your daughter.'

'Christ, Stephen, Bella's *four*.'

'Sorry.' Considine yawned. 'Not been at her desk since first thing.'

'She has been working though, right?'

'No idea.' Considine held up his hands. 'If I see her I'll point her in your direction.' He chewed away, looking around the office like he was sizing it up for sleeping spots. 'Bloody Mac's taken the Python with him.'

'It is a pool car.'

'Even so, I don't want to get lumped with the *Volvo* again.'

Considine spat it out like a Catholic saying Satan. 'Anyhoo, I was down at the forensics lab, speaking to your goth mate.' He held up photocopies of the notes. 'They match. Typography, paper stock, even the newspapers they were taken from, *The Sun* and the *Daily Mail*. No prints, no danger we can trace anything.' He checked his dark-grey notebook. 'The good news is they reckon the paper was unbleached recycled. Quite unusual in these parts.'

'Interesting.'

Considine burped, giving a waft of mint and second-hand kebab. 'Want me to dig into it, then?'

'Fill your boots.'

'Can you—'

'No, DS MacDonald has it.'

'Fine.' Considine slouched off. 'See you.'

Vicky watched him go, shaking her head. *Prick will be the death of me.* She reclined in her chair and stared up at the ceiling tiles. More water damage than tile.

'There it is.' Karen sat at her desk and picked up her bottle of Dr Pepper. She shook it, the dark liquid fizzing up to the lid just before she tightened it. 'MacDonald is a complete arsehole.'

'What's he done?'

'Made me meet him at the front door just to give me a page of scribbles.' Karen held up a sheet of paper. 'Supposed to be for some briefing with Raven. He asked me to type them up for him.' She handed it to Vicky. 'That mean anything to you?'

Vicky had a go, but she was right; it was just scribbles. Lines, casually drawn boxes and squiggly writing. 'Why you?'

'You told him I was the best. Thanks a bunch.'

'Sure you'll decipher it soon enough.'

'Aye, right.' Karen propped it in front of her monitor. 'So. Tonight?'

'I've got a gram of coke. Might hit some bars in town, find a seedy businessman, then shag him blind.'

'And in reality?'

Vicky took a deep breath. 'Watch some more *Breaking Bad*.'

'Can't believe you're still on that. *Better Call Saul* is even—'

Karen tapped her nose. 'Oh, I get it. Put Bella to bed early then straight in the bath with that new eighteen-incher from monster dildos dot com?'

'Karen!' Vicky clocked Zoey sloping back into the room. *Thank God she's got headphones on.*

'Your knicker drawer must be like an Ann Summers clear-out sale.'

'*Karen.*' Vicky stabbed a finger at her. 'Get back to your hieroglyphics.'

'Right, right.' Karen focused on MacDonald's page and started typing. 'Bzzzzzzzzzzzzzzzzzzzz.'

'Grow up.' Vicky got up and walked over to Zoey, sitting behind her desk, Beats headphones on, focused on a video on her laptop. 'I was looking for you earlier.'

Zoey lowered her headphones to rest around her neck.

'I said I was looking for you.'

Nothing, just stayed looking at the screen.

Vicky tugged at her T-shirt. 'Zoey?'

She jumped. 'Jesus. Sorry.' She stabbed her finger at her laptop. 'Look, ma'am. I've found something.' She pressed one of the keys and the video started at the beginning in full-screen.

The laptop screen went dark. A light switched on, revealing the cage in the industrial unit.

Vicky pressed a finger against the screen. 'Is this Rachel and Paul?'

Zoey just nodded.

The camera focused on Paul staggering around the cage, smeared with excrement, silenced with a gag, struggling to cover his chemically erect penis with his hands.

Rachel lay behind him, belly down, blank eyes staring into space.

A black leather-gloved finger appeared in front of the camera, pointing at Paul. 'There he goes. He's just about ready. You'll see why they call it doggy style.' The distorted voice was deep — the laptop's speaker struggled to replicate the sound.

Another voice, same effect but slightly higher: 'Right.'

'What's up?'

'Nothing.'

The camera moved closer to the cage. The hand reached out and started rattling the frame. 'Go on, boy, get it up her.' Then the finger pointed at the cage. 'What's he doing?'

'This is a bit too cruel.'

'They're animals. There's nothing cruel about it.' Again, the gloved hand rattled the cage.

Paul bared his teeth at the camera.

The video bleached white with a loud clicking sound, then shot back to darkness before recovering the image of the couple in the cage. The clicking repeated, but now the hand was by the cage. Just within view at the bottom of the screen was a Taser, its two probes alive with electric blue sparks.

'Don't make me use this again.'

Paul's gaze moved from the Taser to his sister, lying prone at his feet. He started breathing faster, on the edge of hyperventilation.

'Christ's sake. We'll never get these two to breed at this rate.' The Taser sparked again — the gloved hand held it jammed against the bars. The voice kept laughing, the sound deep and unnatural.

The camera tracked Rachel crawling to the far corner of the cage, tucking herself into the foetal position.

'Want to be a good boy for daddy?'

Paul glared at the camera again, a primal moan coming from his chest.

The screen froze on Paul's eyes, wide with fear, staring straight at the camera. Then some text appeared across the image:

DOG BREEDING IS EVIL.

SIBLINGS DON'T HAVE A CHOICE WHETHER THEY'RE BRED WITH EACH OTHER.

THE 10,000 PUGS IN THE UK HAVE THE GENETIC DIVER-SITY OF 50 INDIVIDUALS.

MEANWHILE, 9,000 DOGS A YEAR ARE PUT DOWN BECAUSE HOMES CAN'T BE FOUND.

The video faded to black.

Zoey tapped the screen. 'This is on YouTube. The story is out there.'

10

Forrester swallowed as the video finished on his computer screen. He slumped back in his chair, blowing air up his face. 'You did say there was a camera.' He stretched out his back. 'What was the flashing thing?'

'It's a Taser.' Zoey flicked to another window on her screen, showing a gun manufacturer's website. 'If you remove the cartridge it doesn't send out the spikes, just acts like a cattle prod. The reason it looks like that is it's overloading the camera's sensor.'

'Unbelievable.' Forrester drummed on the desk then shot a wink at Zoey. 'Just as well we got you in, eh?'

Head still spinning, Vicky turned to Zoey. 'Those voices...'

'They're scrambled, ma'am.'

'I heard. Can you descramble them?'

'It's called a voice changer, ma'am. I've seen it before. It's next to impossible to descramble. That's why they use them. It's a complex series of Fourier—'

Vicky folded her arms. 'In English, please.'

'Sorry.' Zoey licked her lips, took a few seconds to parse geek in layman's terms. 'They change the pitch of the voice, distort it, add phase, ring modulation and so on. You can still work out the words, just not who said it.'

'Can you get back to the original?'

'We'd need to know exactly what they've applied to it. The only way to know is to have the original recording. Without it, we'd just be guessing. Worse still, we might create a voice that sounds like someone else. Either way, I doubt it'd be admissible as evidence. What they've done is like shuffling cards then gluing them to the ceiling. Maybe. After you'd torn them apart and stuck them together. As triangles.'

'Okay, I get it. Can you find who posted it?'

'Already done.' Zoey nodded, a sly grin on her face. 'Got an address too.'

~

VICKY WAITED IN THE PYTHON, parked by a patch of waste ground in Hilltown, across from a bookmaker and two takeaways. 'That it over there?'

Considine checked his notebook then nodded. Still looked so pleased he'd snatched the car from MacDonald's grip. 'Certainly the address Zoey gave us.'

'Sheltered housing?'

'Don't shoot the messenger.'

A panda car pulled in a couple of spaces ahead and a thickset uniform got out. 'Vicky Dodds, again.' PC Colin Woods, Karen's husband.

'Afternoon, Colin.' Vicky walked over, crunching across the loose gravel. 'This is DC Considine.'

Woods narrowed his eyes at him. 'Karen's told me all about you.'

'Has she?' Considine dusted off his shoulder. Couldn't take his eyes off Colin's birthmark and didn't seem to mind if he noticed. 'You the heavies, then?'

'Son, back off a bit, eh?' Colin thumbed at his colleague, a matchstick man with size fifteen feet. He'd be no use on a Saturday night in Menzieshill. 'Vicky, this is PC Soutar.'

Matchstick took off his hat. Poor guy's hair was in patches, just tufts left. 'So, what're you needing proper coppers for?'

'We've traced an IP address to a Brian Morton.' Vicky waved in the direction of the flats. 'Lives in the ground floor flat over there.' She looked Matchstick up and down. 'So we need you and your muscle to bring him in for questioning.'

'Come on, then.'

Vicky held him back. 'Waiting on— Ah.'

A dark-red sports car trundled to a halt, so low it was almost kissing the ground. Jenny Morgan got out with a spring. The car matched her hair perfectly. 'I like an audience for an entrance.'

Colin rolled his eyes at her. 'That us, Vicks?' He waited for a nod then rubbed his hands together. 'Let's get this over with, then.'

Vicky followed down the hill then up the ramp to the flat entrance on Ann Street. A dark wood door blocked their entry. She pressed the buzzer for flat two, holding it for a few seconds. Jenny was already checking her nails.

'Yo?'

'This is the police.' Vicky raised an eyebrow at Considine. 'We need a word with a Brian Morton.'

'Not without a warrant.'

'Sir, is Mr Morton in or not?'

The line went quiet.

Vicky pressed the buzzer again. The door clicked open.

A man stood in the doorway, muscular arms folded above his shirt-and-jumper combo. A quiff like it was moulded. He pushed his glasses up his nose. 'Need to see some ID.'

Vicky flashed her warrant card. 'Brian Morton?'

'That's my brother. What's he done?'

'We need to speak to him in relation to an inquiry.'

A buzzing came from the hall behind. A morbidly obese man navigated a mobility scooter, his jowls sagging, the fabric of his shell suit stretched tight. 'What's going on, John?'

'It's the police, Brian.' John Morton lowered his head to his brother. 'Have you been an idiot on the internet again?'

'Officers, please escort Mr Morton to the police station.' Vicky waited as the two uniforms secured Brian. Considine stood near John. *Useless.*

Vicky pushed into the flat taking Jenny with her. 'What a bloody shower.'

'Tell me about it.' Jenny's eyes bulged. 'Oh. My. God.' She got down on her knees in front of a computer, a giant black mass with glowing blue tubes that looked like it should be on *Star Trek*. 'I am worshipping at the temple of a higher being.'

'Quit it, Jen.' Vicky shook her head. 'What is it?'

'This is a gaming rig, my friend.' Jenny caressed the monitor with a gloved hand. 'Water-cooled. 4K screen. GTX1080?'

Brian sat in the doorway, shrugging like it was obvious.

'Oh, Vicky, you should see the *Witcher 3* on something like this.' Jenny bit her bottom lip. 'Even you'd—'

'Can you get anything off it?'

'I want to get pregnant off it.' Jenny hit the space bar. 'It's not locked.' She pulled out her own laptop. 'Give me half an hour and I'll get one of my laddies to clone the hard drive for you.'

'Nooooo!' Screaming from outside. Brian was rocking back in his chair, then threw Matchstick to the ground. From sitting. Looked like he was going to try the same with Colin if he went anywhere near him.

'Stay here.' Vicky ran out of the flat.

Brian was a kicking and screaming mass of fat and shell suit in a mobility scooter. 'That's my computer!'

Colin Woods was in a crouch. 'Well Vicks, you're going to have to give us a hand getting Jabba the Hutt back to Tattooine.'

Brian scowled at him. 'Jabba was never on Tatt—'

'Shh.' Colin put a finger to Brian's lips, then gradually pushed him up so his scooter was level. 'Now, are you going to play nice or do I have to smash your computer into tiny pieces?'

'If anyone touches that, I'll kill them!'

Colin clicked a button on the scooter and pushed Brian away. 'Keep telling yourself that, son.'

～

VICKY SAT in the interview room, staring at the lawyer. 'Ms Nelson-Caird, your client needs to start co-operating with us.'

'Mr Morton hasn't committed a crime, Sergeant.' Kelly Nelson-Caird seemed to have one of those mouths that lags behind the brain.

Vicky glanced at Considine who was still silent as instructed. 'If you'll let him speak, I might be able to determine that for myself.'

'Very well.' Nelson-Caird snorted. 'Can you please outline the offences you believe my client *may* have committed?'

Vicky laid her hands on the table and focused on Brian. He was heavily out of breath, sweat dripped from his lank hair. She leaned forward on both elbows. 'Mr Morton, you uploaded a video to YouTube, didn't you?'

Brian violently shook his head. Hard to say whether in rejection of the allegation or merely due to a muscle spasm. The man did not look well. And he did not look at Vicky. 'I don't know what you're talking about.'

'Mr Morton, please give me your full attention.'

Brian angled his head slightly. 'I said I don't know what you're talking about.'

'The user who posted it is called Muse1991.' Vicky produced a sheet of paper. 'We traced the account to your IP address.'

'Doesn't prove anything.' Brian picked it up. 'You can mask IP addresses.'

'So, you know a bit about computers?'

Brian swallowed. 'A bit.'

Vicky leaned back in her chair. 'My analyst tells me this IP address wasn't masked.'

Nelson-Caird frowned. 'Are you suggesting my client is here as a result of a trace on an IP address?'

'Correct. She traced it to Brian's email account too.'

'And you know it's completely accurate? Someone could be posting on there and making it point at my client. This could be a smokescreen to implicate Mr Morton. Thus, the evidence you present is inconclusive at best. At worst, it is deliberate fabrication.'

'We'll have to agree to disagree on that.' Vicky felt sweat trickle down her spine. 'Mr Morton, why did you post that video?'

'I don't know what you're talking about.'

Vicky's blouse was sticking to her back. 'Can you account for your movements on Wednesday evening?'

'I'm housebound.'

'And yet here you are.'

'The only reason I'm here is because you removed me from my mobility scooter and put me in this.' Brian slapped his fists off the extra-large wheelchair, his breathing quickening. 'I was in hospital on Wednesday afternoon. Having a check-up.' He looked at the lawyer, almost pleading with her. Nelson-Caird just shrugged. He focused on the table. 'I'm getting a gastric band fitted. It was a check-up to make sure my body's still fit for it. The tests took all afternoon.'

'Name of the surgeon?'

Brian gripped the handles of the wheelchair tight. 'John will remember.'

Vicky held his stare in silence then made a note to ask. 'And what about this afternoon? I'm interested in the time between two and two thirty.'

'I was at home having lunch.'

'Using your computer?'

Brian let out a sigh.

'Mr Morton, we're checking with your internet provider so don't lie. Our analysts are trawling through your computer now.'

Brian wiped his brow, now soaked with sweat. 'I was.'

Vicky picked up the sheet of paper and turned it over. 'And you posted this video, didn't you?'

'No.'

'You also posted a message saying *"They got what was coming 2 them LOL"*?'

'No.'

'You didn't reply *"PMSL"* to a post saying *"Wouldn't take one of their pups!"*?'

Brian shook his head. 'No.'

Nelson-Caird licked her lips, smudging her lipstick. She leaned across and whispered in his ear.

'But I didn't do it.'

Vicky interrupted the legal counsel. 'Could anyone else have access to your computer?'

'No.'

'Not your brother?'

Brian laughed. 'John doesn't even know how to turn it on.'

'Where did you get the video?'

'I didn't do it!'

'Remember that we're searching your hard drive.'

'Someone emailed me it.'

'And you just posted it?'

Brian's head slumped.

'Without thinking it through?'

Brian hit the desk. 'This is persecution.'

'Of what?'

'Of obese people.'

'Mr Morton, don't flatter yourself. Your, shall we say, impressive bulk is of no relevance here. I've asked you questions relating to your internet usage, which links to a crime we're investigating.'

Nelson-Caird rubbed her forehead. 'Sergeant, can we pause this interview, please?'

'Interview terminated at sixteen oh nine.' Vicky reached forward and pressed the stop button on the recorder. She got to her feet and left the room. She led Considine down the corridor. 'Any idea what PMSL stands for, Stephen?'

'Pissing Myself Laughing.'

'Shouldn't it be PML?'

Considine shrugged. 'Americans.'

'Come on. Let's speak to his brother.'

~

'I NEED TO TAKE BRIAN HOME.' John Morton sat in the waiting area, arms clutched tight to his chest.

Vicky opened the door to an interview room adjacent to the one Brian was still in. 'If you'll just join us in here, sir?'

John got to his feet and followed her in. 'I need to take him home.'

'I hear you.' Vicky waited for Considine to shut the door. 'We need to take a statement from you regarding your brother's activities.'

'Is Brian under arrest?'

'Not yet.'

'You need to let him go.'

'He's uploaded a video taken during a kidnapping.'

'Ah, shite.' John gripped his knees. 'What's on the video?'

'The victims were forced to . . . do things they didn't want to. We liberated them yesterday afternoon. Your brother posted it on YouTube today.'

John fidgeted on the plastic chair. 'What proof have you got?'

'We've traced a user account back to his IP address.' Vicky produced a copy of the sheet she'd shown Brian. 'Here.'

'What's an IP address?'

'Internet Protocol address. It's a unique code given when your computer connects to the internet. Your Internet Service Provider can point us to the individual using one at any given time.' Vicky pushed another sheet across the table. 'Does that look like the sort of thing he'd post?'

John carefully inspected them. 'Maybe.'

'Is your brother into animal rights?'

'Animal welfare, certainly.' John leaned forward on the table and took off his glasses before rubbing his eyes. 'He's a vegetarian. Hates animal cruelty. All of his cakes are made with free-range eggs...'

'Cakes?'

John put his glasses back on. 'Brian pretty much lives off desserts. Cheesecakes, gateaux, that sort of thing. If I don't fill a trolley with frozen cakes on a Saturday, it'll be a week of tantrums. He's worse than a child.'

'Well, in between his feeding sessions, your brother found the time and energy to post a video of a criminal act.'

'You're absolutely sure it was him?'

'Unless you've got evidence that he wasn't using his computer at the time these messages were posted? Maybe it was you?'

'I was meeting a client. Used to be a journalist, but I've got my own publicity company now. I popped in to see Brian after I finished. That's when you lot came blundering in.'

'Mr Morton, we just want Brian to tell us who filmed it.'

'I take it Brian's not been very forthcoming?'

'Would we be asking you if he had been?'

John chuckled.

'Mr Morton, could he be involved in this?'

'Look at him.' John started cleaning his glasses on his jumper. 'He can't leave the house without me launching a military operation. That computer's all he's good at.'

'How good exactly?'

'I don't know. I'm next to useless myself. I can check my emails and get on Schoolbook, but that's pretty much it.'

'Where was your brother on Wednesday evening?'

'Ninewells.' John swallowed. 'Appointment for his gastric band fitting. Last hope for him. Did you see the guy in Livingston who died last week? Brian's now the fifth-heaviest person in Britain.' He pushed his glasses back up his nose. 'Look, Brian's an idiot, okay? His heart's in the right place but... I moved back here after Mum died and I'm all he's got. He's just lonely, you know?'

'Mr Morton, do you mind detailing your movements on Wednesday afternoon?'

'Do I need a lawyer?'

'We simply need to eliminate you from our list of suspects.'

'Why am I even under suspicion?'

'Mr Morton, everyone in Scotland and the north of England is under suspicion until we rule them out.'

'I was with Brian at the hospital.' John took a few seconds to clear his throat. 'Then my mate Greg drove me down to Armadale in West Lothian to the Speedway.'

Vicky glanced at Considine, who took the hint and started writing. 'Speedway?'

'Team motorbike racing. The Edinburgh Monarchs race there ever since the greyhound track in the city centre was shut down. I got into it when I lived down south. The Rye House Rockets. Ask my mate, Greg. He'll confirm it.'

'Okay.' Vicky inspected her notebook for anything not asked. *All out of ideas. Time to wrap it up.* 'This is a serious crime. Your brother may be involved. I'll discuss this with the Senior Investigating Officer and let you know the next steps.'

'Just make sure he gets something to eat.'

'What?'

'His stomach will be eating itself. He needs to eat every couple of hours.'

'*Needs* to, does he?'

'Brian's not a well man. Looking after him's almost a full-time job. I've done it since Mum died. It's not been easy. Can I see him?'

'That's not going to happen. He's going to be in here for a while before we charge him.'

~

VICKY FOUND Forrester in the Obs Suite next door. 'Take it you heard that?'

'Most of it.' Forrester leaned back in the chair. 'Brian sounds like he knows what he's doing. Think he's our guy?'

'Either way, he's not giving up any names.'

'Nope, he's not.' Forrester took a slurp of coffee. 'And his brother?'

Vicky thought it through, trying to block out the acrid tang filling her nostrils. 'He doesn't strike me as the canine justice warrior type.'

'So where do you want to go from here, Vicky?'

'Well, we could keep him in.'

'What if he has a heart attack?' Forrester put his feet up on the desk and stared into his mug, his nose wrinkling. 'I'm in enough shit as it is.'

'Or we let him go.' Vicky sighed. 'Put surveillance on him.'

'So young Considine and the Three Amigos lose their weekends?' Forrester folded his arms. 'Hell of an OT bill and for what?'

'Brian's probably thirty stone, maybe more. Unless he's wearing a fat suit like in that Gwyneth Paltrow film, he's clearly not abducted Rachel or her brother.'

Forrester wiped his mug with a paper towel then poured himself some coffee. 'But he posted that video, ergo he knows who recorded it?'

'Right.' Vicky slumped back in her chair. 'He's into animal welfare and—'

The door opened and MacDonald slipped in, smiling as he supped coffee. 'Don't mind me.'

'Vicky...' Forrester laughed. 'Following that logic, we could arrest the staff at every dog pound in a hundred miles of here. What good would it do?'

She bunched up her ponytail, tightening the rubber band.

MacDonald got in first. 'Whoever kidnapped Rachel and Paul filmed them. Forced them to have sex. Then Brian posted it on YouTube. Right?' He didn't wait for a response. 'Next they'll get the press and news all over it to spread their message.' He smoothed out his blue tie. 'It's all about creating fear. Meaning a terror group's behind this.'

Forrester nodded slowly. 'So, Mac, who?'

'Like I said, I've got contacts in the NCA.' MacDonald flipped through his notebook, shaking his head. 'Their watch lists are all Irish and Islamic, no active animal rights cells at present in Scotland or the north of England. They're generally more interested in people poisoning reservoirs, blowing up hotels, sending anthrax to abortion clinics, that kind of thing. They deem this a vigilante action.' He snapped the notebook shut. 'But. I'm thinking the National Wildlife Crime Unit might bite. They're nationwide and specialise in this sort of thing. Based down in Livingston. I could drive down this afternoon?'

Forrester was already on his feet. 'I'll join you.'

'Excellent.' MacDonald opened the door. 'I'll go and claim the Py— Subaru.'

Vicky waited for him to leave, eyebrows raised. 'And while you two are re-enacting Lethal Weapon, do we let Brian go?'

Another knock on the door. Jenny Morgan stood there, hand on hip, red hair coiled like a snake. 'There you are, Vicks. I've got something for you-hoo.'

Forrester motioned towards his just-empty chair. 'Good news?'

'The best.' Jenny perched on the front of the chair, laptop resting on her knees. 'So, we've been looking through his machine. What a *stallion*. Anyway, young Brian is an avid user of the dark net, where predators love to hide. Pirates, drug dealers, child pornographers.' She bit her lip. 'As well as YouTube, he's posted this video to a forum called xbeast, in a message chain called *Animal Rites*, as in last rites. Seven users have posted comments in support of it. So far.'

Forrester squinted at her screen. 'Terrorists?'

'That's your mystery. I just give you the rope to hang yourselves with.'

Forrester leaned forward, arms folded. 'Can we trace them?'

'We can and we are.' Jenny almost smiled as she took her laptop back. 'I've got three in Dundee and four in Fife. Brian is obviously one and Zoey's going through his internet history now.' She checked her laptop with a frown. 'The other two users have the same IP which I've traced to a location on the Perth Road. Looks like it belongs to a married couple, Sandy and Polly Muirhead.'

'Right-o.' Forrester focused on Jenny. 'Fifers?'

'It's fine, David. I passed them to Glenrothes.'

'Jenny...' Forrester's eyes clamped shut. 'This is our case, okay?'

'You were all busy. I thought you'd—'

Forrester sighed. 'What do you have on them?'

'Bunch of schoolgirls in Cupar, would you believe? Their

parents and teachers aren't going to be impressed when half of the Glenrothes MIT pitch up at the school.'

Forrester let her leave the room with a glare.

'Sir?' Vicky grabbed Forrester's shoulder. 'What are we doing about Brian Morton?'

'Should he stay or should he go?' Forrester hummed a tune. 'Okay. Let him go—'

'Sir!'

'Vicky, you're right. we need to see who he leads us to.' Forrester beamed wide. 'As good as Mac and you are, Raven's given me Alan Laing to help. I'll get him running surveillance on the other two from Dundee and this fat bastard.'

Vicky let out a deep breath.

'I never disagree with you, Doddsy.' Forrester shrugged into his suit jacket. 'Now, can you get down to Cupar and scare the living crap out of these schoolgirls?'

11

The first houses of Cupar came into view, along with a wave of near-stationary traffic. Not that Considine slowed during his approach, just waiting until the last minute to slam on the brakes. 'Would've been here already if Mac hadn't taken the Python.'

Vicky braced herself against the dashboard. 'What's the point in being a sergeant if we can't call dibs on the pool cars?'

'It's not right, though.' Considine took a hard right past a block of council buildings then turned left into what passed for the town's main shopping area, pulling up outside a bakery. 'Bet he doesn't know that little rat run.'

'Well done, Stephen. You know Cupar.' Vicky got out and made her way to the police station across the road.

Considine rushed after her with a few effortless strides. 'That bakery looked amazing. Mind if I get my piece now?'

'It's your cholesterol.'

'Hey, I work out.'

'You hide it well in those loose-fit clothes. I'll get this started.'

'Sarge.' Considine skipped back down the road, like Bella heading for tablet at her grandmother's. *Hard to figure out who's the more childish.*

With a sigh, Vicky opened the door to the station, eyes sweeping around the waiting room. 'DS Reid?'

'For my many, many sins.' A large man was wandering around, listening to his phone but not talking. Shaved head, no neck, dark suit taut around his massive shoulders. He killed the call and pocketed the phone. Still no smile. 'Sergeant Dodds, I presume?'

'My pet DC is off clogging his arteries.' Vicky nodded at the door. 'Can I see them then?'

'Through here.' Reid opened the security door with a swipe. 'We've got the run of the interview rooms.' He led Vicky through the station, the wallpaper frayed around fist-sized holes in the plaster. Looked like the place had taken more than the proverbial beating. Reid opened the door to an observation suite, four screens showing videos of interviews, a teenage girl in each. Three were in floods of tears, the fourth with her eyes locked shut.

Reid lowered his bulk on the nearest chair with a grace that belied his size. 'Take a seat.'

'I'd prefer if we led the interview.'

'Would you now?' Reid kicked out his feet and leaned back on the chair then unmuted a monitor.

A dark-haired schoolgirl smeared a hand across her cheeks, smudging tears and make-up. 'I swear I've not *done* anything.'

'My client has told you all she knows.' Her lawyer leaned forward, a tomato ketchup stain running down the left sleeve of his tweed jacket. 'I suggest that you let her get back to her lessons.'

'Your client has been a very naughty girl.' A female DC gave the sort of smile Vicky used to think beat lawyers in those situations. 'Now, Chrissie, what do you—'

Reid muted it again and sat forward. 'To think we came up from Glenrothes for this...'

Vicky treated him to her best apologetic smile. 'What have you got from them?'

Reid stared at her, seemingly confused, then got out a notebook and flicked through it. 'Very little. Don't know what you expected.' He turned the page in his notebook. 'So far, they've all denied even being on this ex-beef thing.'

'xbeast.'

'Whatever. They've denied it all.'

'Got their laptops in?'

'They weren't very happy about it, as you can imagine. Sent them to my old pal Jenny Morgan for processing.' Reid pointed to the top-left screen, to the girl with her eyes still shut. 'Especially this lassie here. Just sat like that. Won't speak.'

Vicky focused on the screen. 'Can I have a word?'

'No, you can't.'

'This is *my* case.'

'Should've thought about that before you passed it down to us.'

'We didn't. Jenny Morgan made a mistake.' Vicky leaned forward, steepling her fingers. 'Your guys aren't getting anything out of her. Let me try.'

'I don't get why the great and the good from Scumdee are so interested in some daft wee lassies?'

'Says the man from Glenrothes.'

That got a smile from him, at least.

Vicky leaned back in her chair, arms folded. 'My DI is down in Livingston speaking to the anti-terror squad about this case.'

'And you think Hazel, Chrissie, Amanda and Hermione are *terrorists*?'

'If you'd just let me—'

The door creaked open and Considine bumbled in, still chewing. Pastry flakes all over his suit jacket, a rim of milk around his lips. He gave Vicky a nod as he sat.

She tried to avoid scowling or shaking her head as she focused on Reid again. 'Do you know if any of them have access to a black saloon?'

Reid gave a shrug. 'Not to my knowledge.'

'We'll look into it, then.' Vicky let Considine know with a raised eyebrow. He nodded, and she looked back at Reid. 'Are we speaking to any boyfriends? Might've been using their girlfriend's laptop.'

Reid picked up a biro and made a note. 'I'll see what we can do on that score.' He left the room without another word.

Superb.

Vicky pressed her mobile to her ear, the ringing tone drilling into her bones. Then replaced by the drone of motorway driving. 'Sir, I'm in Cupar and—'

Forrester cut her off with a sigh. 'Is it William Reid?'

'Didn't know that was his first name, but yes.'

'Two ticks.' Silence.

Superb...

Reid came back into the room, giving Vicky a hard stare. 'I'm not in the habit of—' His phone beeped. He got it out, his chubby fingers stabbing at the screen. He thumped down in a chair and kept typing. 'Didn't say your gaffer was David Forrester.'

'So I can speak to her?'

Reid pocketed his phone with a bored sigh then casually turned his back and headed for the door. 'Your wish is my command.'

Hermione Johnston's jaw ended with a hook, like her father was the man in the moon. Her eyes were as tightly closed as a suspect's lips after legal advice.

'I bet you get a lot of stick for the name Hermione.' Vicky got her to open her eyes at least. 'Your parents were Harry Potter fans, right?'

'*Atonement*, actually.' Hermione cleared her throat. Her name was the least of her worries. *Growing up in Cupar with an accent as English as Sunday lunch, cricket and warm beer. Poor thing.* 'My parents named me after a character in an Ian McEwan book, before they'd heard of Harry Potter. Mother's an English teacher in St Andrews.'

'Still, you must get stick.'

A slight flicker of laughter cut through Hermione's sigh. 'I'm one of *five* Hermiones in my year.'

'Look, I can sympathise. My daughter's called Bella and I named her before I'd heard of all that *Twilight* rubbish. I hope, by the time she gets to high school, nobody remembers the films or books.'

Hermione nodded slowly. 'Don't even have a middle name I could use.'

'Same with my Bella.' Vicky smiled, holding Hermione's gaze for a few seconds. 'You know why you're here, don't you?'

Hermione nodded again, but Vicky had lost the eye contact. 'That video.' She shook her head. 'I just saw it. I didn't post it.'

'You know who did, don't you?'

'No.'

Vicky waved at the door. 'What about your pals?'

'They're as disgusted about it as I was.' She glanced over at her lawyer. 'Should I be telling her this?'

The lawyer balanced his disinterest with the likelihood that his client wasn't going to see a charge. Gave a slight shrug.

Hermione leaned across the table, the wood digging into her flat chest, the fire of the righteous burning in her eyes. 'You know about pugs?'

'I've heard a few things.'

'Some woman spoke to us in the street a few months ago. Saturday afternoon, we were hanging out by the bakers. She gave us a leaflet about inbreeding. It's sick what they—'

'Do you still have the leaflet?'

'Mother threw it out.'

'Who was this woman?'

'Can't remember. She was *so* right, though. Hazel and I checked it out and it's totally true. It shouldn't be allowed. They get these dogs to have sex with their siblings. Just for money? Can you believe that?'

'Like I say, I've heard a few things about pugs and their problems.'

Considine butted in. 'So how did you go from reading a leaflet to using TOR to access to the dark net so you could watch films of—'

'Don't you see?' Hermione threw her arms in the air. 'It's like the Bible. Eye for an eye and all that? They're evil. Shouldn't they get punished for it?'

'How did you find xbeast?'

'It was on the leaflet. Instructions on how to access it. Had to get Becky's boyfriend to help us. He's a bit Asperger's.'

'Did this woman try and recruit you into a terror group?'

'She wasn't a *Muslim*, you racist.'

'Islam isn't a race.' Vicky let out a groan. 'Did she—'

'I'm not going to help you anymore. What that woman was doing to those dogs is hideous and she deserves everything she gets.'

'What about her brother? He didn't breed dogs.'

'Collateral damage.' Hermione shrugged, cool teenage indifference. 'Sorry.'

Vicky stared at her long and hard. *An inch of progress, maybe. Her and her mates aren't kidnapping people, but someone was making noise about pugs and breeders like Rachel. Meaning they were careless, meaning they'd slip up again.*

Sod it, Reid's welcome to her.

'You know that Sergeant Ennis *hated* driving over water.' Considine eased the car onto the Tay Road Bridge, electronic dance music playing at a low volume. 'Used to hit a ton going over this. Mad bastard.' He slammed the steering wheel. 'Not that this piece of shit can get over seventy without crying.'

'Mac has the Python.' Vicky shut her eyes. 'Get over it.'

'Hard to get over it. We were made to be together.'

The wide river foamed beneath them, a few small boats bobbing in the brown water beneath dark, dark clouds. The car juddered as it powered over the long bridge, illuminated in a series of pale spotlights by rows of tall lampposts. Its sister rail bridge curved away to the left, soon lost in the grey murk.

Dundee sprawled at the other end, the site for the new Victoria and Albert museum sucking in as much of the surrounding land as it did local conversation. *Luckily nobody's tried to set me up with someone called Albert yet.*

On the hill to the left, the Wellcome and Bios buildings flanked the older university tower, the famous Dundee multis now mostly replaced by houses.

She let out a sigh. 'Seems like every year there are less multis.'

Considine glanced at her. 'You mean fewer.'

'Fewer?'

'Fewer multis, Sarge. Less doesn't apply to numbers.'

Vicky raised an eyebrow. 'Maybe I've misjudged you, Stephen.'

Considine shrugged. 'Not the first time that's happened with an older woman.'

Vicky shot him a glare. 'Anyway, there are *fewer* multis every year.'

'And that's a good thing. Pain in the arse having to climb the stairs when the lifts are out—and they *always* are—only to find whichever scumbag you're after isn't even in.'

Vicky chuckled. 'I took Bella to see some getting torn down last year.'

'Felt good, didn't it?'

'Felt like a metaphor . . . like we can all start over.'

'Poetry doesn't belong in Dundee, Sarge.' Considine glanced at her. 'So, what do you think of these schoolgirls?'

'Reid's welcome to them. He'll get nowhere.'

'Been thinking.'

'I wouldn't recommend it.'

'This woman handing out leaflets. That wifey at the animal shelter kept trying that with us. You think she's...?'

Vicky reached into her pocket for the crumpled leaflet on defective pugs. It was sympathetic to the plight of the animals, not judgmental about the breeders or angry with the ignorant owners. 'Not sure I buy it.'

'What about those newspaper articles?'

'Eh?' Vicky scowled at him. 'What articles?'

'Ah, crap.' Considine ran a hand across his face as they

approached some slow traffic at the Dundee end. 'I showed them to Mac.'

'And we're so alike...' Vicky got out her phone and opened the browser. 'What articles?'

'Search for Alison McFarlane and Wee Boab.'

Vicky tapped them in and waited. The top article was an interview with Alison McFarlane, chasing the tail of the Gary Black news story. 'You expect me to read the whole thing?'

'And they say that lack of concentration is a failing in the young.' Considine looked over at her screen as he set off again. Almost hit the barrier. Grabbed the wheel and righted the car.

'Stephen!'

'Wouldn't have happened in the Python, I swear.' Considine looked like he was sweating now. The car stopped vibrating as they crossed onto the Dundee end of the bridge and descended to street level. 'The bit that gets me, Sarge, is where she says pug breeding is a form of cruelty.'

Vicky flicked down the page and found it.

'*These breeders should be strung up.*'

'TRY TO STOP ME.' Vicky opened the door and pushed into the small office.

Alison McFarlane and Yvonne Welsh shot to their feet, like they were doing something they shouldn't.

'Get your knickers back on, ladies.' Vicky took a seat in front of the desk and waited for Considine to settle down. 'Need to ask you a few questions about something.'

Alison perched on her desk chair and smiled. 'Pray tell?'

Vicky reached into her handbag and showed them the article. 'Do you remember this?'

Just a glance at it. 'Of course.'

'As you can imagine, we're interested in anyone who may have a bone to pick with Mrs Hay. The comments you made in this article were quite inflammatory, and I quote: "*They should be strung up.*"'

'I was just making a general point about dog breeding.' Alison exchanged a look with Yvonne, still standing. 'There are more than enough animals to go around.'

'Stringing someone up is a serious offence, as is locking them naked in a cage.'

Alison covered her mouth then dropped her hands into her lap. 'Is that what happened to Mrs Hay?'

'It is.' Vicky held up the article on her phone again. 'So, going back to this?'

Alison stared at the phone like she could read it. 'We were heavily involved with this particular case. That was the third or fourth incident of NME we had from their kennel. Even with all the improvements they've made, pugs are particularly prone to inbreeding. We see quite a lot of it in the smaller dogs.'

'Not that any breeds are acceptable, but...' Yvonne took a deep breath. 'Pugs are so heavily bred that it kills them.' She stabbed the air with her pen. 'This NME condition... Their brains get inflamed because of the way they look. We can't cure it, but as Alison says, we can help the dogs. Normally, they get put down within weeks of diagnosis, but with some medication we can make them comfortable for the short time they have left.'

Vicky scanned the article again. 'But you said all breeding is evil.'

Alison sat back in her chair and fiddled with her necklace. 'Particularly pugs, though.' She sat forward. 'Do you know much about biology?'

'Very little.'

Considine raised a hand. 'I did it at uni.'

Alison leaned across the desk. 'All dogs are grey wolves that have been selected for morphological features present in a small part of their DNA.'

'How they look.' Considine nodded. 'If loads of dog breeds interbred over and over again enough times, you'd end up back with a kind of wolf thing.'

'Precisely.' Alison smiled. 'Dogs have been bred to be machines over the years, much like cattle and horses. Collies or Bull Mastiffs, for instance. Certain characteristics were chosen like they were designing them. Jack Russells so they can go down rabbit holes. Repeatedly mated the smallest dogs with the smallest over and over again.' She slumped back in her chair. 'With pugs, however, it's purely aesthetic, not functional. You find a dog that looks strange and mate it with another one that looks similar. Do that enough times and eventually you'll get a pug.'

Considine chanced a glance at Vicky. 'Trouble is, the funny-looking ones are brothers and sisters. Which leads to hardly any variety in their DNA, which means they're at higher risk of cancers and weird shit like that NME thing.'

'It's hereditary. Usually from a dodgy breeding pair breeding too closely.' Yvonne grimaced. 'Dodgy is putting it mildly. If one of the dogs has it, the pups will have it, too.'

'The people who make money from the poor animals always cut corners.' Alison clenched her fists. 'Makes my blood boil.'

'Enough to hand out leaflets about the evils of pugs to schoolgirls?'

She frowned. 'Our leaflets are purely informational.'

'Never linked to any dark net sites?'

'Dark what?'

Vicky stared at her hard. 'Are you involved with a domestic terror cell?'

'Excuse me?' Alison glowered at her. 'We're done here.'

'And I'm tempted to take you to the station for further questioning.' Vicky waited for Alison to smile, backing down. 'Have you ever handed out leaflets in Cupar?'

'Coupar Angus?'

'No, the one in Fife.'

'Why would I?'

Considine's hunch was crumbling. 'Can you account for your whereabouts between four p.m. on Wednesday and midnight yesterday?'

'I was working here.'

'We were both here.' Yvonne perched on the edge of the desk, wringing her hands. 'I don't know what you're trying to do. We're just helping animals. Working all the hours God sends for very little pay.'

'I understand.' Vicky made a note. 'I just want to make sure you're not harming people at the same time.'

'Believe me, the less we have to do with people the better.'

'I DOUBT THEY'RE INVOLVED.' Vicky opened the passenger door and slumped in her chair. 'They're not behind this.'

'You seemed to think otherwise.' Considine sat behind the pool Volvo's wheel. 'Their alibi though, Sarge. Just the pair of them to vouch for each other's whereabouts?'

'I never like that.' She thought it through.

Is he onto something? Alison has no solid alibi, but a lot of hatred against Rachel Hay. Rachel as the target makes a hell of a lot of sense, especially given the fact she has a brother — makes their message easier.

Vicky's phone rang before he could say anything else — Forrester. 'Afternoon, sir.'

'Doddsy, can you do me a favour? Still stuck in bloody Livingston all afternoon. Just got back in the car and my phone's filled up with messages. Some daft bastard journalist has called. Says she got sent the video before it went on YouTube.'

'Do you want me to—'

'She's in the nick already. Get in there and boot the shite out of her for me.'

12

'I got an email. A link to some video footage.' Anita Skinner folded her arms, her wristwatch sliding up to the middle of her forearm. Mid-thirties, her blue eyes seemed to shimmer under the interview room lighting. 'That's my story.'

Vicky raised her eyebrows. 'It just fell into your hands?'

'Are you implying I'm involved in this?'

'Are you?'

'I won't even dignify such *outrageous* nonsense with a reply. Why would I come to you voluntarily if I was in any way involved?'

'A diversion?'

'Christ on a moped...' Anita tossed her hair back, exasperation written all over her carefully made-up face. 'I've *told* you, someone sent me the links. A stranger.' She reached across the table for her laptop. 'If you look at my laptop, you'll see.'

Vicky tried to disarm her with a winsome smile. Tried and failed, so she resorted to subjugating politeness. 'You click on every anonymously sent link you receive?'

'God, I was just hoping to find a good story.' Anita closed her eyes and took a deep breath. When she opened her eyes again, she was the consummate professional. 'I'm a journalist.' She pointed at the screen — *"Rachel Hay's crimes"*. 'Are you telling me *you* wouldn't open that?'

Vicky scowled at her. 'Do you know who sent it?'

'Of course not!' Anita gasped. 'Just look at my computer!'

Vicky nodded at Considine. 'Constable can you do the honours, please?'

'Sure.' Considine snapped on a pair of nitrile gloves and took the laptop from her, a black machine looking a good few years old. He worked at the machine for a few seconds, then swivelled the machine round for Vicky, frowning. 'There's no sender.'

'I know.' Anita tugged her left earlobe. 'That's what made me suspicious. That's why I called.'

Vicky leaned over and checked the email. The link was the YouTube link, not something on the dark net.

Nothing to further the case, except...

Except that they were now going public. Emailing journalists. Getting the story out there.

'Get Zoey on it.' After a heavy pause, Vicky turned her attention back on Anita, staring her down. 'Ms Skinner, my IT analyst will look into this. If you've been up to anything else on there, you need to tell me now.'

Anita balled her fists. 'I. Just. Clicked. The. Link.'

'Then you've no reason to worry.'

'Well.' Anita took a breath. 'I... published it.'

Vicky shut her eyes. She opened them again, glowering at Anita. 'Where?'

'My blog. So what?'

Vicky rubbed her tongue across her teeth. 'And how many people read your blog?'

Anita shrugged. 'Maybe a hundred?'

Vicky looked up at the ceiling, noticing a flicker from the dull strip light. 'So, you published the video showing—'

'I just posted the link. Christ, I'm not an idiot.'

'It showed a brother and sister trapped in a cage as someone with a taser forces them to have sex.'

Anita couldn't look at her. 'You're trying to... Look, I'm a journalist. I'm just looking for the story. If you're burying something, that's a story.'

'We're not burying anything, Anita.' Vicky flexed her fingers, silently counting to ten. 'We're *protecting* people.'

Anita held Vicky's gaze for all of five seconds. Then she buried her head in her hands. 'You don't know how hard it is out there. Papers are sacking people left, right and centre. I was made redundant last year and freelance work is crap. My blog's the only thing I've got left. I can't afford my rent, so I'm going to be chucked out of my flat. I posted this and my hits went through the roof. My phone hasn't stopped ringing. Ten *thousand* shares on Schoolbook.'

'Thought you said you only had a hundred people reading it?'

'That's right, but...' Anita shrugged. 'They're mainly journalists and editors. And it automatically publishes onto Twitter and Schoolbook.'

Superb...

'You idiot.' Vicky thumped the desk. 'The reason terrorists do this sort of thing is to scare the living shit out of people. We've kept this to ourselves to stop that happening. You're as bad as them.'

Silence.

'Look, I'm not involved here, okay?' Anita's eyes were gleaming with tears. *Some hardcore journalist she was.*

'You've let the world know about these revenge videos. If we don't find the people behind this, guess who we'll be hanging out to dry.'

VICKY SLAMMED the interview room door and left Anita alone with her mistakes and regrets. 'Absolute idiot.'

Considine nodded.

The Obs Suite door opened and DCI John Raven appeared, focused on his brand new BlackBerry. Not the tallest of men, but all about image — shiny grey suit, striped shirt and black tie. He nodded at Vicky, then gestured into the Obs Suite. 'A word.'

He watched? Just, superb.

Vicky joined him, her heart thudding. 'Sir.'

'Well.' Raven pointed at the monitor in the Obs Suit, still focused on his BlackBerry like it was 2005 again, his thumbs stabbing the keyboard. 'That lassie's causing us a bucketload of trouble. I've asked to get her blog taken down, but hey ho, never easy, is it?'

'Never, sir.'

'Never ever.' Tap, tap, tap, both thumbs working away. 'Anyway, we're giving a news conference now, Sergeant. Trouble is, David's down in Livingston speaking to some Red Squirrel Protection Squad or some nonsense. Need you to help me.'

'. . . spokeswoman had this to say. "On Thursday we, uh, received a call-out to Invergowrie to the west of the city. A woman ha—" '

Vicky muted the canteen telly and walked back to her table. Place was dead, just the cleaner squeaking his way round the servery.

Considine sat opposite and opened a can of Sprite. 'You not like hearing your own voice, Sarge?'

'Does anyone?'

'DCI Raven certainly seems to.'

'And DCs looking to make DS shouldn't be saying that aloud.'

'Of course.' Considine broke eye contact, pink blotches climbing his neck. 'Zoey's not getting any joy tracing Anita Skinner's mystery email. She did find copies sent to other journalists.'

Vicky drained her can of Diet Coke. 'You get anywhere with John Morton?'

'What, his alibi?' Considine shuffled through his notebook. 'Some uniform gadgie popped in to ask his mate about it. Boy lives in Fintry, name of Greg. Confirmed that John *was* at the Speedway. Got the tickets for it. John paid for the petrol.'

'Okay, then.'

Considine checked his watch. 'Ah, hot balls. I'm late.' He got up and marched off.

Vicky crumpled her can. Couldn't get Raven's words out of her mind.

"And make sure you get some bloody media training. Every second word shouldn't be um or ah."

Prick.

Someone waved their hands in front of Vicky's face. 'Earth to Vicky?' Karen.

Vicky sat up, yawning. 'Sorry.'

Karen sat down with a fresh Dr Pepper. 'What's up?'

'Just distracted. I hate news conferences. Especially when I'm not prepared for them.' Vicky smoothed out the sheet of paper in front of her. 'Look at my hair. And I've got Bella's breakfast all over my blouse.'

'You look good on TV.'

Vicky scowled at her. 'I look like I weigh twenty stone.'

'I mean it.' Karen leaned forward. 'You look good.'

'For my age?'

'No, generally. Tying your hair up suits you.'

Vicky fiddled with her ponytail. 'I doubt anything'll come from it, anyway.' She rubbed her pulsing vein. 'My neck's killing me again.'

'Did you try those bras I recommended?'

'Made no difference. I think it's stress related.'

'Paracetamol.' Karen opened her bottle and let the fizz out. 'Or Ibuprofen.' She took a drink, eyes locked on Vicky. 'Thought any more about tonight?'

Vicky frowned at her. 'What's tonight?'

'Curry?'

'I don't like curry.'

'Bzzzzzzz.'

'*Karen.*'

'Look, Robert's nice. Okay? Colin's a shite squash player, but he's a great judge of character.' She took another drink and smiled. 'But, of course, you're interested in DS MacDonald.'

'No way!'

'Shut up, of course you are.'

Vicky stared up at the ceiling again, at the thick extract pipes leading to the window. *The things you notice when you're looking for a way out.* 'You think I should give it a go?'

'Nothing ventured, nothing gained.'

'What about Bella?'

'Colin's mum's looking after our two. Have a nice sleepover. Give your mum and dad some time off.'

Vicky smoothed down her trousers. 'Look, I don't know if Bella's—'

'Focus on yourself for once.'

Vicky tried to swallow, felt a big lump in her throat. 'I always think about how I'm letting her down...' Her eyes were hot with tears. 'I'm... Jesus.'

'Hey, hey, it's okay.' Karen reached across the table and wrapped her warm fingers around Vicky's blocks of ice. 'It might be good for Bella to have a father figure around. But for that to happen, you need to start dating again.'

'Let me think about it, okay?'

'Not too long.'

Someone cleared their throat and Karen broke off. MacDonald, gesturing at one of the spare chairs. 'Mind if I sit here, ladies?'

'Not at all.' Karen shifted her tray aside. 'I was just telling Vicky how sexy she looked in that news conference. Don't you agree?'

MacDonald coughed, then focused on his coffee mug. 'Sure, I've seen worse.'

Vicky glared at her empty can. 'Thank you.'

Another cough. 'No, no, I didn't mean to criticise your performance. You were fine.' MacDonald shook his head. 'I was thinking of the public impact. This is a nation of animal lovers. It's going to be hard to convince them of the need to punish vigilantes who avenge animal cruelty.'

Karen leaned on one hand. 'You got any pets, Sarge?'

'I'd love a dog one day, but it'd be cruel keeping it in a flat.' MacDonald coughed, slowly recovering from his blunder. 'Have you been keeping yourself busy?'

'Looking into these cages.' Karen sat up. 'Got to call someone about it.' She winked at Vicky as she stood. 'I'll see you later, okay?'

Forrester marched across the canteen and settled between Mac and Vicky, his hand stuck in a packet of Quavers. 'I'm bloody starving.'

'Don't they have shops in Livingston?'

'Not so's you'd notice. Mac managed to get us totally lost there. Bloody nightmare, that place. It's like Glenrothes with weegies instead of Fifers.' Forrester munched a mouthful. 'Heard the presser on the radio back. Let me know if you need any media training. Got the budget for it.'

'Piss off, sir.'

'Raven's already spoken to you, hasn't he?'

'Something about ums and ahs.'

'Happens to the best of us. Should've heard Raven at last year's inspectors' party. Chief Constable grabbed him and started asking about Tayside. He could barely speak.' Forrester lifted the bag up and inhaled the rest without much chewing. 'Anyway, it's Friday night, I'm knackered and I'm going to the pub for a pint after this.' He nodded at MacDonald, his mouth a mush of crisp. 'Right-o. Since your ill-fated press conference, the phones have started going mental. Mac, can you—?'

'Consider it done.'

'You want to update Vicky?'

'Okay.' MacDonald unfolded his arms and shoved his hands in his pockets. 'Turns out the National Wildlife Crime Unit were pretty helpful. They've got a couple of officers on secondment from the Met's National Domestic Extremism and Disorder Intelligence Unit.' A grin flickered across his lips. 'That's a mouthful, isn't it?'

Vicky winced at Karen's nine-inch joke again. And her vibrator. 'Are they treating this as terrorism?'

'Not as such. Happy with the arm's-reach approach. They've seen what we've got and aren't overly concerned. Until we get evidence of a political agenda, they're happy for it to be a "CID crime". The guy actually did air quotes.'

'We'll keep in touch with them over the next few days.' Forrester started folding his crisp bag into a triangle. 'Hopefully it'll just die out.'

'Even though the video's out there? Even though it's been blogged?'

'Even though.' Forrester held up his phone. 'Press boy tells me that *The Courier* and the *Press and Journal* are planning to run it on their front pages tomorrow. A few others have it inside. He's talked them down from including screen grabs, but still.' He shuddered. 'Did you speak to that journalist?'

'Doubt she's involved.'

Forrester shook his head. 'Half of Scotland seems to have got that bloody email, she was the only one daft enough to publish it. That media officer boy, can't mind his name, he's been going spare trying to keep a lid on it. Had to get the Chief Constable to have a word with our friends in the fourth estate.'

'An unofficial gag order?'

'Let's say it's like bloody whack-a-mole — hit one and another pops up.' Forrester tore open a second bag of crisps. 'How did you get on in Fife?'

'They're not involved.' Vicky scowled. 'I suspect that someone tried to recruit them to a terror cell.'

'Now that is interesting.'

'Our suspect is denying it.'

'Typical.' Forrester scratched the back of his head, then narrowed his eyes at Vicky. 'Anything more on fatso?'

'I'm not sure that's appropriate language, sir. And no. He's gone home and stayed there.'

'Right-o.' Forrester stared at the wall for a few seconds. 'Well, it's not like he'll run away. That nightmare lawyer of his was on the phone shouting the odds about human rights.' He shrugged his shoulders. 'I made it seem like she was the reason he was getting out. Told me that if we charged everyone who'd been stupid on the internet, half of Dundee would be in the cells.'

'There's a difference between stupidity and incitements to violence, sir.'

'Quite.' MacDonald tutted. 'Hopefully Brian will lead us to his accomplice.'

'Speaking of which...' Vicky looked up at Forrester. 'Are we keeping Zoey on?'

'For another week, unless we solve it before then.'

MacDonald took a deep breath and checked his watch. 'You need me to run the surveillance over the weekend?'

'Just the day shift. Laing's got the night.' Forrester got to his feet. 'Right-o, I think we've made some good progress today, considering what we're up against. Let's see what the weekend brings. No lives in immediate peril just now. We've done a cracking job to get where we are, so we should be pleased with that. Okay?' Without another word, he left them to it.

MacDonald grinned at Vicky as he got up. 'What a first week, eh?'

She led out of the canteen, dumping her tray by the entrance. 'Tell me about it.'

'Fancy a drink?'

Vicky pursed her lips, sorely tempted. She checked her watch — just about enough time to make it home to tuck Bella in. 'Sorry, but I've really got to head home.'

'I'll not take it personally.' MacDonald stopped by their office space, held her gaze for a few seconds then checked his own watch. 'Anyway, I'll wait around and see where Forrester is going for his pint.'

'Have a good one, anyway.' Vicky went over to her desk to put on her coat. She could feel MacDonald's gaze following her.

Karen winked at her as she did up her coat. 'Any decision about tonight, Vicks?'

'Just that I need a drink.'

'Bzzzzzzzzzz.'

13

Someone thumped the front door.

Vicky froze. *Who the hell is that?* Bella was in the living room, transfixed by the TV. Vicky crept through the kitchen into the hall. She peered through the spyglass then let out a groan as she tore open the door.

Karen stood there, hair pinned back, necklace hovering over cavernous cleavage. 'Right you. We're staging an intervention.'

'Kaz, not tonight.'

Mum was behind her. 'We don't care, Victoria. Karen called me. We'll babysit.'

'Kaz!'

'Come on, Vicks. You're going half-demented here on your own. Some wine, some curry.'

Vicky tutted, but her heart wasn't in the feigned indignation.

'Come on, Victoria.' Mum stepped round Karen. 'You need to get yourself ready.' Vicky stepped aside to let Mum into the house. 'I'm doing this on one condition.' She gave a stern look. 'You tell me how it goes tonight.'

Vicky hugged her. 'I don't know what I'd do without you, Mum.'

'You and me both.' Mum went through the living room. Bella

was propped up against the back of the sofa, eyes locked on the TV screen. 'Granny!' She did her little happy dance.

'Hey, Bella. Get your shoes on, okay?'

'Okay!'

Mum grabbed her backpack and led outside. As though revived by the cold air, Bella sprinted along the short drive into her gran's arms. She opened the car's back door. 'Come on, you. Let's get you buckled in.'

Vicky squatted and cuddled Bella.

'I love you, Mummy.'

'I love you too, sweet pea.' Vicky kissed her hair then waited, arms folded against the cold, while Mum put Bella in the car.

Mum slammed the door and gripped Vicky's shoulders. 'She'll be fine. We'll be fine. I'll see you tomorrow. Okay?'

Vicky gave a salute. 'Yes, boss.'

Mum got in and drove off, Bella waving her arms in a dance as they trundled up to the main road.

Vicky got a taste of Karen's perfume and tried to act like it wasn't happening. 'I've no idea what to wear.'

'You'll be fine Vicks, you always are. Jeans and a clingy top — show off your boobs.'

'It's not just the clothes.' Vicky slumped against the wall. 'I don't know, Kaz. This just feels too much.'

'You're going to be fine. I'll be there, okay?'

'It's been so long since I've been on a date.' Vicky bit her bottom lip. 'What do I say? "Hi — I catch criminals for a living. Oh, and I'm a shitty single mother"?'

'Stop putting yourself down. You're quite something, Vicks. Not many people could cope with your life.'

'I don't.'

'Of course you do. You and Bella are great. And Tinkle. Come on, Vicks.' Karen left a pause. 'You've got nothing to lose, okay? Some nice wine and a curry. And if you think he's lovely . . .'

Vicky allowed herself a chuckle. 'That's what I'm worried about.'

'YOU'LL LOVE IT, PRINCESS.' The lad in front of Vicky on the bus was sixteen at most, head shaved, ears pierced, mobile blaring out some tuneless hip-hop. Chatting on another phone. 'I'll get you some vodka, got a half-Q. We're sorted, ken?'

Vicky pulled at the seat back, trying to nudge the little twat. 'Can I arrest him for noise pollution?'

'Vicks!' Karen grabbed her hand. Gave a fresh wave of her perfume. 'Will you simmer down?'

'Hard to, Kaz.' Vicky was scratching her fingernails off her palms.

'You're nervous, aren't you?'

Vicky bit her lip again, getting lipstick on her teeth already. 'I'm not the world's biggest curry fan, but we'll see how it goes.'

Karen rolled her eyes. 'I meant about Robert.'

'I know.'

'So, *are* you nervous?'

Vicky blushed. 'A bit.'

The bus rolled around the corner and stopped at the lights outside Broughty Ferry library. The Gulistan was almost exactly halfway between bus stops.

'Have a wee bit of dope.' Another Eminem track started up. 'Then I'll slide my fingers right—'

'Kaz, this is our stop.' Vicky got up and went downstairs, clocking the ned checking her out as she descended. She smiled as she got off the bus and sucked in the cool evening air. A short man with red hair walking a dog stopped to give her the once over.

Karen bounced off the bus, shaking her head. 'What's got into you?'

'Six and two threes between this stop and the next one.' Vicky set off along Queen Street, catching herself in the reflection from the bus shelter. *Fat and dumpy and ARRGH.* 'Could do with a walk.'

'That flouncy top's the right choice.' Karen was almost charging ahead now. 'Might live to regret the fuck-me boots, though.'

'Too flirty?'

'No!'

'Too much make-up?'

'Too late!' Karen stopped outside the curry house. 'Come on, Vicks. Keep the head, aye?' She entered the curry house leaving Vicky outside.

Her heart beat faster with every second.

The bus trundled past, the hip-hop ned pressing his nose against the window to get another good look at her. *Maybe I'm not too bad.*

Get over yourself — taking compliments from a wee prick like him.

She pushed through the front door. A half-dozen waiters milled around, though it seemed fairly quiet for a Friday night. Smelled amazing, though. Sharp spices mixed with dark charcoal. Gentle sitar music floating from the big speakers mounted to the ceiling. Karen was at a table in the far corner, sitting on the opposite side from Colin.

Vicky walked over to the table. 'Evening, Col.'

'Good God!' Colin inspected her before glancing at his wife. His large frame was pressed into a tight shirt, the sort of pattern he'd never have chosen for himself. White shirt with a collar that matched his birthmark. Like it was a deliberate provocation. 'Robert'll be drooling when he sees you, Vicks.'

Vicky hung her leather jacket on the back of the chair and sat next to Karen.

'I bet Kaz you wouldn't turn up.' Colin thumbed behind him. 'Robert's at the bar.'

A middle-aged man collected some pints, the flash off his balding head distracting Vicky from his toothless smile. When he caught her eye, he gave her a lurid wink.

Vicky almost walked off there and then.

Colin got up and tossed his napkin on the table. 'What can I get you, Vicks?'

'Bacardi and Coke.'

'Coming right up.'

Karen leaned back in her seat. 'First time I've seen you have full-fat Coke in ages.'

Vicky shrugged. 'Thought I'd push the boat out a bit.'

Colin reappeared and set down two pints of red beer on the table. 'Just off for a sla— to the toilet.'

Then Robert appeared, carrying the ladies' drinks. Not the bald-headed Methuselah she'd seen. Maybe ten years older than Vicky, but *fit*. And he still had his own hair. Stonewashed blue jeans with a red gingham shirt, wiry hair sticking out of the open collar. He handed a glass of rosé to Karen and a tall glass to Vicky, before offering her his hand as he sat. 'Robert Hamilton.'

She shook it. 'Vicky Dodds.'

Robert sat, almost spilling his pint as he nudged the table leg. 'Whoops.' He took a big slurp, taking it below the danger line. Then he flashed his eyebrows. 'I'm sure Karen will have told you everything about me.'

Vicky nudged her. 'What, when she's not talking about herself?'

'Vicks!' Karen play-slapped her hand. 'I'm not that bad, am I?'

Colin returned, drying his hands on his jeans. 'Bit of a mission to the bo— toilets. Practically have to cross the Tay Road Bridge.'

Robert bellowed with laughter. 'I'll bear that in mind.'

'I've broken the seal now.' Colin took a sip of beer and gasped. 'Oh, that's nice. Cheers, Robert.'

'You chose it.'

'So I did.' Colin chuckled. 'You been here before, Vicks?'

'Dad's family used to talk about it in the eighties, when this was the place to go.'

Colin frowned. 'They were out in India for a bit, aye?'

'Dad was born in Calcutta.'

Robert took a gulp of beer. 'Wow.'

Vicky did a dramatic wince. 'I could've got you with my "I'm half-Indian" wind-up there.'

Robert smiled. 'Maybe you can try it on later?'

'I'll do that.' Vicky tapped her nose. 'Hey, Robert, did you know my father's Indian?'

Robert chuckled. 'Gosh, Vicky. You don't look half-Indian.'

'His parents were both from Dundee. They worked in the jute business. Boom, boom.'

'Never tire of hearing that.' Colin yawned as he put his pint glass down, half-empty already, and picked up a menu. 'Who's for a starter?'

Vicky checked the listing — under-eating when drinking was never a good idea. 'I'm going for the chicken saag.'

'Nothing too hot for me, either.' Robert checked his menu. 'Which one's saag?'

'Lots of spinach.'

'Right, I know the one.'

The waiter appeared. 'Please?'

Colin gave a him a broad grin. 'One chicken saag, a chicken tikka masala and a lamb phall. Robert?'

Robert held up his menu. 'Is the chicken free-range, do you know?'

'It is, sir. I can show you the box?'

'Chicken biryani, then.'

The waiter scribbled it down. 'Rice or naans, please?'

Colin leaned back in his chair, hands clasped behind his head, every inch the alpha male on day release. 'Two naans, garlic and plain, and two portions of pilau rice?'

'Very good, sir.' The waiter left them.

'I wanted a peshwari naan.' Karen shook her head at Colin as she took a drink of wine. 'And that phall's too hot for you. Remember last time? You were on the bog for a week.'

'Who can finish a curry, though?'

Vicky glanced at Robert. 'I didn't think to ask.'

Karen frowned. 'Ask what?'

'If the chicken was free-range.'

Robert shrugged. 'I try to avoid animal cruelty.'

Vicky tilted her head at him. 'As chance would have it, we're dealing with that very thing at work just now.'

'You're a police officer as well, right?'

'Detective Sergeant.' Vicky took another sip. 'For my sins.'

Robert grinned at Colin. 'Outranks you, then?'

'Don't I know it.'

'SHOULD HAVE SEEN HIM, ROBERT.' Colin was at the far end of the living room, fiddling with a tablet, queuing up enough music to last a week of partying. 'Boy must've been about forty stone. Vicky did her psycho bitch stuff on him. This poor disabled guy.'

Vicky rolled her eyes. 'He wasn't disabled, just obese.'

'You're not denying the psycho bitch stuff, though?'

Vicky laughed. 'Too late now.'

'Then me and this skinny wee poo—'

'There we go again.' Vicky took a sip of wine and settled back in Karen's sofa. 'Colin's talking shop again.'

'Always does.' Karen held out the bottle of rosé. 'Top up?'

'Don't mind if I do.' Vicky leaned forward on the sofa and held out her glass. She made eye contact with Robert, but he broke it off.

Karen topped it up, eyebrows gesturing to Robert. 'Well?'

Vicky looked around the room. 'I like what you've done. Looks fresher.'

Karen's hand shot to her mouth. 'Tell me you've been here since we repainted it?'

'I don't think so.'

'Colin!' Karen called over to her husband. 'When did we paint this room?'

'May.' He stayed focused on the tablet. 'Just before we went to Tenerife. My arm was still—'

'My God.' Karen slumped on the sofa next to Vicky. 'That's shocking.'

'You know how it is. I've been busy with Bella and we both work. And everything.'

'Nice try at dodging the question.' Karen raised an eyebrow. 'You know I was asking what you think of Robert.'

Vicky shrugged. 'Seems okay.'

'I don't get you, missus.'

'What's to get? I'm too busy to get into anything right now.'

'Is that *really* it?'

'Maybe.'

'Aye, and maybe not.' Karen took a sip. 'What's going on in that head of yours?'

Vicky played with her ponytail, avoiding her friend's quizzical look.

'How long's it been since—?'

'Four and a half years... It's just—'

'Vicks, quit it with the "it's just". You've had enough time. More than enough time. You know that, right?'

'I do, it's just—'

Karen elbowed her side. 'No. More. Okay?'

Vicky laughed, but it quickly turned into a grimace. 'I worry about who I'm letting in... I don't want another arsehole.'

Karen nodded over at the men. 'Robert's nice.'

'Yeah, but I've only known him five minutes.'

'Here we go, Detective Sergeant Victoria Dodds is back on duty.'

The music changed — a blast of staccato guitar-bass-drums followed by a sinister voice. Vicky frowned at the stereo. 'Is that Green Day?'

'Ten points to Doddsy.' Colin held up the tablet, showing the album's cartoon cover. '*Dookie*. Their best album.'

Vicky sat and took a sip of wine, her foot tapping to the music. 'I saw them at T in the Park.'

Karen tapped her nose. 'Another diversion.'

'You got me bang to rights.' Vicky put her glass on the coffee table, almost missing the edge of the coaster. 'I deal with so many arseholes each week, most of them male. It's hard for me to trust a man these days.' The track changed and Vicky scowled. 'Is that *Pearl Jam*?'

Colin chuckled. 'Best band ever, Vicks.'

'An old favourite.' Robert held up his hands. 'Don't hold it against me.'

'I'll try not to.' Vicky grinned. 'My brother called them a bad Red Hot Chili Peppers covers band fronted by that guy from Hootie and the Blowfish.'

Robert winced. 'That's a bit harsh.'

'Accurate, though.' Vicky picked up the wine glass and took a sip.

Nobody spoke. Robert shot a nervous glance at Vicky, before Colin showed him something on the tablet.

Karen leaned over and tipped the remaining dribble into her glass. 'Avoiding again.'

'Come on . . .'

'I'm serious. Robert's lovely — you should give him a go.'

'He's over there hiding from me with Colin and Eddie Vedder.'

'Well, you're a frightening police officer. And you've tucked yourself into your tightest top to show off your rather — dare I say it — bombastic boobs.'

'You can talk, Kaz. No idea how you run with them on duty.'

'A sports bra.' Karen adjusted her top down a few inches to show yet more cleavage. 'Maybe he's intimidated.'

'Is that all?'

'Maybe I should've told you earlier.' Karen held up her glass and stared through the bottom like she was searching for lost pirate treasure in there. 'He's a widower.'

Vicky rubbed her forehead, the vein in her neck pulsing harder than the music.

Karen drained her glass. 'His wife died last year.'

'So I'm looking for broken biscuits in love's bargain basement?'

'Hardly. I'm just saying, he's not one of those bad guys.'

'Unless he killed his wife.'

'With cancer?'

'Ouch.'

'He's got a wee boy.' Karen looked over at the men again. 'Jamie. Sweet kid.'

'This just gets worse.' Vicky put her head in her hands and groaned. 'I mean, what an awful name. Poor kid.'

'Right, that's it, you're talking to him.'

'Kaz . . .'

'Enough.' Karen held up her empty glass and cleared her throat just as the music switched track. 'But I'll need to get another bottle.' She called over to Colin. 'Come and help me with the cheese.'

'I'm stuffed after that curry, Kaz.'

'Now.'

Colin scowled at his tablet, then his gaze shifted back to Karen. 'Oh, right. Aye.' He handed the tablet to Robert and followed her into the kitchen.

Robert rested the gadget on top of the stereo and turned the volume down before smiling at Vicky, deep ridges on his forehead.

Vicky hesitated, then returned the smile. 'So, you like Pearl Jam?'

'They were my favourite band when I was a teenager. I had the ripped jeans, the plaid shirt, the long hair, the five-string bass.'

'Don't remind me. I was a grunge kid too.'

'This was a non-album single, I think, or maybe it was on a compilation.'

'Wasn't it on that *Singles* film?'

'Oh, Christ. I forgot about that.' Robert took a sip of beer. 'I saw them in London with my mates, back in the day. We caught the coach down and hung around the bus station overnight, waiting for the first one back. Mark's genius plan was to stay at the YMCA.'

'Oh my God.'

'Gets worse. His plan was to hop in a taxi and ask to be taken to the nearest one. Guy didn't know where it was.'

'I kind of liked them at school, but they've not aged well.'

'I beg to differ, but as long as you don't say the same about me, I won't question your taste.' Robert came over, the sofa creaking as he sat on the arm. He nodded at the kitchen. 'Not exactly subtle, are they?'

'On her last appraisal form, Karen spelled it S-U-T-I-L. I thought that was bad enough, but those two haven't even heard of the word.'

Robert chuckled. 'You're her boss, right?'

'Sort of. It's complicated.'

'You guys working on anything interesting just now? Colin mentioned an animal cruelty case with a really fat guy?'

'Aye, this case is as close as the job comes to being interesting, I suppose. We saved some people before they died, which doesn't usually happen. And I'm learning about lots of deviant internet stuff.'

'Oh, I'm useless with computers.'

'Me too.' Vicky stared into her glass. 'My brother works for the police, doing that sort of thing. Before he got ill.'

'I'm sorry to hear that... What happened?'

'ME. CFS. They don't really know. One thing I do know is he used to absolutely destroy the energy drinks, so he could pull really long shifts. Until he broke. Could really do with him on this case.'

'Why, what's it like?'

Vicky raised her eyebrows. 'Why the sudden interest?'

'I wouldn't say it's sudden. Just a case of Colin and Kaz dominating conversation and me not getting to ask you about yourself.'

'Before they left the room, I think the only words I've said to you were my name, and I was hard pushed to get my surname in.'

Robert laughed. 'No, my interest comes from being an avid reader of detective books. Especially Allan Guthrie. He's a local writer, more or less. Hasn't done anything in a while, mind.'

'Never heard of him.'

'That's a character reference if ever I saw one. Anyway, reading crime novels when you're a copper must be like a busman's holiday, I imagine.'

'I read trashy shit, when I've got the time.' Vicky drained her glass. 'So, Karen said you're a teacher?'

'I'm a PE teacher at Monifieth High.'

'PE? Not my strongest subject.'

'It's what I was good at. Got diagnosed with dyslexia when I was sixteen and the damage had been done by then. I didn't read a book until I was twenty. I just couldn't concentrate. Now I can't put them down.'

'That must have been hard.'

'I managed to get through my exams okay in the end. Got into Moray House in Edinburgh.'

'That's pretty good.'

'PE and secondary education aren't exactly rocket science.' Robert pulled an ancient Nokia out of his pocket and placed it on the table. 'Sorry to reveal my luddite tendencies so early on, but it's getting stuck in my jeans pocket. I'm too used to wearing trackie bottoms all day.'

Vicky smiled just as Colin paced back into the room, a bottle of Prosecco in his hand. 'Right, bottoms up, you wee shaggers!'

VICKY STOPPED OUTSIDE HER HOUSE, reaching into her handbag to retrieve her keys. 'This is me.'

Robert raised his eyebrows. 'Oh.'

'Thanks for walking me home. Even though you live next door to them.'

Robert raised his shoulders and pushed his hands into his pockets. 'I wouldn't let you walk home alone.'

'I'm a police officer.' Vicky tried to steady herself on her feet. *Those bloody heels. Okay, maybe the booze played a part, too. A tiny part.* She reached over and pecked Robert on the cheek. 'Very chivalrous of you, though.'

He looked down Westfield Street, past Vicky's house towards the park at the end.

She folded her arms. Was he angling for something?

He blinked a few times. 'Do you want to go for a drink some time?'

'I'm a bit busy just now.'

'Oh.'

'I'm not brushing you off, I'm just being honest.' She tottered forward and patted his arm. 'And I'm not going to invite you in for coffee, if that's what you're after.'

'It's cool. I'm a tea man.'

'Well, I'm not inviting you in for a cup of tea.'

'I'm not—'

Vicky touched his arm. 'Relax.'

'So, will I see you again?'

She reached into her purse and got out a business card. 'Call me.'

He took it. 'Thanks.'

She winked, then whispered. 'Don't tell Colin or Kaz.' She fumbled with her keys, eventually getting the lock to turn. 'Goodnight, Robert.'

'Night, Vicky.'

She blew him a kiss and shut the door behind her, then leaned against it.

What the hell am I doing?

DAY 3

Saturday
2nd April 2016

14

Vicky woke up, her mouth dry. She reached to the bedside table for her glass of water. Empty. She squinted at the alarm clock. 7:04.

What woke her up?

Her phone buzzed again. *Bastard thing. Should've left it downstairs.*

She checked the display. A text:

THSI IS MY NR. ROBERT X

She grinned as she thought of the ancient Nokia Robert had pulled from his pocket at Karen's.

The X . . .

She texted back.

HEY ROBERT. FANCY A DRINK *WITHOUT* KAZ AND COLIN? VICKY X

She sat for a minute, heart pounding, as she waited for a response, eyes locked on the screen.

Buzz.

TOMOROW?

Tomorrow? Moving a bit fast... Then again, I barely spoke a word to him with Karen there and he seems nice. Not an immediate fail, anyway. Nice enough, as Mum might say.

Before she knew it, her fingers were typing out a reply:

STAG'S HEAD @7?

Vicky swallowed, back to waiting.
The phone buzzed again.

ITS A D8!!! R

A banging noise came from downstairs. Someone at the door.

Her heart fluttered. She jumped out of bed, tugging her dressing gown around her as she raced downstairs, narrowly avoiding stepping on Tinkle's little fat body bouncing up the stairs to the warmth of Vicky's bed.

A figure misted in the door glass, knocking again.

Vicky opened it, blinking at the early morning light. 'Dad?'

'Morning.' He held up his old toolbox. 'I've come to put those shelves up in Bella's room.'

Vicky rested a hand on her face. 'Dad, it's *seven* on a Saturday.'

'Well, I was up anyway. Thought I'd get out and be useful.' He barged past her into the house.

On the street, Mum helped Bella out of the back seat. As soon as she was free of the seat belt, Bella raced up to Vicky and hugged her leg. 'I love you, Mummy.'

Vicky crouched to kiss her daughter on the forehead. 'I love you too, Bells.'

'Need a jobbie!' Bella dashed inside.

Vicky frowned at her mother as she approached. 'What's up with her?'

'She wouldn't go at ours this morning after Andrew told her about the jobbie monster.'

'Oh.' Vicky shook her head smiling, then nodded back at the house. 'How was she last night?'

'Good as gold. How was—'

'Got a stinking hangover, Mum. And it's early.'

Mum gave her a coy smile. 'It went well, then?'

'Might need you to babysit tomorrow night?'

Mum grabbed her in a hug. 'I hope this man's worth it, Victoria.' She checked her watch. 'I'd better go. I've got scones in the oven. The girls are coming round at nine.'

Vicky patted her arm. 'Thanks for looking after her.'

'You're still due me an account of what transpired last night, Victoria.' And with that, Mum was gone.

Vicky went back inside and hunted for her father. The thumping in the kitchen gave him away.

Dad was tearing through the cupboards. 'Can't find any coffee?'

'I don't drink coffee.'

'Of course you don't. Have you got any in?'

Vicky tightened the belt around her gown. 'I'll make you some.'

'There's a good girl. I've had my porridge, but a coffee would be a much-appreciated digestive aid. Doctor's orders, eh?'

Vicky ignored the attempt at levity as she filled the kettle. She found a coffee jar at the back of the cupboard, the granules a bit gunged up. *It'll do.* 'Milk and two still?'

'Your mother's got me on these *sweeteners*.' Dad seated himself on a stool at the breakfast bar and produced a small white box. 'Not too bad in coffee, just don't try to eat them.'

'If you say so.' Vicky poured milk over the instant coffee granules and started making a paste as the water boiled, the sharp aroma stinging her nostrils and bringing back fond memories. 'Remember when me and Andrew were wee and we used to dunk biscuits in your coffee?'

'Like it was yesterday.'

The kettle clicked off and she filled the mug. 'There you go, Dad.'

'Here's cheers.' He popped in four sweeteners before taking a drink, not even wincing at the temperature. 'How's work?'

'So, you still miss the force then?'

'Never retire, Vicky.' Dad shook his head. 'It's a *nightmare*. I keep waking in the middle of the night thinking about some old case from the nineties, and people who'd want to get me. It's hard to switch off.' He took another sip. 'Anyway, tell me about your case.'

She pressed her eyes back into the sockets. 'Nothing fits together.'

'Ah, chaos. The bit I loved about being a detective.'

'Any sage advice on restoring order?'

'Threatening to kick the shit out of them usually helped.' Dad slurped at his coffee. 'That or kicking the shit out of them.'

'Dad!'

He laughed. 'Oh, you really are after advice. Well, speaking to people helps. Usually someone's done something stupid some-where along the line. What is this case, anyway?'

'A brother and sister were abducted. I rescued them.'

'Saw that in the paper. *You* found them?'

'Press conference was a disaster. Raven told me to get media training.'

'I remember when he was a spotty wee wanker. Now he's just a wee wanker.'

Vicky reached into the fridge for the two-litre bottle of Diet Coke. She poured out a glass and took a sip — almost entirely flat. Needed at least another fifty litres before she felt better. 'I'll take Bella up Dundee Law today and tire her out.'

'Not by driving up.'

'I know. I'll walk up from Lochee.'

'That's what me and your mother did every weekend. Get you and Andrew to run around and exhaust yourselves.' His eyes dark-ened as he gazed into his cup. 'Now look at him.'

'Not that I'm much better.' Vicky stared into her glass, only a couple of bubbles dancing on the surface. 'Dumping Bella on you guys all the time. I'm such a shit mother.' Tears stung her eyes, images of Bella asleep in her bed creeping all over her. 'Why am I such a mess?'

Dad got up and held her in his arms. 'Hey there, baby girl, that's no way to be.'

Vicky took a trembling breath. 'I'm ruining her life, Dad.'

'Bella's *fine*.' He stroked his daughter's back slowly, just like when she was a teenager, heart broken by some idiot boy. 'And don't worry about your mother.' He stood back and held her out at arm's reach. 'Pissing her off's my job.' He waited for her grin. 'She's always like that and besides, looking after Bella keeps us young.' He stared into space. 'And it takes your mother's mind off your brother.'

'You know Andrew was back at work yesterday?'

'I heard. This ME, or whatever it is, it's killing your mother seeing him like that.'

'Quite a pair we turned out to be.'

Dad stroked her arm. 'We're proud of you both. Never forget that.'

'Grandad!'

Dad spun round and lifted Bella up in his arms, twirling her around the small kitchen. 'How's my girl?'

'Mummy, can we catch baddies today?'

Dad beamed at Vicky. 'Another chip off the old block.'

'Up, Mummy!'

Leaning against the railings at the top of Dundee Law, bracing herself against the wind, Vicky looked down at Bella. 'We are up.'

'No, up!' Bella grabbed the railings with her gloved fists. 'Up on the metal things!'

'It's not safe.'

'My wee leggies are sleeping.'

Vicky lifted Bella up and rested her on the railing, both forearms firmly hooked under her oxters to keep her safe.

Dark clouds loomed overhead, a heavy curtain hanging over

Perth in the west. South was clear and bright blue, across the urban sprawl of Dundee all the way to the Tay with its twin bridges over to Fife.

Her legs tingled from the walk up, but it was still bitterly cold, an arctic blast carrying stale smoke from somewhere.

Bella pointed to the river. 'Where's that?'

'That's the River Tay. The land is Fife.'

'Five?'

'No, Fife. It's where Auntie Karen and Uncle Colin come from. It's why they say "aye" and not "eh".'

'Oh, eh ken.' Bella giggled. *Dad was teaching her Dundonian again. Christ.* 'Isn't Cameron from Fumdernland? Not Five?'

'Dunfermline is part of Fife.'

'Oh.' Bella scanned the panorama like she could see that far. 'Where're the baddies?'

'There aren't any up here.'

'Oh.'

'Is that why you didn't want to come up?'

'Grandad said my wee leggies wouldn't make it up.' She flashed a toothy smile. 'I did, though.'

'Why did you think there would be baddies up here?'

'Grandad said this is a jail.'

'The Law Hill hasn't been a prison.' Vicky smiled. 'Not for a long time.'

Bella pointed at the war memorial. 'What's that?'

'That helps us remember people like Granny's Uncle Jimmy who died in the war.' Vicky lifted her down from the railings. 'How was playgroup this week?'

'Caitlin and Jayden were my best pals. They gave me football stickers. I like Arsenal.' Bella looked up at the memorial. 'Mummy, why haven't I got a daddy?'

'You've got a mummy, Bells. Isn't that enough?'

'Stinky Simon said Hayden has a daddy but not a mummy and Ross has two mummies.'

Vicky's phone rang. *Saved by the bell.* She tucked Bella between her legs before getting out her phone and checking the display. Dad. 'You haven't burnt the house down, have you?'

He laughed down the line. 'Not yet, but your cat's not speaking to me. I only tried to stroke her.'

'She's a cat, Dad. Let her come to you. Why are you calling?'

'You couldn't pop into that place on the Kingsway on your way home, could you? Seem to have lost my eight-mil screws.'

Vicky rubbed her face, her thick gloves catching her cheek. 'Couldn't you have done that before you came round this morning? The shop would've opened at—'

'Ach, you know how it is, Vicky. Your mother was rushing me. Scones in the oven and all that. Come on, be a good girl.'

'Right, fine. I'll get some. Bye.' She pocketed her phone and crouched down, looking through the railings across the southern edge of Dundee, gently resting her head on Bella's. 'Have you been a good girl?'

'No.'

'Why not?'

'I've not helped Mummy catch any baddies yet.'

'Well, let's get a hot chocolate, shall we?'

'Mummy!' Bella slapped her mother on the thigh. 'I want to see the owls!'

A stall housed a collection of poor-looking birds of prey — owls, kites and a few others Vicky didn't recognise.

'Come on, Bella.' Vicky lifted her up, her police training stretching to breaking amid the hostile stares from the other customers milling around the Fixit DIY entrance.

'Noooooo!' Bella screeched like one of the birds, kicking out at Vicky. 'NOOOOOO!'

The rat-faced proprietor sidled over, shoulders twisting. 'I can let your girl see the birds for half price if you keep her quiet.'

Vicky frowned at the guy's smirk, then glanced around at the

crowd taking a rather obvious interest in their little tête-à-tête.
'Well, much as I'd like to make you regret those words, no thanks.'

He pointed a disgusted finger at Bella. 'She seems to have
other plans.'

'*She* had a giant hot chocolate and her blood sugar level's
collapsing.' Vicky barged past him, carrying Bella into the store.
'Come on, Bells, that man's a baddie.'

Little fists pounded on her back. 'Mummy! I want to see the
birdies!'

Vicky hurried around the store, soon losing her bearings as
Bella screamed.

*Shouldn't have let her act all grown-up like Mummy and have a
deluxe hot chocolate. Not that Mummy's a grown-up.*

They ended up in the paint aisle, then the kitchens. Vicky
doubled back and crossed the aisle. *There they were. Screws. Eight
mil — was that the drill size or the screw size?* She grabbed both bags
and raced to the tills. The self-service was free, so she scanned the
bags, Bella clinging tight, her tears slicking onto Vicky's shoulder.
Muttered words about Mr Owl. Vicky put Bella down so she could
pay, then led her out of the store.

Bella stopped by the bird display, tiny hands rubbing at her
eyes. 'Grandad would let me see them.'

'Then Mummy will have words with Grandad.'

'Why won't you let me see the birds?'

Vicky took a deep breath, the knot in her neck tightening. An
image of Rachel and Paul in their cage flashed up in front of her
mind's eye. 'Because the birds don't want to be there, Bells.'

'Are they sore?'

'Very sore. They're in agony.' Vicky took her hand, making sure
to be extra gentle. 'Come on, let's go get our shopping.'

'Why's this called the Riverside, Mummy?'

Vicky stood by the freezer in Tesco, cold air blasting out and chilling her tear-soaked shirt. She pointed past the tills. 'That's the river we were looking at up on the Law.'

'River Five?'

'River Tay.' Vicky held out a packet of free-range chicken Kievs. 'Shall we have these for tea?'

'I like eating at Granny's.' Bella folded her arms around her chest. 'I get soup there.'

'I don't believe you for a second, little Miss Naughty. What do you really eat?'

'Biscuits.' Bella giggled. 'And sausages. And chicken nuggets. And tablet!'

'Did Granny tell you to say soup?'

Bella pouted. 'Maybe.'

Vicky pushed the trolley towards the next aisle. *Thank God the tantrum's over.*

Bella stopped in her tracks. 'Are those the baddies?'

Vicky followed the line of her finger to four teenagers huddling round the PlayStation games. 'I don't know.' Her phone rang. She got it out, expecting another errand from Dad.

Considine instead. *What the hell does he want?*

'You on today, Sarge?'

'Day off. What's up?'

'Well, you've just walked into a covert surveillance.'

'What are you talking about?'

'Brian Morton is at the Riverside Tesco.'

'I'm allowed to go to the supermarket, for God's sake. It's a public space.'

'Either way, Forrester wants you out of there.' And he was gone.

Vicky pocketed the phone, eyes shut. 'Sh— sugar.' She opened them, looking around for Brian or his brother. No sign of either.

Load of nonsense.

She wheeled the trolley over to the tills. Ahead, two middle-aged women stood chatting, heads craning back in laughter, their trolleys blocking the aisle. Vicky barged past, shoving her trolley into one of them.

She got a wild glare. 'Excuse me!'

'Sorry.' Vicky pushed through and headed towards the tills, Bella bobbing up and down in the child's seat.

A mobility scooter came round the corner just ahead of her, Brian Morton's flab rolling over the sides. John Morton pushed a trolley loaded with cakes — artisan brands Vicky could never afford. John stood at the end of the aisle gesticulating at his brother.

I've got every right to be here.

Vicky pushed the trolley out of the front door, getting a fresh waft of the bakery's cloying fresh bread smells. Bella skipped alongside as they walked back to the car.

By the front door, DS Johnny Laing sat in a dark grey Mondeo, eyes hidden behind shades, elbow resting on the open window. He was a big lad, farmer big, his suit stretching at the buttons of his tartan shirt. Parked next to her car.

He nodded as Vicky approached. 'Let me know when you're done making an arse of my obbo.'

'I'm allowed to be here, you wanker.' Vicky allowed herself to breathe as she unlocked her car. Trying to act cool, not to blow Laing's cover. Not that he wasn't doing a great job of it himself. 'Have they done anything today?'

'Nothing. Quiet day in while the Three Amigos scratch their balls outside. Young Zoey's not found any other dodgy web traffic from them.' Laing looked at Bella, in the middle of a little dance. 'That your kid?'

Vicky lifted Bella into her car seat. 'What's going on, Johnny?'

'Precious little. Took fatso ages to drive that thing down from the Hilltown.' Laing frowned. 'Take even longer getting back up, I suppose. Maybe get a cab. Easier to tail.'

'*Sergeant.*' Forrester joined them, scowling, and got in Laing's passenger seat. 'They *made* you.' *Talking like they were in a Jason Bourne film...*

'It's a supermarket.' Vicky opened the boot and dumped a bag in. 'I'm allowed to be here.'

'Well, sort of. Problem is, Kirk's mic picked them up talking about you. Thought they were under surveillance.'

'I'm just *shopping*.'

'Either way, our obbo's gubbed.' Forrester huffed out a sigh then focused on Laing. 'Right, Johnny, you can get off to Dens Park and watch our boys getting stuffed by St Johnstone.'

Laing looked like someone had shat in his cornflakes or at least stolen a half-day's double time. 'Sure?'

'Sure.' Forrester folded his arms. 'I'm in enough hot water without burning money. Thank you very much.' He stormed off towards a blue BMW.

'Got out of bed the wrong side, Vicks.' Laing snarled at her. 'I could've done with that OT.'

'Maybe cut down on the gambling, then?' Vicky got in, slamming the door and the central locking button.

'Mummy, was that man a baddie?'

'No, he's Mummy's boss. Shall we go home and get some soup?'

'Soup's my favourite.' Bella grinned wide. 'Tablet soup.'

VICKY SAT on the edge of Bella's bed. The small Cinderella lamp on the pine chest of drawers lit up the Disney posters covering the walls. 'Night-night, sweet pea.'

Bella struggled to keep her eyes open as Vicky kissed her on the forehead. 'Will we catch baddies tomorrow?'

'Don't worry about that, little princess. We'll do some fun stuff, okay?'

'Isn't catching baddies fun?'

'Not all the time.' Vicky reached over to kiss her again, holding her close for a few seconds, wishing they had a lot more time.

'Sleepy, Mummy. Night-night.'

'Goodnight.' Vicky left the room and stood outside Bella's door.

She waited, listening as her breathing slowed. Then she wiped the tears from her cheek and trudged down the stairs.

In the kitchen, she reached into the fridge for the bottle of wine. Stared at it until her eyes filled with tears again. She went over to the sink and tipped it out, the sweet tang fading as she turned on the tap.

Bella's life is just passing her by.

Remember giving birth like it was yesterday, Karen holding my hand tight. Where had the years gone? Before I know it, Bella will be leaving home and I'll have nothing but memories of tucking her in.

Something scratched at the back door, like it was going to slice through the wood. Vicky let Tinkle in, the cat shivering from the rain. Vicky blinked away the tears and picked up Tinkle to cuddle her for a few seconds. *Spend more time with her than Bella.* She put her on the counter and fetched the half-full tin of cat food from the fridge. The meaty stink almost made her retch as she spooned it into the bowl.

Vicky stood there watching the cat eat. *Tinkle, another life in which I play a minor role at most, though the half-feral tabby probably doesn't care. Though she has softened to the point where she can be picked up and handled. When she's hungry.*

Tinkle was at the opposite end of the spectrum from the animals Rachel Hay was selling, no human hands guiding her genetics. Whoever rescued her took her from a feral colony which suffered the same levels of inbreeding.

All Vicky could see was Rachel Hay lying in the hospital bed. Paul almost catatonic.

Whoever was behind it is beyond sick. What they tried to force Rachel and Paul to do . . .

Christ.

DAY 4

Sunday
3rd April 2016

15

Vicky walked along Bruce Drive, heels clicking on the pavement, coat tugged tight around her, breath misting in the late morning air. She took a deep breath and stared at the door.

Up ahead, Bella pushed the door open and skipped inside Vicky's parents' house. *Little madam...*

Something chimed in her bag. Her Airwave. *Bloody thing should be at work.* She got it out and had a look. A photo message, Vicky at the press conference, all twenty stone and bad hair. Underneath:

'HUNTER'S FARM, BARRY. NOW.'

She checked the sender but couldn't make sense of any of it. Looked like she'd sent it.

What the hell? Barry's just down the road, five-minute drive, if that. Add another five to get my car and—

No. This is my day off. Probably Laing or Considine playing a joke, getting me back for killing their OT bonanza.

She put the handset away and went inside, cooking smells greeting her from the kitchen — lamb, maybe? 'I'm here!'

Bella wandered out of the bathroom. 'Poo won't flush.'

Vicky bent down to hug her again and hid her smile behind the girl's head. 'I'll have a look in a minute.' She straightened up. 'Come on, let's see what Granny's been cooking.'

'Good! I'm *really* hungry!' Bella skipped ahead.

Vicky sniffed the air, still couldn't place the roasting meat. 'What we having, Mum?'

Mum leaned against the solid oak cabinet, letting her apron come free. 'Roast pork.'

'I love the way you say it like it rhymes with hawk.'

'What about the way she says oven?' Andrew leaned in the door frame, tightening the belt on his dressing gown. He plodded into the room and took a seat opposite Vicky at the kitchen table. 'Morning. Afternoon. Whatever.'

Mum prodded her cooking fork at him. 'You're a cheeky so and so, Andrew Dodds.'

'What's a so-and-so, Granny?'

'Your uncle.'

'When's lunch?'

Mum beamed as she hunkered down to cuddle Bella. 'It'll be hours, poppet.'

'I just had porridge for breakfast. Mummy's isn't as good as Grandad's!'

'Nothing can be!' Dad swooped in, picked Bella up and carried her through the conservatory into the garden.

'Somebody's full of beans today.' Andrew pursed his lips as he looked out the window. 'Wish I had ten per cent of that energy.'

Vicky reached across the table to stroke his forearm. 'You got home okay?'

'Thanks for leaving me in the car park. Heard you found them.'

'We did. You shouldn't have been at work.'

'Not got much choice.' Andrew shrugged. 'I'm so skint you wouldn't believe it. Why else do you think I'm back here?'

'Oh.'

Seeing her brother like that made Vicky's gut wrench. 'I was thinking of taking Bella up to Crombie.'

'How far round?'

'All the way, probably.'

'Better give it a miss.' Andrew smiled, though it was at least half a grimace. He slumped forward onto his elbows, nostrils twitching. 'Thought I smelled coffee, Mum?'

'Drinking coffee is what got you into this state in the first place, Andrew Dodds.'

'Mum, there's no link between coffee and ME.'

'I know that, Andrew, but you pushed yourself too hard and you broke down. They shouldn't have let you do it. You'll look after yourself while you're under my roof.'

Andrew stared at her. 'The only time I feel normal is when I have coffee.'

'Just remember what it feels like the next day, son. And the day after that.'

Andrew rubbed his beard and blew a raspberry through his lips. 'How's Zoey doing?'

'Okay, I suppose.'

'You're jealous.' Andrew grinned. 'Nice little lady like that, getting all the attention.'

'Shut up, Andrew.' Vicky glowered at him, feeling like she was fifteen again.

Mum huffed by the cooker, pulling a tray of spitting potatoes out of the oven. 'Right, I'll go and see what Bella and George are up to.' She walked off through the conservatory.

Vicky nodded after her. 'Still talking to herself, then?'

'Getting worse.'

Vicky stared out of the window across the old dump towards Barry. The message scratched at her scalp, pins and needles flashing. She reached into her bag for her Airwave and put it on the table. 'I got a weird message. Wonder if you can see who's winding me up?'

Andrew leaned over and started thumbing away at the device.

Mum reappeared, Dad and Bella trailing behind. Vicky

couldn't tell who looked more disappointed to have their playtime cut short.

'Can we catch baddies today, Mummy?'

Vicky reached over to kiss Bella. 'After lunch maybe.'

'Will you help us, Uncle Andrew?' Bella tugged at his sleeve. 'Grandad's going to kick their bums!'

Andrew was still checking the Airwave. 'If Grandad's helping, you don't need me or your Mummy.'

Bella snuggled in close to Vicky. 'I'll always need Mummy.'

'Thank you.' Vicky kissed her on the head. 'Go and wash your hands. There's a good girl.'

'Okay.' Bella skipped out to the hall.

Mum put a pot of tea in the middle of the table. 'Go and get dressed, Andrew. You're worse than Bella.'

He was still fiddling with the Airwave, his tongue sticking out his mouth. 'You think one of your colleagues is winding you up?'

'Those wankers are blaming me for messing up a surveillance yesterday.'

'Well.' Andrew passed it back. 'Problem is, that message came from outside the network.'

'What does that—?' Vicky frowned. 'The Airwave scanner?'

'Likely.' He shrugged. 'Ach, it's Jenny's job now.'

'You're saying I shouldn't ignore it, right?'

'It's not far, sis...'

'I'll be back soon.' Vicky got up and left the room, dialling Karen as she walked along the corridor.

HUNTER'S FARM was about a mile up the new road to the A92, not that it was that new anymore. The sign was expensively designed, tasteful, with a cute egg in cream. A Georgian farmhouse hid behind a thick evergreen hedge.

Vicky parked behind a maroon Volvo and got out.

'You took your time getting here.' Karen was leaning against her car, arms folded. 'So?'

'What?'

'Did you show Robert your tits?'

'That top you got me to wear meant I was showing them to everyone.'

'Vicks...'

'Kaz, I want to check this out then find out who's sent me that bloody message. Okay?'

Karen narrowed her eyes at Vicky. 'You'll keep.'

Vicky set off up the path towards the farmhouse, her feet crunching on the gravel. The wind whistled past, sounded like singing. She stopped by the front door and looked inside. No signs of life, not even a radio or telly.

Karen battered the door. 'Tell me everything.'

Vicky looked in the window, squinting. 'Kaz, there's nothing to tell.'

'But you let Robert walk you home even though he lives next door.' Karen folded her arms. 'Did you . . . ?'

'No.'

'No?'

'*No.*'

'Vicky . . .'

'What?'

'Did you ask him in for coffee?'

'No.'

'Come on. Are you losing your mojo?'

Vicky stepped away from the house and hit the door. 'I gave him my number.'

'Oh, good.' Karen grinned. 'Did he do anything with it?'

'He texted me his yesterday morning.'

'And you really didn't shag him?'

'No! I'm not that sort of girl.'

'Bullshit. So, are you seeing him again?'

Vicky averted her eyes. 'Doubt it.'

Karen waved her arms in the air like she was drowning. 'Oh my God!'

Vicky bit her lip. 'I'm having another crisis of confidence.'

'When did the last one end? I'm struggling to keep up.'

'Ha bloody ha.' Vicky sighed as she paced over to the yard at the side of the house, stopping at a lane leading to some dark farm buildings, maybe ten or twelve, paired off each side of the path. She set off down the lane. 'Come on.'

'Seriously, you're not going to—'

'Musisz mi pomóc!' A man mountain stood halfway down, fists clenched. Shaved head, dark beard trimmed to a thin strip. Topless, bulging muscles over a drooping pot belly. 'Nie mogę znaleźć Pan Huntera lub jego rodziny!'

Noise. Polish noise. Worried noise.

Except for "Hunter".

Vicky dashed over to him and got out her warrant card. She pointed at her chest. 'Police. DS Vicky Dodds.'

He tapped his own chest. 'Janek.'

Vicky smiled at him. 'Janek, is Mr Hunter okay?'

Janek threw his arms in the air. 'He... I can't find. Sorry, my English not so fantastic.'

'Better than my Polish.' Vicky glanced at Karen. 'What's happened?'

'I turn up at usual time but Mr Hunter not here.' Janek started walking towards the buildings. 'He always here. He always... crack the whip.' He led them further down the lane, between stacks of wooden outbuildings with pitched roofs. The eerie sound of grouped hens sounded like howling wind.

So — not singing, then. Hens.

Janek bolted for it.

Shit.

Vicky ran after him, stopping by a door. Janek was looking at something. A bit of paper.

Shit, shit, shit.

Vicky snatched it off him — another note, matching the style of the three previous ones.

NOT SO COMFY, IS IT?

HOPE THAT 24 HOURS OR SO IN ONE OF THESE DOESN'T DAMAGE YOU LIKE ONE YEAR DOES TO THE BIRDS.
 FEATHERS = HAIR.
 HOPE YOU START TO RESPECT THE BEAUTIFUL CREATURES.

Her gut clenched. *Another abduction. And whoever did it lured me here. Shit. The press conference means I'm now the public face, a target on my back.*

Karen grabbed Janek's arm. 'Can you help us get in?'

'Yes, yes, yes.' Janek patted himself down and found some keys in his front pocket. He held them up. 'Yes!' He unlocked the door and pushed it open.

A sharp blast of bird shit stung Vicky's nose, mixed with something meaty. *Bacon?* 'Do you have pigs here?'

'Pigs?'

Vicky oinked.

'Wieprzowy.' Janek nodded then shook his head. 'No... pigs? Just chickens.' He flicked a switch.

The light clicked on, each flash illuminating the long room. Maybe thousands of hens crammed tight in tiny wicker cages, rows and rows of uncollected eggs underneath them. Two birds climbed to the top of the rest in one cage before falling back down. They were bald and deformed, barely had a beak to feed with.

Vicky stopped Janek from going first.

Karen shook her head as she followed her through. 'Makes you want to get free-range eggs, doesn't it?'

'I do.'

The calls of the hens were almost deafening. But there was something else. Not the chickens screaming. Girls' voices. Coming from the end of the row.

Vicky sped up.

Against the far wall, wedged next to a hen run, two metal cages. The left-hand cage contained two girls, not much older than Bella. Heads shaved, naked. Two adults in the other, both naked. A woman at the front, wild-eyed, hands covering her chest and groin, mouth taped up. Behind her, a man lay in the corner, barely moving, hands clamped to his face.

Vicky looked around, breathing heavily now, desperate fingers fumbling with the locks.

'They're welded shut.' Karen hit the locks. 'There's got to be something we can do.'

'Ty draniu!' Janek stood behind them, waving his hand in the air. 'This is still on!'

On the table next to him, a glowing metal strip fizzed behind a bracket with three large holes.

'What the hell is that?'

'Hot knife machine.' Janek held out a hand like it could stab him from there. He tapped his nose. 'Debeaking. Very fast. Hundreds in an hour.'

Karen was reaching through the bars. The woman let her tear the tape off.

'They used it on him!' The mother's face was up to the bars of the cage, her haircut patchier than the kids, blonde tufts catching in the light. 'Graeme won't let me see!' He curled into a tighter ball.

'Vicks...' Karen held out another note.

WHETHER IT'S FROM SHOCK IN FRONT OF THE MACHINE OR STARVATION/DEHYDRATION COS THEY'VE BEEN MUTILATED, **BEAK TRIMMING KILLS.** BE THANKFUL YOU'RE STILL ALIVE.

The woman tugged at the man's arm, twisting him round. The tip of his nose was a blackened stump, at least a centimetre shorter than it should've been.

Vicky tasted sick in her throat, realising what the bacon was. The acrid tang of human flesh. 'They've debeaked him.'

16

—————

Back outside, Vicky sucked in fresh morning air, trying to get rid of the reek from inside. *Six buildings, all full of hens. Thousands of birds suffering inside.* Her gut churned at the thought.

And Graeme Hunter... His nose burnt off like one of his birds. Eye for an eye. Tooth for a tooth. One nose for a thousand beaks.

'You okay?' Karen didn't look it herself, her face as green as her hoodie.

'Not really.' Vicky sat on a low wall. Listened to the birds calling for their freedom. 'Let's hope there's some sort of security system here.'

'Called a fire engine but the Carnoustie lot are attending a fire on Carlogie Road.' Karen held up her phone. 'Poor bastards. Stuck in there.'

A shiver crawled up Vicky's spine. 'Where's Janek?'

'With a pair of uniforms.' Karen joined Vicky on the wall. 'Think he's involved?'

'Doubt it. He seemed frightened more than anything else.'

'One of the uniforms has a Polish wife, managed to speak to him. Janek wondered if they're being targeted by some racists or whatever. He's got mates in Dundee who've got into fights with locals.'

'This isn't that sort of crime.'

'No, it's not.' Karen clutched her phone in her hands. 'Anyway, I've sent a photo to my cage guy, but they look like a match to the one in Dryburgh.'

'We're missing two then?'

Sirens blared nearby, blue lights pulsing near the farmhouse. A pair of male paramedics raced towards them lugging a gurney between them. Karen set off.

Vicky stared into space trying to weigh up the options. Her Airwave weighed heavy in her hands.

Someone sent me here. That photo, that message. Someone targeting me, involving me deep in the case.

Definitely need to get Jenny to check my Airwave, see if she can back up Andrew's assessment, maybe even take it one step further.

She hit dial and put her phone to her ear.

VICKY'S AIRWAVE CRACKLED. 'Fire engine's just turned up, Sarge.'

A fire engine joined the long row of official vehicles — two panda cars, an ambulance and the Scenes of Crime van. Karen and her paramedic chums set off towards it.

'I can see it.' Vicky killed the call and tossed the handset to Jenny Morgan. 'Finally get them out of there.'

'You're not getting any less impatient.'

'Too many negatives for a Sunday lunchtime, Jen.' Vicky tried to peer into the farm but just caught a few SOCOs getting into their crime scene suits. 'How many of your lot are here?'

'Twenty. Better hope there's no other crime in Tayside today.' Jenny was focused on the Airwave. 'Well, I agree with your brother. It's an external message. Problem is...' She clicked her tongue. 'I've just got no idea what I'm doing.'

'But Andrew does.'

'Correctamundo.' Jenny gritted her teeth. 'And he's off the park.'

'Can anyone else help?'

'Three guys coming up from Edinburgh.' Jenny sighed as she set the device down. 'But I need Andrew. You need someone who knows what they're doing.'

'Is this a prank?'

'You should tell Forrester.'

'Right.'

'But you don't trust him, do you?'

'Trust who?' Forrester finished zipping up his crime scene suit. 'Considine.'

'Right.' Forrester pulled on a pair of gloves and nodded at Jenny. 'One of your lot was looking for you.'

'Cheers.' Jenny got up and wandered off.

The rain started up, small droplets dotting the ground, raising the ozone smell.

'She freaks me out.' Forrester shoved a mask onto the top of his head. 'Heard they burnt the boy's nose off... That can't be right, can it?'

'Now he knows exactly what his chickens feel.'

'Tell me you're not sympathising with them.'

Vicky stared at him. 'All those hens, even you'd start to think about it.'

'How did you find this guy?' Forrester frowned at her. 'Popping over for a dozen free-range double-yolkers?'

'Hardly.' Vicky scowled at him. 'It's battery hens in there.'

'Ah for the love of—' Forrester frowned behind Vicky. 'Mac, take a look at this.' He waved the note.

'I've not got a suit on, sir.' MacDonald stepped forward. 'I can see it's another note, though.'

'Get round the nearby farms. Put out a call for information.' Forrester grimaced.

MacDonald nodded. 'Jenny Morgan told me she found a couple of human hairs near the note. Wouldn't think twice about it, but the colours don't match the family or that Polish guy.'

'His name is Janek.' Vicky looked over at him. 'Janek.'

'Well, check his story. Fine-tooth comb, Mac.'

'You'll need to exclude me and Karen Woods.'

'Right, right.' Forrester put his goggles on. 'So. Why were you here?'

Just then, the paramedics carried a gurney away. Karen jogged alongside Mrs Hunter.

'Right-o, I'm going to see what's what here.' Forrester walked towards the farm buildings. 'Vicky, follow them up to Ninewells and speak to her, okay?'

~

'THREE.' Vicky stepped inside the lift and grabbed the rail. 'Same as Rachel Hay and her brother.'

Considine pressed the button. The lift shuddered as it started to climb. 'At this rate, we'll fill the hospital by the end of the month.'

The doors ground open. Dr Rankine stood at the reception, hands on hips. 'DS Dodds.'

Vicky exhaled. 'How's Mr Hunter doing?'

'He's in surgery now.' Rankine rubbed at her nose, some unconscious reaction. 'Unfortunately, there's no question of reattaching anything, more a case for rhinoplasty. The machine burnt away a lot of the flesh and cartilage, and the heat cauterised the wound.'

Vicky nodded, torn between sympathy and anger. 'Can we speak to Mrs Hunter yet?'

'Rhona. Her name is Rhona.' Rankine shook her head. 'She's suffering from exhaustion and dehydration, but she should be able to answer a few questions. Just don't push her too hard.' She led them into the ward and opened a curtain. 'Mrs Hunter?'

Rhona lay on a bed, a drip in her arm, eyes blank, a hand clasped to her scalp, tiny dots of stubble covering her cranium amongst the blonde tufts. 'How are my babies?'

'They're fine.' Rankine checked her chart, nodding slowly. 'We're just keeping them in for observation.'

'And Graeme?'

'He's in surgery just now.'

Rhona wiped a tear from her face.

'I'll let you know as soon as I hear anything. Meanwhile, the police want to ask a few questions.' Rankine left them with a smile.

Vicky sat next to the bed, Considine on the other side. 'Mrs Hunter, I'm with the Major Investigation Team. We want to find who did this.' She got out her notebook. 'Can you describe what happened this morning?'

'I was in the kitchen with the kids. Graeme was mucking out the duck house, listening to *The Archers* on the radio. We've got about thirty Indian Runners and they get *filthy*.' Rhona swallowed hard, her eyes shutting, as if she was back there. 'Then... Then a car pulled up. People get lost out our way all the time. We're a bit off the main road, but people don't realise the dual carriageway to Dundee is less than a mile further up.' Her eyes widened as she took a breath. 'Graeme went over to the car and—'

'Do you remember what kind it was?'

'Black thing.' Rhona shrugged. 'I'm afraid I don't know much about vehicles without tyres weighing thirty stone.'

Vicky got out the sample photos of the car from Dryburgh Industrial Estate. 'Was it any of these?'

'That sort of thing. Could be any of them, though. I'm sorry.'

Vicky made a note. 'Did you see who was in the car?'

'A man. He got out and grabbed Graeme from behind. I couldn't see his face or anything. Next I know, the driver's out of the car, balaclava on, knife in his hand. They came inside and threatened us.'

'Were they both wearing balaclavas?'

'When I saw them. Just saw their eyes.'

'What colour were they?'

'I can't remember. I'm sorry.'

'Don't worry. Can you give us a physical description?'

'Like what?'

'Well, were they male?'

'One was definitely a man. The other, I don't know.' Rhona rubbed her forehead with her palm, her fingers coming to rest on the stubble. 'It could've been a woman or maybe a—' she leaned forward with great effort, '—*homosexual*.'

Vicky buried her face in her notebook. 'What makes you say that?'

'The walk. It could've been a woman, but I got the impression it was a man.'

Vicky made another note, less for investigative procedure than to show she was taking the bigot seriously. 'And you were in the kitchen?'

'I just stood there, couldn't do anything. If only I'd got Graeme's shotgun . . .'

'Did they speak to you?'

'Barely said a word, and what they did say sounded garbled. Really deep and rough. It all happened so fast. They brought Graeme inside the house and shoved us in the kitchen. They...' Rhona's hand started shaking. 'The man got these cages out of the car and put them in one of our barns. The driver kept us in the kitchen for half an hour. Must've taken all that time to assemble them.' She ran a hand over her head, tugging at the remaining tufts. 'Then they took us over and...'

Vicky waited, giving her the space and time she needed.

Tears welled in Rhona's eyes. 'They shoved the girls into a cage and welded the door shut.'

'Did they look like professional welders?'

'I wouldn't know. They put me in a different cage. One of them shoved a knife in my face, while the other—' She broke off, her eyes screwed up tight, and yet the tears leaked down her face. 'I'm sorry, I—'

'It's okay.' Vicky smiled at her but kept her distance. 'Take your time.'

'Graeme's hot knife.' Rhona clenched her jaw. 'Stuck his head against it.' She shut her eyes again. 'The sound of him screaming, the smell... I'll take it to the grave.' She opened her eyes, full of fury and rage. 'They bundled Graeme into the cage with me. He'd passed out by then. They welded it shut and left us in the dark with the hens.'

Vicky wrote it down. 'Did they record this?'

'I don't think so.' Mrs Hunter gave her a dazed look. For a moment she seemed to consider something, then shook her head and stared Vicky straight in the eye. 'Get these bastards for me.'

'I LOVE THIS MAP.' Forrester walked over and slumped behind his desk. Couldn't take his eyes off the huge map. He traced his finger over the area around Barry, a triangular bulge just after the Tay met the North Sea. The map didn't have the new road on it, just a winding thing terminating near the farm. 'The cages match.'

'Two kidnappings in the space of five days. Impressive.' Forrester slurped from a navy coffee mug. 'So why were you there?'

Vicky swallowed the sour taste in her mouth and tossed her Airwave at him. 'Someone sent me a message.'

Forrester frowned at it, holding it far from his face. 'A photo of you?'

'Andrew reckons it's from whoever's hacking the network.'

'But why you?'

Vicky shrugged. 'Because I'm the face of this.'

'Eh?'

'Raven forced me to speak to the press on Friday. If you and Mac hadn't gone to Livingston, maybe it would've gone to you instead?'

'So you just pitched up there with DC Woods?'

'I thought it was Laing getting back at me for killing his OT after the thing at Tesco.'

'Vicky, Vicky, Vicky. Call me first, okay?'

'Right. Right, I'm sorry. I should've.' Vicky's brain rattled as she processed the case. 'Hang on. If it's the same people... Irene

Henderson described three people kidnapping Paul Joyce. Definitely one female. Rhona Hunter saw a male and an androgynous person.'

'So the woman's dropped out?' Forrester nodded slowly. 'But that's at least two consistent descriptions, though.' He got up and went over to his coveted map, slurping coffee. 'It's pretty far out of the way, isn't it?'

Vicky pointed at where the farm was. 'She saw a black car.'

'Right-o.' Forrester shook his head, grimacing as he took a sip of coffee. He pointed at the map around Dryburgh. 'Mac's laddies have been going through the industrial estate CCTV. Nothing. The number plate's come up blank on the ANPR, which means they didn't go through the Kingsway or the Riverside.'

'Meaning we don't have anything.'

'No, and they're committing more crimes.'

Vicky shook her head. 'Nothing from the surveillance?'

'You mean after you ballsed it up?'

'You want me to apologise for shopping at Tesco?'

Forrester winked. 'Asda's so much better.' He put his mug down on Rankine's desk. 'Laing was seething when I called it off.'

'I'm not going to apologise to him. Did you get anything on the brothers?'

'Aside from the excursion to Tesco, neither left home yesterday. Them clocking you means that, if he is involved, he'll warn his mates.'

'Right. That's your logic?'

'Vicky, I have to beg Raven for every single penny. Johnny Laing sitting on his arse with four DCs costs a bloody fortune. And we've got precious little intel on those two.' Forrester tapped on the Hilltown. 'Loving this map. Loving it.'

'Remember we spoke to those schoolgirls in Cupar? Wasn't there another couple who might've been posting on xbeast?'

'The Muirheads. Live just off the Perth Road. Haven't spoken to them yet.'

Vicky folded her arms. 'And that's not suspicious?'

17

Vicky pulled off the Perth Road onto one of the better streets in Dundee, a short row of old stone houses, and parked behind a blue BMW. 'There's MacDonald. What the hell is he doing here?'

'The 1-Series?' Considine laughed. 'That's a hairdresser's car.'

'Listen to yourself...' Vicky got out, headed straight over and sat in the seat behind MacDonald. 'Why are you here, Euan?'

Considine got in the seat behind Karen Woods. 'Mac, nice motor, my man.'

Vicky grinned at MacDonald. 'Stephen was just saying this is a hairdresser's car.'

MacDonald twisted round to glare at Considine. 'That right?'

'You're not disagreeing, are you?'

MacDonald chuckled then glanced at the time display on the dashboard. 'We've been here half an hour and there's no movement.'

Vicky leaned forward to block out any more banter from Considine. 'Forrester know you're here?'

'I can do what I want.' MacDonald folded his arms. 'Why do you ask?'

'Never mind. You found them yet?'

Karen frowned. 'Been round the garden, looked in the windows. Nobody's home.'

'So you're just waiting?'

MacDonald opened his mouth to speak.

Karen tapped the passenger window. 'Here we go.'

A dark red Fiat pulled onto the street, headlights on, and pulled in by the house.

'That him?' MacDonald opened his door, got out and rapped on the passenger window before Vicky had a chance to assume control of the situation.

The window wound down.

MacDonald raised his eyebrows at the driver. 'Mr Muirhead?'

'Who?'

'Detective Sergeant Euan MacDonald of Police Scotland. Can we have a word?'

'What's this about?'

'Better discuss this inside, sir.'

The man got out of his car and locked the door, his movements weary. 'What are you talking about?'

'Is your wife home, Mr Muirhead?'

'My name is Jim Parrott. Not Muirhead.'

'Right.' MacDonald tilted his head to one side, then the other. 'So why are you here?'

'Buying a turntable off a boy.' Parrott shrugged. 'Gumtree ad. Old Rotel job with a diamond stylus.'

MacDonald shook his head. 'On you go.'

Parrott set off across the road, hands in pockets, heading away from the Muirhead house. Even had a record bag over his shoulder.

MacDonald drummed the car roof. 'Where the hell are they?'

Vicky leaned back against the car. 'Have you run their names through your Wildlife Crime Unit leads?'

'Happy to do that, Mac.' Considine clapped his shoulder. 'Want me to?'

Vicky rolled her eyes at Karen. *If he stuck his tongue any further up MacDonald's arse, he could clean his teeth for him.*

'Calm the beans.' MacDonald bit his lip. 'Got a lead from them. There's an undercover operative involved, so we're treading on eggshells.' He cleared his throat. 'Commune near Redford called Phorever Love, spelled with a Ph.'

Vicky smirked. 'Sounds like a Shamen song.'

'Showing your age there, Vicky.' Karen gave her a cheeky wink. 'What's the link, Mac?'

'Wildlife guys wouldn't give us even that.' MacDonald sniffed, audibly put out by the interruption of his lecture. 'Something like commercial sensitivity.'

'You and Karen stay here.' Vicky stared at MacDonald, searching for any acknowledgement. 'Stephen and I will head there.' She got a shrug from MacDonald. 'And call your mate and check for me, okay?'

～

'So, I was thinking.' Considine turned right just before the turning to Crombie Park, instead heading deeper into the Angus wilderness. He powered through Carmyllie, getting closer to the speed limit every second. 'You know this development I've got to do to get to DS? Do you mind if I take over managing Zoey?'

Vicky had to look out of the window to suppress a laugh. 'She's not interested in you, Stephen.'

Considine swallowed as he turned down a country lane, passing entrances to two large farms on opposite sides of the road, before taking a right along a single track. 'If memory serves...' He trundled on for a few minutes, the car's suspension rocking them like crash test dummies. 'Thank God we took the Python.'

'Don't call it that. Seriously.'

His grin turned sour as he slowed by a set of large walls, barbed wire along the top, a steel gate blocking the entrance, "Phorever Love" graffitied in pink and red.

'Doesn't look like much love's going on in there. It's like something out of *The Walking Dead*.'

'I seriously hope there are no zombies in there.'

'Zombies or not, it's not exactly what I was expecting from a hippie commune.' She pointed to a passing bay on the left. 'Pull in.'

Considine slowed to a halt, but left the engine running.

'Can't the Python turn itself off?'

Considine twisted the key in the ignition and the silence returned. 'I regret telling you.'

'What you should really be regretting is that you ever called it that.'

'Whatever.' Considine couldn't even look in her direction. She almost felt sorry for him. 'Anything from Mac?'

Vicky checked her phone. Nothing. She hit dial. Answered immediately. 'Mac, we're here. You got anywhere yet?'

'Literally just off the phone with him.' MacDonald yawned. 'Sorry, late night. That group is a commune. An off-grid kind of deal. Very active in campaigning. Do a lot of picketing. A few years ago, they stopped delivery lorries getting to Hunter's Farm for a week.'

Vicky looked over at the gates. 'Seriously?'

'I'm not in the habit of joking.' MacDonald yawned again. 'He did say they've been investigating a group of cyberterrorists who took down a few company websites, including a GMO company in Midlothian and a cattle feed company in Paisley. Sites were down for over two weeks. Hacked a few meat companies' Twitter accounts and so on. Made them all look like idiots. They might be based there.'

Vicky took another look. *Explains the barbed wire.* 'So, what's the link to this Muirhead couple?'

'Polly Muirhead is supposed to be their lawyer. Hence the corporate sensitivity.'

Vicky tried playing the logic through her head. 'That fits. Okay, I'll let you know how it goes.'

Considine was already out of the car and walking over to the gates. He knocked on the corrugated iron then shook his hand in the air. 'Ow.'

'Don't know your own strength, eh?' Vicky joined him by the entrance. Locked tight.

The gate slid open. Two men stood there, arms folded, wearing army surplus gear. The older had blond dreadlocks tugged back into a ponytail, while the younger one's shaved head was more soldier than Buddhist. Both had dark shadows under their eyes.

Dreadlocks sniffed at them. 'Can I help?'

'Looking for Sandy and Polly Muirhead.'

'Very pleased for you, sweetness.' Dreadlocks gave her a good once over. 'If you're looking for them, they're bound to have a nice fun time. Smashing tits you've got, love.'

Skinhead shook his head, laughing. 'Listen, can I tell them who's asking for them?'

Vicky held out her warrant card. 'DS Vicky Dodds.'

Dreadlocks didn't hold out a paw, but his leer slipped off his face. 'I run this place. Kevin Simmers.'

'So go and get them.'

Dreadlocks laughed. 'No. Goodbye.'

'We're investigating two vigilante actions in the Tayside area. They appear to have been committed against people with a public record of animal cruelty. Know anything about it?'

Skinhead edged closer, before his associate could close the gate. 'Going to ask nicely. Get to fuck.'

Vicky narrowed her eyes at him. 'And who would you be?'

Skinhead towered over her. Had a real menacing air about him. That or his eyes were just too close together. 'None of your business.'

Vicky stood her ground. 'Just bring Mr and Mrs Muirhead out here.'

'They're not here.'

'You just said they were.'

'I'm a liar.' Skinhead winked at her. 'Don't trust me.'

'We've got intelligence linking your group to these crimes.'

Skinhead laughed. 'The police have intelligence?'

'Very funny.' She stepped closer to him. He towered over her, but she'd stopped caring. 'My understanding is you picketed Hunter's Farm in Barry. That correct?'

Skinhead shrugged. 'Might've done.'

'Someone trapped the family in cages. Know anything about it?'

Skinhead glanced at his leader. 'Want me to get rid of them, Kevin?'

'Andy, leave it.' Simmers shook his head. 'Officers, we're a strictly pacifist group. Now, how can I help?'

Vicky smiled at him. 'I just need to speak to Mr and Mrs Muirhead. Going to bring them out?'

Simmers let out a slow breath, then nodded at his underling. Skinhead clicked his fingers and a couple walked out.

A grey-haired man with glasses, maybe early forties. Not too out of shape.

And his wife... Talk about androgynous. As tall as her husband, just the expensive haircut and blouse identifying her gender.

Definitely candidates.

THE STENCH of Brian Morton's stale sweat lingered in the interview room even after the weekend. Vicky sat at the interview room table, gave MacDonald a nod to take the lead.

He cleared his throat. 'For the record, please state your name and occupation.'

'Polly Muirhead.' She was androgynous — a woman's face on a girl's body. 'I'm a solicitor at Gray and Leech in Dundee.'

MacDonald gave Polly Muirhead's lawyer a smile. 'And for the—'

'Fergus Duncan.' Without looking up, the lawyer tapped at a high-end smartphone. Dark pinstripe suit, tangerine tie. Aiming for Dundee United's colours, but the orange was a perfect match for the flaring acne covering his neck and face. 'I'm also employed by Gray and Leech.'

MacDonald let his glare linger, not that Duncan was going to look up again. He switched his attention to Polly. 'Mrs Muirhead, we're investigating two abductions perpetrated by an as-yet-unidentified group which may or may not have an animal welfare agenda.'

'And?'

'We believe you may be attached to said group.' MacDonald handed them some stills from the leaked video. 'We further believe that—'

'You think *I* am involved in *this*?' Polly scowled at her lawyer.

Duncan glanced up from his mobile, a frown etched on his forehead. 'These are strong accusations.'

'For which we have proof.'

Duncan smirked. 'And I'm sure this sort of thing can be tampered with.'

Vicky gave him a level stare. 'Our work is sound.'

Duncan's smirk faded, but the smugness remained. 'Take your word for it.'

Vicky turned to Polly. 'Do you have a user account on the xbeast site?'

Polly stared hard at Vicky, her blues burning. Easy to imagine them peeping out of a balaclava. 'Fine.' She exhaled. 'I'm a member of a group. It's not a crim—'

'Polly.' Duncan leaned over to her and whispered in her ear. Then he once again smirked at Vicky. 'My client wishes to make it clear that, while she indeed has a user account on the website in question, it is a safe haven for animal welfare discussion.'

Vicky opened her notebook. 'Mrs Muirhead, did you post a comment stating *"They didn't go far enough"*?'

Polly swallowed. Then nodded slowly.

Vicky leaned back in her chair and let an uncomfortable silence set in.

'Look, I'm a vegan.' Polly squirmed in her seat. 'I deplore animal cruelty. I give half of my time *pro bono* to animal welfare charities. My husband pays our bills and I give most of my salary to these charities. Those are just words. I was angry at what she'd done to those dogs.' She stared at the ceiling. 'Being filmed naked in a cage is nothing compared to the crimes committed by that woman.' She pointed at the still. 'Rachel Hay.'

'So you know her name.'

'It's all over the video file.' Polly raised a finger. 'Which I didn't post.'

'You said it was Rachel Hay who perpetrated the crimes. Not her brother. What makes you say that?'

'I already told you. It was on the file.'

Vicky held up the screen grab. 'It just says "Rachel and Paul".'

Polly looked at the printout again, then her eyes seemed to slip out of focus. After a moment, she shook her head. 'I've never heard of her brother, but I know all about Rachel Hay. You should be investigating her, not me.' Her voice dropped to a low hiss. 'She should be rotting in prison for what she did to those poor animals.'

'You know where she lives?'

'No.'

'Ever follow her daily dog-walking route?'

'What? No!' Polly clasped the collar of her cream blouse. 'I just saw that story in the papers. That woman got what was coming to her. I don't think anyone can disagree with that.'

'And yet you deny any involvement?'

'Sergeant, I've got sympathies with PETA. That doesn't mean I'll blow up a vivisection laboratory.' Polly let her collar go. 'I told you that my professional time is divided between client work and *pro bono* work with certain charities. That yields far more positive results than locking some daft woman and her brother in a cage. I'm trying to educate the wider public, not entrap them.'

'Know a Brian Morton?'

Polly narrowed her eyes. 'Should I?'

'He's another user of xbeast. One who uploaded the video in question to YouTube.'

Polly coughed, staring at the table top. 'Well, aside from my husband, I don't know any other group members. It's anonymous for a reason.'

'Okay, so where were you between three p.m. and midnight on Wednesday?'

'I was at work until after six.' Polly glanced at Duncan. 'Fergus can confirm that.'

'We were in a conference with the firm's partners. I can—'

'And after that?'

'I met my husband for dinner with friends.' Polly bit her lip. 'We went to the Rep theatre to see "*And Then There Were None*".'

Sounds like our suspects list.

Vicky sat back and folded her arms, eyebrows raised.

'It was very good. Based on an Agatha Christie novel. Look, I've got the ticket stubs in my purse if you don't believe me.'

'We'll need to take them in as evidence.'

With a sigh Polly reached for her handbag, rummaging through it for her purse. She handed over two tickets, the paper torn at the edges, and tossed them in the middle of the table.

The stubs looked genuine enough, not that Vicky was an expert. Or that they proved they were actually there. 'Now, these friends you—?'

'Simon and Emma Hagger.' Polly took a sheet of paper from Duncan and wrote on it before passing it to Vicky. 'This is their address.'

Vicky checked it — the arse end of Broughty Ferry. Another Considine task.

Polly hugged her shoulders tight. 'Fergus, I'm feeling quite stressed by this.'

Duncan tapped at his phone's plastic case. 'Noted.'

'Imagine what Graeme Hunter and his family are going through.' MacDonald stared at Polly then at her lawyer. 'Trapped inside a pair of tiny cages. Mr Hunter lost most of his nose.'

'I've got *nothing* to do with this.' Not a flicker of sympathy.

Definitely hiding something. Just... what?

Vicky drilled a deep glare into Polly. 'Where were you this morning?'

'First thing, Sandy and I...' Polly shrugged. 'We went for a walk through the glens then I had a meeting.'

'At the Phorever Love commune out by Redford?'

Polly didn't respond.

Vicky raised her hands, then let them drop back on the table with a bang. 'We picked you up there!'

'We...' Polly blinked, the frequency quickening with every silent second. 'Fine.'

'You said this was work related, but both of you went?'

Polly cleared her throat and the tough lawyer in her was back. 'It was part of my *pro bono* work for the firm. Sandy accompanied me, that's all. They're a small operation and I'm helping them deal with some complex contracts.'

'What do these contracts relate to?'

'They're *confidential*.' Duncan narrowed his eyes at her. 'Covered under an NDA which—'

'I get it.' Vicky glanced at him. 'You do know that place is linked to cyberterrorist activities?'

'Sergeant, Polly's billable work is developing a number of tech start-ups and other small businesses in a depressed area. Helping rejuvenate the Angus economy is all it is.'

'Not hacking into the Twitter accounts of meat companies?'

'My client has stated the reason for their visit.' Duncan spun his phone on the desk. 'The action now rests with you to verify that, should you wish.'

'Oh, we will.' Vicky resisted the impulse to throw Duncan's phone against the wall but only just. 'We'll start with your employers.'

'And as an employee, I can confirm it's true.' The lawyer rolled his eyes. 'The details are covered by client confidentiality.'

'Naturally we'll need a partner in the firm to confirm that, not just a lowly member of staff.'

18

'E uan?' Vicky had to jog to catch up with MacDonald, weaving between a couple of uniforms coming the other way. 'Mac!'

'Oh, Vicky.' MacDonald shrugged and leaned against the corridor wall. 'That could've gone better.'

'I watched that interview.' Considine joined them, hands deep in his pockets. 'Think you nailed it, eh?'

'You can think that...' MacDonald chuckled. 'We need to destroy those alibis.'

'Agreed.' Vicky smiled at Considine. 'Stephen, can you...?'

'Already on it.' Considine gave a mock salute then strode off down the corridor. 'And I'm taking the Python.'

'What a boy.' MacDonald drummed his fingers on the door-frame. 'And I mean boy. Seems a bit grim. Can we trust him all on his own?'

Vicky replied with a half-smile. 'I have problems with trust at the best of times.'

'And at the worst?'

'Let's just wait and see what he comes back with.'

'Sweet Fanny Adams, no doubt. Lawyers, got to love 'em.'

Vicky nibbled at her lip before stepping forward to avoid an officer hurtling down the corridor. She was within a foot of MacDonald.

MacDonald shook his head. 'Vicky, I just caught my guy on the golf course. He's doing me a favour. Said it'll be tomorrow before—'

'*Tomorrow*?' Vicky stepped away from him, arms out wide. 'Mac, people are—'

'I know, Vicky. I know. Look, their undercover lad speaks to his handler every Monday. After that they'll maybe start giving us supporting evidence.'

'Can't you try and—'

'I can try, but I'm not promising.'

'Right. So we'll just *wait* till he gets back to you then, and hope nobody else gets abducted?'

'We're doing all we can.' MacDonald looked back down the corridor. 'You want to double-team Sandy Muirhead?'

'Nicest offer I've had all week.'

'*TERRORISM*?' Sandy Muirhead dropped his hands on the interview table, his cufflinks rattling off the plastic surface. 'Polly's just trying to do some good in the world!'

'You and Mrs Muirhead post some inflammatory things on parts of the internet we're monitoring for terrorist activity.' MacDonald sat there, grinning wide. 'And you're associating with groups we have connected to domestic terror.'

Fergus Duncan was sitting next to Muirhead, a grin on his face as he fiddled with his mobile. 'My clients are very busy people, so if we can get to some sort of point?'

Vicky tugged at her blouse collar. One look at Muirhead and she felt like she was already drawing on her last reserve of fake politeness. She took a breath. 'All we're looking for is to establish your where-abouts between three p.m. and midnight on Wednesday night.'

Muirhead looked up from her chest, flicking his tongue over

his lips. 'We were at dinner with friends. Simon and Emma Hagger. Then we went to the theatre.'

'We're verifying that story.'

'Good.' Muirhead stared at her, eyelids flickering. 'You'll find that it's true.'

'Let's move on to today. First thing.'

'I was at work.'

'On a Sunday?'

'I'm an accountant. I had some bits and pieces to finish ahead of tomorrow.'

'Where is this office?'

'Whitehall Crescent.'

'Can anyone vouch for your presence?'

'My secretary, I suppose. She was there, too.'

'And after you were at work?'

'Polly picked me up and we went out into the glens. Then Polly had a client visit at this Phorever Love place.'

It all married up so nicely with his wife's tale. Even added some detail about being at work on a Sunday.

Vicky sat back in her chair and smoothed down her trousers. 'Mr Muirhead, this is your chance to change your story.'

Muirhead exhaled through his nose, loud and long. 'It's the truth.'

'And we need to make sure of that.'

'Sergeant.' Duncan tossed his phone on the table. 'Please desist from baseless insinuations until you've bothered to validate the story.'

MacDonald's hard-bastard mask had slipped revealing traces of bitter disappointment, like his team had lost a cup final he'd bet his mortgage on winning. Or at least like Vicky's dad after yet another Dundee United defeat. He just shrugged.

'Is that it?' Muirhead held up his wrist and made a show of staring at his watch. 'Are we free to go?'

Vicky sat back, struggling to think of another line of questioning. Until the alibi fell apart, she had to keep them on that side of the line. Looking like some masked perpetrators wasn't enough. She got to her feet. 'For now.'

Muirhead creased his forehead, yet the wrinkles soon smoothed out again as a smile spread over his smug face.

'You will, of course, have to remain in the country.'

Muirhead's face creased up again. 'But we're going on holiday next week!'

MacDonald frowned. 'Where to?'

'Riga. In Latvia.' Muirhead kept smiling. 'My wife and I are making an effort to visit every country in Europe. That's the four-teenth on our list.'

'Sounds nice.' Vicky got to her feet, scraping her chair across the floor. 'Trouble is, you'll be stuck at thirteen until we've confirmed your alibis.'

VICKY SAT in the corner of the Auld Cludgie Café, keeping well clear of the Sunday lunch queue at the counter. MacDonald wasn't so lucky, almost growling as the server seemed to make the teas and serve soups all on her own. 'How's it going out in Barry?'

'Shite.' Forrester almost growled. 'Bloody perfect crime, Doddsy. Nobody saw anything, place is so far from civilisation.'

'Carnoustie's hardly civilised.'

'True enough.' Forrester gave a thumbs up across the café. 'Tell you, Mac's some boy.' He grinned like a father on the touchline as his son scored. 'How you getting on with him?'

'Rough diamond, maybe. Though he could just be a load of coal.'

'Your glass is empty, Doddsy. Not even half.' Forrester smiled at MacDonald as he set their drinks down. 'Cheers, Mac.'

'No bother.' MacDonald sat next to Vicky, almost brushing his leg against hers.

Almost?

Forrester took his coffee, leaving Vicky's can and glass on the tray. 'So, these Muirheads are giving us sod all, right?'

'Deny, deny, deny.' MacDonald nudged Vicky's leg with his foot. Didn't even apologise. 'And that lawyer doesn't help.'

'Fergus Duncan the third.' Forrester shook his head. 'Dealt with his old man a few times. Slimy bastard.'

'Should've kept up the surveillance on the Mortons.' Vicky narrowed her eyes as she opened her can and poured. 'Then we'd know. Might've avoided the attack at the farm.'

'Level with me here, do you honestly think the Muirheads are involved?'

Vicky nodded. 'Yes.'

MacDonald was shaking his head. 'No.'

'Right-o.' Forrester chuckled, then his forehead knitted tight. 'Well, which is it?'

MacDonald gestured to Vicky. 'Ladies first.'

Sexist prick.

Vicky composed herself, taking her time to think through her logic with something other than a gut reaction. 'Polly Muirhead fits the profile of the androgynous perpetrator. She's like a pre-teen stretched out. I can't remember the last time I didn't have curves.'

'And what curves.' MacDonald coughed. 'Isn't Sandy a bit short, though?' The hard bastard was back in control, giving her a strong look rather than lust. 'And he's got pretty small hands. Hard to see them kidnapping anyone let alone overpowering a farmer.' His blue eyes darted about. 'We shouldn't base our suspects list on the flaky descriptions we've got so far.'

'It's not just that.' Vicky took a drink, buying time. 'Polly's aware of Rachel's past controversies. And she gives money and professional time to animal charities.' She put her glass down again, the contents slopping over the side. 'And this Phorever Love group. They're up to all sorts according to Mac's guy. They pick-eted Hunter's farm.'

'That's true.' MacDonald checked his phone. 'Still waiting, by the way.'

'I'd say they fit our profile. There's a link to both cases.'

Forrester nodded before looking at MacDonald. 'Okay, Mac. Tell us why they're not suspects?'

'Two things. First, this is a lawyer and an accountant not a couple of tree-hugging hippies. They might be vegans and sympathetic with PETA, but they seem like lovers not fighters, if you catch my drift.'

Forrester peered over his coffee mug. 'All mouth and no trousers.'

'Exactly what I— hang on.' MacDonald tapped at his phone. 'That's Considine. That other couple confirmed the alibi for Wednesday night.'

Forrester set his mug down. 'One nil to Mac, then.'

Vicky drained her can and crumpled it. 'I still think we should be including them.'

'Even with alibis?' MacDonald frowned. 'Why do you think they're lying?'

'This is Considine we're talking about. He's probably gone to the wrong people, heard no and told us yes.'

Vicky's phone rang — unknown number. Could be anyone. Could be nothing, too, but never worth the risk. 'Better take this.' She walked off and left them to it. 'Hello?'

'Is that Vicky Dodds?' Male. English accent, maybe London.

'Speaking.'

'This is Andy Salewicz.'

Vicky frowned, trying to recall the name. 'Going to have to help me here.'

'I met you this morning. At Phorever Love.'

The skinhead. And he has my mobile number. Superb...

Vicky switched her mobile to her right hand so she could log the call in her notebook. 'Are you going to threaten me on behalf of Mr Simmers again?'

'This isn't about that.' He paused. 'DI Andy Salewicz. I work for the Met's Domestic Extremist Team.'

'Seriously?'

'Seriously.' He laughed. 'I'm undercover at Phorever Love. I'm in a garden centre in Brechin. Supposed to be collecting ten wheelbarrows, but I got peckish and went for some soup, if you know what I mean.'

'You use your real name?'

'Saves hassle with the cover. My cover story needed military service — I did three tours of Iraq. Besides, I don't want someone blurting out my real name in Tesco, do I?'

'Well, that was an impressive display this morning. I had you tagged as hired muscle.'

'I'll take that as a compliment.' Another warm laugh. 'My boss asked me to call you or DS MacDonald. I can put a face to your name, so I called you. What's your interest in Phorever Love?'

'Two suspects potentially involved in an animal justice campaign. Kidnapping a pug breeder and trying to get her brother to... And burning a hen farmer's nose off.'

'I saw that on the news.' Sounded like Salewicz was outside now. 'The reason I'm at Phorever Love is we got wind of a plot to poison a reservoir near Edinburgh. Six months of deep cover and Simmers is only just starting to trust me. Turns out this lot aren't involved.' He sniffed. 'They *are* involved in drugs, though. They've got a meth lab up in the Highlands.'

'Like in *"Breaking Bad"*?'

Salewicz laughed. 'I was halfway through the last series before I got put on this, so *please* don't spoil the end.' He chuckled again. 'My handler told me to stay here and help the NCA to pursue the drug lead. Might be a dead end for you.'

'We've got Polly and Sandy Muirhead in—'

'Them. They're frequent visitors here. Only thing is...' Salewicz exhaled into the speaker, the distortion crackling in Vicky's ear. 'Be careful. It's ultra-sensitive. When I ran their names past my handler...' He snorted. 'There's a red flag next to them. The NHTU warned him off.'

'The National Human Trafficking Unit?' Vicky waited for a grunted agreement. 'Why are they looking into them?'

'Their vice remit. Drugs go hand in hand with vice, I'm afraid, and that's all I can tell you. Simmers is shrewd despite the dreadlocks. They've lawyered up like Walter White in *Breaking Bad*.'

'Polly Muirhead?'

'Got it in one.'

'What is she protecting for them?'

'Your guess is as good as mine.'

'Can you look into it for me?'

'I can try.'

'Got anything on this cyber angle?'

'Precious little. They hired someone externally, but— Well, we don't know who.'

'Does the name Brian Morton mean anything to you?'

Another speaker rattling sigh. 'Again, precious little.'

'Big fat guy on a scooter.'

'Sorry.'

'What about Kelly Nelson-Caird?'

No reply. He'd already hung up. Vicky turned back and put her phone on the table.

'Look Mac, that's the end of the matter, okay? We've got a job to do, let's do it.' Forrester took a slurp of coffee and glanced at Vicky's mobile. 'Who was that?'

'Salewicz. He's undercover at Phorever Love. Reckons the Muirheads are frequent visitors. Polly's repping them legally. Up to... some dodgy shit.' She held up a hand. 'There's a vice angle.'

'Curious...' MacDonald shot a glance at Forrester. 'I know people who worked in the predecessor of that squad in Strathclyde, the old Vice and Trafficking Unit. Could check it out?'

'Do it.' Forrester made a loose fist and tapped his pursed lips with his knuckles. 'But be careful not to blow anyone's cover. People's lives are at stake here.'

Forrester sucked air through his fist. 'See you back over the road.' He got up and left them to it.

MacDonald finished his coffee. 'Vice investigations usually trump everyone else's.'

'I guess.' Vicky pointed a finger at Forrester as he passed the window, already on his phone to someone. 'This cyberterrorism angle. We'll have to wait till tomorrow to pick up with Zoey, won't we?'

MacDonald pushed his mug away. 'I persuaded her to come in today.'

'She's keen.'

'Don't know the half of it.' MacDonald coughed into his fist. 'Anyway, let me pick up with my contacts. Might be something in the vice angle. Probably nothing that'll help us with this case, but it'd be nice to do that Fergus Duncan chump with something.'

'Sounds good.' Vicky grinned at him. 'And please tell me whatever you find.'

'No secrets with me.'

19

Zoey got to her feet, Beats strapped to her head like an old policeman's helmet, her perfect lips mouthing some lyrics. Vicky blocked her, motioning to take her headphones off. 'Need some help.'

Zoey tugged her hair, avoiding eye contact. 'Is it that dark net stuff because I could do with a couple of hours, to be honest.'

'Not that.' Vicky shrugged, then beckoned her over to their desks. 'Cyberterrorism at Phorever Love.'

Zoey blinked a few times. 'I spoke to DC Considine, but he—'

'Come to me or DS MacDonald in future, okay?'

'Okay.' She glanced over at Forrester's office door. 'He's a bit of a cock, isn't he?'

'He's the whole penis and the balls.' Vicky took a deep breath. 'What have you got?'

'I was down with the Forensic guys.' Zoey got out her laptop and hit the keys. 'We did a search on the known activities of your cyberterrorist group.' She glanced at Vicky then away again. 'I managed to match some stuff.' She leaned back in her chair and raised her eyebrows. 'I tied the IP addresses from the cyberterror-ists to Phorever Love.'

Vicky paused, trying to process it. 'But?'

'I've not got any real people.' Zoey kicked her heels. 'I'm working on it, but—'

'The Muirheads?'

'Tried their home address. Not them.'

Vicky glanced at Zoey. 'But the Muirheads are active posters on xbeast, right?'

'They are, but I still can't trace anything to them. Sorry.' Zoey nibbled her lips. 'But... Wait, one of them's been on xbeast. Oh, I've got him!'

Vicky sat in Brian Morton's living room amid bare magnolia walls. The curtain was drawn, a naked bulb hanging from the ceiling the only source of light. 'Mr Morton, do you know anything about a group near Redford called Phorever Love?'

Brian sighed and closed his eyes. 'John!'

His brother kept staring at the TV.

MacDonald was loitering by the window overlooking the main street, Hilltown buses rumbling outside. 'You sure you don't know anything about it yourself, Brian?'

Brian's breathing quickened. 'I've no idea what you're talking about.' His face reddened. 'I've never heard of Redmond.'

'Redford. It's near Forfar.'

Brian slammed a fist against his scooter. 'Do I look like I can get there?'

MacDonald shrugged. 'Decent battery life on those things.'

'I know absolutely nothing about this Love Forever group.'

'Phorever Love. It's spelled with a "ph".'

Brian ran a hand through his hair, damp with sweat. 'I still don't know anything.'

'See, members of the group posted on xbeast.' Vicky crossed her legs. 'They organised a campaign against a place near Barry called Hunter's Farm. Do you watch the news, Brian?'

Brian shook his head and glanced at his brother. 'The only time the telly's on in here is when he's around.'

John was still watching the news, unperturbed by the repeated references to him.

Vicky marvelled at his composure. She leaned towards Brian. 'You took great delight in what happened to Rachel Hay and Paul Joyce.'

Brian tightened his grip on the arm supports. 'Whoever did this has done *nothing* wrong.'

'Kidnapping's against the law. That means it's wrong.'

MacDonald left the window and stood over Brian. 'And it's not just kidnapping anymore. They burnt off someone's nose.'

Brian pounded the scooter again. 'I don't know anything about it!' He kept pleading with his brother, who just ignored him.

'Come on.' Vicky uncrossed her legs and got to her feet. 'We'll need to get Mr Morton down to the station. Better call in back-up again.'

John looked over from the TV. 'This isn't good for Brian's heart.'

Vicky smiled at him. 'Then it's in his interests to answer our questions, isn't it?'

'If he says he doesn't know, he doesn't know.'

'Your brother posted a video of someone in a cage being tortured. That's direct involvement. He can help us find these people before they do it again.'

'I'm not going to.' Brian slammed his fist on the scooter again. 'These people are heroes.'

'He doesn't mean that.' John held up his hands. 'Brian's heart's in the right place. He's just interested in helping the animals. That's right isn't it, Brian?'

Brian pouted. 'I just want people to stop it.'

'We all do.' Vicky nodded. 'We all do.'

Brian glowered at her. 'You're not doing anything about it though, are you?'

MacDonald crouched in front of the scooter. 'There's an IT

analyst working full-time on this. If you've been a naughty boy on there, it's in your interest to tell us now. Okay?'

John tilted his head at Vicky. 'Can I have a private word, please?'

'Mac, call in back-up.' She followed John into the kitchen. About a dozen empty cheesecake and gateaux boxes sat on the counter, giving off a sickly-sweet aroma. Looking was enough to give you diabetes. 'Tell me he doesn't—'

'That's just this morning's.' John started putting the boxes in the recycling. 'It's all he'll eat since Mum died. I've just not got the patience she had or the time to deal with it. Does that make me a bad person?'

Vicky rested against the counter, the chipped wood digging into the palms of her hands. 'I'm not sure I'm qualified to comment on family compromises.'

'He has tantrums like he's a kid.'

'I can relate to that.' Vicky frowned. 'There's nothing wrong with his mental health, is there?'

'No. I mean, there's got to be a mental cause for...' John held up a cheesecake box, scrunching it between his fingers. 'You should see him destroy one of these. *Man Vs Food* has nothing on him.'

'Much as I feel for you, I assume you didn't call me in here to tell me about your brother's eating habits?'

'Right.' John stuffed the last box in the recycling bin, the lid not quite shutting. 'Our old man died from a heart attack.'

'Sorry to hear that.'

'He was an arsehole.' John pushed his glasses up his nose. 'I don't want my brother dying. As much of a nightmare as he is, he's all I've got left. How can I help?'

'Your brother may see these animal justice crusaders as heroes, but people have been abducted and tortured.'

'I don't give a shit about all this animal crap, okay?' John's forehead creased. 'I *do* give a shit about my brother. I almost had to take him to hospital on Friday night after you let him go.'

Vicky pushed herself off the counter. 'We think he knows who's done this.'

John licked his lips as he stared at the door to the living room. 'How about I speak to him for you?'

Vicky stared at him, letting the silence build.

Raised voices came from the living room. Brian was screaming at MacDonald. 'Get away from me!'

'This is what I have to put up with.' John waved his hand at the door. 'His blood sugar level is up and down like a whore's knickers because of those cakes.'

'How about you stop feeding him them?'

John pointed at her. 'You're welcome to look after him.'

'I'll pass, thanks.' Vicky rested her hands against the counter again — the last thing she needed in this case was a coronary. 'Speak to him and see what he can help us with.' She handed him her business card. 'In case your brother ate the last one.'

VICKY HELD the station's front door. 'What did you ask him to make him scream like that?'

'Nothing.' MacDonald shrugged as he entered. 'He was just ranting.' He swiped through the security door, the lock clunking as it released. 'Muttering to himself like I wasn't even there. Mad stuff about not going back to the police station. He was just talking himself into a frothy fit. Thought he was going to keel over there and then.' He frowned, leaning against the door. 'What's his story, anyway?'

'Morbidly obese. He lives off frozen desserts. His brother showed me.'

'Christ.' MacDonald started off down the corridor. He opened the door to the stairwell and started climbing the steps, their footsteps echoed around the tight space.

MacDonald accelerated up the last few steps to hold the door open. 'According to the witness statements, we've got three perps. One average bloke, one woman and someone of indiscriminate gender. Brian doesn't fit the profile of any of them.'

'Zoey found a link between him and these cyberterrorists.'

'It's hardly conclusive, is it?'

'The way I'm thinking, he's their IT support.'

'A terror group's help desk.' MacDonald laughed.

Vicky waited in the corridor outside their office space. Zoey was tapping at a laptop, ever-present headphones on. 'Let's do some more digging.' She joined Zoey at the desk, hand on hip. 'Made any more progress?'

'Been flat out, ma'am.' Zoey swallowed. She flicked an eyebrow up at MacDonald before focusing on her laptop again. 'Still nothing.' She glanced at Forrester's shut door, his voice droning through the scarred wood. 'The DI asked me to look into something.'

Superb... If it's not clowns below, it's jokers above...

Vicky sat next to her. 'I don't want to put you in a difficult situation, but I need you to focus on that, okay?'

Zoey took her headphones off and tossed them on the desk. 'Keep your knickers on.'

'What did Forrester get you to do?'

'Check that journalist's emails.'

'Anita Skinner?' Vicky looked around, the nerve in her neck loosening off a touch. 'Why?'

'Search me, ma'am. I got her site taken down, but he's worried she'll... I don't know.'

'It's hardly the highest priority.' Vicky got to her feet again, steeling herself for another shouting match with Forrester. 'I'll sort it out, okay?'

'Hang on.' Zoey tapped her screen, flicking through the poison pen letters and a screen grab from the video. 'She did publish the notes on her blog.'

Vicky scanned them. Looked like photos of the originals. 'How the hell did she do this? Did she see them before they were delivered?'

'Not sure. She got them sent from an anonymous account.'

'How do you know that?'

'I—' Zoey cleared her throat, '—installed some friendly malware on her laptop.'

'Is that legal?'

'Well, it's not *strictly* illegal.'

VICKY WALKED along the Perth Road and got in the silver Golf's passenger side. 'No Amigo helping you, Johnny?'

'Buchan's getting us some bridies.' Laing was slumped low behind the wheel. Looked like it hurt, but it was effective. Vicky couldn't see him from outside the car. The car was stuffed with Sunday tabloids, Pringles tins and half-drunk bottles of Pepsi Max. Absolutely stank, too. 'Have to head to the Murraygate on a Sunday, mind.'

'Or Forfar.'

'Nobody wants to go to Forfar, Vicks.' Laing sat up in his seat. 'Anyway, what's this lassie done?'

'Been a naughty girl.' Vicky peered up at the tenements, hard to work out which was Anita Skinner's. 'You seen her?'

'Thought we'd lucked out when she had a shower, but she shut the curtains.'

Vicky spotted the flat, the curtains still drawn. 'She's definitely in there?'

'Calm the beans, doll. She's there. Walked her dog at one. Buchan followed her. Poor bastard had to sit on a park bench while she got a phone call.'

'Any idea who she was speaking to?'

'Nope. Buchan got lost in his book on chess openings, though. Almost missed her getting up.' He shook his head. 'Just like his uncle.'

'Never met him.'

'Used to be Dundee but works in Edinburgh now. Runs their uniform through there. Still keeps an eye on his nephew.' Laing shot her a cheeky wink. 'And they say nepotism is dead, eh?'

'My dad was a cop.'

'Tell me about it. Dirty old bastard.'

Vicky thwacked him with a Sunday Sun. 'That's my dad!'

Laing shielded himself from more attacks. 'Still a pervert.'

Vicky punched him in the side. 'What the hell do you mean by that!'

'Nothing! I swear!'

Before she could inflict any more damage, Vicky's Airwave chirruped. Hopefully Forrester apologising for being a twat earlier.

A photo. Vicky and Bella at the Fixit DIY store on Saturday afternoon.

Laing was looking at her screen, his face white. 'Jesus Vicks, what's that?'

'Someone sent me a message. I got another one this morning.'

'That shite in Barry? Christ, you need to find out who sent that.'

A text appeared on the Airwave. *"The egg is in the nest."*

Bella!

Vicky got out and put her phone to her ear, stomping away from the car. Went to voicemail. She killed the call and redialled as she ran to her car. 'Come on, come on, come on.' She snapped on her seatbelt and checked the Bluetooth. Still not connected. Still ringing in her ear. She stuck her key in the ignition and started the engine.

Click. Bedlam in the background. 'Victoria?'

'Mum, is—'

'Victoria, what's—'

'Is Bella okay?'

'Bella? She's fine.'

Vicky slumped back in her seat. 'Jesus.' She swallowed hard. 'Are you at home?'

'We've been watching "The Little Mermaid". Again.'

'She's definitely with you?'

'She's with your father just now.' Sounded like Mum rapped on the kitchen window. 'She's fine. They're playing in the garden. When can I expect you?'

'I'll be here all day at this rate.' Vicky turned the key back. 'Let me know if anyone asks for Bella.'

'Are you okay?'

'I'm fine, Mum.'

'Like that is it? I see.' A pause, filled with Bella singing in the background. 'Well, let us know when you deign to grace us with your presence.' Click and she was gone.

Vicky stared down the Perth Road at Laing's car. *Maybe Anita Skinner spotted him. Maybe she had nothing to do with the case.*

What the hell am I doing? Running around, chasing my tail.

She eyed the Airwave on the passenger seat.

Chasing my tail while someone sends me Airwave messages. Stalking me while I put suspects under surveillance. Is it one of them? Anita Skinner? Brian Morton? Polly Muirhead?

She grabbed the Airwave and checked the message again.

"The egg is in the nest."

Feels like the Barry message that morning, so avoiding it isn't an option. But...

What the hell did it mean?

'Robert says hi.'

'Karen...' Vicky got out of her car. The DIY store loomed over the car park, corrugated steel painted grey and orange, wind battering the row of trees shielding it from the road. Still had the feel of a late eighties B&Q despite the paint job.

'Good for him.' Vicky clenched her jaw and handed her the Airwave. 'Have a look at this.'

Karen took the Airwave, her mouth hanging wider with each second. Then she curled up her tongue. 'Someone's stalking you?'

'Bella had a tantrum here yesterday.' Vicky took the Airwave back then set off across the car park. 'She wanted to see the owls.'

'Cameron did a similar thing a few weeks ago. Little bugger.'

'Bella had a massive hot chocolate, too. My fault.' Vicky set off towards the display. Quiet, just a pair of kids staring wide-eyed at the birds chained to their cage. A van sat behind, with enough ventilation fans to keep a whole load in.

The proprietor swaggered over, his leather coat almost touching the ground. Greasy hair, long at the sides, short straight fringe. He sniffed. 'You again, eh? That your granddaughter yesterday?'

'My *daughter*.'

Bird man frowned at Karen. 'You not her daughter?'

'Quit it.' Vicky showed her warrant card. 'DS Vicky Dodds. What's your name, sir?'

'Kyle Ramsay. And you can clear off.' Ramsay spread his arms wide to take in the full extent of his empire. 'This is all legit.'

'Not everyone might agree with what you're doing.'

'I paid a small fortune for these birds. I own them, all right? Nobody tells me what to do with them. *Nobody*.'

'I'm not here to—'

'Not talking about you, doll.' Ramsay held up a poison pen letter.

Vicky snatched it off him.

"YOUR BIRDS OF PREY DISPLAY IS IMMORAL. STOP IT. NOW. OR ELSE."

20

Vicky frowned at Ramsay. 'Where did you find this?'

'On my van this morning.' Ramsay made a "come on" gesture — arms stretched out, fingers flapping towards him. 'Some punks threatening me. I'd like to see them try.'

Vicky recognised his type, saw it every Saturday night on the beat. But she persisted anyway. 'Has anyone threatened you face-to-face, Mr Ramsay?'

'What?' Ramsay scowled at her. 'I pay my way, okay? Me and my birds aren't harming anyone.'

'That's not—' Vicky sighed. 'People might deem your display to be cruel.'

'Cruel?' Ramsay snorted. '*Cruel?* If they did, I'd smash their teeth in.' He snarled at her. 'I've got customers to attend to.' Without another word he turned and made for the kids gazing at the birds.

Not getting anywhere...

Vicky handed the note to Karen. 'Get this verified by Forensics, would you?'

'Can you say "please"?' She put the sheet in an evidence bag. 'Why have they switched to warning people all of a sudden?'

'No idea. *"Your Birds of Prey display is immoral. Stop it. Now. Or else."* The 'or else' bit worries me.'

'Come on.' Vicky entered the shop. Fresh sawdust smells mixed with jazz funk sounds. Two middle-aged men in Fixit aprons hung around the tills, oblivious to the winding queue of irate punters.

A manager hovered in the background, before he was accosted by a white-haired man with a frown and open mouth.

Vicky relieved him with her warrant card. 'Looking for the manager.'

'Gordon Christie.' Tall, skinny, no older than late twenties. He smiled at the customer. 'Sorry sir, I need to deal with this.'

'But I've got a boiler hanging half off the wall.'

'James!' Christie attracted one of the aproned duo over. 'Can you deal with this customer? And get Ian to open that till!' He walked off, beckoning Vicky and Karen away from the entrance. 'What's up?'

'Need a word about the display outside.'

Christie shrugged. 'It stays.'

'Excuse me?' Vicky grabbed the note off Karen and waved it in front of his face. 'This was on his van. Don't you watch the news?'

'The display stays. Chief Exec's orders. His idea in the first place.' Christie held up a hand. 'Before you ask, our headquarters are over by Camperdown Park.'

~

LIGHT STREAMED through a clear glass door at the end of the long corridor, lined with moody photos of stores similar to the one they'd just visited — night shots with cars and lights blurring in front of the buildings.

Willis Stewart, Group CEO.

The receptionist knocked before popping her head round the door. 'That's the police for you now, sir.'

'Send them in.' Stewart's voice was deep and loud, a bizarre contrast to the person — a skinny man whose gold watch looked heavier than he did. Thinning hair on top but thick at the sides.

Vicky took a seat in front of his desk. Behind, a window spanning the full width looked over the cars and lorries hurtling down the Kingsway. 'We need to—'

'I'll stop you there.' Stewart sat back in his chair, the mechanism grinding underneath him. 'Gordon Christie's been on the phone. You're not—'

'Sir, you need to take this seriously.'

'Let me tell you a story.' Stewart sat forward, puny elbows resting on the desk. 'I bought that store, our flagship, from B&Q when they opened their Warehouse up the other end of the Kingsway. Swung deals for a few more in Glasgow, Edinburgh, Dunfermline and Aberdeen not long after. I'm moving into Preston, Newcastle, Manchester and Carlisle. This is a big business and I'm on the board of six other companies. I didn't achieve that by listening to threats.'

'You need to remove the display before—'

'No!' Stewart swung round in his chair to look out of the window. 'That's the end of the matter.'

'I'd advise that you listen to me, sir.'

'Why?' He perked up. 'I'm on the board of Bios, you know? They're joining the FTSE in the next few months. I think I know more than some *cop*.'

Vicky felt the throb in her neck. 'Look at these.' She produced her copy of the notes they'd received so far. 'People suffered when these notes were left. That's why you need to take this threat seriously.'

'Sergeant, my family has a long history of falconry.' Stewart leaned over his desk. 'I refuse to throw it all away just like—' he clicked his fingers, '—that.'

'You can surely stop the display for a week or so, can't you?'

'No.'

'No?'

'*No.*'

'I'm sorry you see it that way, Mr Stewart.' Vicky got to her feet, the nerve really throbbing now. 'I'll have to refer this matter to my superior officers. Your actions are endangering members of the public.'

Stewart looked at a laptop on his desk. 'Shut the door behind you, please.'

Vicky almost tore it off its hinges as they left.

~

VICKY GOT out and crossed the station car park, her nerve as tight as a piano wire. Karen was lagging behind.

Sergeant Tommy Davies nodded in recognition as she passed through reception. 'Afternoon, Vicks. Seen Charlie?'

'Who's Charlie?' Vicky swiped through the security door.

'Never mind.'

Vicky headed down the hallway.

Halfway down the corridor MacDonald was thumping a vending machine, his fingers rattling the change door as he caught sight of her. 'Vicky.'

She stepped aside letting Karen pass behind, a smirk on her face. 'Is Forrester in?'

'Upstairs.' MacDonald shoogled around in the machine's innards. 'I just want a bloody drink.'

A WakeyWakey can was jammed on the second bottom row.

Vicky checked the usual pitfalls — bags of crisps blocking the fall of a can, an errant empty space in the shelf. Nothing. She looked around. The corridor was empty. 'You didn't see this.' She gripped the edges of the machine and gave it a rattling shake. The can popped down into the funnel in the middle. 'There you go.'

'Cheers.' MacDonald bent down to retrieve it. 'I'll have to remember that.'

'The moody machine or my special touch?' She tapped it again with her foot then started off down the corridor.

'The latter. I hope I'll have plenty of opportunity to witness it again.' MacDonald held open the door to the stairwell, grinning over the lid of the small can as he sipped.

Vicky started climbing the stairs, the nerve in her neck tightened again. If this case wasn't closed soon, she'd die of a stroke first.

'Sarge, Mac.' Considine was on the landing looking pleased with himself. 'Just back from Mr Muirhead's place of work.'

Vicky nudged past him. 'Get anything?'

'Nothing that made me think they're behind it.'

'What about anything that made you think they're not?'

'Well, the boy's secretary showed me his diary.' Considine held up a sheet of prints from a computer calendar. 'I was a bit of an arse and got to see the CCTV — all time-stamped, of course. He was there when he said he was.'

'Get it in the case file, then.'

'Will do.' Considine trotted downstairs, away from the case file.

Vicky watched him go, his footsteps ringing. 'See what we're dealing with.'

'And he thinks he's DS calibre?' MacDonald pointed back into the office space, scowling. 'What's that wanker's name again?'

Vicky followed his gesture and groaned. 'DS Johnny Laing. And you're right — he is a wanker. Never play pool with him.' She smiled and wandered over to Laing. 'Johnny, you get anything on Anita Skinner?'

'Square root of hee haw.' Laing leaned in close. 'You seen Big Time Charlie? Supposed to have a meeting with him.'

Vicky frowned. 'Excuse me?'

'The new boy?'

'DS MacDonald?'

Laing shrugged. 'Aye, that boy fancies himself even more than he does your—'

'He's out in the corridor.'

'Much obliged.' Laing sighed as he sauntered off.

Big Time Charlie...

Vicky smirked. Then she saw Forrester approaching. She pointed at his office and followed him in, shutting the door behind her.

Forrester hung his jacket on his coat rack. He picked up his coffee machine's jug, murky water swilling over the sides, and dumped it on the table. 'What's up?'

'Fixit DIY just received a note about their birds of prey display.'

'Aw, Christ. Is anyone hurt?'

'Not yet.' Vicky rested against the back of a chair, fingers tight against the fabric. 'The store manager was a dick about it and the CEO isn't going to do anything.'

Forrester stopped fiddling with his filter papers, his head dropping. 'The CEO?' He tipped ground coffee into the hatch. 'So, I guess you're here to get me to escalate it?'

'PLEASE, HAVE A SEAT.' ACC Helen Queensberry took off her uniform jacket and rested it on the back of the desk chair. Looked like she ran a marathon every day. Sweated like it too, her standard-issue blouse was soaked through. She sat between Vicky and Forrester, fanning her face. 'Thanks for joining us, David. DS Dodds, I don't believe we've had the pleasure?'

'Pleasure's all mine.' Vicky offered her hand, tensing her wrist to control the trembling.

Queensberry shook it. 'Okay, so it's never fun and joy when you're here, David?' She smiled at Forrester. 'This is about Willis Stewart, am I right?'

'How did you know?'

Queensberry took a sip of coffee. 'He phoned me. Said you'd try and pull some shit.'

'Ma'am, with all due respect, he's the one pulling shit.' Forrester showed her a copy of the note. 'This matches the others we've got.'

'Dryburgh.'

'And Barry.'

'Barry? That's yours?' Queensberry's eyebrows shot up. 'What's Willis saying?'

Vicky butted in. 'Mr Stewart's being pig-headed. Some

nonsense about falconry being in his family since the time of Christ or something.' That got a grin. 'The store's been warned and we're ahead for the first time.'

'And we don't want it becoming something else.' Queensberry brushed sweat from her forehead. 'Right, right. I'll speak to Willis about it.'

'Ma'am...' Vicky tilted her head at Queensberry. 'It might be more advisable to *do* something rather than talk, if you'll excuse me saying so. We should close the display. Now.'

Queensberry shut her eyes, then nodded. 'I'll inform Willis.'

Forrester was on his feet, almost bowing at the ACC. 'Thanks, ma'am.'

Queensberry shook her head at him. 'David, stop being such a toad.'

'A TOAD.' Forrester flicked the indicator to right and waited for the roundabout traffic to let him through. He slumped back in his seat. 'What a bloody day.'

Vicky rested her elbows on the armrests. 'Having fun?'

'I stopped having fun the day I got the promotion to Detective Inspector.' Forrester jolted across the roundabout and hit the Fixit car park. 'Why did she call me a toad?'

Can't possibly imagine...

Vicky had her finger over the seatbelt release as Forrester trundled towards the store. Forrester stopped and she clicked then shot out of the car, stomping across the tarmac.

Gordon Christie was by the entrance, smoothing down his tie. 'Wondered how long it would take.'

Vicky made for him. 'Sir, we're here—'

'Willis warned me.' Christie stepped forward, hands deep in his pockets. 'He said I was to go kicking and screaming if you threatened. But I'm not doing that for a *bird* display.'

No sign of Ramsay by his display. Just a pair of sad owls in cages. 'Where is Mr Ramsay?'

'He put that up an hour ago.' Christie pointed at a sign pinned to the side:

"BACK IN FIVE"

'Did you send him home?'

'He usually gets his lunch about now. The guy's got some metabolism, I tell you.' He leaned in close. 'Listen, you think there's something in all of this?'

'You ever seen what a debeaking machine does to a man?'

Christie swallowed. 'I don't want to get involved in this. Kyle's a bit of an acquired taste.'

'And then some.' Vicky exhaled slowly. *Fifty-five minutes over a five-minute sign. That's not good.* 'We need to speak to him. Got his address?'

VICKY GOT out onto Baldovan Terrace and looked down the long row of tenements pockmarked with satellite dishes, the parking bays mostly filled with work vans. She crossed the road to the tenement door and ran her finger down the list. *K. Ramsay.* Bingo. She tried the flat buzzer. No answer.

Forrester stayed by his car.

Vicky cupped her hands round her eyes, peering into the window of the dark ground-floor flat. Just an unmade bed. The other window showed a settee and an Xbox lying in front of a TV. She took a step back and looked up and down the street. She pressed the buzzer again and waited.

No answer.

She tried the buzzer next to it, *G. Scrimgeour.*

A burst of static from the speaker. 'Who's that?'

'Police.' Vicky leaned against the wall, tipping her head towards the microphone. 'I'm looking for Kyle Ramsay.'

'Never heard of him.'

'He's your neighbour. Can we have a word?'

The door buzzed open.

Vicky entered the stairwell, illuminated by shafts of light falling through a roof window.

'Gordon Scrimgeour.' A wiry man in a tracksuit and Dundee FC shirt stood across the corridor, arms folded, guarding his flat door. 'I've not seen that chump today.'

'Have you heard anything?'

Scrimgeour frowned. 'Bit of a commotion an hour ago. Got me out of my pit. On a *Sunday* afternoon. Had a heavy session last night, I tell you. Didn't see anything, before you ask.'

'But you heard something?'

'A car maybe.' Scrimgeour shrugged. 'Dunno. Could've been one of them cars the kids have buggered about with, I suppose. Loud exhaust on it, anyway.' He waved out to the street. 'The laddie's van's here, though.'

An unmarked white van, ventilation equipment protruding from the back.

Vicky walked over and peered through the small back window. Rows of tiny cages inside, some of them containing birds. A big cage sat at the back, in the gloom. She smiled at Scrimgeour. 'Thanks for your time, sir.'

'Is he going to get into trouble?'

'I seriously hope so.' She handed Scrimgeour her card. 'Call me when he turns up.'

Scrimgeour wandered back inside the tenement, scratching his bottom.

'You see that in there?' Forrester tapped at the van window, startling Vicky. 'It's barbaric.'

Vicky tried the door. Locked. Couldn't see anyone inside, though. The bonnet was cool. She wandered round to the back and tried the back door. Locked, as well. She went round the passenger side.

A note was pinned to the side.

"HAS THE EGG HATCHED?"

Forrester squinted at it. 'What the hell does that mean?'

Vicky peered inside.

A flash of movement. Vicky caught sight of a balaclava. The engine roared and the van shot off.

∼

'Sir! What the hell are you doing?'

Forrester pulled out into the oncoming lane, his teeth clenched tight. 'What does it look like? I'm trying to get round the van!'

Vicky fought her instinct, trying to keep her eyes open.

A man was behind the wheel steering the van along Lochee Road. Heading out of Dundee. Then he was gone as Forrester overtook.

'Got you, you bastard!' Forrester pulled back in front of the van.

Vicky swivelled round, her seatbelt lacerating her left breast. Got a better view of the driver but still couldn't get much.

He tugged the wheel hard right and the van disappeared.

'Shite!' Forrester slammed on the brakes.

Vicky flew back, her side hitting the dashboard, the belt digging into her armpit.

'Hold tight!'

The gearbox clunked then the car spun round, the tyres squealing again.

Vicky tried to move but she was held fast.

Forrester powered down the lane into an empty car park. No sign of the van. 'Where the hell is it?' He stopped across three spaces.

Vicky got hold of her seatbelt control and let go. She tumbled into the footwell, then hauled the door open and got out. Took another look around, no sign of Kyle Ramsay's van. She jogged across the car park following Forrester.

Dudhope Castle towered over them, its white walls in an L-shape. A group of people had assembled next to a patch of lavender.

'DS Dodds.' Vicky flashed her warrant card. 'What's going on?'

The nearest uniformed workman took off his hard hat and squared his shoulders. His eyes bulged at her ID.

Vicky's nose twitched. She smelt something, couldn't quite place it. 'What's that smell?' She pushed through the crowd to see what had attracted their attention.

Kyle Ramsay's van was on the grass, the engine idling. No sign of the driver. The back door hung open, the birds squealing and squawking. Ramsay lay in the middle groaning, naked. His hands and feet were tied up, his mouth covered in tape. His skin was heavily bruised, dark purple blotches all over his chest and face. Four birds sat on his chest, pecking away. Deep gouges had been sliced out of his legs and arms. Blood dripped onto the floor.

21

Vicky stepped away from the paramedics, letting them take Kyle Ramsay away. An SSPCA van trundled up and Forrester broke off, heading to give them orders. All he was good for.

'World's gone mad, I tell you.' The lead gardener sniffed, a big oaf called Fleming, then gurned at her, gnashing his remaining three teeth. 'Turn my back for a second to have my piece. Next thing I know, abracadabra, a van's slaloming over my bed. I just dug that!'

'You see the driver?'

'Boy just ran away. Had a balaclava on.'

Just bloody missed them.

Fleming's tongue crawled over the stumps next to his good teeth. 'Never thought I'd see the day I play a part in a gay magic show.'

Vicky coughed to cover a laugh. 'Did you open the door?'

'Nah, it was hanging open. Your nudie was just lying there like a floor show in Las bloody Vegas.' Fleming put his phone to his ear; Vicky hadn't heard it ring. 'Nobody there.' He scowled at it, then at Vicky. 'Why've they done this to the boy?'

'We think it's because he runs a birds of prey display at Fixit

DIY.' Vicky's stomach curdled from the smell. 'Someone's taken a strong dislike to it.' She looked around the car park, surrounded by mature beech and oak trees. Behind, the white-harled walls of a castle. 'What is this place?'

'Council offices.' He gestured around the small group. 'My boys look after the park and the offices. Do a fine job, if I say so myself.' He laughed. 'Queerest thing, though. This place used to have a menagerie. Birds and animals in cages and that. My grandpa used to bring us here.'

Vicky narrowed her eyes at him. 'I'll need you to give a statement, okay?' She gave him a smile and headed towards the uniforms milling around Forrester and the van.

A female SSPCA officer was looking inside the van. She looked back as Vicky approached. 'We'll take them in while the owner recovers.'

'Thanks.' Forrester flashed a smile then headed towards the police officers, shaking his head at Vicky. 'We almost bloody had him.'

'Don't have to tell me, sir.'

Forrester cleared his throat then grinned wide. 'Okay, lads and lassies. I need you going door-to-door.' He pointed at the castle. 'Every room in that place.' Then at Fleming. 'And start with laughing boy there, okay?' He nodded slowly. 'This circus act stops today.'

VICKY CLOCKED Rankine in the waiting area, frowning at her phone. The boiled-cabbage stink mixed with dentist smells. 'Hey.'

Dr Rankine looked up, her face like she'd just sucked a lemon dry. She shuddered then walked over to Vicky. 'We're just cleaning him now. It'll be a while.'

Vicky tried to peer past her, but the door swung shut. 'But he's okay, right?'

'He's an obstreperous sod and he's been savagely beaten, but he'll survive.'

'Beaten?'

'Punched, I would say. There's an indentation of a sovereign ring on what little pectoral muscle he has.'

'Can you get an imprint?'

'Already on top of it.' Rankine clapped her shoulder then frowned at the door as a scowling male nurse lumbered through.

Vicky looked inside and almost lost her lunch.

Kyle Ramsay lay on the bed, his torso blocked by a male nurse dabbing at his wounds. His face was purple and red, bandaged but free of excrement. Except for the lingering smell.

'Fuck off.'

'That's not very nice.' Vicky sat on the chair next to him, smiling. 'We want to find who did this to you.'

'Fuck off, you tramp. You're trying to close my display!'

'Mr Ramsay, this is—'

'Fucking rob the kids of the joy of seeing a wild creature? You can live with yourself doing that, eh?'

'We want to stop whoever's doing this.' Vicky kept her smile on, but it was cracking round the edges. 'You're not the first, but I'd rather you were the last.'

'You did this to me, you fucking witch.' Ramsay held up a shaking hand 'I mind you and your little daughter yesterday. Mind her fucking tantrums, wanting to see my fucking owls. You stopped her, you tramp. Your own daughter. Just five fucking quid to see her wee face light up.'

'Sir, I'd rather you didn't use that language.'

'Fuck off. I'm not going to help you. Trying to steal my livelihood. Police fucking conspiracy.'

Vicky locked eyes with Rankine. *How to get this prick onside and stop others suffering?* 'Sir, we've recovered your birds.'

'All of them?' Ramsay sat up. 'You need to make sure.' He rubbed at his bruises, prodding a red patch under his right eye. 'They can't get free. They can't handle the wild.' He slammed a fist onto his thigh. 'Cats will eat them!'

'We'll check you're not missing any.' Vicky couldn't keep her eyes off the wounds on his legs and arms. 'You were pecked by your own birds, weren't you?'

'No.' Ramsay sniffed. 'Maybe. Bite the fucking arm that fucking feeds you.' He shot her a hard glare. 'I'm making a good living out of those animals. But you don't like it, you filthy pigs. Fucking police state, man.'

'We believe this was done by vigilantes, Mr Ramsay.'

'Well, I didn't see anything.'

'Just take me through what happened.'

Ramsay lay back down, wincing. 'I got back to my crib, away get some ramen. Some punk knocked me over with their fucking car. Pushed me to the ground, then kicked and kicked and fucking kicked. Next thing I know, I'm in the back of the van, wee Doad and Benny are pecking at me and some toothless prick is checking out my junk.'

'WE SHOULD CHARGE STEWART.' Vicky sat at Rankine's desk. The chair's lumbar support setting was high enough to cause back pain. 'This is his fault.'

'You know what he'll say, Vicky. The boy Ramsay had already pissed off by the time we got there, so he didn't *technically* disobey our advice.'

'Come on. Of course he did. He was a complete nightmare about it.'

'Well, Queensberry's not answering my calls.' Forrester frowned as he checked the wall map again. 'I asked Raven to get one of these. Wouldn't approve the budget. Police bloody Scotland, I swear. Tell you, Vicky. Bloody Strathclyde chumps thinking they can treat the whole bloody country like a county.'

'Want me to tell the Chief?' MacDonald was in the doorway, his jaw clenched. 'I used to golf with him.'

'Shite.' Forrester smacked a hand to his forehead. 'I was venting, Mac. Didn't mean anything by it.'

MacDonald's frown deepened. Then he laughed. 'It's cool,

David. To be honest I agree with you. Can't get anything done these days.'

'Damn right.'

MacDonald leaned forward on the desk. 'Think we should bring in the Muirheads?'

'What?' Forrester gave him a scowl. 'Why? Their alibis stacked up. It's not them.'

MacDonald joined Forrester by the map, circling the park not far from Bell Street station.

Forrester checked his watch. 'Right. Vicky, I need you to write everything up. Every last detail, okay? Then get home. Need you back in early doors tomorrow, fresh as a daisy.'

Vicky sat there, open-mouthed. 'Seriously?'

'Seriously. Mac, I'll see you downstairs.' Forrester marched off, taking one last envious look at the map on the wall.

MacDonald made to follow but stopped in the doorway. 'You okay?'

She stared at him, soaking in his eyes and his rough stubble. Then she let out a sigh.

MacDonald scratched the stubble on his chin. 'Look, once you've finished your homework, fancy going for a pint?'

'A pint of gin.' Vicky smiled, feeling sliced in two. 'Maybe tomorrow?'

MacDonald made his hand into a gun, shooting it at her. '*Definitely* tomorrow.'

22

Vicky stopped outside the Stag's Head and checked her watch — five past seven and no sign of Robert. Ten minutes, then she was gone.

Daylight was slowly dying, the stream of traffic on Carnoustie's long High Street navigating the single-file parking system that so infuriated her dad. A couple of hundred metres away a crane overlooked the demolition of her old primary school, like her old head teacher watching the passing of yet another generation.

A green Volvo pulled in ahead of her and flashed its lights.

'Bloody hell.' Vicky leaned down at the open driver-side window. 'Karen, what're you doing here?'

'Driving home.'

'This isn't the way.'

'Thought you could keep it from us?' Karen did her tongue tube thing. 'Robert told Colin. Asked for tips on how to talk to you without you biting his head off.'

'Not that Colin would know.'

'True enough.' Karen looked her up and down. 'But when he takes one look at you, he'll do anything to put a ring on it.'

'Kaz...' Vicky looked at the ground. A ball of chewing gum was flattened out at the edge of the pavement. 'I can't handle any more rejection.'

'You've not even had one date with the guy and you're thinking of when he'll dump you?'

'It's how my brain works.'

'You can start by stopping those thoughts.' Karen gripped Vicky's cheek between thumb and forefinger. 'Most men would kill to have you. Robert's keen!'

Vicky smiled, her cheek pleasantly warm where it had just been pinched. She spotted Robert across the street as he entered the pub, his black leather jacket matching her own. 'I'd better go.'

'Never noticed before, but he's got a really nice bum.'

'Christ Kaz, don't you ever stop?'

'Never.' Karen flicked the indicator. 'See you tomorrow.'

Vicky stepped back and watched her drive off. *No secrets...* Deep sigh, count to ten, a break in traffic, and she skipped across the road then into the pub.

Robert was standing at the bar, phone in hand. He waved when he saw her. 'Was just about to call you.'

Vicky leaned against the bar unsure whether to offer a hand, peck his cheek or what. She kissed him near the ear, lips pressing baby-smooth skin. No aftershave, just a nice clean smell. 'Nice to see you. You look good.'

'Oh, really? Thank you.'

'You're welcome... Want to return the compliment?'

'Sorry, yes I do, actually.' Robert put his phone away. 'You look... ravishing.' He laughed. 'What can I get you?'

'Bacardi and Coke, please.'

Robert turned to the barman, midway through pouring a pint of something dark brown, and got a nod.

'I'll bring them over, pal.'

Across the empty bar, Vicky spotted a huddle of men her age. All beer bellies and bald spots, watching the preamble to some football match on the large TV.

She got a leery wink.

Scrape some of the lard and years off, might even look a bit like—

Christ. He's not aged well. To think I—

Vicky sat so she couldn't see him.

Robert perched on a stool and thumbed behind him. 'Do you know that lot?'

'I think I recognise a couple of them from school.' Vicky shrugged. 'If that's hi— *them*, they've filled out a bit.' She looked around the room, blushing. 'They've done this place up. We used to call it the Slag's Bed.' She raised her hand in panic. 'Not that I was the slag.'

'Perish the thought.'

The barman appeared with their drinks.

'Thanks.' Robert raised his glass before taking a gulp. 'So, you grew up in Car-snooty?'

'I hate it when people call it that.'

'It's what we called it in Arbroath.'

She smirked. 'Everything's relative, I suppose.'

'So, did you?'

'What, have a slag's bed?'

'No.' He laughed. 'Grow up in Carnoustie.'

'I've not grown up.' She took a sip of her dark drink. *Too many shit jokes. Just like her old man...* 'Kinloch Primary then the high school up the road. Then Aberdeen Uni.'

'And you came back?'

'For my sins.' Vicky stared into her glass. 'Got a job with Tayside Police as was. Lived in Dundee for a bit, working the Hilltown. *Brutal.* My boyfriend at the time wrote for *The Courier*.'

'I've always liked Carnoustie.' Robert took a drink. 'Moved here to get a new start...' He took another sip, then stared at the table top for a few seconds. 'My wife died last year.'

The nerve in her neck twanged. 'I'm sorry to hear that.'

'Cancer. And mercifully quick, to be honest.' Robert stared into space. 'Took years with my uncle, constant false hope and constant setbacks. He was like a dog that couldn't stop pissing on the carpet. Felt like we were keeping him alive for my aunt's sake.' He took another drink. 'With Moira, there was no option of chemo. Died a month after she was diagnosed. Sorry if that sounds... I don't know. Grief will do that to you. You focus on enjoying what you had, rather than what you've lost.'

Vicky looked at him until he met her eye. 'Even so, I'm sorry for your loss.'

'Thank you, it was...' Tears welled in his eyes. 'The hardest part was all the bloody admin I had to do after she'd gone. I just wanted to lie in bed for a month, remembering the good times. Instead I had so much crap to do. Had to be there for Jamie. I pulled myself together and took him away, toured the Highlands and Islands. Standing on Kirkwall harbour one Sunday, watching this poor wee laddie playing the trumpet in a howling Orkney wind... Felt so futile. That's when I decided to sell up and move.'

Vicky didn't know how to respond. 'You chose well. Corbie Drive's a nice street.'

'Seems to be a real community there. And Kaz and Colin seem like good people.'

'I wish I could afford to live there.' She took a sip. 'Not all of us have new-build houses in Dunfermline that rich bankers in Edinburgh want to buy for double what you paid.'

'Not that you're bitter.' Robert finished his pint. 'Your house isn't so bad.'

'You think? I'm a police officer and I live in the worst bit of Carnoustie.'

'Still better than the best of Arbroath.'

She laughed, thankful for the comic relief. 'Hardly, but I'll take it.' She checked the bar was free. 'Can I get you another?'

He handed her his empty. 'The Ossian, please.'

Vicky took his glass to the bar, finishing hers as she waited for their drinks.

Glancing round at Robert, this time seeing him with sober eyes, she revised his age down. Maybe not even forty. He seemed less nervous than on Saturday. It suited him.

The conversation got so serious so quickly. I could run. She looked at the door. *I could just leave.*

Then she caught a fresh leer from Craig Norrie. Her ex from high school. Fat and bloated and still a total wanker.

As if on cue, the barman put the drinks in front of her. Decision made. She paid and returned to the table.

Robert took his glass of ale and toasted her. 'Cheers.'

She clinked glasses and smiled at him. 'Billy Connolly's first gig was supposed to be in here. He was in the Territorial Army, staying at the camp at Barry.'

'Never knew that.' Robert took a long drink. 'Saw you on TV at lunchtime. That press conference from Friday. Impressive work.'

'You think so? I kept stumbling over my words. My boss's boss got me to book a media training course. A *whole* week's worth.'

Robert offered her a gracious smile. 'You looked fine to me.'

'I made a complete mess of it.' She took a drink. 'You know, when I've got my warrant card I'm really confident. Outside of work? Complete mess. And on camera? Train wreck.'

'Talking to a camera's hard.' Robert chuckled. 'I did a community outreach project with our school and Arbroath Football Club. A video to encourage kids to exercise. I *hated* it. Made an utter arse of myself, much to the amusement of, well everybody. It's on YouTube. Kids wind me up about it daily.'

'Sounds like a noble thing to do, though.'

'It was.' Robert took a drink. Looked like it tasted like cat piss. 'How's the case going?'

'Well, I'm not really supposed to talk about it. But... It's three now.'

'Three? It was just a brother and sister then this thing in Barry?'

'I can't go into it. Seriously.'

'You think they've been targeted by vigilantes? A terror cell?'

'I can't talk about it, sorry.'

'Right. Doesn't bear thinking about.' Robert sniffed. 'Wouldn't blame them, though.' He put his glass back on the table. 'Have you got any pets?'

'Just a scraggly little cat.'

'What's he called?'

'*She* answers to Tinkle when she answers at all. She's as

complicated as her owner.' Vicky took a big drink. 'How about you?'

'Two retired greyhounds. They're lovely, but I have to go home to walk them every lunchtime, and one of them doesn't like being left alone.' He laughed. 'She's why we got the other one.'

'Had them long?'

'A few years. They were Moira's.' He sat back and held up his hands. 'Sorry, I wasn't going to mention her and now I've brought her up twice. It's not like I haven't grieved and moved on. If that's the right way to put it.'

'Don't worry, I'm not policing your every word.'

His turn to be grateful. 'I just don't want to give you the wrong impression. Kaz and Colin kind of forced us into this blind date business on Friday night.' He held up his hands. 'Not that I'd need to be forced to go on a date with you.' He stared at the table. 'I like you. It's why I texted you. It's why I'm here.'

'Thank you. Compliment received and happily returned.'

Robert finished his pint, still avoiding eye contact. He tapped her half-full glass, touching her finger as though by accident. 'Another?'

'Sorry, my mum's babysitting Bella.' Vicky swallowed, biting her lip. 'She's my daughter. I should let her get home.'

'I didn't know.'

Vicky picked up on a slight frown. 'Is she a problem?'

'No, not at all.' He shook his head then finally looked at her with a grin. 'Did you get her name from *Twilight*?'

'Not you as well.' Vicky pointed a finger at him. 'And before you start, I hadn't even heard of that bloody book when I had her.'

'Sincerest apologies.'

'She's great, but she's a bit too much like me. Prone to tantrums, shall we say.' She finished her glass. 'I worry how badly I'm messing her up.'

'Why on Earth?' Robert frowned. 'You seem like you'd be a good mother.'

'Kind of you to say, but I rely on my own parents to look after her.'

'I know the feeling. Jamie's... Well.'

'Named after Jamie Bell?' Vicky smiled. 'Our children are meant for each other.'

Robert laughed. 'Let's see if their parents work out first, shall we?' His smile broadened as he leaned closer. 'Listen, you're probably fed up of the Bacardi, do you fancy some of the nice wine I've got in my fridge?'

Vicky sat there, weighing up the choice. *Go to Robert's or relieve Mum from babysitting?* She got out her phone and texted her mum. 'Okay.'

'—WITH HIS GRANDMOTHER TONIGHT.' Robert led them into the hall. His greyhounds raced through from the living room and started jumping like mad, tails wagging, mouths open. Robert tugged at the collars. 'I'll just put these two outside.' He hauled the dogs into the kitchen, their claws scratching the floor. The patio doors slid open and shut again. He licked his lips, the kitchen spotlights catching his hair, just the right side of silver fox. 'Anyway.' He got a bottle of wine out of the fridge and snapped the foil off.

'One you prepared earlier?'

'Always got some white in there.' Robert licked his lips as he plunged the corkscrew deep and twisted hard. 'Never know when I'll need a hit.' He poured out two healthy glasses and set them down on the counter.

Vicky took a sip of wine. Tasted *really* good. 'Have you got school tomorrow?'

'I do, but Mondays are pretty light for me...'

'Deliberately so?' Vicky waited for a nod then took another drink. 'Do you enjoy teaching?'

'I do, but... PE's a weird subject. There's nothing quite like it. All the kids get it in first and second year. Bit of a nightmare. You're forcing the... fat kids to do cross country. Half the girls in the class have their period every week in swimming. What are the chances of that?'

'Don't.' Vicky wagged a finger at him. 'The boys in my class were practically wanking themselves off at the girls in the pool. It was *horrible*.'

Robert laughed. 'Tried to split the sexes in swimming classes, but the jobsworths who do the timetable knocked it back.' He took another drink of wine. 'Most kids we're just forcing to do it and teaching them to hate exercise. It only gets interesting with Standard Grade and Higher pupils. They can run and they play football because they're good at it, not because their dad wants the next David Beckham to pay off his mortgage.'

'Is Jamie going to pay off your mortgage?'

'Not by playing football.' Robert smiled at her. 'He's a maths prodigy. He'll be an accountant or something.' The smile thinned. 'That's Moira's genes.' He splashed some more wine in his glass. 'Course, I was a decent player back in the day. On Dundee's books as a teenager. Never made it, obviously. Went to uni instead.'

'When was this?'

'You're trying to calculate my age, aren't you?'

She shrugged. 'Maybe.'

'I'm forty-one, Vicky.'

'Well, I'm thirty-five.' Vicky took a sip of wine. Robert splashed more in her glass. 'Are you trying to get me drunk?'

'You're doing a very good job of it yourself.'

'Pretty much the only thing I'm good at.' Vicky took a sip. 'Career and a kid, not easy to manage.' She shrugged. 'Mum and Dad help out way more than they should.'

Robert took a long drink. 'Bella's father doesn't help out, then?'

Vicky looked away. 'Alan lives in Edinburgh now.'

'I didn't realise.' Robert raised his eyebrows. He stared into his glass for a few seconds. 'And he's not on the scene?'

'Never has been, really. Doesn't even... want to know about her.'

'Oh.'

Vicky sipped her wine. 'It's better for all concerned, trust me.

We'd only been going out for a few months when he got a job offer in Edinburgh. I found out I was pregnant, but I was settled here. He didn't want to stay in Dundee. Or with me and my daughter.'

'He doesn't want her in his life?'

'It's fine. I'd much rather bring up Bella on my own than have to deal with him and his nonsense.'

'Did you ever . . . You know?'

'Think about abortion?'

Robert scratched his neck.

'Every day at bedtime.' Vicky smiled. 'Only joking. Of course I thought about it, but I couldn't bring myself to go through it. It's been really hard, but I've only regretted it every day since she was born.' She shut her eyes. 'I didn't mean that. I'm a cop. Gallows humour is how we cope. Hard to switch it off.'

'I get that.' Robert took a big dent out of his glass and pointed through to the living room. 'Shall we have a comfy seat?'

'Go on.'

Vicky stood up, almost toppling over. She held out her arm for Robert to take. Instead, he put his hand on her arm and kissed her gently on the lips.

VICKY GOT out of bed and crossed the room, tugging the dressing gown around her naked body. Far too tight.

'Not bad for your age.' Robert grinned at her through the darkened room, just one sidelight on.

She blushed. 'Back in a minute.' She went into the bathroom, locked the door behind her and leaned against the door. Deep breath. She dropped the condom into the bin, the teat filled with semen, millions of half-Roberts swimming around. It stank of her. She lifted the toilet lid and sat on the seat, head in her hands.

Alone in a strange bathroom. 'Shit, shit, shit.'

What the hell am I doing?

Bottom line, can I commit to anyone beyond myself and my daugh-

ter? And even if I can make room for a bit of romance in my life, what about taking on a son?

Her breath came in short bursts as she felt the weight of the responsibility crushing her lungs. She peed and flushed the toilet before splashing cold water on her face. In the mirror, her face was pink and blotchy, her make-up smudged. She went back through and sat on the bed.

Robert snuggled up to her, kissing her neck. 'I enjoyed that.'

Vicky froze. 'You know I can't stay, right?'

'Of course. Bella's got to come first.'

'Oh.' Vicky turned towards him. 'Thank you. That's... That's very considerate of you. I appreciate it, really...' She turned away again.

'But?'

She hesitated. Another deep breath. 'I need to let Mum get home and...'

'You can just wipe your cock on the curtains and clear off.'

She slapped him on the chest. 'Robert!'

'I'm joking!' Robert brushed her hair aside and started stroking her neck, not far from that nerve.

Vicky glanced at the clock: 22.33. 'I've got to go.'

'Hint taken.' Robert got up. He slid his boxers on, then the first leg of his trousers, hopping as he put on the second one. He was much more athletic than she'd initially thought — his abs were tight, his shoulders firm.

Vicky looked down at her own stomach poking out of the gown. Not so good.

'Well, that's me.' Robert slid his shirt on and pulled his belt tight. 'I take it you want to slip out like a thief in the night?'

'You can tell you're a nineties boy.'

'Eh? That's a Rolling Stones song.'

'I thought it was Take That.'

'All this talk of grunge is just a cover, isn't it? You're really a pop girl.'

'No comment.' Vicky picked up her bra and hauled it on, clipping it in place then pulling up the straps. She got up and pulled her top on, then her jeans. *Where the hell are my boots?*

Under the bed. She kicked her left boot on, then the right and stood up a few inches taller.

Robert reached over, rather than down, and kissed her on the lips. 'I like you, Vicky.'

'Okay.' She pulled back with an instant blush, but before he could get the wrong impression she leaned back in for another, longer kiss. Then broke off, keeping eye contact.

A smile flashed on his lips. 'Do you want to come here for dinner tomorrow night?'

'That's... quite soon.'

Robert gave her a puppy-dog face, lip out, eyes wide. 'Don't you want to see me?'

Vicky turned back to face him and couldn't help laughing. 'Sod it, it's a date. I'll get Mum to look after Bella.'

'You could bring her, if you want.'

'Spending an evening with two small kids isn't a date, it's crowd control.'

'Agreed.' His dogs scrabbled at the back door. Robert set off towards the kitchen. 'See you tomorrow.'

'Looking forward to it.' With a wink and a smile, she walked off into the night.

Mum stood in the sitting room doorway, coat already on. 'Well?'

'Well what?' Vicky hung up her coat. 'Is Bella asleep?'

'She is. Poor wee thing fell asleep watching TV.' Mum beamed. 'We saw you on the news. They put up some footage of you giving a press conference on Friday. Bella was so happy.'

'That makes one of us.'

'Oh please, you came across so well, Victoria. I'm very proud of you.' Mum screwed up her eyes. 'How was your date?'

'Fine.'

'Are you seeing him again?'

'Maybe.'

'Oh my God!' Mum hugged her tight, but Vicky batted her back. 'Just allow me to be happy for you.'

'Okay, just this once.' Vicky put her arms around her. 'Is the only good thing about my life the fact I've been on a date?'

'No!' Mum broke off and stood back, looking her in the eye. 'Why would you think that?'

'You just go on about how bad I am, Mum. About how I need a man?'

'Victoria, I know how hard it is for you and Bella on your own. You're doing a brilliant job of raising my wee girl. It's just that your father and I aren't going to be around forever.'

Vicky rubbed a hand across her face, trying to stop her eyes welling up. 'Don't say that, Mum.'

'I just want you to be happy, Victoria. Okay?'

'Okay, Mum.' Vicky coughed, her voice thick with tears.

'I'll need to collect your father from the Kinloch. God knows what state he's got himself into.'

'I'll drop Bella off at eight tomorrow, if that's alright with you?'

'That's fine.'

Vicky bit her lip. 'Can Bella stay with you tomorrow night?'

'Another date?'

Vicky nodded. 'Of course!' Mum looked to the heavens, her eyes suddenly clear as day. 'Thank God.'

'Mum, not even God can sort out my love life.' Vicky pecked her on the cheek.

Mum let herself out, grinning as she shut the door behind her.

Vicky took a deep breath, then another.

In less than twenty-four hours, I'll meet Robert's son and dig myself a deeper hole.

Sure, he seemed to have his heart in the right place and we just... but...

Do I even like him?

She climbed the stairs, making for Bella's room. A thin shaft of light flashed across the floor, illuminating just enough of the bed to make her wonder how there was enough room for Bella with all those cuddly toys piled on the pillow.

Vicky knelt and gently kissed her daughter on the top of her head.

Bella's eyes flickered open. 'Mummy catched baddies on telly.'

DAY 5

Monday
4th April 2016

23

The radio alarm blared out REM's *Shiny Happy People.*

Vicky slammed her hand down on it, her boob falling free with the movement. She looked down, wondering where her vest top was. She was naked.

Robert.

She turned back over. What the hell am I doing?

The clock radio read 7.00.

She squinted, spotting her dressing gown on the floor then reached down to get it, tugging it on. Then she sat up, trying to clear her head.

Her phone buzzed, rumbling on her chest of drawers.

A text from Robert — *Hd nice n8. R* She put it back. *Whatever he might have going for him, texting clearly isn't one of Robert's skills.*

'Mummy!'

Vicky reached out to grab Bella as she jumped on the bed. 'Somebody's full of beans today.'

'Had good sleeps, Mummy. Can I catch baddies with you today?'

'Mummy's got to catch baddies on her own, sweet pea.'

'I missed you yesterday.'

Vicky kissed her head. 'Me too.'

'HUNGRY, MUMMY!' Bella bounced in the back of the car, her seat rattling as much as her mouth. 'My wee tummy's empty!'

'Not long now.' Vicky drove down the long straight of Barry Road against the flow of traffic. Bella sang all the way through the corner bend and past Vicky's first police station.

As they turned into Bruce Drive, Bella stopped singing and punched the door beside her. 'Where's my daddy?'

Shit, shit, shit.

She was hangry...

Vicky choked. 'It's okay, Bella.'

'I want my daddy!'

Vicky turned left towards her parents' house, then sped along the street, angling her rear-view to keep an eye on her daughter. 'Bella, you don't have a daddy. It's just you, me and Tinkle. And Granny and Grandad.'

'I want my daddy!' Bella punched the door again. 'I want my daddy!'

Vicky parked outside her old house, got out and pulled Bella out of her seat, hugging her tight. 'It's okay, baby.'

'Why do I not have a daddy?'

'You're a special girl, Bells.'

'Stinky Simon said everyone has a daddy.'

'Well, you're a very special girl, Bells.' Vicky pulled her in even tighter. 'Bells and whistles. Remember?' She stood there for a few seconds, smelling Bella's clean hair. 'Shall we get Granny to fill up your wee tummy?'

'O-kay.' Accompanied by a little stomp.

Vicky walked up the drive and knocked on the front door.

Mum came out in her dressing gown, tired eyes squinting into the light. 'Is that you, Victoria?'

'Hey, Mum.'

Mum helped Bella up the steps, a smile was twitching at the corners of her mouth. 'How's my girl?'

'My wee tummy's empty, Granny.'

'Well go inside, Bella. Grandad's just making porridge.'

'Yay!' Bella skipped past her into the dark house.

Vicky let out a breath. 'I'm giving you a tantrum warning.'

'Her daddy again, I take it?' Mum shrugged. 'You've made your bed, Victoria.'

'Thanks...' Vicky got back in her car and slumped in the chair. Mum and Bella in the living room, waving out at her. She gave a friendly wave back, but her heart wasn't in it.

Would give anything just to take Bella away and cuddle her all day. Spend some actual time with her. Instead of everyone stealing that time away.

Her Airwave chimed on the passenger seat. Another message.

Shit.

A new photo, Vicky chatting to the Fixit DIY manager. And text:

"THE BEST WAY TO SERVE EGGS IS FROZEN."

VICKY PULLED into the car park at the Fixit DIY store and parked next to a police car near the entrance, its blue lights still flashing. She got out and crossed the car park.

Colin Woods snipped the end of the crime tape as she approached. 'This is getting beyond the joke, Vicks.'

'What's happened?'

Colin frowned as he inspected her. 'You look a bit different today.'

Vicky blushed. 'Just tired.' She nodded at the building. 'What's going on?'

'I just came on my shift when I got a call-out.' Colin waved behind the tape. 'The store manager was chained to the front of the shop.'

Vicky started off across the concourse. 'Is he still alive?'

'Calm the beans, Vicky.' Colin laughed. 'Christ, Vicks, do you think it'd just be you on your lonesome if there was a body? This place would be swarming with C&A suits if it was a murder. Poor boy's naked, and it was a cold night. Some doctor from Ninewells is with him.'

She stopped by the door.

Dr Rankine was kneeling on the floor. Gordon Christie was moaning next to her, bound in a semi-recumbent posture to the DIY store. Looked like the same chains that Kyle Ramsay used to secure his birds. The man was naked except for his underpants.

A note flapped down from him:

"LISTEN TO US. LOSE THE BIRDS, SET THEM FREE. OTHERWISE WE'RE NOT RESPONSIBLE FOR WHAT WE DO NEXT. YOU'VE GOT TILL LUNCHTIME. YOU'VE SEEN WHAT WE CAN DO."

24

Vicky tried to focus. *Christie needs help. Now.* 'What can I do?'

PC Soutar appeared from the store entrance, his stick arms opening some Fixit packaging. He held up a hacksaw, catching the blue glow from the police car, and started slicing at the knot of chains around Christie.

'Sergeant, we need to get him warm.' Rankine got to her feet and smiled at Vicky. A glance at Christie wiped it from her face. 'It was four degrees last night with no cloud cover until the rain started just after six. He's suffering from hypothermia. We need to get him somewhere warm fast or he'll die.'

'How long has he got?'

'Minutes.'

'An ambulance will take too long, right?'

Rankine stared into space.

Vicky snapped her fingers at Rankine. 'An ambulance will take too long, right?'

'Far too long.' Rankine bit her lip. 'I've got something in my car which might help.' She shook her head. 'It's not going to do it.'

Vicky grabbed her arms, tried to shake her. 'Will the store office be warm enough?'

'Maybe.' Rankine frowned, eyes still on Christie. 'Why?'

Vicky picked up the bag at Soutar's feet. 'Did you get this from inside?'

'Found the keys by the door.' Soutar looked like he knew what he was doing with a saw. Made a change from his policing. 'Was I not supposed to?'

'No, just hurry!'

Soutar started sawing harder. Something tinkled to the concrete. 'There we go!'

Vicky patted him on the arm. 'Follow me.' She jogged over to the front door.

Colin and Soutar carried Christie over, his shaking arms draped round their shoulders.

Vicky tramped through the store, triggering a trail of lights. She found a door marked "Manager" and thanked the heavens that it had a gas fire. She turned it up full and hammered the ignition until blue flames climbed up the front.

Colin and Soutar helped Christie through the door. His body was shaking hard, teeth chattering. Rankine appeared clutching a shell suit and helped Christie into it.

Vicky looked around for something to do. The room was tiny, yet crammed full with four desks, green-screen terminals perched on top. She shut the door before wheeling the fire over. 'I need to ask him some questions.'

Rankine zipped up the front of the jacket and fastened the Velcro. 'You can try.' She got up. 'I need to find a kettle or coffee machine.'

Vicky knelt in front of Christie. 'I'm going to need to ask you a few questions, okay?'

Christie nodded through his shivering. 'Th-th-th-that's f-f-f-fine.'

'Mr Christie. What's the last thing you remember?'

'L-l-l-locking up.'

'What time was this?'

'T-t-t-ten. J-j-j-just affffffffter.'

'What happened?'

Christie struggled for breath. 'H-h-h-hit on head.'

Rankine knelt in front of him, clutching a steaming cup of hot water. She held it out for Christie but he just stuck his face over the steam.

Vicky ignored her. 'Did you see who attacked you?'

'M-m-m-m-m-man.'

'Was he tall?'

Christie nodded. Looked more like a seizure, but Vicky had to press on.

'What was he wearing?'

'B-b-b-b-b-b-balac-c-c-c-clava.'

'Was there anyone else?'

He hugged his body tighter and shook his head.

'Thanks.' She exhaled slowly. 'My colleagues will take a full statement from you later.'

He gave a slight nod, his teeth clacking together.

Rankine glanced at Vicky, then at Christie. 'There's an ambulance on its way to take you to hospital.'

'SOUNDS like it went well last night.' Karen tilted her head as she got out of her green Volvo. 'I take it your top drawer didn't get opened?'

'Only for a condom.'

'Oh my God!'

'No, we did at Robert's.' Vicky turned away from the DIY store. 'Karen, a man's almost died here.'

'And you saved him. Well done.' Karen gripped her cheek and pinched. 'Are you seeing him again?'

'Dinner tonight.'

'Squeeee!'

'Kaz, I swear if you make that noise one more time, I'll never speak to you again.'

Karen laughed. 'Sorry.' She frowned at Colin as he sauntered over. 'Who found him?'

'Some boy at the Asda round the back spotted him. He's in the canteen the now, but I'll follow up with him later just to make sure there's no funny business.'

Vicky pointed at Karen. 'One for you, my dear.'

'Come on, Vicks!'

'Eyes on the prize.'

Karen shook her head as she wandered off. *Serve her right.*

A four-by-four pulled up alongside them. Willis Stewart got out and ran towards them, eyes bulging. 'Is Gordon okay?'

'Sir, this is a crime scene.' Colin held him back. 'I need you to vacate the area, sir.'

'Don't you know who I am?'

'I don't sir, but I need you to calm down and keep back.'

Stewart pushed Colin's arms away. 'I'm the Chief Executive of this company!'

Colin raised his eyebrows at Vicky. 'What do you think?'

Vicky clenched her fists. *Stewart ignored the warning, and this is what happened.* 'He needs to stay here.'

'But—'

Vicky put a finger to her lip. 'No buts, Mr Stewart. Understood?'

'This is—'

'Sir, I need you to back off.'

Stewart huffed out a sigh. A man who wasn't used to being told what to do. He looked... nervous. 'How's Gordon doing?'

'He's not going to die, Mr Stewart.'

'That's good.'

'That's *lucky*.' She scowled at Stewart. 'I normally hate to say I told you so, but...'

'Your Assistant Chief Constable told me so as well. As I've told—'

'Is there active CCTV here?'

Stewart pinched the point of his chin. 'There's a camera round the back. The one at the front is out of action.'

'You should've got rid of the birds.' Vicky got in his face. 'You could've prevented this.'

'I refuse to negotiate with terrorists.' Stewart stared her down. 'The birds are staying.'

'I hope you can live with yourself.'

'This might not be—'

Vicky waved the note in front of his face. 'This is related. This is your fault.'

Stewart's shoulders slumped.

~

Vicky looked around the car park. Just familiar faces. SOCOs dusting and photographing. Paramedics wheeling Christie away, his teeth still chattering. Uniformed cops trying to keep the crowd at bay. Journalists, photographers and a BBC news crew. 'What a mess.'

Jenny Morgan looked up at Vicky, frowning. Her red hair caught the early sunlight shining across the car park, the early commuters backing up on the nearby Kingsway already. She put down Vicky's Airwave, resting it between her knobbly knees like Karen's son when told to stop playing his DS. 'Still can't get anything on this, though.'

'This is the third time, Jen.' Vicky sat next to her on the metal bench, cold enough to cause piles with about two seconds contact. She leaned back on the chair and exhaled, her breath misting in the air. 'Someone's stalking me.'

'And it's not that deadbeat of an ex.' Jenny got to her feet and stuffed the Airwave in a bag. 'I need to take this, of course.'

'Naturally.' Vicky leaned forward. 'There's nothing you can—'

Wait. Up there. A flash of light and not from the SOCOs.

Vicky pushed herself to her feet and stormed off through the scrum, barging past Colin Woods and his skinny partner. Another flash.

Jen's right. Someone's stalking me. And here they are, taking more photos. More messages to lure me to crime scenes.

Vicky swung round the other side of the Scenes of Crime van

and peeked out. Another flash, more aimed at the shop than her. No doubt get it back in a message to her Airwave.

A woman, though. Probably a woman. Not many curves or bumps. But...

Vicky snatched the camera out of their hands, jerking the strap as it flew from their neck. Then she grabbed their right wrist and twisted, mangling the arm behind their back.

'Give me that back!'

The voice. Vicky knew it from somewhere.

A stray flash from a SOCO camera caught the photographer's face.

Vicky bent her over the van's bonnet. 'Anita Skinner, I'm arresting you for—'

'I've not done anything!'

'—say anything, but it may harm your—'

'This is bollocks!' More wriggling. 'I've not done anything!'

'—mention when questioned something which—'

'I'm not photographing you!'

'—say may be—' Vicky stopped. 'What did you say?'

'Why would I photograph *you*?'

Vicky let her grip slacken off. 'So you can send me messages.'

'Are you mental?' Anita waved over at the store. 'This is for my blog. You think I can afford a photographer? I heard about an attack, of course I'm heading down.'

'Doddsy!' A hand grabbed hers from behind. Forrester, frowning at her. 'What the hell are you doing?'

Vicky pointed at Anita. 'She's stalking me!'

'Okay...' Forrester smiled at Anita, then waved at Karen. 'DC Woods, can you take her away, please?'

'I want my camera.'

Vicky let it go. It thudded off the concrete.

'Jesus!' Anita lurched forward.

Karen took her arm and pushed her face down. 'Stop!'

'Come on.' Forrester grabbed Vicky's arm and led her away. 'Laing's laddies have been on her all night. She got here twenty minutes after you.'

Vicky looked over at Anita as she was pushed into the back of a police car. 'Shit.'

'So here's the thing. A little birdie tells me you got another message.'

'Jenny.'

'Vicky, no matter how bad you feel, you can't assault journalists.' Forrester gave her a level gaze. 'Okay?'

'Sir, I can't just let people photo—'

'Stop.' Forrester folded his arms. 'We need to sort this out. Our Airwave network isn't secure and someone, for whatever reason, is sending you messages related to this bloody case. Now it might just be a coincidence or—'

'We need to—'

'Vicky!' Forrester shook her shoulders. 'Jenny's looking into it for me. Meanwhile, there are some very nice people sitting in my office just now who'd love to speak to you.'

VICKY WALKED through the almost empty office space, just Zoey lost in the world of her laptop, and knocked on Forrester's door. She waited, getting a look from Zoey.

'Just a minute!' The voice boomed through the wood. The door trundled open like a crypt opening in a horror film. Rather than a vampire, a tall man in a brown suit, his lime green tie and pink shirt already making Vicky's eyes hurt. 'DS Dodds. I've been expecting you.' He stepped aside. 'Come.'

Vicky slipped past and sat in her usual chair.

'My name is Superintendent Marcus Ogilvie.' He swayed over to sit behind Forrester's desk and tapped at a laptop. 'Now. While I work for—' he did air quotes, his eyes rolling out of focus, '—"The Complaints", this isn't about you, okay?'

'Who is it about, then?'

'Whoever is, mm, sending you these Airwave messages.' Ogilvie rubbed at his right eye, really pressing it hard. 'Now. This isn't a formal interview, but... Well. This morning's events have, mm, somewhat, yes, accelerated things. Shall we say?'

'Whatever you say.'

'Mm.' Ogilvie wrote another sentence on his laptop. 'Now. Your boss, DI Forrester, he, mm, he called us up yesterday. After you received, mm, a message?'

Vicky didn't reply. *Let him spill his story and correct later.*

'Now I gather that you've got more of these, mm, messages?'

Is there something wrong with him or is he just trying to annoy me?

'Said messages drew you not only to Barry but also to, mm, the, mm, DIY store.'

'Fixit.'

'Right, right. Right.' More typing. 'And now... Well, mm, another message?'

Vicky gave him the satisfaction of a nod.

'Now, this message led you back to, mm, the DIY store, where poor Mr Christie was freezing to death.'

'We saved his life.'

'Mm.'

'I'm not sending these messages.'

'Did I say anything about it? Mm?' Ogilvie waited, his tongue gliding round his mouth. 'But. Your brother knows how the system works, mm?'

'Excuse me?' Vicky was on her feet, fists balled. 'My *brother*?'

'Mm.' Another glance at the laptop. 'Andrew Kevin Dodds.'

'You think he's doing this?'

'Sit, please.' Ogilvie waited until she complied. 'Andrew has the necessary knowledge and the skills, Sergeant.'

'Someone involved with these attacks is targeting me!'

'And that's definitely not your brother?'

'Of course not. He's ill.'

'Mm.' Ogilvie's tongue batted between the sides of his mouth, fast and loud. 'Of course.' He picked up a sheet of paper and slid it across the table. 'Have a look at this, mm?'

Vicky glanced at it. Then took another, longer look. Her name and bank details, next to a transaction dated four years ago. 'What's this?'

'You made a sizeable donation to an animal rescue charity. Brown Street Kennels, run by Dundee City Council.'

'I took in a cat. Tinkle.'

'Of course. And the standard fee for such was fifty pounds.' He glanced at his laptop, 'Not fifteen hundred.'

Vicky bit her lip, drawing blood. 'Should I have a lawyer or Federation Rep in here?'

'This isn't a formal interview, Sergeant.'

'But you're investigating me?'

'Correction, we're not investigating you. DI Forrester, as part of this case, is investigating people with strong sympathies to, mm, animal charities. It's a scattergun approach, I know, but sometimes these things, mm, pay off? Now, you made that donation. I'd like you to explain it.'

Vicky exhaled slowly. 'My ex gave me some money. Cash. So I gave it to them when I rescued Tinkle.'

The door trundled open and Forrester appeared carrying a long cardboard pipe. He plonked it down and started fussing with his coffee machine. 'Don't mind me.'

Ogilvie looked like he did mind. Very much. 'Well, we'll just have to leave it there and see where the investigation gets us, mm?' He packed up his laptop to the sounds of coffee grounds being tipped into a bin then set off, nodding at Forrester as he left. 'David.'

Vicky stayed sitting, her fury building. 'Thanks for landing me in the shit.'

'Wasn't my intention, Vicky.' Forrester cleared his throat as the first hiss came from the coffee maker. 'I want us to cast the net wide. We're already searching far and wide for this black car. Beyond that, though, we've nothing. So, Raven asked me to get a list of anyone in the Tayside area with sympathies to animal charities or other welfare groups. Large donations, activities on marches, that sort of thing.'

'And my name came up.'

'Young Zoey found it, yeah.'

'You think I'm involved?'

'I'll take your word for it, Vicky. Always will do. If you say you're not, you're not.'

Vicky stared at him hard for a few seconds. *So much for trust.* 'I'm not involved.'

'Then I believe you.' Forrester smiled at her. 'You're at risk, though.'

Bella...

Vicky got up and smoothed down her trousers. 'Want me to head home?'

'I want you to do whatever you need, Vicky. But I'm kind of short-staffed.'

VICKY LEANED back in her chair, made it squeak as she spun round to look through the smudged window, the jute mill opposite lit up.

Am I at risk? Is someone targeting me or am I just a conduit?

All those messages about eggs. The photo. Would they go after Bella? If they did, would Dad still be able to protect her? Would Mum?

'Sorry.' Zoey pulled the headphones down to rest on her shoulders. 'What was that?'

'Didn't say anything.'

Zoey clicked her tongue a few times. 'Pretty sure you did.'

'Sorry.' Her head hit the rest as she slumped back. 'DI Forrester said you have a list of charity donors?'

'You want a print?'

'Please.'

'Mac only wants it on paper. Hates reading on a screen.' Zoey tapped her keys. 'That's it printing.'

'Thanks.'

But Zoey had already stuck her headphones back on.

Vicky walked over to the printer as it worked through the sheets and looked across at Considine poring over a file. 'How are you getting on, Stephen?'

'Getting there, Sarge.' Considine closed the file and got up to stretch his back. 'See you in a minute. I need to do some chasing.'

Vicky watched him leave, sighing as he closed the door. Forrester was still in his office, the booming sound of a phone call.

Betrayal.

Someone's targeting me and Forrester hung me out to dry.

She grabbed the paper off the printer, still hot, and walked back to her desk. She shuffled aside the endless transcripts of the witness statements and interviews and shit. Last night's report, three hours of tedium. She collected it and picked up the first page of Zoey's list. Her tired eyes scanned it.

She spotted a healthy donation from Polly Muirhead just above Gary Black's two grand — the refund from Rachel Hay.

But the next name made her stop.

Robert Hamilton.

25

Vicky sat on the toilet seat lid, elbows on her knees. 'Shit, shit, shit.' She clutched the damning sheet again.

ROBERT HAMILTON, 18 CORBIE DRIVE, CARNOUSTIE.

The donation was for ten grand.

Ten grand.

She tried to keep her breathing under control.

Robert was a good guy, wasn't he?

Then again, asking all those questions about the case... Getting close to Colin and Karen and me. Coincidence?

Asking the waiter in the Gulistan for free-range chicken. His retired greyhounds.

None of it's evidence, but maybe it's why I'm being targeted. We didn't have a tail on him so he could be the one following me, taking photos of me and Bella.

She bit her lip. *What the hell am I going to do?*

'Sorry, sir, my sort-of boyfriend might be behind this.'

'Right-o.'

'And he's got suspicious ties to the victims. Oh, and he gave a load of cash to the animal rescue place down the road.'

'Never mind, that's less than we've got on the Muirheads.'

She found herself laughing. Unlikely though that outcome was, her mind games helped.

What the hell am I going to do? 'Shit, shit, shit.'

'Are you all right in there?'

Vicky blushed at the sound of the lilting voice. 'I'm fine, Zoey.'

'You don't sound it.'

'Too much Diet Coke, I think.'

'Ugh. Too much information.'

The door shut.

Had Zoey heard my conversation with myself? I don't even know if I spoke it aloud or not.

She got to her feet and straightened her blouse.

Need to be professional. Go through the rest of the list, find any likelier suspects.

Yeah, keep telling yourself that.

BACK IN THEIR OFFICE, Forrester's door was open. He stood against the wall, grinning like Bella on Christmas morning. 'Come here.'

Vicky walked over, heart thudding. 'What's up?'

'Ta-da!' Forrester pointed at the wall. A massive Ordnance Survey map of Dundee and its surrounding area, the familiar open mouth of the Tay to the wedge at Barry. Covered Perth in the west. 'It's beautiful, isn't it?'

Vicky shrugged. 'Sir, I need to—'

'Should've got it centred closer to Perth.' Forrester tilted his head to the side. 'There's too much sea on this.'

'Sir?'

'I need to catch up with Ogilvie and Jenny Morgan, okay?' Forrester patted her on the shoulder. 'Unless it's urgent?'

Very.

She shook her head. 'I'll catch you later.'

'Right-o.' Forrester grabbed his jacket and charged off.

Vicky trudged back to her desk and slumped in her seat. Hard rain battered the windows.

Weakling.

Coward.

Zoey dropped her headphones on her desk. 'Ma'am, you need to see this.'

Vicky pinched the bridge of her nose, the nerve pulsing in her neck. 'What is it?'

'A video of Kyle Ramsay.'

Vicky jolted round to her desk. On the screen, birdcages on both sides of a narrow corridor. In the middle, birds were pecking seeds off Ramsay's naked torso. He looked unconscious but wriggled at each bite.

The image froze, Kyle Ramsay's face a rictus as a falcon's beak bit into his thighs. Then text appeared, one word at a time.

"WANT TO KNOW WHY?"

'It's on YouTube.' Zoey tapped the screen. 'Thousands of hits every minute.'

'So the message is finally getting out.' Vicky rubbed her forehead. 'Who posted it? Brian Morton?'

'That's the thing — the audit trails are totally masked. They're clearly learning from what we're doing. It could be him, but we've no way of proving it.'

Then more words:

"HERE'S WHY."

The video shifted to some CCTV footage of a shopfront, cages filled with birds. 19.12, 2015-10-17.

Kyle Ramsay sloped into the picture and reached into a cage for an owl, grabbing its feet and tugging it out of the cage. The bird flapped its wings manically, trying to escape. Then Ramsay punched it with his free hand, cracking it right in the face. The bird stopped struggling and flopped in his hand, dropping to the ground. Ramsay started panicking, hands behind his head.

Freeze frame and new text:

"IN 2015, THIS MAN WAS BANNED FROM KEEPING BIRDS FOR FIVE YEARS."

It cut to footage of Ramsay outside Fixit DIY, timestamped two days ago.

"YET HERE HE IS, KEEPING BIRDS IN 2016."

~

RANKINE LEANED back against the wall, though Vicky and Forrester towered over her. 'Anyway, you can speak to Mr Ramsay, but.' She glanced at Vicky. 'Let's just say we've not been able to wash his mouth out.'

'Heard about that.' Forrester sniffed. 'This boy's a sick, sick puppy.'

Rankine nodded. 'It's like he saw that Hitchcock film and decided to...'

Vicky set off towards Ramsay's room. Sick bastard was given his own room. *After all he'd done, what happened to him was the least he deserved.*

He took one look at her. 'You can get to fuck.'

'Mr Ramsay, I need to ask you about killing an owl.'

'Fuck yourself, you stinking bitch. I'm not talking to you or any other pig cu—'

~

'—OR SOMETHING.' Gordon Christie sat up in his bed, the machines beeping. 'I've told that lassie everything there is to tell.' A shiver ran down his legs. Seemed to intensify as it went, until his feet looked like they were plugged into the mains. Then they stopped and he sucked in breath. 'I'm still frozen, man. Can feel it in my *bones.*'

Vicky sat next to the bed. 'We need to ask you about Kyle Ramsay.'

'He's got nothing to do with this.'

'We have eviden—'

'Absolutely nothing, you hear me?' Christie had another shiver attack. 'He wasn't even there when they took me.'

'We think he was the target.' Vicky held up the photocopied note. 'We understand he killed an owl.'

'Shite.' Christie slumped back in his bed, like he'd lost all muscle control. 'That's nothing to do with this.'

'You employed him despite being on the SSPCA cruelty list.' Vicky showed him a still from the video. 'He punched an owl to death. And, of course, Kyle Ramsay isn't his real name is it?'

'Shit.'

'When you search for Douglas Scott, his real name, you find rather a lot of animal cruelty crimes. Mostly against birds. So. How did he get a job outside your shop?'

'The CEO wanted him.' Christie massaged his leg. 'And when Willis wants something, he gets it. Kyle was just the operator. His brother owned the company. Lives out near Montrose.'

Vicky got to her feet and nodded at Forrester. 'Think we should pay him a visit.'

'I HATE IT WHEN LORRIES OVERTAKE.' Considine kept the Python right up the tail of the lorry until he turned left off the main road through Montrose, heading out of town along the northern shore of the tidal basin they'd just crossed. 'Slows down the advanced drivers.'

'Live and let live, Stephen. We're not in a hurry.'

'So why are your hands drumming on the dashboard?'

Vicky stopped, unaware she'd been doing it.

Considine grinned as he swerved out into oncoming traffic before cutting back in, stuck behind the tractor. The sort of angry driving Vicky's dad used to practise as soon as anything went slightly wrong with the car or his children.

Vicky held up the road atlas. 'I told you to take a left about a mile back.'

'I should be able to get through the back way, though.'

'If only you'd—'

'I *don't* need a *satnav*.' Considine glared at her. 'I know where I'm going.' He kept on down the road, heading towards the glens and the distant mountains.

'You're lost, aren't you?'

'Maybe.' Considine slowed to a stop at the side of the road. 'Crap.' He did a three-point turn, making a Range Rover brake sharply, and shot back the way they'd come. 'So. Left here?'

'No, right.'

Considine turned down a country lane, its single track leading deep into the early spring green. 'You think this guy's actually done something?'

'That's what I want to find out, Stephen. He's covering for his brother. I want to know why.'

'Someone attacked him because he killed an owl.' Considine shook his head. 'Animal cruelty. Complete bollocks.'

Vicky glowered at him. 'People are being kidnapped and disfigured, Constable.'

'Don't get me wrong — I want to catch them. I just don't get why they're doing it. Animals are just food.' Considine patted the steering wheel. 'We haven't exactly needed carthorses since the invention of the internal combustion engine, have we?'

Vicky just shook her head.

After a few hundred yards, they passed a farm on the right, a monolithic granite farmhouse sitting beside giant steel silos. 'This it?'

'Next one.'

Considine ploughed on. The lane lost its tarmac and the car bumped along the wild farm path, not that it slowed him down. They got to a stone cottage almost hidden behind a thick beech hedge.

The greyhound traps were visible from a distance, twelve long strips of grass surrounded by chicken wire, a small kennel at the end of each one. A couple of dogs paced around one in the middle, but the rest seemed empty. The house behind the kennels was typical of the area — multiple extensions quadrupling the size of an old stone cottage.

Vicky felt the twang in her neck — Robert and his retired greyhounds, taking the dogs away from the cruelty and exploitation.

Considine pulled into the long pebble driveway beside the house.

Vicky got out of the car, crunched up the path and rang the doorbell, an electronic buzz just audible through the door. She took in the house, the eaves hanging over their heads. No sign of movement inside.

One of the dogs barked, a weird 'Hooo!' sound.

Considine stood next to her, scratching his crotch.

'You okay, Constable?'

'Never better.'

Vicky hit the bell again. No answer.

'Nooooo!'

She glanced at Considine. 'Did you hear that?'

'With bells on.' Considine grabbed the handle and twisted. 'Door's open. Shall we—'

Vicky barged past him into a poky wee hall, dark red walls. Cigars and fried bacon. And a loud thrumming noise. She paced over the dark green carpet towards the sound. An oak-floored living room, a muted TV in the corner in front of some IKEA chairs.

'Nooooo!'

Came from the door on the left. She followed Considine down another hallway. The grinding got louder. Considine tore open a door.

'Nooooo!' A man was on his knees, cradling another man. A treadmill whirred round above them. 'Help!'

The man he was cradling flopped to the ground. Navy tracksuit, drenched in sweat. One arm raised up, handcuffed to the treadmill. Dead eyes stared out at them.

26

'Hard not to think it's a murder.' Vicky squinted into the distance at some uniforms chatting casually at the far side of the house. 'Handcuffed to a treadmill?'

Forrester stood outside the front door, jaw clenched. 'We got a name for this guy?'

'Micky Scott. Douglas Scott's brother, AKA Kyle Ramsay.' Vicky waved over at Micky Scott's son, letting a female uniform help him into a car. 'Son found him not long before we got here.'

'Think it's just a sex game gone wrong?'

'I know your love life's racier than mine, sir, but handcuffed to a *treadmill*? Really?'

Forrester gave her a reprimanding look. 'You know what I mean.'

'I don't think so, no. Who gets sexually excited by running?'

'Takes all sorts, Doddsy.'

'Handcuffs imply premeditation. Implies murder.'

The pathologist's massive arse squelched out of her Saab, followed by the rest of her, oddly thin and toned. Shirley Arbuthnott waddled over to the house with a nod.

'Good luck getting that into a crime scene suit, love.' Forrester stopped watching Arbuthnott's bottom and stared at Vicky. 'I'm thinking heart attack. Have to wait for Big-arse Arbuthnott to get him on the slab back in bonny Dundee.'

'You want to treat it as murder?'

'Not my call. I'll have to see Raven, but that's how I'll be advising him.' Forrester folded his arms. 'You want to have a word with the boy's son?'

VICKY WALKED through Alec Scott's home and stopped by the sofa.

Alec Scott sat there, rubbing his thinning hairline and staring into space. The sitting room was dark, thick curtains covering the windows, a couple of sidelights shining up the stone walls. The back wall was a kitchen area, decent-looking appliances and units. 'Mr Scott?'

'I've never felt anything so cold in my life.' Alec Scott blinked, pupils dilated. Looked barely twenty, his hair cut into a short Mohican. 'Can't believe it. Supposed to chat about my dogs, but he never showed up.' He bit his lip. 'I called him. Nothing. Thought he'd stood me up. But it's not like him to not call or text. So I drove out and...' He took a few seconds to steady himself, eyes moist. 'Dad was lying on the treadmill. Well, just off it, like he'd fallen over. Bastard thing was still running. Thought he'd knocked himself out.' He shut his eyes. 'He was dead. Stone-cold dead. *Handcuffed* to the treadmill.'

'Sorry to ask you this.' Vicky gave him a sympathetic smile. 'Did your father possess any handcuffs?'

Alec's eyes widened. 'Not that I know of.'

'But your father liked to exercise?'

'Big style. Played for Dundee in the eighties. Had to give it up but ran every morning trying to keep in shape, not like some of these old pros you see on the telly.'

'Can I ask about your mother?'

Alec shook his head, not a second's hesitation to think it through. 'No.'

'What do you mean?'

'I mean...' Alec bit a fingernail then sighed. 'She died when I was ten. Cancer. Dad didn't remarry.'

'Any other family in the area? Brothers or sisters?'

'I'm an only child. Dad's older brother died of a heart attack two years ago. That's it.'

'No other family?'

'Well.' Alec sniffed. 'Dad's got a kid brother. Douglas, but he calls himself Kyle for some reason. Can't stand the guy.'

'Were they close?'

'Look, Dad's a good guy.'

'I understand. Did your father have many friends in the area?'

'None that spring to mind.'

'Much of a drinker?'

'Teetotal.'

'And what about your father's professional life?'

'After the football, Dad took up greyhound training to earn a crust.'

And the noise at the back of Vicky's skull started to ring like a bell.

'Train them myself.' Alec stared out of the window at some similar kennels to his father's home. 'Six dogs, two bitches. Dad's got forty-three. Not all of them his, of course.' He set his glare on her. 'I'll look after them, don't you worry.' He shrugged. 'Have to see what's in the old boy's will, but...'

'You don't stand to inherit?'

'Never came up. Not even sure he's got one.'

'Anyone in the greyhound business he had any run-ins with?'

'Not that I can think of.'

'Are you sure?'

'Well.' Alec sighed, his tension sagging with his shoulders. 'Dad had a few arguments with a couple of guys in the Newcastle area.'

'What kind of run-ins?'

'Race fees, prize money, stuff like that. The usual.'

'No accusations of cruelty?'

'Eh? If anything, Dad's too soft on them. Need a firm hand.'

'Any names?'

'Listen, I like working with the dogs and that's it. Dad kept me away from the gangsters who run the meets. Sorry.'

Vicky made a note to get a search done for contacts with 0191 numbers. She lifted out a tattered photocopy of the first note. 'Ever seen a note like this?'

Alec scowled at the page. 'Nope. Why?'

'This case might be connected to a few others relating to animal cruelty.'

'I thought I recognised you.' Alec squinted at her, giving her the once over. 'You were on the telly the other day.' His gaze finally left her chest. 'Wait, you think someone's killed my old boy because he raced dogs?'

'Is it likely?'

He averted his eyes. 'Don't buy it.'

'Never had any protestors, hate mail, anything like that?'

'Never.'

~

CONSIDINE PULLED up outside Micky Scott's house. Vicky got out before he'd killed the engine.

Forrester was outside the house, shaking his head as she approached. 'Bloody hell.'

Vicky stopped next to him, Considine right behind her. 'What's going on?'

Forrester sighed. 'Raven.' That's all he could say, by the looks of it. 'Come on.' He crunched down the path.

Raven's gaze swept over them. 'Right, David.' He wrestled with his hair, the Angus breeze blowing the combover back the way. 'Okay, I've had a chance to put my arms around this.' He crossed his forearms, the sleeves of his suit jacket riding up his thick forearms, and gave Forrester a tight nod. 'I want us to treat this as a murder, okay?'

'I agree.' Forrester glanced at Vicky then back at Raven. 'You think this is connected to the others?'

'What do you think David?'

Forrester shrugged. 'They all involve vigilante action against animal cruelty. This guy trained greyhounds. I think it's wise to link them.'

'There's no note, is there?'

'No, but...' Forrester held up a hand. 'The crimes have been escalating. They started by abducting a brother and sister. Then they chopped off a farmer's nose. Last night, they got that boy's birds to peck him. Then almost freezing his boss to death this morning — if it hadn't been for Vicky, that boy would be in the morgue. Now they've killed the bird guy's brother, a greyhound trainer...'

Raven held his gaze. 'You're saying they've crossed the line from abduction and threat to murder?'

'Something like that. We should treat them as linked.'

'Okay.' Raven's glare became a wink by the time he focused on MacDonald. 'I don't disagree. I want us on the front foot, okay? Euan, can you schedule some time for you and me to chat with the NCA? This is clearly their case.'

MacDonald nodded slowly. 'Sir.'

'Let's get ahead of the curve.' Raven walked off with MacDonald, deep in a conversation that for once didn't involve Dundee United. His phone rang and he stopped to answer it.

Vicky turned to Forrester, lips pursed. 'What do you make of that, sir?'

'I need a coffee.' Forrester scowled. 'Sod it. I need a bottle of whisky in it.'

'David!' Raven called over. 'Arbuthnott's starting the PM. Can you attend?'

Forrester raised his eyes at Vicky.

∿

Focus on the victim.

The man lying on the slab, dead eyes staring up at the ceiling. Mouth hanging open, locked in place by rigor mortis.

Arbuthnott spoke into a microphone in a low tone, evading Vicky's gaze.

Vicky took in the skinny body again. Very little body fat. Must've run on that treadmill most days. Angus weather and drivers meant a serious runner needed it.

'Okay.' Arbuthnott cleared her throat. Took a few goes, then she waddled round to Vicky's side of the table, her massive arse almost pressing into Vicky's thigh. Didn't seem to have any sensation in it. 'Okay, you'll be glad to know that Mr Scott died of a heart attack, most likely from the running he'd been doing on his treadmill.'

'Why would I be glad?'

'Well, if he'd died running on a treadmill and it wasn't a heart attack, we'd be dealing with a bigger mystery than how they built the pyramids.' Arbuthnott frowned. 'Though I did discuss that with your brother the other day. He told me that they were built using seasonal labour? Thousands of Egyptians working the Nile in the summer who didn't have any work in winter. Floated the stones down the Nile.' She shook her head. 'Of course it's not.' Then she leaned back against the morgue's wall, cushioning herself with her buttocks. 'I put time of death at between nine p.m. and ten p.m. last night.'

'We found him at half past ten this morning.' Vicky swallowed hard. 'Twelve hours.'

'Doesn't bear thinking about.' Arbuthnott chuckled. 'I'd hate to die alone. At least one of my five kids should see me right.'

'Right.' Vicky paced round the other side of the table and stared into Scott's eyes. His left wrist was scarred where the handcuffs had been. 'So, he was cuffed to the treadmill and died of a heart attack. How do you force someone to run?'

'Like this.' Arbuthnott rolled Scott onto his side and slammed him on his front with a strength belying her figure. Then she caressed his back like a shiatsu masseur. 'See these?'

Thick lumps lined Scott's left hip, like bone ridges. Some on the other side, but much smaller.

'Is that bone?'

Arbuthnott frowned. 'Do *you* think the pyramids were built by seasonal labour?'

Vicky couldn't take her eyes off the present mystery. 'Is that bone?'

'I just can't believe it.'

'I'll get Andrew to send you some YouTube links.' Vicky hovered her finger over the lump. 'For the third time, is this bone?'

'Muscle spasms.'

'Muscle spasms?'

'Quite. Flummoxed me for a bit until I realised what we're dealing with. He died with these, they didn't stop spasming, and when my old friend rigor mortis set in, well. What you see is what you get. A Taser set in drive-stun mode.' Arbuthnott pointed an imaginary device in the air and made a rumbling noise. 'And applied with some force, I should add.' She frowned. 'I didn't know this until twenty minutes ago, but drive-stun mode is—'

'—when the Taser is used without the cartridge, so the electrodes don't fire.' Vicky crouched down to level with Scott's back. 'Makes it just like a cattle prod.'

Arbuthnott pouted, disappointed her womansplaining was ruined. 'Well, you're quite the expert.'

'Our first case involved a Taser in drive-stun mode. No injuries like this, though.'

'Well.' Arbuthnott brightened. 'What appears to have happened is said Taser was held up to the body and repeatedly sparked.'

'Meaning?'

'Meaning, Sergeant, that we can deduce that Mr Scott had been running under extreme duress, to the point where he suffered a coronary.'

'Back to the heart attack. Back to murder.'

'Quite. But someone forced it on him.' Arbuthnott walked off, shaking her head. 'Floating the blocks down the Nile. As if.'

∽

'Michael Scott is a good man.' Willis Stewart rubbed his fingers together. His office was glowing in the afternoon sunshine. The photo of the Kingsway store was missing from the wall, like the shame of the attack was the fault of the building. 'I can't believe he's dead. Jesus.'

'We're treating it as murder.' Vicky let the word sink in for a few seconds. 'We believe it's connected—'

'You think everything's connected. Just because I received a note doesn't mean—'

'What happened to Mr Ramsay and Mr Christie is directly connected to that note. You were warned. There are videos of Mr Ramsay's torture online.'

Stewart looked away, wilting under the heat of her glare. 'That's no proof.'

'You knew that Mr Ramsay was convicted of animal cruelty, didn't you?'

'That's preposterous.' Still couldn't look at her. 'It's all above board.'

'Kyle Ramsay's real name is Douglas Scott.'

'What?'

'He's Michael Scott's brother.' Vicky didn't like herself for it, but she felt a tingle of joy at getting one over on Stewart. 'His company was owned by Michael. They tricked you.'

'I refuse to—'

The office door thunked open. A teenage boy stood to attention, hands behind his back, legs square. Fourteen, fifteen. A mess of acne, bumfluff and hormones. A shock of thick hair crawled across his face, almost hiding his eyes. Almost. They widened as he took in Vicky. Then back at his father. 'Daddy, I need—'

'Calum, I'm busy.' Stewart sat up ramrod straight and waved his son away. 'Can you go and see your mother. Isn't she with you?'

'Of course.' Calum looked over at Vicky and smiled, but his focus was on her chest. 'I'll see you later, Daddy.' And he was gone.

Filthy little bastard. Male gaze, indeed.

Vicky turned back to Stewart. 'Douglas Scott AKA Kyle Ramsay changed his name and used his brother to hoodwink you.'

'I... Well.' Stewart looked out of his office window towards the Kingsway. 'Used to own a greyhound Micky trained. A bitch. Champion for a year, then it started running in lame. Micky said he'd... get rid of her for me.'

Vicky's gut burned. 'And did he?'

'I *owned* that dog, she was mine.' Stewart's eyebrows flew up, heading to the same trajectory as his hairline. 'So I took her in. Made a great pet for ten years. Until, well.' His Adam's apple bobbed. 'She passed on.'

'I'm sorry to hear that.'

Stewart's cheek throbbed. 'Sergeant, are you just here to upset me or is there some point to this visit?'

'I just wanted you to know the truth. Maybe get some closure on why your store has been targeted.'

Stewart's mouth hung open. 'Oh. Well. Thanks. I appreciate it.'

VICKY PAID for her cheese and tomato sandwich. *Can't face any meat. Or poultry. Or fish.* She looked around the canteen, hoping for a seat on her own.

Wait. Is that Andrew?

She walked over with a smirk on her face and gripped his shoulder with her free hand. 'Andrew Dodds, come with me.'

His hands shot up to his chest and his tablet clattered off the table. 'Jesus, Vicks.' He let out a deep breath. 'Thought it was—'

'Should've seen your face.' She looked at the pile of stuff next to him — a plastic sandwich tub, folded-up crisp packet, squashed can of WakeyWakey. 'Mind if I join you?'

Still panting, Andrew pushed his stuff to the side. 'Mum made my lunch.'

Vicky sat opposite and tore open her sandwich wrapper. 'Even packs energy drinks, does she?'

'Keep quiet about that.'

'Maybe.' Vicky tapped the can. 'You know what Mum'll say, don't you?'

'Yeah, "You'll take bad, Andrew Dodds, just you mark my words."'

'Glad she can focus on someone else's failings for once.' Vicky grinned, pointing at his shirt and tie. 'You been in court today or something?'

'It's your fault I'm in. Your bloody Airwave messages.'

'Oh. Ogilvie?'

'Who?'

'The Complaints? Professional Standards and Ethics or whatever they're called this week?'

'Why would they be after me?' Andrew scowled at her, oblivious of the investigation into him. 'Jenny got me in. She's working me like a bastard. I'm shattered.'

'There's really nobody else?'

'I know.' Andrew cracked his knuckles. 'I'm the best at what I do.'

Vicky laughed. 'Is that so?' She started on the second half of her sandwich. 'Look, the Complaints are investigating you. Interviewed me this morning about these bloody messages I'm getting on my Airwave.'

'That's what Jenny's got me looking at. Why are they investigating me?'

'Because you're the best at what you do?'

'Funny.' Didn't look like it was. 'Oh, your name came up this morning.'

Vicky took another bite of sandwich. 'What have I done now?'

'Undercover guy. Andy Salewicz or something.'

'He's not going to be undercover for long at this rate.' Vicky chewed slowly. 'What was he after?'

'The Tetra scanner, what else? Checking to see if this commune up in the glens are using it.'

Superb...

Cheeky bastard didn't mention it to me.

'And are they?'

'Can't tell.'

'Thought you were the best at what you do?'

'It's not that simple. These guys don't want to be found.'

'Are you okay?'

'Like I said, I'm absolutely knackered, but it's good to be working again. I'm at an ME doctor all day, if you must know.

'We should get lunch one day.'

'This *is* lunch.'

'No, a proper lunch. With forks and knives and manners.'

He laughed then forced a burp. 'Have to teach me some.'

VICKY PUT two ibuprofen in her hand, swallowing them with a single glug of Diet Coke. She took in the evening skyline, street-lights and tail lights pointing west to the sun setting over Perth and its surrounding hills, a warm, golden glow taking the edge off her sour mood. She walked back to her desk, but Forrester was sitting on it talking to MacDonald. Just Considine and Zoey in the office, everyone else out.

'I don't know.' Forrester blew a long breath through puffed up cheeks. 'It's the fact nobody's taking credit. Why?'

'It's a new group.' Vicky sat between them. 'That right, Mac?'

'MO doesn't match any known group, that's for sure.' MacDonald perched against his desk. 'Trouble is, Raven didn't get to fob this off on the NCA. So we're lumbered with it.'

'Fantastic.' Forrester let out a breath and returned his attention to Vicky. 'We're getting nowhere out in Montrose. Square root of bugger all. Raven was asking what searching we've done for this car.'

'We've been doing nothing but.' Vicky kicked the desk. Least she thought it was the desk. Could've been MacDonald.

'The Three Amigos were looking into it.' MacDonald rummaged through his navy notebook. 'Got a list of everyone with a black Lexus, Mercedes, Audi or BMW saloon in Tayside, cross-referenced with being in the vicinity of Dryburgh Industrial Estate between delivery of those cages and the abduction of Paul or Rachel.'

'I'm going to regret asking this, but can you speak to all of them?'

'That's over a hundred cars, sir. OT bill will be colossal.'

'I know, but it needs to be done.' Forrester stared into space, like he was imagining ways to hide the bill from Raven. 'What about the press side of things? Has Micky Scott been in the papers?'

'I had a look, but.' MacDonald flashed up his eyebrows. 'That theory was just a guess by Vicky, right?'

'It fits, though.'

'It *did*. Doesn't look like—'

'Sorry, Mac.' Considine swung round in his chair and got a glower for his trouble. 'Couldn't help but overhear. I just found out the SSPCA took a court action against a company called Red Mountain Racing. Michael Scott's company.'

'Oh, good Christ. What were they doing?'

Considine smirked. 'He was having his retired dogs put down instead of rehoming them. Not illegal, but it's frowned on.'

Vicky felt that spear in her gut again. Micky Scott offering to get rid of Willis Stewart's dog.

'Micky Scott isn't mentioned in the news reports.' Considine nudged Zoey. 'But if you do a quick Google . . .'

She pulled headphones out of her ears. 'What?'

MacDonald tapped her laptop. 'Google "Red Mountain Racing" for me.'

Zoey's fingers were a blur on the keyboard and trackpad. 'There.'

Her screen showed an amateur-looking page, the left side filled with an aggressive shot of a muzzled greyhound mid-race, the right with a panting dog being walked around on a lead by a small boy. Might even be a young Alec Scott.

Considine tapped at the bottom of the screen. 'Name and address there, see?'

MacDonald exhaled. 'What does that tell us?'

Considine scratched his scalp. 'They're still targeting people they find in the news?'

Vicky massaged her neck — it felt like the ibuprofen was finally helping.

Zoey was nodding to herself, one hand toying with her headphones while the other fiddled with her laptop. 'You guys might want to look at this.' She dragged a window from her laptop screen to the monitor on her desk. 'My guy in the Met's been monitoring the account that posted the earlier video. It's just uploaded this.'

A YouTube page, the video already playing in black. The screen lightened, revealing a figure running on a treadmill. A man, thin and athletic, his gait hobbling on the left.

Vicky leaned forward to get a better look. 'Looks like Micky Scott.'

MacDonald nodded.

A male voice called out from behind the camera, deep and distorted. 'Keep up!'

A spark of light flashed in front of the camera.

Micky Scott ran faster, trying to put distance between himself and the device.

A hand reached over and adjusted the controls. 'Come on, boy! Faster, boy, faster!'

Vicky got a flash of the lumps on Micky Scott's back as the Taser dug in and sparked again. She tapped at the screen. 'That's a Taser.'

Forrester frowned at MacDonald. 'How are you progressing with the "Taser as MO" angle?'

'Nothing so far, sir. One guy in Birmingham with previous, but he's currently inside for armed robbery with a normal gun.'

Onscreen, Scott fell to his knees, clutching his chest. The treadmill kept going, dragging him down, his left hand remaining in place, held firm by the handcuffs as the belt kept turning round.

The sound cut and the camera moved to Scott's body lying on the floor. The image froze and text bounced in.

DOG RACING IS MURDER.

OFFICIALLY, 9,000 GREYHOUNDS A YEAR RETIRE FROM
RACING.
UNOFFICIALLY, 40,000 ARE DROWNED, SHOT OR BEATEN TO
DEATH WHEN THEY DON'T MAKE THE GRADE.
MICKY SCOTT DID THIS TO OVER 500 DOGS.
DOESN'T LOOK LIKE HE MADE THE GRADE, DOES IT?

27

'Hey, sis.' Andrew leaned back in his office chair, sipping another can of WakeyWakey. He grinned at Zoey, skulking next to Vicky. 'Ms Jones, you really should marry me.'

Zoey hid behind her fringe and held out her engagement ring. 'I'm spoken for?'

'A damn shame.' Andrew switched his smile to his sister. 'So, Vicks, what brings you down here?'

'You know.' Vicky rested on the edge of his desk. 'The IP addresses Zoey just sent you.'

'You know I like a mystery in my life.' Andrew looked at his screen, his fingers a blur on the keyboard.

'Like Shirley Arbuthnott?'

Andrew stopped dead. 'Who?' He didn't make eye contact.

'The pathologist. Told me you were telling her about your pyramid theory.'

'It's not a theory.' Andrew gasped. 'And besides, she thinks it was *aliens*.' He started hammering the keyboard again. After a grunt, he clicked the mouse and pointed at the screen. 'Okay, so I've been looking at these YouTube links Zoey sent me. The first one we know was posted by one Brian Morton. You need this urgently, because—'

'We found a body this morning. A greyhound trainer. We think it's connected.'

'Okay.' Andrew screwed up his face like something off a shit sitcom. 'Anyway. The second and third ones... Man, that's some brutal stuff. And I worked the kiddie porn shift for three years. The IP addresses are nonsense. Whoever's doing this is *good*.'

Zoey tutted. 'That's where I got to.'

'Well, snap. Means we're stuck.'

Vicky let out a slow sigh. 'Thought you were the best at what you do?'

'Don't use my words against me, Vicks. I'm an ill man.'

Zoey frowned. 'What's up with you?'

'Nothing. I'm quite a catch, I'll have you know.'

'Bet you are.' Zoey turned to Vicky, brushing her hair out of her eye. 'See, I told you he couldn't help.' She started walking off.

'Wait!' Andrew waved his hands at them. 'I'm just...' He was back at the keyboard. 'This is a shot in the dark but it might just— I AM INVINCIBLE!' He shot to his feet and punched the air. Then slumped back in his seat, wheezing. 'Shit.'

Zoey was ignoring him, all her attention on the screen. 'Are you okay?'

'I'm perfect. Your greyhound trainer video. I've traced it to an IP address.' Andrew ran his finger down the list. 'Bam, there we go. Does this name mean anything to you?'

MARIANNE SMITH STOOD in the middle of the Living Garden giving a talk to a group of teenage schoolchildren. She stopped talking as Vicky approached, clearly vexed but putting on a smile for her audience. 'Can you all take a five-minute break?' She checked her watch. 'Back here at three thirty.'

The group dispersed, three of the nearest kids retrieving smartphones from their bags, eyes instantly lit up by the screens. Amazingly, none of them bumped into Vicky or Considine.

'Sergeant.' Marianne's jaw clenched as she looked at the flanking uniformed officers. 'How can I help today?'

'Just a few questions.'

'I'm in the middle of something.' Marianne folded her arms, glancing at her students. 'You can have five minutes.'

'We'll need longer than that, I'm afraid.'

Marianne settled her gaze on Vicky. 'What's this about?'

'We need to do this in a police station.'

'Please, can you come back later?'

'Ms Smith, I need you to accompany us to the station.'

'And if I refuse?'

'I'll arrest you.'

Marianne remained silent as her gaze bounced between the two police officers.

Considine stepped forward. 'Ms Smith, can you come with me, please?'

Marianne took a deep breath. 'I need to arrange for a colleague to finish the talk.'

VICKY CLEARED her throat and glanced at Considine, sitting beside her, writing every word in his grey notebook. 'Ms Smith, can you account for your movements this morning?'

Marianne glanced at Nelson-Caird, who motioned for her to reply. She scratched at the desk with a fingernail, her breathing fast. 'I was at work.'

'When did you leave home?'

'Em, about ten. I travel late to avoid the traffic. I was doing some preparation for the class I was teaching when you so rudely interrupted me.'

'Can anyone confirm this?'

Marianne shook her head. 'I live alone.'

'So, you were in your house all morning?'

'Until I left, yes.'

'Okay, well that fits with what we know.' Vicky waited for Marianne to narrow her eyes. 'Someone posted some videos on the internet showing certain criminal actions perpetrated over the last few days. We've tracked them back to your internet account.' She showed a print. 'Do you deny posting this video?'

Marianne scanned the page. 'Of course I deny it.'

'How do you explain it tracing to your home address?'

'My client has answered the question.' Kelly Nelson-Caird sat back in her chair next to Marianne Smith, furiously gesticulating as she spoke. 'It wasn't her.'

Vicky pushed a sheet across the desk, visible to both Marianne and Nelson-Caird. 'Our tech department traced that user to an IP address, which led us to a Virgin Media account in Cupar.' She pointed to a highlighted section. 'This is your home address and landline number, right?'

Marianne swallowed. 'That doesn't mean anything.'

'But it's yours?'

Nelson-Caird narrowed her eyes at Vicky. 'Move on.'

Vicky leaned back in her chair. 'What did you do yesterday?'

'I was working.'

'And not at home?'

'Correct.' Marianne brushed her eyes with her thumbs. 'I was there from lunchtime until just after ten.'

Tallied with the timeline. 'You got home at ten o'clock then posted a video relating to the abduction of one Kyle Ramsay, AKA Douglas Scott.'

'This is—'

'Sergeant.' Nelson-Caird bobbed forward on her chair, all righteous indignation. 'My client has been more than helpful. I suggest that you let her go?'

Vicky pushed another sheet in front of them. 'Ms Smith, we're investigating the murder of one Michael Scott, a greyhound trainer who lived near Montrose.' She tapped the page. 'This video showed his death. Someone murdered him at nine o'clock last night.'

Marianne glanced at her lawyer then gave a shrug. 'You can check with my admin manager at the Hutton Institute. Otherwise, you can have my mobile phone and see where I was.'

Vicky kept staring at Marianne. 'Were you involved in what happened to him?'

'I've never even been to Montrose.'

'But you know people who'd like to cause harm to a greyhound trainer?'

'Lots of people. I don't know anyone who'd actually carry it out, though.'

'A video of his death was posted today.' Vicky exhaled slowly. 'Ms Smith, you posted it, didn't you?'

'Sergeant.' The corners of Marianne's lips curled up in a saccharine smile. 'Much as I'd dearly love to assist you in your investigations, I'm afraid I'm not involved.'

FORRESTER WAS in the observation suite next to the interview room. 'In here.'

Vicky followed him in and leaned against the far wall, watching Marianne and Nelson-Caird whisper in each other's ears on the screen. 'I take it you watched that?'

'Oh, aye.' Forrester creaked back in his chair, drumming his fingers on the table, eyes on MacDonald. 'I'm trying not to read too much into her having the same lawyer as Brian Morton.' He stopped the drumming and cracked his knuckles instead. 'What's your next play?'

'She posted that video. We can arrest her. Then we can search her property. I expect we'll find sufficient evidence to convict.'

Forrester exhaled slowly. 'Right-o.' He put his feet on the desk. 'You really think she's the criminal genius behind all this?'

'She's got a connection to Rachel Hay.'

'I remember.' Forrester wasn't buying it, though. 'You seriously think we can sell her dogs wrecking that garden as a motive?'

'It's a connection, I didn't say it was a motive. Could've just put her on her radar.' Vicky couldn't stay in the same place for too long. 'Sir, we've got witness statements for three people directly involved in these cases. One of the assailants is a woman.'

'Is that enough, though? A woman did it, the end?'

'It's a start. We can do her for posting that video.'

'We've not done Brian Morton for the first one.'

'Because we don't think he's a perpetrator.'

Forrester rocked forward in his chair. 'Who do we—'

Considine rapped on the door. 'Sorry to interrupt, sir, but DS MacDonald asked me to do a background check on Marianne Smith?'

Forrester beckoned him in. 'Go on.'

Considine shut the door behind him. 'This is just preliminary stuff, sir, but apparently she's a bit of an agitator. Been moved on from protesting down the Murraygate on a Saturday afternoon a couple of times, handing out flyers, collecting signatures, shouting on a megaphone. And the NCA have a file on her. Won't give it to me.'

'Right-o.' Forrester gazed at a spot over their heads for a moment, then nodded. 'This is promising. I'll get on to the NCA and see if they'll pass this file to me.' He glanced at Vicky. 'Sergeant, do what you need to.'

VICKY TOOK A DEEP BREATH. 'Marianne Smith, I'm arresting you under sections one and two of the Terrorism Act 2006, namely "Encouragement of terrorism" and "Disseminating terrorist publications". You are not obliged to say anything, but anything you do say will be noted and may be used in evidence. Do you understand?'

Marianne shook her head. 'No, I don't.'

'Ms Smith, do you understand the fact you're being cautioned?'

'I do.'

'Do you have anything to say?'

Marianne slumped in her chair. 'I made those comments.' She shrugged. 'I'm involved in animal rights groups. So what? It's not a crime.'

'People have been harmed in the execution of these acts. Micky Scott *died*.'

'Are these people innocent?'

'Are you a judge or just the executioner? Did you attack Rachel Hay because she's a dog breeder? Or Graeme Hunter because of his hens? Did you make Micky Scott have a heart attack?'

'I had absolutely nothing to do with what happened to them.'

'You're denying your involvement?'

Marianne puckered her lips. 'Sergeant, as you yourself stated, I have the right to silence.'

~

MacDonald yawned. 'Shattered.'

Vicky looked around the room. A bundle of Fifer uniforms were tearing into anything they could find and not taking great care about where it was supposed to be returned.

Not that there was much order to the place. Marianne Smith's house was a big bookcase. Even the bedroom was filled with them. Political textbooks, mainly. Nothing out of the ordinary. Well, so far. Ten biographies of Margaret Thatcher, though?

She opened a desk drawer and peered inside. Nothing. She shut the drawer. It wobbled. She eased it out again, then pressed it. Something rattled and it clunked to the floor. She knelt down and reached her gloved hand inside. A hessian sack lay in a secret compartment. She took it out.

'What the hell is that?' MacDonald was on his knees in front of her. Looked like he was trying to put a ring on it.

Vicky eased the bag around a bundle of books.

MacDonald reached over and took the top one. 'What the hell is this? "When They Give Up Their Right to Life: How to Stop Abortion Before It Starts".' He flicked through it. 'How to firebomb an abortion clinic without getting caught.'

Vicky looked through the rest. 'Not just American domestic terror. Got some animal rights groups here. Real nasty stuff.'

MacDonald held up a book with a KKK member in full white garb, arm raised in a Nazi salute. "Blood And Soil: Take back the Homeland". Something flapped out of it and he picked it up. Couldn't stop himself grinning. 'One of the schoolgirls you spoke to in Cupar reckoned someone tried to recruit her to some group. Right?' He held out a leaflet. 'Was it like this?'

Vicky checked it. A diatribe against pugs and their breeders. Links to a dark net TOR address. 'It's a match.'

'Looks like she's been handing them out.' MacDonald held up a bunch of them. 'We can get her for this.'

Marianne Smith cowered next to her lawyer, eyes red, deep bags underneath them. 'So, can I go?'

MacDonald leaned across the table. 'Ms Smith, we have just completed a search of your house.'

Marianne stared at her lawyer. 'Can they do that?' She got a nod from her lawyer, Kelly Nelson-Caird.

'Very interesting.' MacDonald produced a ream of paper in a large evidence bag and tapped the sheet. 'Some paper stock matching the notes found at the crime scenes.'

Marianne blinked. 'But that's just paper.'

'Quite unusual paper, though. Just a single supplier in the Tayside area, and it's not available for general sale on the internet.'

'This is inadmissible as direct evidence against my client.' Nelson-Caird wagged a finger at him. 'Unless you can demonstrate these notes came from *her* supply of paper, you—'

'Care to explain these?' MacDonald produced a stack of books, all bound in evidence bags. 'These all concern domestic terror.'

'My doctoral thesis was on domestic terror in Ireland, Spain and Germany in the seventies.' Marianne swallowed. 'I like to keep up to date on the topic.'

'These ones don't appear to have anything to do with the IRA,

ETA or Baader-Meinhof.' MacDonald picked up a book and inspected the cover. 'They *do* have detailed analyses of methods used in issue-specific terrorism. You name it. Actions against abortion clinics or vivisectionists in America. Completely unrelated to nationalist or communist groups.'

'No comment.'

'Did you abduct Mrs Rachel Hay from near your place of work and lock her in a steel cage in a unit on the Dryburgh Industrial Estate in Dundee?'

'No comment.'

'Did you abduct Mr Paul Joyce and lock him in a steel cage in a unit on the Dryburgh Industrial Estate in Dundee?'

'No comment.'

'Did you attempt to force Mrs Hay and Mr Joyce to have sexual intercourse while locked in said cage?'

Nelson-Caird's nostrils twitched as her gaze shifted to her client.

Marianne rubbed her eyes, tears welling up. 'No comment.'

'Did you record this act with a video camera and subsequently post the video online?'

Marianne closed her eyes, then blinked away a few tears and stared at the ceiling. 'No comment.'

'Ms Smith, did you break into Hunter's Farm in Barry and forcibly lock Mr Graeme Hunter, Mrs Rhona Hunter, Miss Amelie Hunter and Miss Grace Hunter in a steel cage?'

Tears slid down Marianne's face. 'No comment.'

'Ms Smith, did you forcibly apply a hot knife machine to Mr Hunter's nose?'

'My God.' Marianne tugged at the collar of her T-shirt, eyes wide. 'No comment.'

'Ms Smith, do you know one Brian Morton of Ann Street, Hilltown, Dundee?'

'No comment.'

Nelson-Caird tapped her thumb on the table top. 'Mr Morton is also a client of mine.'

'I'm aware of that. I haven't made any comment on the fact you represent two suspects in the same case.'

'Do you really wish to have that on the record, Sergeant?'

Vicky folded her arms. 'Do you?'

'My firm has a wide range of clients. Some are fee-paying, like Ms Smith here, while others are legal aid, like Mr Morton. My client base isn't pertinent to your investigation.'

'We'll see.' MacDonald adjusted his tie. 'Ms Smith, we've now had two threats made by your group, both relating to these birds. One crime's already been committed. Does it have to be mass murder before you'll help us?'

Marianne glanced at Nelson-Caird. 'No comment.'

MacDonald patted his giant file, eyes locked on Marianne. 'You know that we're investigating your involvement in these crimes.' He passed Nelson-Caird the statement. 'This is from a schoolgirl in Cupar.'

The remaining energy drained out of Marianne. Her eyes went dead, her skin pallid. She nodded.

'She told us someone tried to get her to join a group. It was you, wasn't it?' MacDonald didn't get a reply. He put his copy down on the table. 'What group is this?'

'I don't know what she's talking about.' Marianne's voice was barely a whisper. 'Children... They get fantasies in their heads, don't they?'

'Fantasies about marrying that bloke from One Direction? Maybe.' MacDonald's grin darkened. His ears twitched. 'Fantasies about being recruited to terrorist groups in Fife? Bit more difficult to make that up, wouldn't you agree?'

'That's a *lie*.'

'There's a terrorist group perpetrating acts against known animal welfare abusers. That wouldn't be the same group, would it?'

'No comment.'

'You're under caution. This is your chance to clear yourself. Gone are the days when silence was the voice of innocence.'

She bristled at the literary taunt. 'Do you know what I'm going through? I'm still detained without charge.'

'You've been cautioned.'

'Because I had some books in my home?'

'Those books aren't the sort you can buy with One-Click on Amazon, are they? You have to be in the inner circle.'

'I've spoken to Gemma at numerous events in Cupar.' Marianne lowered her gaze. 'She's a lovely girl, but I swear I never tried to recruit her.'

'Meaning you've tried to recruit other people?'

'No! There's no group!'

'Now, now, no need to shout.' MacDonald leaned back in his chair. 'We've got a series of crimes committed against people with a public record of animal cruelty. Somehow, it went from three suspects to two. Bit of a coincidence, isn't it?'

Marianne snorted. 'You're clutching at straws.'

Nelson-Caird leaned across the desk. 'I suggest you alter your line of inquiry, Sergeant.'

MacDonald opened the file in front of him, casually flicking through the pages. 'Are you involved in any animal rights groups, any at all?'

'No.'

MacDonald pushed a sheet across the table. 'This is heavily redacted, of course, but it clearly shows your membership in several nasty groups.' He dropped the file on the table. 'This is a serious crime, Ms Smith. You're in over your head, aren't you?'

Marianne smacked her open hand on the table. 'I've got no sympathy with any of the victims.'

28

Vicky led MacDonald along the corridor, her brain still reeling. 'You think it's her?'

MacDonald took a final sip of coffee and scowled. 'Got to be. We just don't know who she's doing it with.'

'What about her and the Muirheads?'

MacDonald rubbed his chin. 'They've got alibis, though.'

'People lie.'

'Don't they just.' MacDonald set his cup down on the window sill, grinning. 'Well, they fit the description. You think the androgynous person could be Polly Muirhead?'

Vicky looked back down the corridor towards the interview room. 'She's tall and not particularly curvy.'

MacDonald's eyes swarmed over Vicky's body. 'Certainly fits the bill.' Then they pierced her eyes. 'So, how's about that drink once we've finished up tonight?'

Someone approached from behind, a ragged military march. Squeezed Vicky's shoulder and punched MacDonald on the arm. Forrester, grinning. 'I'll join you. We've just charged Marianne Smith. Time for a wee celebration.'

~

VICKY RESTED her head on the back of the booth, watching MacDonald ease through the crowded Old Bank Bar to the toilet.

Forrester was fiddling with his mobile.

Vicky took a sip of Bacardi and Coke. *Tastes like a bloody double...* 'What do you think of MacDonald?'

'What do I think?' Forrester took a sip of whisky then puckered his lips, still focused on his phone. 'Well, I hope we've not got another cowboy on our hands.'

'I doubt he's as bad as Ennis.'

'Tell you Vicky, him going off on the sick meant I didn't have to sack him. Had a few meetings with Raven about it.'

'Sure you should be telling me this?'

'I know I can trust you.' Forrester looked around the pub. 'Can't figure out who told Ennis he was on borrowed time and made him get a sick note. Stress, I tell you...'

MacDonald was snaking his way to the bar. The large clock hanging over him read quarter to eight.

Vicky clenched her jaw. 'Shite, is that the time?

Forrester grinned at her. 'You going to turn into a pumpkin or something?'

She grabbed her phone and pushed her way through the pub, already dialling Robert's number.

'Hello?'

'Robert, it's Vicky.' She joined the smokers on Reform Street, the long street bookended by the McManus Gallery at one end and the Caird Hall at the other. Both lit up, pretty much all Dundee had going for it.

Half an hour and I could be back in Carnoustie. Eating Robert's food, drinking his wine.

The man who might be involved in this.

Through the window, MacDonald was putting more drinks on the table. He caught her eye and raised a fresh glass with a smile.

I need to keep a distance.

She swallowed hard, tried to smile, tried to make it sound convincing. 'Look, something's come up at work. Sorry, but I have to bail.'

'Oh.' Robert left a long pause. 'I saw something on the news. Are you involved in that?'

'Afraid so.' Vicky locked eyes with a woman roughly her age, tarted up for a Monday night out on the town. 'Thought I'd still be able to make it, but I've got to interview a suspect and—'

'I understand. I'll stick the casserole in the fridge. Give me a call when you're on your way.'

Vicky felt herself blush. 'It'll be tomorrow.'

'Oh, okay. Good luck, then.'

Vicky killed the call and leaned back against the wall.

That felt harder than it should.

'You've got some style, honey.' The nearest smoker nudged an elbow into Vicky's arm, her chubby face encased in make-up. 'Blowing him off like that.'

Vicky vaguely recognised her from an adjacent table. 'Excuse me?'

'Lying to your husband like that.' She blew out a cloud of smoke and nodded through the window. MacDonald was laughing at Forrester's joke. 'You letting Mr Right there into your knickers tonight?'

Vicky gave her a polite smile. 'Naturally.'

'Damn. Had my eyes on him. Nice arse.'

Vicky chuckled as she went back inside then dumped her phone in her handbag as she sat.

MacDonald nodded at her bag. 'Who were you on the phone to?'

'A friend. Where's Forrester?'

'Toilet.'

MacDonald handed her a glass, dark liquid fizzing around the ice cubes. 'Here you go.'

Vicky emptied her previous drink. 'I *was* going to head home.' She wrapped her hands around the new one. 'Course, now I'll have to get the bus. But the night's still young.'

'Even though we have work tomorrow?' MacDonald took a sip of beer and finished his glass. He pushed it over to touch Vicky's. 'Dundee used to have one or two decent clubs, right?'

'Euan, it's a Monday.'

'The Mardi still open?'

'Long gone. Not that it was decent.'

'The Mardi Gras.' MacDonald laughed as he reached for his fresh pint. 'Been there a few times.'

'I forgot you were from around these parts.'

'The accent, right?'

'Right.' Vicky took a sip from her new drink. *Definitely a double.* 'I used to go out dancing but that was before...'

'Before what?'

Vicky coughed. 'Before I became a DS.'

'I know the feeling. Trying to show you're mature, set an example.' MacDonald took a long drink. 'Bet you looked good on the dance floor, though.'

Forrester bumped down on the bench with a deep sigh. 'Bloody carnage in there. Smells like an open sewer.' He sank his fresh whisky in one go. 'Right, I need to get home.' He got to his feet, fighting his suit jacket, and gave an exaggerated wink. 'RED PANTY NIGHT! Now, you pair better follow my example, okay?' He frowned. 'Not about the knickers. I mean about clearing off. In at eight tomorrow. Strong coffee and breath mints, am I clear?'

'Right.' MacDonald watched Forrester trundle out of the bar. He took a sip from his pint. 'So?'

Vicky's turn to avoid his eye. She glanced at the food menu on the table. 'I'm starving.'

'Me too. Trouble is, the kitchen shut early.'

Vicky finished her drink and bounced to her feet. 'Come on, then.' She sashayed out of the bar into the cool night air, MacDonald hot on her heels. In amongst the smoke, she got a waft of MacDonald's namesake's burgers and chips.

The smoker from earlier was still out, sucking hard on another cigarette. She winked as they passed.

Vicky looked up and down Reform Street, then did a one-eighty and stared at Dundee High, its brightly lit pillars beckoning them to the end of the street. Near the clubs.

'Fancy a curry, Vicky?'

'Let's get something a bit more Dundee.' She set off towards the lights, rubbing her hands together. 'Chips, cheese and coleslaw.'

He laughed. 'Peak Dundee.'

'There's a good place on Panmure Street.' Vicky glanced at the back of the McManus Galleries. 'I saw someone eating a mince roll last week.'

'A *mince roll*?'

'My dad used to have a Scotch pie on a roll. Ate the pastry off the top and the bottom, then stuck it on a buttered morning roll and smeared it with tomato ketchup.'

MacDonald nodded slowly. 'Sounds less like a meal than a father-daughter bonding experience, right?'

Vicky's heart jumped. He was the first one she'd ever told that story to who actually got the point. She wrapped her arms around her waist, bracing herself against the cold. 'Freezing.'

MacDonald smirked. 'Zoey did say you're a cold bitch.'

Vicky shrugged. 'I kind of am.'

He laughed, then turned and looked her right in the eyes. 'Doesn't bother you?'

'The downside of being a sergeant.'

'Tell me about it.' MacDonald buttoned up his suit jacket. 'Wonder what they think of me.'

She choked. 'They call you "Big Time Charlie".'

'Doesn't surprise me.' MacDonald smiled. He stepped forward and kissed her gently on the lips. As he pulled away again she locked her eyes on his, then tilted her head to the side and leaned forward, ever so slowly, until her mouth connected with his. He raised his arms, pulled her into a warm embrace, hands on her arse, his tongue exploring—

'Get stuck in there, son!'

They broke off, Vicky stepping back, away from him and his tongue and hands and fingers.

A group of lads in rugby shirts walked along the street, clapping and whistling at them.

What the hell am I doing? Vicky stared at the pavement. 'I need to go.' She flagged down a passing taxi.

MacDonald frowned. 'See you tomorrow?'

'Of course.' Vicky got in the cab, hauling the door shut before she could change her mind and do something that would hurt even more than the pending hangover. 'Carnoustie.'

The driver rubbed his hands together as he set off. 'It's my lucky night.'

Vicky slumped back in the seat, finding little comfort in the knowledge that there was at least one man she was making happy tonight.

'THAT YOU AWAKE, PRINCESS?'

Vicky woke up bleary-eyed, the rumble of the taxi going right up her spine. Took her a few seconds to recognise Monifieth passing through the window, the Tesco set back from the road, then that little square that used to have the video shop on it. Tempting to get the driver to stop for chips. She sat up and rubbed the sleep from her eyes. The cheeky bastard had taken the low road — must've seen her fall asleep when they were still in Dundee and decided to get a few extra quid out of his lucky night.

Her tongue stuck to the roof of her mouth.

MacDonald...

Did I really kiss him?

Shit, shit, shit.

Should've gone to Robert's. Only he was involved in the case, wasn't he? I need to have it out with him. Sort this out.

'Shit, shit, shit.'

'You all right back there, princess? Fifty quid if you chuck up.'

'I'm fine.' Vicky took a deep breath. 'Can you drop me at Corbie Drive?'

'Won't save you anything.'

'I know that.'

The driver took a left at the new roundabout and trundled along the old main road through Barry. He turned into Corbie Drive, boxy grey houses and their triangular roofs. 'Twenty quid, princess.'

Vicky handed him the money. 'Have a good night.' As she got out, the cold air hit her hard. She started shivering. Rubbing her arms, she tottered into Karen's cul-de-sac.

Sorry, Robert, I didn't get held up at work. And I got off with my colleague. Are you involved in this case?

Karen's house was at the end, the lights on, the telly flickering in the corner. Robert lived next door, shared a drive with Karen.

Vicky stopped dead.

In Robert's drive was a black Audi saloon.

DAY 6

Tuesday
5th April 2016

29

The briefing was already underway, so Vicky skulked around the back of the Incident Room, hoping not to be noticed. She perched on the edge of a desk, the corner needling her thigh through her trousers.

Considine was just next to her. He leaned over and whispered in her ear. 'You're late.'

She glared at him. 'Do as I say, not as I do.'

At the front, Forrester locked eyes with her, his jaw crunching through some mints. Then he was off, jabbing a finger on the whiteboard. 'Moving swiftly on, we've got the forensics back from Hunter's Farm. We found a hair in the barn of the battery hen farm where the family were trapped. Unfortunately, the DNA doesn't match anything we've got on record, including Marianne Smith.'

MacDonald was next to him, forehead knitted tight, avoiding looking anywhere near Vicky. 'What about Polly Muirhead?'

'Since we haven't arrested her, Sergeant, we don't have her DNA on record.'

MacDonald took a sip of coffee through the lid. 'Right.'

'Okay, let's wrap this up.' Forrester looked around the room. 'The violent lengths these animal rights activists are prepared to go to are escalating. I want us to do everything we can to catch them before they strike again.' He took a deep breath. 'We can do it. Okay?'

The room exploded with white noise. Vicky stood up slowly.

Considine leaned in to her. 'You and Big Time Charlie, eh?'

Vicky panicked. Her gaze shooting across the room to MacDonald. He was heading her way. 'What do you mean?'

'Investigating the Muirheads today. Honestly think they're—'

'I'll see you later.' Vicky shot off through the sea of bodies in the opposite direction but hardly managed three steps before she bumped into someone.

Karen wasn't letting her past. 'Christ, Vicks, you look like you need a breakfast.'

'YOUR CAR WAS HERE when I got in?'

'Long story.' Vicky opened the door to the Auld Cludgie Café in a daze, sucking in the familiar tang of coffee and frying bacon.

'I'll get it.' Karen headed over to the counter.

'Cheers.' Vicky walked over to the window and slumped in a seat, the nerve in her neck thumping in sync with her headache.

What a mess.

The end of Reform Street.

MacDonald kissing me. Then running off.

And I'm paired with him on the job again. Shit, shit, shit.

Vicky picked up the morning's *Courier* from an adjacent table and flicked through the news. A few thousand words on Gordon Christie and Micky Scott. Two in one day.

And another photo of me at the press conference... Christ.

She piled up the empty plates on the table, pushed them to the side, the spoons chinking in the cups. Then put her head in her hands, catching her sleeve in a puddle of tea.

What the hell am I doing?

Bella's going through a serious spell of daddy issues, and now my love life is...

Why did I sleep with Robert? Did I lead him on? Is it my commitment phobia kicking in? Move on to the next shiny thing?

No, that's not me. Robert's... potentially involved. Definitely a suspect. Definitely someone I should raise on the case.

Karen sat opposite and slid a bacon roll across the table, the plate rattling. 'Butter and bacon at breaking point.'

'Perfect.' Vicky tore open a sachet of brown sauce and squirted it on the roll. She took a large bite, savouring the liquid butter mixing with the crispy bacon. 'Just. Perfect.'

'Okay, Vicks, so why was your car here?'

Vicky chewed slower, savouring it before the full inquisition started. 'I went out with Forrester and MacDonald for a drink after work last night.' She let out a shallow breath, eyes on the plate. 'Left my car here and got a taxi home. Bus in this morning.'

'You cancelled on Robert, didn't you?' Karen put her head in her hands. 'Let me guess — by text? Classy.'

'No! I phoned him.' Vicky stared into space. A draught from the door sent a shiver up her spine. She mopped up the fat from her plate with the last bit of the roll. 'Kaz, I need to—'

'Morning, ladies.' MacDonald walked past the table, raising a finger in recognition before going up to the counter to order.

'You can see why they call him Big Time Charlie.' Karen leaned across the table. 'Total wanker, right?'

Vicky blushed. 'I got off with him last night.'

Karen gawped at Vicky. 'You're a complete idiot.'

'I know.'

'Robert's a nice guy.'

'And that's the problem. I've never been one for the nice guy, have I?'

Karen looked across the café. 'I see your point...'

'I've no idea what I'm doing, Kaz.'

'Have you told MacDonald about Bella?'

Vicky's blush deepened. Must be what a hot flush feels like. 'No.'

'What about Robert?'

'He knows all about her.'

'I said you were being an idiot when you let Alan go.'

'I didn't let him go, Kaz. He pissed off and left me, three months pregnant.' She hit the table. 'He's a *worm* and I don't want him anywhere near Bella.' She wiped a tear from her eye. 'Bella's better off never knowing him.' She wiped another tear away as she glanced back at MacDonald. Now he was bantering with the barista.

Is he the sort to take in a four-year-old and her damaged mother?

With a quiet sigh, she pushed her empty plate away. 'I'm worried Robert's involved in this case.'

Karen rolled her eyes. 'Now you're getting hysterical.'

'I'm serious. You know he's into this animal welfare stuff, right? I found him on a donation list yesterday. And he's got a black Audi.'

'Are you serious?'

'You haven't noticed?'

'I hadn't thought about it, no.'

'Here's my thinking. Tell me if I'm being an idiot. First, he's been tapping me for information. You and Colin too. Almost like he's keeping an eye on the case.'

'I want to shake you.' Karen shook her fists in the air. 'As soon as a guy gets close, you run a mile.'

'I know, but...' Vicky gave her an apologetic smile. 'I should raise it in the case log, shouldn't I?'

'Christ, Vicky. Are you sure?'

'If I'm wrong, fair enough. But if I'm right?'

'I know.' Karen's slow nod was the first sign that Vicky was maybe onto something.

Vicky finished her roll in merciful silence, broken when Considine breezed past the counter, slapping MacDonald on the shoulder like they were best mates.

MacDonald wandered over to their table but stayed standing, an ambiguous smile playing on his lips. 'Morning, Vicky.'

'Euan.' She glanced at Karen. 'What's wrong with Forrester's coffee?'

'He reuses the grounds over the day.' MacDonald stared at his cup. 'It's pretty rank.'

She laughed. 'We're supposed to be checking out the Muirheads, right?'

'That we are.'

Vicky kept her eyes on Karen. Who was sticking her tongue into her cheek, pushing it in and out, in and out...

'Thing is...' MacDonald thumbed back at the counter. 'Young Considine checked their alibis.'

All MacDonald needed was the look between Vicky and Karen.

'Like that, is it?' MacDonald took a sip of coffee. 'I'll get him to recheck it, then.'

'Always wise to triple-check his work.'

'Sure thing.' MacDonald's mouth hung open. 'Em, just wondering if we—'

'Later.' Vicky grabbed her bag and left the café.

DS LAING WAS READING the paper, picking at his teeth with his pinkie. He looked up at Vicky. 'Doddsy, whatever it is, I'm busy.'

'Bollocks you are.' Vicky snatched his paper off him and tossed it in the recycling. 'I need to add a new suspect to the case log.'

Laing blew air at the ceiling, his fat lips vibrating. *Guy was allergic to work.* He leaned forward, shirt buttons straining. He clicked his pen. Could almost see the dust flashing off. 'Fire away.'

'Robert Hamilton. He appeared on the list of significant donors to the animal shelter on Brown Street.' Vicky held out a finger. 'Not the council one.'

'There were over four hundred people on that list. Including yourself. Want me to add them all?'

'Just him.'

'Got any, like, evidence?'

'He owns a black Audi saloon.'

Laing raised his eyebrows, his lined forehead creasing further, then scanned a page of notes. 'Robert Hamilton, Robert Hamilton, Robert Hamilton . . . Here we go. He's on our list of car owners. He's on for this afternoon.' He circled the name. 'Think I should bring him in sooner?'

Vicky swallowed. 'I would.'

Laing took his time making a note. 'Big Time Charlie's behind you.'

'Oh?'

MacDonald was charging towards them, his face stern.

'Cheers, Johnny.' Vicky nodded at Laing and met MacDonald by a column, keeping it between them. Nobody within earshot.

'Look, Vicky, about last—'

'Euan, we need to progress the case.'

'Right.' MacDonald frowned. 'Well. The alibis Considine supposedly checked. Like you said, full of holes. Lots of alleged phone calls and vague looks.' He opened his notebook and flicked through. 'But that's by the by, we can manage that. Sunday night is where it gets interesting. The Muirheads were at a dinner party in Broughty Ferry but left early. Half seven.'

'Wait a second.' Vicky frowned, trying to clear her head enough to visualise her timeline. 'Christie was attacked at the back of eight, wasn't he? So, they could have done it?'

'Take about five minutes that time of night.' MacDonald got out a tablet computer. 'The one that's pissed me off is last Wednesday when Rachel and Paul were taken. They were supposed to be at the Rep. Considine, to his credit, had acquired the CCTV footage. Trouble is the daft sod didn't check it.' He held up the tablet. 'Watch this.'

Vicky recognised the Rep theatre. She shrugged off memories of school trips there to see the panto, though it was all literary fantasy instead of thigh-slapping camp.

A crowd of people, chatting. In the middle, a middle-aged couple were ringed in red, staring straight at the camera. The man was heavily overweight, the woman a few rungs above him on the attractiveness ladder.

MacDonald paused the video and zoomed in. 'The couple they were meeting. Simon and Emma Hagger.'

Vicky stared at the photo, playing *Where's Wally?* with it. Couldn't see anyone remotely like the Muirheads. 'Where are they?'

'That's the thing. There's half an hour here, plus fifteen minutes of intermission. No sign of Sandy or Polly Muirhead.'

'So let's bring them in.'

MacDonald smiled. 'Sandy's already here.'

30

'That slimy creep.' Vicky checked her watch as she waited outside the interview room. 'He's getting one more minute, then...'

MacDonald looked up from his notebook. 'You dealt with Fergus Duncan before?'

'Once. Like I said, slimy creep.'

The door opened, and Fergus Duncan appeared wagging a finger at Vicky. 'A word in private, Sergeant?'

Vicky let MacDonald enter the room, leaving the door wide open. Sandy Muirhead was in there, rubbing sleep from his eyes.

Duncan ran his tongue over his lips. 'You'll be comfortable interviewing just one of my clients today, yes?'

Vicky took another look as the door shut. 'We need to speak to Mrs Muirhead as well.'

'She's in court today.'

'Get her here or I'll send a squad of uniforms over to pick her up.'

'I'll need to arrange cover.' Duncan checked his own watch. 'I'm due in court myself in an hour.'

'Didn't stop you having a lengthy meeting with your client.'

Duncan produced his mobile phone, an expensive-looking

Samsung in a bright orange case. 'I've got your Chief Constable's number on this little baby.'

'Is that supposed to be a threat?'

'One press and I'm through to his personal mobile.' Duncan's finger hovered over the touchscreen of the phone. 'We go way back.'

Vicky got in his face making him step back. 'Cancel your appointment and get Mrs Muirhead in here *immediately*.'

Duncan stared at her. When she refused to back down, he pressed a button on his phone and put it to his ear, gaze still locked on Vicky. Nodding his head, even had time to look her up and down as he killed her career. 'It's Fergus.' He barked out a laugh. 'It's about DS Vicky Dodds.'

Vicky folded her arms, her mouth dry. *Shit, shit, shit.*

Duncan looked over at Vicky, eyes narrowing. 'Polly, I need you to get down here now. I know. Soon as you can.'

What a prick...

Vicky pushed past him into the interview room, only exhaling when she sat.

MacDonald flashed up his eyebrows and mouthed, 'Tape's rolling.'

Vicky straightened her clothes, vaguely aware of Muirhead looking down her low-cut black top. *Should've worn a blouse.*

'Mrs Muirhead's on her way.' Duncan sat opposite, placing his mobile in front of him. 'And you've got the pleasure of my company for the next two hours, should it be required.'

'And what a pleasure it is.' Vicky leaned back in the chair, keeping it casual. 'Wondering if you could help us, Mr Muirhead. Can you confirm your whereabouts on the evening of Wednesday the thirtieth of March?'

'We've already been through this.' Muirhead frowned. 'My wife and I were at the Rep with friends.'

'You're sticking to that, are you?'

Muirhead scowled. 'Are you accusing us of lying?'

Vicky handed over the first photo. 'Can you confirm that

Mr Simon Hagger and Mrs Emma Hagger are present in these photographs?'

'They're in the middle, looking at the camera.'

'And can you confirm that neither you nor your wife are present?'

'We're not.'

'Why would that be?'

Muirhead swallowed. 'Camera angle?'

'Camera angle.' Vicky fanned out another three shots. 'These are from another three cameras placed around the theatre. Are you in these?'

'Maybe we went to the toilet.'

'We've got footage over thirty minutes and a fifteen-minute interval.'

Muirhead kept his focus on the pages. 'We saw that play!' He placed the sheet on the table. 'Polly gave you the ticket stubs!'

Vicky nodded slowly. 'But you weren't there, were you?'

'No comment.'

'Mr Muirhead, your friends will be charged with providing a false alibi. You may wish to consult with your solicitor on this matter.'

Muirhead swallowed hard, eyes bulging as he stared at the table. He leaned in close and whispered.

Duncan peered at Vicky as he placed his mobile on the table, finger poised over the screen. 'My client wishes to end this interview.'

'He's going to answer my question.'

Duncan tapped the screen again. 'Sure?'

Vicky ignored him. 'Mr Muirhead, why did you lie about your whereabouts on Wednesday night?'

'We were supposed to meet Simon and Emma for dinner, then go to the theatre.'

'So you didn't make it?'

'We had an argument. My wife and I are having . . .' Muirhead licked his lips. 'Marital difficulties.' He placed his hands on his bald head. 'We didn't want any of our friends to know about it.'

'This is now a murder case.'

Duncan moved his finger away from his phone. 'Murder?'

Vicky showed him the page with Micky Scott on the treadmill. 'Mr Scott here died of a heart attack.'

'Well it wasn't me!'

'Was it Mrs Muirhead?'

'Sergeant.' Duncan's finger hovered over the dial button. 'Are you going somewhere with this?'

'Mr Muirhead, can you confirm your actual whereabouts last Wednesday evening?'

'I *told* you.' Muirhead shut his eyes. 'My wife and I were at home, arguing.'

VICKY GOT up and started walking around the room, using Polly Muirhead to block Duncan, waving his phone at her but keeping quiet. He knew the interview wasn't being filmed. She cleared her throat. 'Mrs Muirhead, on Sunday evening, you attended a dinner party.'

'That's correct.'

'You and your husband left the dinner party at seven thirty. Correct?'

'No comment.'

'Why did you leave early?'

'No comment.'

'Where did you go?'

'No comment.'

'You didn't go to the Kingsway East Retail Park?'

'My client doesn't wish to go on the record in this matter.'

'You didn't go to the Fixit DIY store, though, right?'

Duncan tapped the mobile again. 'Move on, Sergeant.'

'And yesterday at eleven?'

'I had a client meeting.'

'Where?'

'That's confidential.'

'Sure?'

'My client can't tell you.' Duncan checked his watch, cleared his throat and pushed a document across the table. 'I wish to place it on record that my clients are lodging a formal complaint with Police Scotland as to their treatment here.'

Vicky inspected the first sheet, full of arcane legalese. 'On what grounds?'

'One, corporate sensitivity and two, violation of human rights.'

Vicky raised her hands. 'Mr Duncan, your clients are suspects in three abductions and a murder.'

'This is harassment and I would appreciate it if you'd terminate this interview and let my clients go.'

'You're going nowhere.'

Duncan smirked. 'You probably want to check with your bosses before you make such brash statements.'

Vicky's stare burrowed into Duncan's skull. 'Interview terminated at—'

'YOU GOT A MINUTE?' Vicky slammed Forrester's office door and didn't wait for an answer. She gave him Duncan's letter and took a seat. 'This has gone to the Chief Constable.'

'Raven's had a copy and you know what that means.' Forrester set down his empty mug and rubbed his chin, the stubble making a loud rasping noise like iron filings. 'We need to let them go.'

Vicky ground her teeth. 'Duncan's playing games with us.'

'Believe me, I'm on your side.' Forrester looked up at the ceiling and sighed. 'Have we got *anything* on them?'

'At the moment, their whereabouts at the time in question — *including* for Micky Scott's murder — are completely unaccounted for.'

'I've just had my arse torn open by Raven about this bloody complaint. Until we've got harder evidence, you need to lay off.'

Vicky folded her arms and leaned back against the door. 'Come on, sir.'

Forrester offered her a consoling smile. 'You might think I'm a useless bureaucrat, but I did push back on this.'

'For what it's worth, sir, I never said you were a *useless* bureaucrat.'

'But I'm still a bureaucrat, right?'

'Naturally.' Vicky's smile didn't last long. 'They've *lied* about their whereabouts when two people were abducted.'

'What can we do?' Forrester blew air up his face and scratched the back of his head. 'We're fishing. A false alibi is one thing. Trouble is we don't have anything connecting them to committing those crimes. Anything to link them to Marianne Smith or that Brian Morton lad. If we can even arrest them for something, then the false alibi comes into play. No-one can push back on solid evidence.'

Vicky looked around for a bin to kick. 'This isn't over.'

VICKY STORMED down the corridor and gave the vending machine the kick Forrester's bin hadn't got. A can of Diet Coke slid out.

Shit, shit, shit.

She stuffed a quid in anyway.

Bloody Forrester.

Bloody Fergus Duncan.

Bloody hell.

This isn't over.

Yeah, bullshit. Police Scotland toadying to a legal firm. Letting them walk all over us. Not that we have that much on the Muirheads.

But, still. No smoke without fire.

'Hey, sis.' Andrew was trudging along the corridor, bouncing off the walls, looking like he was still asleep.

She shot over. 'Andrew?'

'Just heading home. Dad's meeting me.'

'Have you been in all night?'

'God no. That Complaints guy interviewed me. Can you believe it?'

'Believe anything. Are you okay?'

'I feel like shit, Vicks, but he believes me. For now.' He trudged down the corridor, every step looking like searing pain.

I should help him get to the car, help him get in.

Sod it, I should get in. Head back to Mum and Dad's for some TLC, spend time with my daughter, let the world go to hell while I recover.

Vicky cracked open her can and took a sip of fizzy, metallic, cold liquid.

Other than slashing Fergus Duncan's tyres, what can I do?

Give up on Sandy and Polly Muirhead?

But they were lying.

Am I so fixated on them because it means Robert's in the clear?

Did it just look like they were guilty? Do I just want to rub Fergus Duncan's face in his own shit?

Her phone rang. She checked the display, didn't recognise the number but answered it anyway. 'Hello?'

'Is that DS Dodds?'

'It is.'

'Hi. It's John Morton.' He yawned. 'Sorry. Look, I'm calling about my brother, Brian. He's not been good over the weekend. I'm asking you to lay off.'

'The problem is your brother's committed a serious crime.'

'So charge him.'

'We plan to.' She sighed. 'Look, just keep him off the internet. Okay?'

'I...' A sigh. 'I'll see what I can do.'

'I'd appreciate that.' Vicky ended the call and stuffed her phone back in her handbag.

Brian was a member of that gang, not frontline but still involved. He uploaded the first video, but we can't pin any of the subsequent activities to him. Maybe he's just an idiot who got carried away.

It has to be the Muirheads. But there's a huge hole in our timeline. Only one person who knows what the Muirheads were up to.

Vicky got out her phone and dialled, leaning against the wall listening to the ringtone, sipping Diet Coke.

'Hello?' Andy Salewicz sounded like he was smiling. Noise in the background, maybe a building site.

'Hi, Andy, it's Vicky. Are you okay to talk?'

'Becky!' Sounded like Salewicz was walking away from the noise. 'Ages since I've heard from my kid sister.'

'I take it it's difficult to talk?'

'You got your card? Took me ages to find one with a dildo on it.'

'I need to know what the Muirheads were doing at Phorever Love.'

'Sorry to hear they're going through a rough patch. We've got a great marriage counsellor here. Expensive but worth it.'

What the hell?

Wait — the argument.

'Are you saying the Muirheads are seeing a counsellor?

'Now I didn't say *that*. But I would recommend her services, sis.' Then his voice changed. 'What the hell are you doing?' Sounded like he'd gone inside.

'I take it you're safe to talk, then?'

'The deal is that I call you.'

'Just tell me what Sandy or Polly were doing yesterday.'

'They were with a marriage counsellor.'

'I need to speak to her.'

'Look, I'm in the middle of something. I've got to go, but I'll call you later, okay? We can have a nice long chat then.'

'I need her name. We think they murdered a greyhound trainer and—'

'Marianne Smith.' Click and he was gone.

31

Vicky stopped outside the interview room and took a deep breath. Her phone buzzed. A text — Salewicz:

YOU ALMOST BLEW MY COVER. I HOPE IT'S WORTH IT. NEVER CALL AGAIN.

Tempted to text the ending to Breaking Bad out of spite.
She knocked on the door and waited.

It opened and MacDonald peered out. Behind him, Polly Muirhead and Fergus Duncan sat on the opposite side. He stepped out, frowning. 'What's up?'

'Got something I need to ask.' Vicky walked into the interview room and took the seat next to MacDonald.

MacDonald took his chair, arms folded, eyes drilling into the suspect. 'DS Victoria Dodds has just entered the room.'

Vicky tried to ignore the threat, but acid burned in her throat. She cleared it and tried for another smile, even more tense than the last. 'Mrs Muirhead, do you know a Marianne Smith?'

Polly's eyes bulged. 'No.'

'You weren't visiting her at Phorever Love yesterday?'

Polly slumped back in her chair and muttered, 'Shit.' She

glanced at her lawyer, but he wasn't looking like he was going to help her. 'She's a marriage counsellor. That's all.'

'That's all?'

'No comment.'

'Mrs Muirhead, your husband's waiting for us in the next room. I'm pretty confident we can get the information out of him.'

Polly folded and unfolded her arms. 'Go on, then.'

'The thing is, Ms Smith is in police custody. We arrested her last night and charged her with terrorist crimes. I reckon she'll be in a more communicative frame of mind.'

Duncan leaned across and whispered in Polly's ear.

She scowled at him. 'Really?'

Duncan nodded. 'I think so.'

Polly coughed, eyes shut.

'We know you're working with her.' MacDonald pushed a sheet of CCTV print across the table. 'A witness provided us with descriptions of her assailants. There was a woman, a man and an androgynous third party. This was yourself and your husband with Ms Smith, correct?'

Her lip curled. 'This has nothing to do with us.'

'Why don't I believe you, then?'

'Listen to me. We were there for marriage guidance. We're going through a rough patch.'

'This fabled argument?'

'You know what it was about, then?'

'Murdering greyhound trainers?'

'What? No.'

'See, these attacks take a lot of organisation.' Vicky held up a sheet of paper. 'Your phone company gave us over a hundred and ten calls between your home and Ms Smith in the last year, going both ways.'

Duncan grasped the edge of the table. 'Polly...'

She stared at the table. 'It was Sandy.'

Vicky struggled to comprehend. 'Was your husband having an affair with Ms Smith?'

Polly shook her head. 'My husband has a thing for... dogging.'

Vicky could only laugh. 'I've heard some very interesting alibis from you so far, but this one takes the biscuit.'

'It's the truth.' Polly's eyes were brimming with tears. 'Christ, I've been living with this shame for so long. Sandy likes . . . having car sex in public places.' She shivered. 'I... I go along with it to please him.'

Vicky turned serious again. 'It doesn't explain why your husband has been calling Ms Smith?'

'We used to... Marianne used to meet up with us and a few others. That's what we were doing at Phorever Love. It's maybe technically swinging, given they have bedrooms and so on.' Polly pinched her nose. 'It's the reason we left the dinner party early. It's where we were when we were supposed to be at the Rep. Sandy's insatiable and... Sandy has particular . . . needs. Our summer holiday was in Riga in Latvia. The prostitutes are cheap and very *liberal* there. And I've had enough. I want out.'

'Assuming this is all true, you've wasted a lot of police time.'

'I'm sorry.' Polly rubbed her face. 'I'm a respectable member of Dundee society. I didn't want this to become public knowledge.'

'We need to confirm this.'

'Speak to Simon Hagger about it. He... He's the one who got Sandy into this deviance in the first place.'

THE HAGGERS' Edwardian bungalow had a mature garden, a bowling-green lawn and two pampas grasses by the road. A decent street in Barnhill, seagulls wheeled above them in the salty sea air.

Vicky walked back from the house and leaned against the Python. 'Why do people who live in a house like that do something so stupid?'

'Boredom?' Considine shrugged. 'The bloke's a bit of a munter, though. You ever seen *Family Guy*?'

'Never heard of it. Why do they call it "dogging"?'

'Isn't it from men pretending they're walking the dog when

they're actually cracking one off as they spy on couples having sex in a car?'

Vicky patted the roof of the car. 'The Python sounds like the sort of car that gets plenty of dogging action.'

Considine laughed. 'I've got an old Volvo for that.'

'You better not get caught.'

'Christ, Sarge, I'm joking.' Considine grinned then pointed back at the house. 'You were pretty bloody-minded in there, Sarge.'

'I'm fed up of getting the runaround by sexual deviants.'

Considine opened the driver door. 'Where to now?'

'Let's get back to the station.'

'COMING UP NEXT on Radio Scotland, we'll have a Scottish writer who moved to Australia eighteen months ago in search of his cousin, who was also his fiancée. The time is five minutes to one.'

Vicky got out of the Python, the tarmac patchy with drying rain. The sky was clear, a dark orange to the south. 'Can you write that up for me?'

'Sarge.' Considine sidled off across the car park.

A blue BMW 1-Series pulled up and parked in a reserved space next to her. MacDonald got out and swiped off a pair of sunglasses in one slick move. 'Vicky.'

She blushed. *My hand stroking his back, his on my neck.* She shook her head to snap out of it. 'Euan.'

'Thanks for that call.' He cleared his throat. 'Just spoke to some contacts in Vice. The Muirheads are part of an anti-dogging operation. No action taken yet, but there's a sting planned for this week on Phorever Love. Better warn Salewicz.'

'Maybe.'

MacDonald smiled. 'That's why Vice didn't want us surveilling them. We'd have put their job at risk.' He ran a hand over his mouth. 'Their holiday checks out, too. Riga's notorious for sex tourism. The eastern-European Thailand.'

Vicky felt herself deflate. *Our only suspects gone. Well. Not our only suspects...* 'So, who's behind all of this?'

'No idea.' MacDonald started off away from the station. 'Fancy a coffee?'

'I'm fine.' Vicky watched him go, tempted to join him.

What the hell am I doing?

He's an idiot. An arrogant prick. And he'll probably be my boss soon. But still...

'Vicky!' Black tracksuit, box-fresh white trainers, silver hair, red face. Robert, thundering towards her, fists clenched.

She walked over. 'What are you doing here?'

Robert stood there, scratching his temple. 'The... Police wanted to interview me. Apparently, I'm a suspect. They think *I'm* involved in this case.' He lowered his head. 'Know why?'

Vicky looked up at the station. 'Should I?'

'Well, you know. We're... And I thought... I don't know.'

'It's just intelligence gathering. Your name is on a list of donors to the animal shelter on Brown Street. And you've got a black car.'

'And that's enough to get called up and told to come in for questioning?'

'Someone died, Robert.' She saw his fury abating slightly. 'It's standard procedure. Okay? That's all. What did you tell them?'

'Moira's will had a clause saying I had to donate a chunk of money to that charity. Jesus Christ, I can't *believe* that's enough to...'

'As long as you told them that and you've got alibis for—'

'*Alibis*? Am I a suspect?'

'If you've nothing to hide, you'll be fine.'

'Bloody hell.' Robert let out a sigh. 'I mean, it could've been worse. Could've been at school. I've got a free morning, so I was in town. It's Jamie's birthday next week and I've no idea what to get him, so I thought I'd go to the toy shops and... Just got a call, get in here. I feel like... I don't know.'

'Robert, are you involved?'

'You don't think that, do you?'

'Just answer.'

'No, I'm not involved.'

'Well, then you'll be fine.'

He shook his head. 'This is—'

Her mobile buzzed in her bag. 'Sorry.' She rummaged around for a few hectic seconds before she found it. Forrester. She swiped the green button. 'Sorry, I'm...' She glanced at Robert. 'I'm meeting a friend.'

'Right.' Forrester paused. 'Well, get your friend to piss off. Some kid's been abducted. And... Ah, shite.'

'What?'

'It's Willis Stewart's boy.'

32

Willis Stewart answered the door, his eyes moist, his grey quiff sculpted to within a hair's breadth of perfection. 'It's you.' He bared his teeth then stepped back from the door. 'Come in.' He led them into the living room, filled almost to the rafters with heavy antique furniture. A few tall pot plants sat in the window, framing a visibly distraught woman. 'Heather, the police are...'

She sat on an armchair, mobile to her ear. 'Call me if he hears anything, okay?' She ended the call and looked up, her face red with tears, spiky hair poking out at odd angles. When she caught sight of the detectives, she got to her feet. 'Have you found Calum?'

'Not yet.' Vicky took a seat as close as she could get. 'We need to ascertain a few facts first. Have you—'

'His phone's off.' Heather's nostrils twitched. 'I've been phoning around his friends' mothers. Nobody's heard from him.'

'Are you sure he's been abducted?'

'Of course I'm sure!' Heather kneaded her forehead. 'He was coming home for lunch. I've got to take him to the dentist, but he... I spoke to the school. They said he left at twelve.'

'Exactly?'

'So they said. There's a bus stop across the road. He should've got here about half past at the latest. Where the hell is he?'

Vicky checked her watch. Over an hour ago. She checked that Considine was at least conscious. 'Do you know what bus he'd be getting?'

'A twelve or a seventy-three, I think. He should get off just at the end of the road.'

Considine nodded and left the room.

Vicky sat forward. 'When was the last time you saw him?'

'This morning. I walked him to the bus stop. He gets the bus to school.'

Vicky remembered the boy in his father's office, wearing that uniform. 'Dundee High, right?'

Heather glared at her husband. 'I didn't want him to go to there, but what can you do?'

'Is it possible Calum could've run away?'

'Of course not.'

'So, he could've bunked off school and gone—'

'No.'

'What do you mean, no?'

'This came through the fax machine.' Heather scowled as she retrieved a sheet of paper from the table next to her.

Vicky snatched it off her.

WE'VE GOT YOUR CHICK.
NOW FOR CLINICAL TRIALS.

Vicky's gut lurched. While it was on shiny fax paper and grainy, it matched the other notes.

Heather pressed her fingertips into her temples. 'He's been kidnapped, hasn't he?'

'This is the same as the other notes you've received.' Vicky shook the page and held Stewart's gaze, waiting until he looked away. 'What does "human trials" mean?'

'The only thing I can think is...' Stewart let out a deep breath. 'I'm on the board of Bios.'

Vicky pinched her nose. 'The vivisectionists?'

'We're *not* vivisectionists.' Stewart punched the wall beside him. 'We're a biosciences business. We're trying to cure cancer and—'

'You don't perform animal experiments?'

'We ... may do.'

Vicky felt a pain in her chest. *It's happening again.* 'You need to be straight with me. Have you had any other warnings?'

'Just the usual nutjobs standing in the way of progress.' Stewart let out another deep breath. 'We've had our fair share of aggro from animal rights activists over the years but, believe me, nobody who would've done this.'

'Why do you say that?'

'Well, why target me? I'm a non-executive director, for crying out loud! It's just two days a month. I just sit on the remuneration panel and, as a captain of industry myself, I make sure they're not jeopardising stakeholders' interests.'

Heather shot to her feet and tugged at Stewart's waistcoat. 'Willis, is this connected to what happened to Gordon?'

'It *can't* be.' Didn't look like even he believed it.

Vicky replied with a raised eyebrow. 'Let's hope not.'

Considine reappeared, walking over and speaking in a low tone: 'Only one stopped in our timeframe. The bus company checked the cameras. Calum didn't get on any of them.'

'Oh my God.' Heather clasped a hand to her mouth, eyes clamped shut. 'Oh my God.' She sunk back into her chair as though suddenly deprived of all support. 'Willis, what the hell have you done?'

'What have *I* done?' Stewart flared his nostrils. 'This has *nothing* to—'

Vicky got between Stewart and his wife. 'Have you received any other notes?'

'I get one or two *every day*. We just ignore them.' Stewart's nostrils flared again. 'People don't understand the good we're doing for society.'

'Even after what happened yesterday to your employees?'

'There was...' Heather sniffed. 'A note came through the fax last night. Said he had to resign from Bios or... I can't remember the exact words.'

Stewart glowered at his wife. 'I burnt it. It's meaningless.'

'Willis, they've got our home fax number!'

Vicky got between them. 'Mr Stewart, two men are in hospital as a result of your connections with animal cruelty.'

Stewart held her gaze for a long moment. 'Find my boy.'

VICKY PARKED the Python in the station car park and focused on Considine. 'Chase up a trace on the number the fax came from, okay?'

Considine nodded. 'Sarge.'

'And dig into Bios for me, okay?'

'Don't you need me there?'

'No, do the legwork, okay? Anyone who's made any threats against them, anything. Okay?' Without waiting for a reply, Vicky hurried along West Bell Street and cut down the lane by Dundee High. The place was swarming with police, uniformed and plain-clothes.

Forrester was in the middle of the throng, sucking on a coffee.

Vicky made a beeline for him. 'Anything?'

Another slug of coffee. 'What do you think?'

'They received a note at the house. Faxed.' Vicky got out the fax and passed it to him. 'It's matching the pattern.'

'Christ. Do people still have fax machines?' Forrester's hand shook as he stared at it. 'For crying out loud.' He finished his coffee and passed the empty to a passing uniform. 'What's the bloody point in press releases if people just ignore these warnings?'

'He gets hundreds a day, sir. He's on the board of Bios. Vivisec-tionists. They experiment on animals.'

'Christ on a bike.' Forrester looked like he was ready for another coffee already. 'What the hell do they mean by clinical trials?'

'Well.'

'I'd cross my fingers but...' Forrester shrugged.

Vicky gestured at the school, the stout pillars at the front of the building distinct from the surrounding ones. 'Left here just before twelve.' She traced a line with her finger from the door underneath the classical Greek portico to the gate in the railings at the front. 'Walked down here then should've waited for the bus just opposite McManus Galleries.' She took in the street, damp with rain. 'But he didn't get on. Considine checked.'

'The boy's been snatched. In broad daylight.' Forrester scowled back towards their police station, a couple of minutes' walk away. 'Right under our noses.'

'No sightings of a black car, I suppose?'

'None yet.'

A car pulled up next to them and ACC Queensberry got out of the back. 'David.' She smiled at Vicky, though it was like she didn't recognise her. 'Have you got the boy?'

'We're still looking, ma'am.' Forrester waved a hand at Vicky. 'Sergeant, I'll take it from here.'

Vicky stared at him hard, then smiled. 'Sir.' She walked off, blood pumping round her body.

Karen jogged over and shook her arm. 'Vicky?'

'What's up?'

'MacDonald's got me going through the bloody bins. Can you believe it?'

'Believe anything. Find anything?'

Karen held up a bag containing a cheap mobile. 'Found this in a bin near the bus stop Calum was supposed to be at.'

Vicky stood outside their office space, holding up the phone in the bag. 'Can you do the usual on it?'

'Oh, Vicks.' Jenny Morgan's perfect nose quivered as she took it. 'This is the fifth item I've had today that's come from inside a bin.'

'Calm it. The evidence bag hasn't.'

'I still need to get at the phone, though.' Jenny held it away from her. 'Right. I'll see what I can do.' She pouted then charged off along the corridor.

Vicky checked her phone for any messages. *Still nothing. Meaning Calum's still missing.*

'Vicky.' MacDonald walked past, holding up a can of Diet Coke. 'That trick with the vending machine worked. Trouble is, it gave me two?' He handed her one. 'You okay?'

'I'm fine.' Vicky cracked it and took a sip, looking around the near-empty office. Zoey was nodding her head to music, Beats headphones clamped to her ears. Considine was grunting next to her, angry at having to think.

MacDonald opened his can. 'Think he's dead?'

'Hope not. Why do you think that?'

'Clinical trials sounds a bit euphemistic.' MacDonald took a dainty sip from his can. 'And they killed Micky Scott.'

Vicky nodded, struck dumb by the memory of the video. 'Looked more like an accident on that video.'

'Putting a man in his fifties on a treadmill and forcing him to sprint is hardly an accidental death.'

'Sarge?' Considine was waving at her. 'You got a sec?'

Vicky wandered over. 'What's up?'

Considine nodded at his computer. 'Been looking into this Bios company?' The corporate website filled his screen, a grey theme with transparent images — a black man and an Asian woman in white lab coats, a white man between them resting his arms on their shoulders, all smiles, all politically correct. 'Pretty generic site, right? No hint of what they actually do.'

'Which is?'

'Well, I've done some digging and had a look at that xbeast site, right?' Considine coughed as he switched to another window. 'Zoey had to help us get on.'

Vicky's Airwave burst into life. 'DC Karen Woods to DS Vicky Dodds.'

'Receiving.' Considine was blushing — clearly had nothing useful to share. 'Safe to talk.'

'Vicks, I'm with Jenny Morgan.' Karen sounded out of breath. 'I've... I've got something. That phone, the burner I found...' She sucked in a deep breath. 'We've been through the call locations. It was used at least ten times in the Fintry area.'

'Fintry?'

'According to the map, there's a load of garages there.'

33

Considine tore up the dual carriageway heading north out of the city, playing fields flying by then swallowed up by post-war houses, the sort that filled Dundee. 'It's still a complete shithole up here.'

'It's better than when I was growing up.'

'Didn't think they had council estates in the nineteenth century.'

'Ha bloody ha. Your jokes are about as good as your driving, young man. You're about to miss another turn. Right here.'

Considine swung a right at the first roundabout heading into Fintry Road. 'Right.'

'Thought you didn't need a Satnav?' Vicky checked the map again and waved a hand round the corner. The buildings switched between long rows of flats and detached houses, most of the small gardens filled with trampolines. 'Next right.'

'Sure? Feels like we're going in a circle.' Considine drove down Fintryside, a row of brown council houses facing into the park, balconies at the front.

Vicky pointed to the right. 'There.'

Considine pulled up behind a Dundee City Council van. A side road led into Finlathen Park, blocked off by a steel fence.

A middle-aged man in white council overalls came over and motioned for Considine to wind down his window. 'One of you DS Dodds?'

Vicky got out of the car and held up her warrant card. 'That's me.'

'Jim Smalls.' He grinned at them as he took off his baseball cap. Had a yellow pencil stuck above his ear. 'I work for the council, ken? We rent these units out to punters to park their cars and... Well, whatever else they want. Ken how it is, eh? So Geena told us that you want to have a wee root around?'

Considine raised an eyebrow. 'We're looking for a black saloon?'

'Check on Autotrader, son.' Smalls chuckled. 'Hope you don't mind me pulling your leg, son.'

'And if I do?' Considine leaned back in his car seat, fixing him with a Hollywood glare. Then he grinned. 'Have you seen any?'

Smalls scratched at the salt-and-pepper stubble on his chin. 'Think there might be one, aye. Could've been shifted, ken?' He gestured across the road. 'If you'll follow me?'

Vicky followed, joining Smalls as he unlocked the gate across the road. Considine was staying in the car. *Prick...* Vicky followed Smalls up the long drive.

Halfway up the steep incline, a long row of lock-ups huddled in the rain, thirty or so single-storey concrete buildings backing on to the park. Mature trees covered the roofs.

'Lucky we've got a skeleton for these.' Smalls fumbled with a long chain of keys until he eventually found the one he was after. He pulled the first garage door open. 'Here we are.'

A matte black Vauxhall Vectra saloon, o8 plates.

Small turned around to Vicky. Then his eyes bulged at something behind her.

She flinched, but a hard object jammed into her back turning her muscles to jelly. Felt like a million volts went through her body. She slumped to the ground unable to brace her fall. Her cheek hit tarmac, her shoulder battering off the kerbstone. She couldn't feel anything but pain roaring through her body. She couldn't move, her arms and legs weren't responding.

Smalls was kneeling on all fours, groaning. Blood dripped from an open wound on his forehead. He toppled over.

An engine roared behind her. She lifted her throbbing head to glance around. The Vectra shot out of the garage, tearing off towards the street. Two heads in the front both obscured by balaclavas.

Vicky took a few deep breaths then slowly got to her feet. 'Considine?'

No sign of him.

Smalls was out of it.

She set off on a careful jog down the hill, fumbling her phone out to call Forrester. 'Sir, I've got a sighting of the car in Finlathen Park. Just by the entrance on Findale Street.'

'Vicky, can—'

'It was in a lock-up. I need an ambulance here and support vehicles now. I'm going to give chase.' She killed the call and set off, her legs starting to work again.

Where the hell is Considine?

She called Considine as she picked up pace. Voicemail.

The path curved round to the left. The Vectra idled at the entrance, engine revving. A figure wearing a balaclava was wrestling with the gates. He spotted Vicky then got back in and the car screeched off.

Another engine roared — Considine was reversing the Python towards her, the engine wailing at a higher pitch than her headache. She got in, tugging the seatbelt on as Considine wrenched the car forward. 'Stephen, you should—'

'Hold tight!' Considine tore down Findale Street, dodging amongst the parked cars. 'It's a Vectra VXR. Sheep in wolf's clothing. The Python will eat it for dinner.' He took the corner fast and tight, sending Vicky flying into the middle of the car, her head greeting the whiplash with another flash of pain.

A thud boomed from the left, just out of sight.

Vicky peered around. 'What the hell was that?'

Considine put his foot down and the Subaru careered around the corner.

The Vectra sat at the end of the road, side on, steam rising from the bonnet. A panda car was wedged into its side, the siren blaring, lights flashing.

Considine screeched to a halt. 'Holy shit.'

Two figures got out of the Vectra, balaclavas askew. For a moment they stood there dazed. Then the moment passed and they bolted down a lane at the back of the houses.

Vicky jumped out of the car, doing her best to ignore the nausea and stay on her feet. 'Come on.' She gave chase down the lane, dodging round a pool of broken glass. The two balaclavas powering ahead of her. One of their prey was starting to lag behind. Tall and muscular but with curvy hips. The androgynous member of the gang — definitely a woman. Familiar, too.

Considine accelerated past Vicky, gaining ground on them. He lurched forward, arms coming round in a rugby-tackle.

Just missed his target's shoulder but somehow managed to catch her feet. As she stumbled, Vicky shoulder-barged into her back, piling to the ground on top of her. Vicky leaned down hard and forced the woman's arm behind her back. She turned to Considine, already back on his feet and glancing around for the other fugitive. She pointed down the lane. 'That way!'

'Right.' He shot off.

Vicky put a knee into her captive's back and pulled out her handcuffs, slapped them round the woman's wrists. 'On your feet. Now.'

The woman got up, shoulders slouching.

Vicky kept one hand on the cuffs as she reached for the balaclava and tore it off in one movement.

Vicky concentrated on the woman's face, struggling to place her. Short dark hair. Her blue eyes couldn't focus on Vicky, staring at the ground instead.

The animal shelter. The expert in NME. The shy woman who preferred animals to people.

Yvonne Welsh.

34

Vicky pushed Yvonne towards one of the recently arrived panda cars and the waiting uniform, her cuffs rattling. 'Take her to Bell Street and get a lawyer in.'

'Sarge.' The uniform ducked Yvonne's head as he pushed her in the back of the car. Seconds later, the car was tearing off towards the city centre.

Vicky sat on a low wall and let out a breath. Everything hurt. She dabbed her cheek, dotted with blood. Her muscles still tingled from the Taser.

Down the road, the Python was still idling next to the battered Vectra, almost cloven in two by the squad car.

'Lost him.' Considine joined Vicky sitting on the wall. 'Too fast for me.'

'You tried.'

'And failed. Think he's gone to ground somewhere?'

'It was definitely a man?'

'Think so.' Considine leaned forward and rubbed at his calf muscles. 'I mean, the one we caught was clearly a lassie but that one, I'd say it was a bloke. It was a blur. Could be anyone.'

'I can't believe it's *her*. Yvonne.' Vicky shook her head. 'We're going to get such a doing over this.'

'What, cos we spoke to her last week? Do me a favour, Sarge. We were all in the dark on this.'

He's probably right.

Considine started stretching off his hamstrings. 'Thing is, Sarge, how did they know we'd be here?'

Vicky tried to think it through.

Assuming it was Robert, then I've not let slip anything about it.

If it was someone else, they had to have...

Oh shit.

Vicky got to her feet and set off towards the pranged Vectra, surrounded by uniforms.

Considine jogged to catch up. 'What's up?'

An ambulance sat beyond, tending to the two uniforms in the squad car. Lucky neither had been killed.

Vicky barged through the wall of officers and leaned inside the front of the car. Leather interior, smelled of menthol cigarettes. One of those Christmas tree air fresheners dangled from the rear-view.

No sign of it.

She looked on the back seat. An old Nokia, the same model as Karen's burner. Next to it, a black box with a red display like something out of *Knight Rider*. Vicky snapped on some gloves and reached for it. Weighed a lot more than it looked.

Considine frowned at the box. 'What's that?'

'A Tetra scanner.'

His eyes bulged. 'You're kidding.'

'Nope. They must've heard Karen's call over the Airwave system saying we'd traced the burner. Then panicked and headed out there. Problem is they got here around the same time as us.' Vicky rubbed at her back right where the Taser had landed.

Considine frowned. 'Network's supposed to be secure, though.'

'You need to pay attention at briefings, Stephen.' Vicky shook her head. 'Turning up on time would be a start.'

∽

'Alright?' Jim Smalls was sitting on the kerbside, a paramedic kneeling behind him and tending to his wound. He chanced a smile at Vicky, but it looked like it hurt. 'You catch them?'

'One of them.' Vicky looked behind him into the darkness inside the lock-up. Looked empty. Then back at Smalls. His wound made her gut clench. 'We'll prosecute him for this.'

'Have to catch him first, doll.'

Vicky grimaced. 'Any idea who rents this?'

'I'd need to check.'

The paramedic gave the impression that Smalls would be heading to hospital first.

'Speak to Geena in the office, see if she can— Ow!' Smalls slapped the paramedic's hand away. 'That's bloody sore!'

The paramedic rolled his eyes. 'Someone's opened your skull, what do you expect?'

Vicky flashed a smile then walked over to the garage. A couple of SOCOs were already dusting around inside. 'You got anything?'

Jenny Morgan pointed at a few boxes by the door. 'I think that's every single Dreamcast game.'

'What the hell is a Dreamcast?'

'The last Sega console. Killed them off, near enough. Highly collectible.' Jenny's hand shifted to another box. 'That one's full of old computers. Going back to an Amiga 500, would you believe? Got another couple in here which are more recent. It's like one of those hoarders on the TV.'

'At least whoever owns this has put them in storage rather than the bin.'

Vicky handed her the Tetra scanner. 'Can you work your magic on this?'

∾

Yvonne Welsh sat hunched over the interview room table, rocking back and forth, eyes closed.

Vicky stared at the recorders, the tapes hissing as they wound round and round and round. Trying to focus.

This is our only chance.

Calum is out there. Every second that passes... human trials could be happening.

Yvonne could be the woman, of course, but she could also pass for the androgynous third member. She was tall and didn't have a particularly large chest. Her hips, however, were clearly feminine. Easy enough to hide in baggy trousers, maybe.

Vicky glanced at MacDonald in a vain attempt at eye contact. 'Ms Welsh, you need to speak to us.'

Yvonne remained silent.

'Do you prefer Yvonne?'

She shrugged.

'You're in a lot of trouble, Yvonne. You know that, don't you?'

No reaction.

Kelly Nelson-Caird wrote long paragraphs in elliptical handwriting.

'Yvonne, a child is missing. Calum Stewart. Whatever grievances you've got against his father, does Calum deserve what you're doing to him?'

Yvonne screwed her eyes tighter, rocking back and forth even faster.

'The car you were driving was spotted at each of the other crime scenes. We've caught you red-handed.'

Yvonne clenched her fists. 'I wasn't driving.'

'Who was?'

Yvonne clenched her jaw.

'Who was with you?'

'No comment.'

'Whoever you're protecting, Yvonne, they're doing you no favours. You're in here alone and they're free. You'll go down for this.' She left a pause. It wasn't filled. 'I don't think you wanted to get into this, did you?'

Yvonne glanced up her.

'It started out as fun, didn't it? Helping animals, maybe. But it's gone *way* beyond that. It's a murder case. Do you really want to face murder charges alone?'

Nothing.

'Yvonne, were you working with Marianne Smith?'

She looked up. 'Who?'

'Marianne Smith.'

She looked away. 'I don't know who that is.'

'On top of the murder, there are kidnapping and abduction charges. On top of those, there are terrorism charges. At least forty years inside, I would imagine. You'll die in prison.'

Yvonne slowly raised her head and stared at the ceiling.

'Are you behind all this?'

'No, I'm not.'

'I didn't think so.' Vicky gave MacDonald a slight nod.

He settled forward on his elbows and flashed a smile. 'Thing is, it's possible we could be lenient with you.' His smile grew as Yvonne's eyebrows rose. 'But we need you to give us whoever's behind this.'

Nelson-Caird whispered in Yvonne's ear, who sat for a few seconds, motionless, before shaking her head. 'My client isn't prepared to listen to any offer.'

MacDonald rolled his eyes. 'Really?'

'I'm afraid so.'

'YOU'RE GOING to have to start answering our questions.' Vicky gave Alison McFarlane a stern look, though her scratched cheek made it sore to even frown. 'Please start with Yvonne Welsh and your relationship with her.'

Alison looked desolate, like she'd no idea her colleague was involved in terror attacks. *Like or actually?* 'We work together.' She crossed her arms. 'But you knew that.'

MacDonald slapped a copy of the case file with his open palm, the thud making her jump in her chair. He licked a finger like he hadn't noticed, then flicked through the pages and stopped a third of the way in. 'You named her as your alibi for the first crime. Trouble is, she either wasn't with you or you were doing it together.'

'Sergeant.' William Flynn adjusted his shirt again, so tight that they could watch the sweat stains under his arms spread by the second. 'My client maintains her statement, albeit without the benefit of it being verifiable.'

MacDonald focused on the lawyer. 'Mr Flynn, your client's implicated in a series of serious crimes, including murder. I'd like to know where she was on Wednesday.'

'I was at work, on my own.'

MacDonald leaned back, almost horizontal. 'Providing a false alibi. Tut tut. It'll be interesting to see the judge's face when you use that as your defence in court.' He nudged the file towards Vicky then rubbed his hands. 'But we'll charge you with that after this interview. Let's focus on the fact you don't have an alibi for the evening of Wednesday the twenty-eighth.'

'My client will amend her statement in due course.'

'But you've got nothing to back up your so-called alibi, have you?'

Flynn blinked a few times before turning to Alison. 'Any work emails?'

Alison shook her head. 'I was checking through the paperwork we receive from our vets, making sure it tallied with our own records.'

Vicky noted it down. 'On a computer?'

'Paper.'

'What about the other times in question? Start with—'

'Sergeant.' Flynn raised a finger. 'We're aware of all the dates you're going to ask my client. She was at work on each of them.'

Vicky stared at Alison. 'Can anyone else verify your whereabouts?'

'Probably not.' Alison wrung her fingers. 'Sorry.'

'Ms McFarlane, are you acquainted with a Polly Muirhead?'

Flynn raised a finger, then thought better of objecting and returned his gaze to the table top.

Alison shook her head. 'Never heard of her.'

'What about Sandy Muirhead?'

'No.'

'Marianne Smith?'

Her eyes widened. 'Never heard of her.'

'You reacted there. Good pals, are you?'

'I used to know someone of that name.' Alison swallowed. 'A long time ago.'

'Interesting.' MacDonald scribbled in his notebook.

Vicky took a deep breath. 'What about a Robert Hamilton?'

'No.' Alison held her gaze. No reaction.

'Okay.' MacDonald clapped his hands and leaned forward until his mouth was a mere inch over the microphone. 'Interview terminated at thirteen thirty-one.' He got to his feet. 'Mr Flynn, Sergeant Davies will take your client downstairs and charge—'

'But she's not involved—'

'False alibi. Sorry. Crime's a crime.' MacDonald led Vicky out of the room.

In the corridor, Considine was sucking up to Forrester outside the Observation Suite.

Forrester tore open a sachet of brown sugar and tipped it into his coffee. 'Constable, give us a minute?'

'Sir.' Considine sloped off.

Forrester watched Considine leave then went back into the Obs Suite. He settled back into his chair. 'I asked you to sort him out, Vicky. He's still a sleekit wee bugger.' He shook his head. 'Anyway, I've got him leading the interviews with Calum's school pals.'

'They're not involved, surely?'

'Probably not, but it makes our wee Python pilot feel important.' Forrester beckoned for MacDonald to shut the door. 'Who's Robert Hamilton?'

'Someone on our donor list.' Vicky felt a twang in her neck, felt MacDonald's scowl drill into her. 'I flagged him with DS Laing this morning.'

'Nothing I should be worried about?'

'Shouldn't think so, sir.'

'Right. Anyway. No sign of Calum still. What a bloody city.'

Forrester took a drink of coffee. 'Either of you reckon McFarlane's involved in this?'

'Possibly.' Vicky watched MacDonald for any suggestion. 'Just don't know how.'

He saved her. 'She works with Yvonne Welsh.' He thumbed at the interview room. 'During that, I caught a reaction when we mentioned Marianne Smith.'

35

MacDonald arched an eyebrow. 'Do you know an Alison McFarlane?'

Marianne Smith clenched her teeth. 'No comment.'

'She knows you.'

'Very pleased for her.'

'One of her close associates is involved with this case. Yvonne Welsh.'

Marianne took her time covering her reaction, but it was still fairly obvious she knew her.

'So we need your help.' Vicky cleared her throat. 'Calum Stewart was abducted today. He's *thirteen*. Whoever took him has threatened him with— We're fearful for his safety.'

'Willis Stewart's son?'

'That's right. We need—'

'The birds of prey were just the tip of the iceberg. Do you really think I care about his son, given what his father does to animals?' The corner of Marianne's lip turned up. 'Mr Stewart is on the board of Bios. Bios have caused untold suffering to pigs and primates among others. Willis was given a few chances to stop it, but he hasn't.'

MacDonald leaned forward. 'Are you admitting your involvement?'

'What I'm saying is, can you really blame whoever's doing this? Willis Stewart's not a good person.'

MacDonald narrowed his eyes. 'What if that was your son out there?'

'Listen. I made a conscious decision in my twenties never to have children. There are far too many people on the planet. Just because your genes or parents or politicians tell you to breed doesn't mean you should. Companies like Bios breed and torture animals just so people can live longer, while the planet collapses under its own weight. If whoever has Mr Stewart's son kills him, is that much of a loss? There'll be hundreds born today to replace him.'

MacDonald slammed his fist on the table.

Vicky grabbed it. 'Come on, Euan.' She leaned over the microphone. 'Interview paused at sixteen oh nine.' She followed him out of the room, leaving Marianne with her lawyer.

MacDonald paced around the corridor. 'Why did you stop me?'

'We're getting nowhere with her.' Vicky folded her arms and leaned against the wall. 'We know she's involved in this, but what we need to focus on now is finding Calum Stewart.'

'You're right, of course. I love a woman with a brain.' MacDonald joined her against the wall. 'Let me get this straight — Marianne was the woman and Yvonne was the androgynous one. Right?'

Vicky nodded. 'Yvonne's done all of the cases, whereas Marianne dropped out.'

'So, who's the man?'

'I don't know.' Vicky's neck throbbed.

It could be Robert.

But it could be Sandy Muirhead, couldn't it? If his dalliances extended to one-on-one sessions with Marianne Smith, maybe they extended to...

It just didn't fit. Polly was the passionate one. She gave her time and salary to good causes. But he supported it.

Vicky stared into space for a moment, then noticed MacDonald's eyes on her chest. 'Us standing here isn't going to find Calum.'

THEIR DESKS WERE EMPTY, just Karen working away.

Vicky sat next to her. 'Have you found who rents that unit?'

'Considine was looking into it.' Her eyes widened. 'Jesus, Vicks, what happened?'

'I'm fine.' Vicky dabbed at her temple. Felt rough like Tinkle's tongue. Very far from fine. 'Any idea where Considine is?'

Karen did her tongue thing again. 'At Dundee High, I think?'

'Right, can you speak to the council, please? Smalls got taken off to hospital. Mentioned someone called Geena?'

'I'll see what I can do.'

Vicky got up and looked around. Zoey was in the corner, hidden behind the pillar, chatting to Andrew. She walked over and spoke to him in an undertone: 'Thought you'd gone home?'

'Halfway along the Kingsway when Jenny called. Said you'd found an Airwave Scanner?'

'And Dad's okay with you coming in to work?'

Andrew shrugged. 'I've had three coffees today just so I can look at that bloody box. And I've not even opened it up yet.'

'You look like shit. You really should go home.'

'Nice to see you too, sis.' Andrew didn't even look up. 'I'm running a diagnostic downstairs against the network, which will hopefully show when they've accessed the network and how. I'll get home once it's finished. Okay?'

'What do you mean, how? They've used that device, right?'

'Vicks, it's not like the old radios. The Airwave network is encrypted, it's not like you just dial in to a frequency and listen. You need the access codes.'

'So they've got a cop's codes?'

'That's what I was alluding to.' Andrew rubbed his neck. 'That's why I got hauled over the coals by that Ogilvie guy. They thought it was *me*. I mean...' He beamed. 'Jenny passed on the stuff from the lock-up. I've been after a Dreamcast for ages.'

'What about the computers?'

Andrew slapped Zoey's back. Sounded like he'd cracked her ribcage. 'Young Miss Jones here is looking at it for me.'

Vicky nodded at her. 'You getting anything?'

Zoey flicked her fringe out of her eyes. 'There's a Dell from two years ago. Still boots up. Managed to get in. Whoever owns this machine was using xbeast.'

Vicky crouched alongside Zoey. 'Who is it?'

'The username is David Hasselhoff. I don't think it's him.' Zoey shrugged. 'I'll be a couple of hours getting an IP address, if we're lucky.' She flipped to another screen, a page of indented text. 'But, they posted this message last night. I didn't spot it till now.'

'WHY ARE THE POLICE LOOKING INTO US? WE'VE NOT COMMITTED A CRIME. DOG BREEDING IS THE CRIME HERE.'

Vicky frowned at it. 'They said "us"?'

'Exactly.' Zoey switched to another document.

'Could be the "athletic we" like in football.' Andrew lifted his coffee mug, dark grey with orange lines, the black Dundee United lion rampant on an orange and white harlequin diamond. 'When I'm talking about a United game, I'd say "we" played well today, even though I was nowhere near the pitch. Kind of like the "royal we", which is shorthand for "God and I". The divine right of kings and all that.'

Vicky slowly nodded. *Makes sense. Doesn't mean they're involved. But they might be.*

Zoey rolled her eyes. 'Andrew, you can leave me now. I know what I'm doing.'

'Fine.' Andrew sidled off, looking like he was in agony.

Vicky stood up, knees creaking, and tapped the screen. 'So whoever posted that dumped a laptop in that garage?'

'Right.

'This is your highest priority.'

'Understood.'

'Vicky?' Karen was on her feet, standing by her desk. 'Just been on the phone with the council. That unit is rented by Brian Morton.'

~

'Go! Go! Go!' Vicky ran across the road following Karen and Considine.

Two uniforms stood either side of Brian Morton's door, another one using the Big Key to batter it in. He got out the way and his mates piled in. Vicky hung back, waiting. Another two uniforms piled in.

'Clear!'

She followed Karen into the hall. The place was quiet aside from the thumps of four uniformed knuckle-draggers. 'Any sign of him?'

'Clear!' Came from the living room.

'Clear!' Bathroom.

'Clear!' Kitchen. 'Anyone want any cheesecake?'

So the bedroom isn't.

Vicky paced over, heart pounding in her chest. Empty. Duvet pulled back, white sheets stained orange and brown, the mattress sagging in the middle. She collapsed against the wall. 'He's not here.'

The uniform standing by the bed tore off his helmet. Colin Woods. 'Afraid not, Vicks.' He walked back into the hall and shouted: 'Clear!'

Vicky grabbed him. 'Get out there and find him, okay?'

'Aye, calm yourself.' Colin shrugged her off and left the room, snapping his helmet back on.

We've missed him. A man the size of a planet riding a bloody mobility scooter, and we've missed him.

Should never have let him go in the first place. So stupid. We knew he was involved, thought he might lure in the others, but he didn't. Instead, he's missing and we've no other leads.

Meanwhile, Calum's out there.

Vicky walked over to the window and leaned against the table, covered in sheets of tinfoil. A framed photo of a yellow Labrador sat in the middle, the dog's panting made it look like it was smiling. She pulled it aside — the table was filled with the sort of electronics shit Andrew had when they were kids — soldering irons, circuit boards, batteries, wires, crocodile clips.

Wait.

What the hell?

Vicky picked up a black metal box, a match for the Tetra scanner they found in the car. It rattled inside, didn't have the screen. But it was the same. She crouched down and found a box full of them. At least fifteen and loads of circuit boards.

Vicky stood and dialled her brother. 'Andrew, I'm in Brian Morton's flat and I've found a load of kit in his bedroom. Talk me through what you'd need to do to build one of those Tetra scanners?'

'Like I told you, building it's not the hard part, decrypting our security is.'

'Have you got anywhere with that yet?'

'No.'

'Right, well I'm standing over a load of tinfoil. Why would—'

Andrew laughed. 'Sounds like he's a conspiracy nut.'

'Andrew, I've found some components, a soldering iron and a load of wires. One of those metal boxes like in that car.'

'Well, that sounds right. Best way would be to stick a Raspberry Pi in it, saves a lot of hassle. I've not taken this one apart, for obvious reasons.' Andrew sighed. 'You know what this means, right?'

'Enlighten me.'

'They've got more than one Airwave scanner out there.'

'Jesus.'

'Still need access codes, sis.'

'Andrew, they've been using it. It's how they knew we'd be there. They've got the codes.'

'That means the whole of Police Scotland is wide open to these pricks.'

'Shit.' Vicky ran a hand across her face. 'Shit, shit, shit.'

Her Airwave blasted out. 'PC Woods to DS Dodds.'

'Sorry, Andrew. I'll speak later.' Vicky killed the call and put her Airwave to her mouth. 'What's up?'

'Vicks, it's Colin Woods. Got hold of fatso.'

VICKY DARTED ALONG THE STREET, passed an idling bus belching out diesel fumes. *Still no sign of—*

There.

Colin Woods stood by a park bench, wrestling with Brian Morton, his scooter almost toppling over. 'Come on, son!'

'Nooooooo!' Brian lashed out with a beefy arm, pushing Colin onto the bench. 'Nooooo!'

Vicky snapped out her baton as she approached. 'Brian, calm down.'

He swung round, staring at her, breathing through his open mouth. 'Nooooo!'

Vicky brandished her baton. Footsteps pounded behind her, heavy like police boots. She stepped forward. 'Are you going to come with me to the police station?'

Brian slumped forward. 'Like you're giving me a choice.'

'I saw what you've been building at your flat. It's over.'

Brian shook his head and slumped in defeat. One of the uniforms stepped round Vicky and snapped cuffs on him. Another had to drive the mobility scooter.

Vicky helped Colin up. 'You okay?'

He was pushing a thumb into his spine. 'I'll live.'

'He was just sitting here?'

'Staring at the bench.'

Vicky frowned at it. Then it clicked. The brass plaque read:

GOLDIE

2002-2008

MY BEST FRIEND FOREVER. BRIAN

~

'HE'S BEEN in the bloody station twenty minutes now.' Forrester stopped pacing. 'What on Earth is he doing?'

'Deliberately taking his time getting up here, sir.' Vicky tapped a foot. 'He was seeing his dog's memorial bench.'

'Christ on a bike. Shall we speak to his lawyer alone? It's Nelson-Caird, right?' Forrester waited for her nod. 'Come on.'

Kelly Nelson-Caird smoothed down the margins of her black notebook. 'Has my client arrived?'

'Which one? You're representing Yvonne Welsh, Marianne Smith and Brian Morton.'

'My clients are all Legal Aid cases. As you should know, Brown, Ward and Martin are the largest Legal Aid practitioners in the city.'

'No win, no fee, right?'

'I beg your pardon?'

'Ambulance chasers.'

'DI Forrester, you should be relieved this exchange is not being recorded.'

'How come you're defending virtually all of the suspects in this case?'

'We're a busy company, and I happen to have been allocated these cases by our office workflow system. I'm more than happy to push them to a colleague if you insist, but that's going to slow things down for you.'

'Wouldn't want to trouble you.'

The door opened and Colin Woods pushed a wheelchair in, its

wheels creaking with the effort. Brian Morton was a dead weight, his body wobbling at each shove of the chair.

Forrester leaned forward to start the interview.

Vicky got up and joined Colin in the corridor. 'How is he?'

'Not said a word. He's just sat there wheezing like he's about to keel over, even though we were the ones doing the heavy lifting. Literally. Took fifteen minutes to get him off his scooter.'

'I'll let you get back on duty.'

'You don't need us to take him back?'

'Don't worry about that.' Vicky raised her eyebrows. 'He's not getting out anytime soon.' With a sigh, she moved off.

Colin grabbed her arm. 'Robert said you bumped dinner with him?'

'You're getting as bad as your wife.' Vicky nudged him off and sat opposite Brian. The guy stank even worse than by the bench, like he'd not washed in weeks.

'DS Victoria Dodds has entered the room.' Forrester sat back and yawned.

Vicky passed a sheet of paper across the table. 'Mr Morton, we retrieved a mobile phone from a crime scene central to the case we're working on.'

No reaction, just slow breathing through his mouth.

'We traced the mobile to a lock-up in Fintry rented by you.' Vicky stabbed a finger at the paper. 'In the lock-up was a car which matches the description of one used in a series of vigilante acts.'

Still nothing.

'Additionally, we found a laptop with a history of posting on xbeast. Is it yours, Brian?'

His head sank, flattening out his jowls as his chin came to rest on a cushion of lard. He scowled at Vicky but didn't say a word.

'Brian, do you know Yvonne Welsh?'

His breathing sped up like a pug in distress.

'Do you know her, Brian? We've got her in custody.'

Brian turned away.

'Is the phone yours, Brian?'

'No.'

'Was it Yvonne's?'

'I don't know an Yvonne.'

Vicky gave him space. He didn't fill it. 'We also found a Tetra scanner. Looks like you've been building them in your flat.'

Brian clamped a hand to his chest and sucked in a deep breath. 'I don't feel well.' He slumped forward in his wheelchair, arms hanging loose by his sides.

36

V icky strode towards the door to their office space, though this time Forrester overtook her just in time to hold it open with a smile. 'Always time for a bit of gallantry.'

MacDonald was talking to Karen and Considine. He looked up as they approached. 'Did you nail him?'

'Even better.' Forrester put on a mock serious face. 'DS Dodds gave him a heart attack.'

MacDonald raised an eyebrow. 'Seriously?'

'Well...' Vicky joined in with her boss's solemn act. 'The jury's still out.'

Still acting like her conspirator, Forrester got out his mobile. 'I'll cover your back with Raven, okay?' He put the phone to his head and walked off.

MacDonald folded his arms. 'What happened?'

'Listen.' Vicky squared her shoulders. Time for the endgame. 'He's faking a heart attack. We were onto him.'

'He posted the videos.'

'Eh? I thought it was Marianne Smith.'

'Come on.' MacDonald walked over and crouched next to Zoey. 'Show DS Dodds.'

'Okay.' Zoey glowered at MacDonald. 'I've got a clone of his laptop now, so it should be much easier.' She patted her machine like a favourite pet then started typing, her fingers blurring over the keyboard, then tapped the screen. 'There's raw WMV files on here.'

Vicky stood behind her gripping the seat back. 'This is reliable?'

'Well, I got a match to one of the accounts posting the videos on YouTube. The Met guys have better gear than I'll ever see, but they still got nowhere. It wasn't until we got his laptop that I could make sure, though.'

'How does Marianne fit into it?'

'They shared the account. Brian was using it at the time, though. This was more intuition than intelligence until I got his computer.' Zoey flashed a laugh at MacDonald. 'You know how I hate being wrong, Mac.'

'Great work all the same.' MacDonald glanced back at Vicky, warning her to back off. 'You got anything else off that laptop?'

'Found a list of dead CCTV cameras. Must be how they kidnapped Calum, right?'

'Makes sense.' MacDonald nodded slowly. 'Anything on who he's working with?'

'Not yet. Found some notes on other attacks. Letting the animals out of Camperdown Zoo. Attacking a racehorse stable. A bomb at Musselburgh and Kelso Racecourses.'

'They're deliberately escalating.' Vicky thought it through. Came up blank.

'Someone had a video camera and recorded Micky Scott's death.' MacDonald stuffed his hands in his pockets. 'Clearly wasn't Brian or we'd have heard his mouth breathing. So, who?'

'What about his brother?'

'We got anything saying it's him?'

'No.' Vicky stared at the screen, filled with prints of the notes. 'We've got Brian. We've got Yvonne. Let's see what she's got to say about it.'

～

VICKY SAT BACK in her chair. 'Ms Welsh, we spoke to Brian.'

Yvonne's eyes shot up. She was holding her breath.

'We know he's been building an Airwave scanner.' Vicky nodded slowly. 'We know he's been posting those videos on YouTube. Trouble is, it's his brother we need to speak to, isn't it?'

Yvonne took a deep breath then looked away. 'I'm saying nothing.'

'See, we can't find John.'

Yvonne frowned but still refused to make eye contact. 'John who?'

'John Morton. Brian's brother. Seems to have disappeared. He was driving when we caught you, wasn't he?'

'No comment.'

'Final answer?'

'No comment.'

'Well, he certainly seems happy for you to take the rap for this.'

Yvonne just glanced at Nelson-Caird.

'This is an offer made on behalf of the Procurator Fiscal.' MacDonald put a sheet of paper in front of the lawyer. 'It guarantees Yvonne immunity from prosecution for charges pertaining to these crimes in exchange for testifying against her collaborators.' He held onto it. 'There are a few provisos in there, stuff like getting counselling, keeping off the internet, not travelling abroad. And we need Calum Stewart back alive.' He let go.

Nelson-Caird lifted the page and slowly read through it. She whispered to Yvonne, loud enough for them to hear: 'I'd take it if I were you.'

Yvonne's eyes stayed focused on the table. 'No.'

Vicky gritted her teeth. 'You're taking the fall for this. Murder, abduction.' She left a pause, letting the word bleed all its horror, while they sat in silence.

Yvonne blanched, paralysed by indecision.

'I think your heart's in the right place, Yvonne, I really do. You wanted to help animals, but you've ended up killing people. By accident. You never wanted to do that, did you?'

Yvonne took the sheet from Nelson-Caird and studied it. She

swallowed hard then sat for a few seconds. When she finally spoke, the words came out in a hollow whisper, her voice hardly recognisable. 'I just wanted to frighten people. Get our message out there.'

'But John didn't?'

Yvonne took a shivering breath. 'He took things too far. Made Micky Scott run for hours.' She flashed her teeth. 'Kept stabbing the Taser at him. Made Kyle Ramsay's owls bite him, gouge him. I didn't like that. We're supposed to be stopping cruelty, not inflicting more ourselves.'

Vicky did her best to keep her voice gentle and sympathetic. 'So why is John doing this?'

'Same as me. He loves animals, hates cruelty.' Yvonne shrugged. 'He works in PR. This is just a campaign for him.'

'Are you an item?'

'No way.' Yvonne scoffed. 'I was at school with Brian. We were, I don't know, a couple? We were fourteen so it doesn't count.' She scratched her cheek. 'Brian wasn't always like he is now, you know? He used to be fit and healthy. It started when he lost his dog.'

'Goldie, right?'

Yvonne frowned. 'How did you know?'

'We found the bench.'

'Their dad was an arsehole, treated Brian like shit. After their parents divorced, Brian was staying with his mother one weekend. She was allergic to animals, though, so Brian couldn't take Goldie. Their dad was away on a boys' weekend, some last-minute thing, so he took Goldie to the Brown Street Kennels. He thought he could just put the dog in on a Friday and get her back on the Monday. Free boarding. But Goldie got rehomed.' She bared her teeth. 'Brian's dad said he tried to get her back but couldn't. The new owner let Brian see the dog occasionally.' She grimaced. 'Then Goldie got run over. Brian just fell apart. That's when he started eating to cope. Eventually that's all he did, apart from messing about on his computer.'

Vicky focused on the wood grain of the table, centring on a particular knot.

We gave her an offer and she gave us the supposed mastermind. Convenient. Is Yvonne throwing John under the bus to save herself and her ex?

Vicky looked up again, straight into Yvonne's eyes. 'John said he was at the Speedway when Rachel and Paul were abducted.'

'He wasn't there.' Yvonne shrugged. 'He planned it all. Getting cages delivered to that building? He knew the security guard's pattern. Easy enough to plan around it.'

'Tell us about the car.'

'John's had it for ages. He bought it when he lived down south. He wasn't happy when you put out a description on the TV news, so he put it in Brian's lock-up. He thought the laptop would lead you to us first.'

'You attacked me at the lock-up, didn't you?'

'That was John.' Yvonne held up her hands. 'Brian heard you were going there on the Airwave and panicked. My car's still parked a couple of streets away.'

Vicky rubbed her forehead. 'We need to speak to John.'

'I honestly don't know where he is.'

Vicky rested her chin on her fist. 'How were you supposed to meet up with John again?'

'He texts me.'

Vicky held up the disposable phone from the car, wrapped in an evidence bag. 'On one of these?'

'Correct.'

Vicky put it down. 'Has he got Calum Stewart?'

'I don't know.' Yvonne avoided her gaze. 'I swear.'

MacDonald took the offer back from them. 'I'll tear this up if you're lying.'

'I helped him abduct Calum.' Tears streaked down Yvonne's cheeks as she reached over for the offer page. 'We waited in John's van and spoke to the kid at the bus stop. Said I'd show him my breasts. John's idea. The kid was thirteen. His little eyes lit up.'

'You say *was* thirteen. Is he dead?'

'*Is* thirteen, Christ.' Yvonne shook her head. 'I swear he's alive. If he's dead, John's killed him since I last saw him. Maybe I can help get him back?'

'Where is he keeping him?'

Yvonne's gaze darted around the room. 'John's been staying with a mate in Fintry.'

37

Vicky stared at the car mirror and nodded. 'Go.' She watched them enter the building then got out, slowly. 'Fingers crossed.'

Figures flashed in the front window. One gave a thumb's up.

'We're on.' Vicky darted across the road, then into the flat.

The place stank of cheap hash. In the living room, a man was on his knees in front of Colin Woods. 'This is the boy.'

Vicky got a good look at him. Late twenties, huge pupils like he'd smoked skunk for twenty years solid. Thin as a whippet. 'What's your name?'

'Greg Wallace.'

'You taking the piss?'

'Eh?'

'The *MasterChef* host?'

'That's my name, doll. Gregor William Wallace.' He tried to get up.

Colin tugged him back down again. 'Looking for John Morton.'

'Not seen him for ages. Weeks.'

'He told us you were at the Speedway on Wednesday.'

'What the hell is Speedway?'

Vicky snarled. *Considine checked the alibi. Turned out to be a load of shite. If he was here, I'd strangle him.* 'Where is he?'

'Guy's like a ghost, peaches.' Greg grinned, his eyes wavering. 'He just slips in and out. Never know when, ken?'

Vicky stormed off, fists clenched.

Bloody Considine. Bloody hell.

VICKY HAULED OPEN the interview room door and got in Yvonne's face. 'Where the hell is he?'

Yvonne backed away. Looked to her lawyer for help. 'I don't know!'

'He wasn't there!'

'Look, he doesn't share a lot with me. Ask Brian?'

'That's not an option. What's he going to do to Calum?' Vicky went into her pocket for a copy of the note from the Stewart house. 'What the hell does *"We're moving to clinical trials."* mean?'

'You know what they do at that Bios company, right? Ever heard of xenotransplantation?'

Vicky narrowed her eyes. 'What do you think?'

'Bios have been taking livers from pigs and sticking them into baboons.'

Vicky tasted sick in her mouth. 'Christ.'

'Supposed to show they can grow pig livers in another species, so they can give them to people who need transplants.'

Vicky swallowed hard. 'Tell me that's not what's in store for Calum Stewart?'

Yvonne pursed her lips.

Vicky sat, head in her hands. *It all pointed towards it.* She had to grab the table to rein in her rage. 'Doesn't excuse what you've done.'

Yvonne cupped her hands at the back of her head and started rocking back and forth.

'Right.' MacDonald held up the sheet. 'You said he's going to experiment on Calum. That deal is worthless unless we find Calum.'

Yvonne stared at the floor, frowning.

Vicky walked back. 'Has he still got an Airwave scanner?'

'I think so. Brian made one for each of us. John had one on him. You've got mine.'

'I've got a plan. Play along or that deal's dead and you're going to prison.' Vicky held up her Airwave. 'DS Dodds to all units. Repeat, the suspect from Findale Place has been released without charge following an interview with Brian Morton.' She locked eyes with Yvonne. 'Morton has died of a heart attack in police custody, but we still seek the whereabouts of his brother, John.'

MacDonald shook his head. 'What the hell are you playing at?'

'The wheels are in motion now.'

The Airwave chirped and repeated the message, this time from Control.

The phone lit up. Vicky looked at Yvonne. 'He's texting. Is that normal?'

Yvonne shrugged.

Vicky smoothed out the bag as she read:

"ARE YOU OKAY TO TALK?"

Her fingers struggled with the buttons on the phone through the evidence bag's plastic. She typed "Free to talk" and hit send. Then she tossed the burner at Yvonne. 'Remember the deal?'

Yvonne stared at the mobile. 'Fine.'

'No funny business. No code words. Plain speak — yes/no as much as possible. Okay?'

'Okay.'

Vicky waited, eyes locked on Yvonne.

The phone rang.

Yvonne pressed the green button through the plastic, then put it on speaker.

'Yvonne?'

'Hi, John.'

'Are you okay?'

'I'm fine.' Yvonne smiled. 'They just let me go. My lawyer said it was something to do with Brian. That he died?'

'I've heard.' John choked, then sniffed down the line. 'Where are you?'

'I've just left the police station.'

'Are they following you?'

'If they are, they're really good. It's quiet here.'

'Where are you going?'

'I don't know. I need to get my car. Then I could meet you at Brian's flat?'

'They've got it covered.'

'I'm scared, John.' Yvonne bit her lip. 'I don't know what to do.'

A pause. Vicky dug her nails into the palms of her hands.

'I'll pick you up. Outside Dundee College on Constitution Road. Fifteen minutes.'

MacDonald's head was nodding to a silent beat.

Yvonne leaned forward. 'Have you still got Calum?'

'He's with me.'

'Is it over?'

'I'm readying him now.' John paused. When he spoke again, the tearfulness was replaced by hard resolution. 'And it's never over, Yvonne.' Click.

Vicky got to her feet. 'You did well.'

Yvonne nodded slowly, her mind clearly elsewhere. 'Thanks.'

'What's important about Dundee College? That building's still shut, right? This isn't a trap, is it?'

Yvonne shook her head. 'John did a journalism course there after school.'

38

Vicky stood shivering outside the old college building, the seven concrete storeys all boarded up ready for sale. Above, the cloudless sky darkened as fast as her mood.

She looked back down at herself. Yvonne's clothes didn't quite fit. The jeans were an inch too long, the hoodie baggy in the wrong places, tight in others. Her sports bra squished her boobs like dolphins in a tuna net.

Christ, stop thinking like them.

Her phone rang. MacDonald. 'You set?'

She glanced along the street to the end of the one-way system to where MacDonald's plainclothes team hung around. 'Her clothes are too big. Feel like I'm trying on my dad's police uniform again.'

'Probably too much information.'

'Just hope my hips and bum aren't a giveaway.'

'Hard not to be distracted by them.'

Headlights came down the hill. The nerve in her neck sparked into life again. She pocketed the phone and put the balaclava on the top of her head, rolled up like a hairnet.

The van pulled in on the other side of the road.

Vicky screwed up her eyes, trying to see if it was John.

The window wound down. The deep voice boomed out. 'Get in, Yvonne.'

Vicky froze.

'Come on!'

Vicky jogged across the road and got in.

The vehicle shot off, John staring at the road as he drove. 'Did anyone follow you?'

Vicky snapped out her baton. 'John Morton, I'm arresting you —'

He smashed his elbow into her cheek, sending her rocking back in the seat. The baton clattered in the footwell. Something crackled to her right, then burnt against her shoulder. Vicky's muscles released, electricity jolting her entire body. For a fraction of a second she went stiff as a board, then limp, limp, limp. Just like in Fintry.

Stupid cow. Knew he had one and you thought a baton would be enough?

Vicky slumped into the seat, unable to move a single muscle.

John accelerated hard. Blue lights ahead of them, sirens from behind. 'Shite.' He tugged the wheel to the left, heading the wrong way down a one-way street, dodging the parked cars on the single-lane road. He sped up, knocking over some wheelie bins as he mounted the pavement. The road curved back round and they powered down the lane at breakneck speed, passing a green gate and a stone wall.

'You won't get away.' *I can speak again.* Vicky clicked her jaw. 'Why are you doing this?'

'Publicity.'

'For the animals or yourself?'

'Both.' John nudged his glasses back up his nose then stabbed her with the Taser again.

Vicky thrashed around for a moment, then slumped even further down the seat. All she could do was watch as this deranged terrorist spun out his final publicity stunt.

Who'd look after Bella?

They shot out of the street. Vicky recognised it — they were back on Constitution Road. They'd done a loop.

Police cars raced up the hill in the wrong direction.

John gained speed as they went downhill, then pulled on to the Marketgait, missing another car by a gasp. He darted into the right-hand lane to overtake a lorry, then cut back in again, the needle hitting ninety. He stomped on the brake pedal, just about squeezing through a roundabout, and then he was off again, the engine howling even louder than Vicky's headache.

Just as she felt her fingers start to respond again, the light cut out. The tunnel! Vicky reached over and tugged the wheel hard left.

John pushed her away and yanked it back.

Too late.

The van crashed into the wall, bounced back, hit the concrete central reservation and went into a screeching spin, the tunnel and other cars blurring.

Smoke in the air, blurred vision, smell of burnt tyres. John let go of the Taser to wrestle the wheel. It landed in the middle of the cabin.

Vicky reached down for it.

John slapped a hand across her face.

Her head spun round and hit the window.

A police car thundered into the front of the van.

Loud bang, airbags out, faces squashed.

Something hit John's side of the van.

They lurched, gravity clawing at Vicky, careening on two wheels, then smashed on the roof.

The seatbelt tore into Vicky's chest. Hanging upside down, she glanced at the driver seat.

John was gone, his door hanging open. Through the crumpled windscreen, she saw him hobbling away between two smashed police cars.

Vicky braced herself and released the seatbelt. She fell to the roof of the vehicle, landing on her shoulders. Something jarred against her neck. The Taser. She put it in the pocket of the hoodie and kicked her door, once, twice, crack and it was open.

She tumbled out on to the hard asphalt. A deep cut in her right hand, pain sparking through the adrenaline. She coughed, leaned on her good hand to push herself off the ground and started after John, clambering over the mangled bonnets of the crashed cars, one a squad car, the other a dark-grey Subaru. Considine was pushed up against the windscreen.

Behind, a wall of yellow hazard lights and blue police sirens blazed out. She ran on, speeding up as she went, ignoring the searing pain in her hand and head.

Beyond the cars, MacDonald came up at John from behind, launched himself into the air headlong and tore him to the ground. Rough landing, a jumble of limbs. John was first to stir. He aimed a fist at MacDonald's head as he got to his knees. The blow sent MacDonald staggering backwards, his head hitting the embankment of the carriageway. She was almost there when John started in with his feet, kicking at MacDonald's prone body.

Vicky stabbed the Taser into John's back.

He fell backwards, a violent spasm gripping him as he landed at her feet. She pressed it into him for a few more seconds then took a swing with her foot, connecting with his balls.

Arms grabbed her from behind. 'Easy, Vicky, easy.' Forrester.

Karen appeared at her side, knelt down and cuffed John.

Forrester helped Vicky over to the wall in the middle of the carriageway. She collapsed against it, focusing on the traffic in the opposite direction. Rubberneckers stared at her and the smashed cars, steam billowing from the bonnets. She smelled a fire.

Calum!

Vicky staggered to her feet and started through the crumpled mess of cars towards the van. She clawed at the back doors.

Forrester gripped the handle of the sliding side door, yanked hard and pulled it open.

Calum lay upside down in the middle of the van, unconscious.

Naked from the waist up, black ink traced the outlines of his organs.

Forrester got in the back and stood on the inverted roof. He felt the boy's neck for a pulse, eyes on Vicky. Sat there for a few seconds. Then let out a breath. 'He's alive.'

Vicky collapsed to her knees, tasting blood in the back of her throat.

39

T he blue lights of the ambulance danced off the tunnel walls. Ahead, a pile-up of destroyed cars like something out of a post-apocalyptic horror, where the heroes have to forage in a destroyed city, just...

Real.

And had just happened. To me.

'Ow.' Vicky winced as a paramedic fussed at the cuts on her hand. Felt like she'd been chewing glass.

'That was good work back there, Vicky.' MacDonald winced as the nurse tightened the bandage on his head. 'Quick thinking.'

'Just relieved we caught him.' Vicky sat on the opposite side, playing with the bandage on her arm. 'How's Considine?'

'Not even a scratch.' MacDonald put a hand towards his wound but got a slap for his troubles. 'The Python's a write-off.'

'Shame.' Vicky grinned through the pain. 'The next one will have to be the Ram.'

MacDonald laughed, then winced and gingerly touched his fingertips to his temple.

Vicky's smiled faded when she spotted the car in amongst the destruction, buckled and twisted. *Could so easily have been fatal.*

What I deserve for getting into that van, almost lost my own life. And Calum's.

Dr Rankine stepped up into the ambulance, eyebrows raised. She grimaced as she sat. 'The good news is that Calum will live. The bad is that he'll be traumatised. Being stuck in the back of the van like that.'

Vicky shook her head. 'Christ, the fear alone...'

'It's only fear, though.' Rankine smiled. 'John Morton didn't get a chance to cut him up.'

'Jesus Christ.'

'You did well, Vicky.' Rankine squeezed Vicky's arm. It hurt. 'Brian Morton had a panic attack. He'll live.' Another squeeze, a sharp pain zapping up Vicky's arm. 'John's balls are still attached after you whacked him. He'll live. You can interview him if you want.'

JOHN MORTON LEANED FORWARD. 'MARIANNE SMITH.'

'She's in charge?'

'Right. She's part of this organisation, doesn't even have a name. Marianne recruited Yvonne a few years back, helped her hand out leaflets. Extreme campaigning, just picketing or leaflets with rabbits covered in blood. Extreme. But it wasn't enough. So Yvonne got my brother involved. Brian's a prodigy with computers. They got him to hack into big pharma companies, seeing what they were really up to. This feed company near Glasgow. Then he was on the dark net, looking for places to talk where you lot wouldn't be listening.'

'You're talking like you're not involved.'

'I wasn't until a few weeks back.' John leaned on his elbows. 'Working in London. It's cut-throat there, they'll let you go like that.' He clicked his fingers. 'Mum died of cancer two months ago. Just after I was made redundant. Someone had to look after Brian, so I'm back in Dundee. Staying in our old house, in Mum's old bed, looking after my brother. A big failure.'

'So you decided to get involved?'

'Right.' Energy sparked in his eyes. 'A few weeks ago, Yvonne and Marianne were round and they started picking on Brian. They were frustrated about how passive it was. Sitting around while Brian found videos of some monkeys getting gassed, sharing it on that xbeast thing. I told them it's preaching to the converted.'

'They didn't mind you being there?'

'I wanted to help. Offered to help. Offered to make it more effective. I came up with this advertising campaign idea. Get their message into the press. We don't care about getting caught. We just want our message out there.' He laughed. 'It worked.'

Vicky stood up. 'I still don't get your motivation.'

'My motivation is that I don't give a fuck. I lost my job, my mother. I saw how the world really is — everything's a race and you're either a loser or a winner. I just wanted to destroy it, bring it to its knees. If I could do some good along the way, then fair enough.' He raised his shoulders. 'I really don't care. Prison will be bliss compared to looking after Brian.'

'I caught you, you shit. Outsmarted you.'

'Oh well done.' John gave a mock clap, slow and building. 'Well done, DS Dodds. You're such a hero.'

'Only thing I don't get is how you accessed the Airwave network.'

John laughed, still clapping. 'Now that would be telling.'

VICKY STORMED through the Forensics area.

Her brother was fiddling with a black box, his forehead creased and his tongue sticking out. 'It's not done yet.' He looked up at her. 'Jesus Christ, Vicks, you look like you've been in a car crash!'

'I have.' Vicky squinted at the box. 'Are you sure someone sold their codes?'

'You know how you lot get new codes every month?' He waved

over at MacDonald, locked deep in conversation with Zoey. 'Well, that box changed code every month, that much we do know.'

'Sure it's not someone behind the scenes?'

'Well, no, I'm not. That's why we're waiting on the diagnostics. It'll work out which codes they've used, hopefully pin it down to a user.' Andrew raised his shoulders. 'But, look. Zoey's looking at it. I'm just helping.'

Vicky took a deep breath. 'You can go home if you want.'

Andrew glared at MacDonald, the old resilience back in his eyes. 'No way.' Then his shoulders slumped. 'I really need to.'

'I can give you a lift?'

'I'll get the bus.' Andrew sidled off and snatched his jacket off the coat stand.

What he's reduced to...

Vicky walked back to MacDonald and Zoey, locked in a deep chat. 'You getting anywhere with that?'

'Your brother's diagnostic is just about done.' Zoey looked over. 'Oh, here we go.'

Just a list of numbers and codes, none of which meant anything to anyone human.

'And?'

'The good news is it looks like someone has sold their codes.' Zoey licked her lips. 'The bad is that I've got a name.' She tapped on the screen. 'Him.'

VICKY PEERED through the window in the Auld Cludgie. *There.* At the table by the toilets, DS Laing sat with Considine, laughing like they were in the pub. Plates piled up in the middle of the table, slurping at coffees.

How could he?

Selling his access codes to terrorists. Murderers.

Vicky sucked in a deep breath. 'You want to lead?'

MacDonald shook his head. 'All yours.'

'Okay.' Vicky took another breath, but her stress level wasn't abating. She opened the door and entered the café. Burnt cheese mixed with rich coffee smells. Radio Tay blared out of the speakers, that really annoying Bee Gees song. She walked over to the table and leaned against it. Couldn't make eye contact. 'You wanting to come in quietly?'

Considine scowled at her. 'What are you talking about?'

Vicky held his gaze. 'I'm not talking to you.' She shifted it to Laing. 'Johnny. We know.'

'Okay...' He was acting cool, just sipping his coffee. 'Know what?'

His mobile was unlocked on the table. Vicky reached for it, but he slapped her hand away. 'What the fuck?'

Vicky grabbed his wrist and yanked him over, all seventeen-odd stone of him thudding to the floor. She pulled his arm back until he gasped, then got in close. 'Selling access codes. How could you?'

'Bullshit!' Laing was squirming, his free hand was reaching for his phone.

'Euan!' Vicky pointed at it. 'Get that.'

'Get off me! Vicks! Have you gone mental? This is— ARGH!'

MacDonald stomped on his wrist as he picked up the mobile.

'That's private!'

MacDonald tapped at the screen. 'What is? Your emails?' He frowned. 'Jesus.'

'What is it?'

'Lots and lots of emails to John Morton, eh?' MacDonald crouched in front of Laing and held the phone out. 'If you're going to email terrorists secret information, don't use your own email account.'

40

'Well.' Forrester sat back in his chair with a sigh. 'Johnny bloody Laing. Can't believe it.'

'I'm shocked, sir.' Vicky shrugged. 'I trained with him, walked the beat with him. Thought he was a mate.'

'Be careful who you trust.' MacDonald raised an eyebrow. 'Reckon we'll get a conviction?'

'They're all going away for a *long* time.'

'Except Yvonne.' Vicky took a deep breath. 'I think she's learnt her lesson.'

'Let's hope so.' Forrester sighed. 'Now, I'd ask you if you wanted a pint, but after last night...'

MacDonald smirked. 'No red panties for you?'

'That's enough about that.' Forrester slurped some coffee, trying to cover his blush. 'Maybe you pair should go out on your own?'

'Okay. See you tomorrow.' Vicky got to her feet, avoiding MacDonald's eye as she followed him out of the office.

He caught up with her just outside. 'I'd ask if you fancied a drink, but I think we need to talk, don't we?'

~

VICKY CLASPED her hands around a glass of Diet Coke and looked out of the Auld Cludgie Café window. Traffic crawled along the Marketgait.

MacDonald sipped his drink, grimacing at the temperature. 'So?'

Vicky stared at the glass. It was empty, the ice almost entirely melted. 'I think I need something stronger.'

'Bacardi?'

'Not the doubles you were buying me last night. I meant coffee.'

'Want me to get you one?'

'No, thanks, I don't... want to be alone right now.' She smiled. 'Tasers are nasty. I've been electrocuted before. I used to help my Dad with his DIY. We were flooring the attic and I accidentally stuck a screwdriver in a live wire. Threw me clean across the room.' Her eyes lost focus at the distant memory, until she shook her head and tightened her ponytail to bring her back to the present. 'Same feeling as this time. My muscles turned to jelly. Nothing I could do. Totally paralysed as he raced away.' She put both hands around the glass, still cool. 'I'm glad it wasn't a gun.' She stared at his cup, deciding she wanted a coffee after all. And something else. She cleared her throat. 'What happened last night, Euan?'

MacDonald rubbed his face. 'You tell me.'

'You kissed me.'

'You kissed me back. Ran your hands all over my body. Then you got a taxi.' MacDonald's gaze dropped to the table. 'What would've happened if those guys hadn't cheered?'

'I don't know.' Vicky stared into her glass. *She did know. Kissing and cuddling and stroking and...* 'What do you think?'

'I was about to ask if you wanted to go back to yours.'

'Why didn't you?'

He shrugged. 'You ran off.'

'I do that.' She shook the glass, swirling the last of the ice cubes around. Over the road, Andrew was standing at the bus stop, waiting in the rain. 'You need to know something, Euan. I've got a daughter.'

MacDonald frowned.

'Her name's Bella. She's four.'

MacDonald glanced at her fingers. 'You don't wear a ring.'

'I'm not married.' Vicky bit her lip, the nerve in her neck starting up again. 'Her father... We're not together. Never were, really.'

'Okay.'

'Euan, you need to be alright with her if we're to get into anything.'

He finished his coffee and checked his watch. 'Quite a lot to take in, you know?'

Bloody typical...

'There you are.' Zoey leaned in and kissed MacDonald on the mouth, lingering. 'Forrester said you'd left?'

'We're just...' MacDonald cleared his throat. 'Closing stuff off.'

'Look, my mum's on her way up. I need to tidy the spare room. You going to help?'

'Just be a sec.'

Another kiss, but she was giving Vicky a warning glare. 'I'll see you in the car, Mac.'

'Right-o.' MacDonald smiled at Zoey and watched her leave.

Vicky swallowed hard, her throat tight. 'You dirty bastard.'

'It's not what you think.'

'You're *living* with her.'

'It's complicated.'

Vicky got up and left him.

Lying bastard.

Dirty, lying bastard.

Dirty, lying, cheating bastard.

∾

'THANKS FOR THE LIFT.' Andrew got out of the car. 'And remember, I was at the doctor.'

'Safe with me, so long as you stop pushing yourself like that.'

He gave a mock salute, then stepped out of the way as a feral four-year-old battered past.

Vicky got out and helped Bella into her car seat. She caught sight of Mum inside their house, but Andrew deflected her focus.

'Did you catch the baddies, Mummy?'

Vicky checked the seatbelt again. 'I did, Bells. For once.'

Bella squealed with delight. 'Mummy's my hero.'

Vicky cuddled her, wincing at the pain but holding on anyway. She'd come too close to never having the privilege again. 'I love you, too.'

'Where are we going, Mummy?'

'Mummy needs to speak to someone.'

VICKY UNDID BELLA'S seatbelt and helped her out of the car, her chest still aching. 'Have you been a good girl for Granny?'

'Granny said so.'

'Granny would, though, wouldn't she? Well, if you've been a good girl you might get to meet a new friend.'

'I've got lots of friends.'

'This might be a special one.'

'Okay.'

Vicky led her up the drive, past the black Audi, and knocked on Robert's door.

He opened the door and frowned. 'Vicky?'

'Hi, Robert.'

The frown turned to a smile when he saw her daughter. 'Are you Bella?'

Bella kicked her foot out. Didn't say anything.

Vicky smiled. 'Can we come in?'

'Sure.' Robert opened the door wide and pushed his dogs back.

Bella covered her face with her hands and started squealing again.

'Come on!' Robert hauled them off inside.

'It's okay, Bells.' Vicky knelt down and patted Bella's shoulders. 'The dogs won't bother you.'

'Sorry about that.' Robert waved his hand at the living room door. 'Sorry the place is such a state.'

Vicky inspected the living room from the doorway. Bookshelves lined three walls, all filled with novels. An expensive hi-fi sat in the corner underneath a large TV. *Jesus, didn't even see it the other night.* 'Tidier than our place.'

Robert's son lay on the ground playing with a Lego set.

'Jamie, this is Bella. Bella's mummy is friends with Daddy.'

The boy sat up, pushing his glasses up his nose. He tilted his head to the side as he inspected Bella. 'Do you like Lego?'

Bella looked up at Vicky. 'Can I play, Mummy?'

'Go on.'

Bella joined Jamie on the floor and began amassing an entire army of bricks.

Robert stared at Vicky, a question forming in his eyes. 'Can I get you a tea or a coffee?'

'I'll make an exception for you. Tea.'

Robert led them through a doorway into the kitchen, went to the sink and filled the kettle.

'This is a nice house, Robert. Seems bigger than Karen's.'

'It's okay, I suppose.' He shrugged. 'Could do with another room or two.'

'How much bigger do you need?'

'I've got a lot of books.' He chucked teabags in the mugs and poured water over them, before mashing them against the sides. 'Milk?'

Vicky nodded, her heart thudding in her chest. What the hell could she say? How could she explain her recent behaviour? 'Lots of milk, please.'

Robert obliged and handed her a mug, his jaw clenched. 'Here you go.'

'Thanks.' Vicky leaned against the counter, put the mug down and pinched her nose. 'Listen, Robert, when you introduced Bella to Jamie, you said I was your friend.'

Robert nodded. 'That's true.'

'Just a friend?'

'I'm not sure... Maybe I could be more one day. If you'd just let me in. Maybe stop reporting me to the police? Maybe be honest with me?'

Vicky concentrated on the rim of her mug. 'One of my colleagues tried to kiss me last night.'

Robert tightened his grip on the handle of his mug. 'Was he successful?'

'I was... not drunk, but...'

'I thought you were working.'

'I had been working. We went for a drink afterwards. Things got out of hand and Euan kissed me and I had to get a taxi home.'

Robert put his mug in the sink. 'Right.'

Vicky grabbed his arm. 'Robert, I'm a mess, okay? I have this commitment phobia. It's one of the long-term consequences from my relationship with Alan, I guess. I can be a cold bitch. I have to . . . I have to flick this switch in my head when I go to work. I have to keep work and home separate. Otherwise, I'd—'

'Vicky, what're you trying to say? Are you letting me down gently?'

She put a hand on his shoulder. 'I'm saying if you'll have me and work through the shit in my head, then I want to give it a go.'

Robert looked her in the eye. He didn't say anything for a few seconds. Then he nodded. 'So let's give it a go.'

READY FOR MORE?

Out now

The second book in the series, FLESH AND BLOOD, is out now — keep reading to the end of this book for a sneak preview.

If you would like to be kept up to date with new releases from Ed James, please sign up to my Readers Club at https://geni.us/EJDmailer

AFTERWORD

Thanks for reading TOOTH & CLAW— I hope you enjoyed the book and Vicky.

Writing and re-writing and re-re-writing and eventually getting it published wouldn't have been possible without the help of a lot of people. In chronological order . . . Thanks to Kitty for helping with the initial idea, alpha reading and moral support throughout; to Pat, Geoff and Rhona for the invaluable feedback on the initial draft; to Allan Guthrie for helping tear the book apart, for teaching me to write properly and for being the best agent I could hope for; thanks to Rhona and Len for invaluable editing, once I'd torn the book apart; and, last but certainly not least, to everyone at Thomas & Mercer for having faith in me and the book, then for returning the rights so graciously.

Ed James,
    Scottish Borders, June 2018

ABOUT ED JAMES

Ed James writes crime-fiction novels, primarily the DI Simon Fenchurch series, set on the gritty streets of East London featuring a detective with little to lose. His Scott Cullen series features a young Edinburgh detective constable investigating crimes from the bottom rung of the career ladder he's desperate to climb.

Formerly an IT project manager, Ed began writing on planes, trains and automobiles to fill his weekly commute to London. He now writes full-time and lives in the Scottish Borders, with his girlfriend and a menagerie of rescued animals.

FLESH & BLOOD

EXCERPT

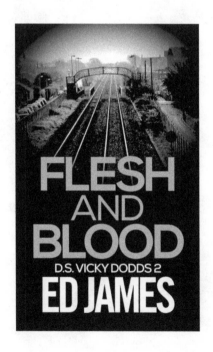

PROLOGUE

An explosion like gunfire makes her look out of the window. Across the dark beach, the fireworks erupt then fade to nothing, leaving a sky dotted with stars, the moon almost full. Then a yellow glow shoots across the sea, leaving a flickering trail in its wake.

She sips the champagne, which tastes sour like beer. Supposed to be good, but it's nowhere near sweet enough for her. Nothing like that stuff they had in Dubai, but it'd do. A wave of goosebumps crawls up her arms. Why didn't she wear something warmer than a summer dress?

The next wave of fireworks lights up Derek's face in the darkness. Mid-brown hair streaked with silver, laughter lines around his eyes. Can't see his toned muscles through his tuxedo, but it shapes the jacket in a nice way. His left arm loops around her waist and his right interlinks around hers and they sip each other's champagne. Her silver fox. All hers.

Something thuds behind her.

She breaks free and swivels away from the window. 'What was that?'

Derek frowns at her. 'Didn't hear anything, babe.'

She rests her glass on the windowsill and squints into the darkness.

Another flash, blue this time, lights up the room. The door is still open, showing the staircase leading back down to the beach. The walls are bright as though it was midday, bare stone with a long crack running down the middle. And it all fizzles away to darkness, just the faint glow from the battery lantern that doesn't reach into the room's corners.

No sign of anyone.

His searching hand smooths over her hip. 'Maybe you're nervous because we're not supposed to be up here.'

She nibbles at her lip. A green-and-red flash on the wall and the door. Nobody there. Right? 'It's probably a bird, isn't it?'

'There are terns and shags round here.'

'*Shags*?'

'It's a type of seabird. We did it at school. Swear it's the truth.'

'Shut up.'

'Seriously.' Derek gets out his bling smartphone and taps at the screen, then shows her a photo of a black seabird standing on a rock, its wings spread wide. 'Huh. Cormorants and shags are closely related, apparently.'

'Well, you've got even more surprising depths.'

He brushes aside the short dress and runs a hand between her legs, catching on the fabric of her knickers. 'I'll show you how deep I can go.'

She slaps his hand away. 'Stop it.'

'Come on.' He sets his champagne flute down next to hers on the windowsill. 'This is supposed to be romantic. God knows I've paid enough for it.'

'I know, it's just...' She looks around and she's shivering now. It's right in her teeth and her bones, down in her marrow.

A shimmering pink light dances across the walls. The room feels way too big and too claustrophobic at the same time.

Nobody there. Just her imagination. Probably the echoes of guilt and paranoia from months and months of keeping secrets from everyone. The reality hasn't caught up with her yet. And maybe it never will. At least not until the sparkling engagement ring on her finger has a wedding one alongside it.

'Sorry. It's just...' With a sigh, she picks up their glasses, both now smudged with her red lipstick, and hands him one, then links their arms again. 'This *is* romantic. Thanks.'

Derek leans in to kiss her and she fights against his tongue, always so over-eager. She opens her eyes.

A flash of fireworks catches a figure in the doorway.

She drops her glass and tries to push away from him. The glass smashes on the stone floor and she's rocked forward. Derek's bulk pins her against the wall.

An arm swings a golf club through the air.

SEARING pain behind her eyes wakes her up, biting at her brain. She tries to move, but can't. The back of her head feels like it's resting against the floor. She's freezing, but everything is on fire. She can barely move her legs. Still got her heels on, the clasps keeping them in place. And something is covering her mouth.

It's deadly silent. The fireworks must've stopped. What time is it? The moon has moved, so it must be hours later.

She can just about make out their attacker standing there, an outline in the moonlight coming in from the window. 'You would've thought, wouldn't you?' He's muttering, his voice deep. 'These people. Their morals, these days. You would've thought they'd learn, wouldn't you?' He looks right at her, but she can't see much. And she definitely doesn't recognise him. 'Why don't you people learn?'

She tries to speak but the gag swallows the sound.

He crouches in front of her and a flash catches in the darkness. A knife, thin like a scalpel rather than Derek's hunting knife. He grabs her by the hair and she tries to wriggle but he's way too strong.

His knees crunch against her ribs and he pins her in place. His thumb holds down her left eyelid. He reaches over with the knife, closer to her eye, and she freezes.

Then he cuts at her eyelid and the pain screams loud.

He pulls the knife away and she tries to move but just can't. Can't do anything. She's so useless, so helpless, and it's like her whole eye is on fire. Liquid fills the socket, little drops. Her own blood.

'Get off her!'

The attacker turns around.

Through a curtain of blood, she can see Derek sitting up, halfway across the room. His shirt is bright white in the dark room, but soaked red. 'You small-cocked wanker!'

The attacker gets off her and stands up with creaking knees. He moves towards Derek. Despite all the searing pain in her head, she knows she needs to do something. Now. So she lashes out with her feet, still bound together. Something bites into her ankles, but she makes contact, her toes connecting with material.

And it's just enough. The attacker stumbles and sprawls forward, landing face-down. He spills the knife and it rolls towards her across the uneven floor.

He's not moving, just lying there.

She should do something. She has to.

Derek is looking at her, his eyes pleading with her.

And the attacker is deadly still. Did she kill him? She doesn't know, but she's got to get them out of here.

So she moves her feet over and a trail of blood runs down her thigh. Another push and she edges her butt over. Then she moves her feet again, and she can just about reach the knife. She picks it up and it's like a scalpel. She reaches down and slashes the blade against the rope and it almost cuts clean through, just a few strands binding her ankles together. She tries to pull her feet apart but whatever the binding is made of, it's holding tight, so she presses the blade against the thread now, and it snaps. She lets out a breath. She can move now. Just like in all those stupid exercise classes, she pushes up to her knees, then hops up to standing.

She tries to cut the bonds on her wrists, but Christ her hands are shaking like crazy. One slip and she'll cut a vein, right? Something drips onto the rope. Blood. She's got to hurry, so she cuts at the rope around her wrists, but it's even harder than freeing her feet. Blood drips down and slicks her fingers. She drops the knife. Christ! She reaches for it again, but something strikes her back.

She stumbles and hits the wall. She hits the floor, crunching up her spine.

'Stay still!' The attacker has the knife again, aiming it at her eye once more. She didn't even see him. 'You have to pay!'

Derek hops over to the attacker and throws himself at him, bashing into him shoulder-first. They go down in a pile near the door.

Should she stay and help Derek?

No, the attacker has the knife again. She's got to get out of here. Got to get help.

She surges forward and leaps over them. Something nicks her neck but she can't stop, so she clatters through the doorway and down the stairs, her heels clicking off the old stone.

Blood runs down her chest from the wound in her throat.

You can buy FLESH AND BLOOD now.

If you'd like to be join my Readers Club and keep up to date on my new releases and get free exclusive content, please join for free at https://geni.us/EJDmailer